THE GALACTIC CHRONICLES

SHADOWS OF THE VOID SERIES

BOOK THREE

J.J. GREEN

INFINITEBOOK

MARS BORN

ONE

Jas went through her training moves. Left jab. Right jab. Right kick. Spin. Left kick. Weave. Right hook. Left hook. Weave. Right kick. She'd made something that vaguely resembled a punching bag from a rolled and taped up bunk mat, and she'd hung it from the ceiling in the starship's dining room. It was the only place on board that was large enough for her to train in. Between meals, she would detach the tables and benches from the floor and stack them against the walls before starting long exercise sessions.

The center of the punching bag contained a long plastic bag filled with water, but the bag wasn't quite heavy enough, and it swung wildly at Jas's last, low kick. She side-stepped as the bag swung back, and she kicked it again, hard, as it passed her. On its second return she punched the bag, grunting with the effort. The bag swung away again, and as it came back, she stepped up to meet it and began jabbing it with increasingly fast blows.

Her brow glistened and her breath came in soft pants. Her arms and legs ached and her knuckles and wrists were sore, but she didn't want to stop. The exercise felt good, though no matter how fast or hard she punched and kicked, the effort didn't dispel her feelings of frustration.

Letting loose something between a gasp and a cry, she jabbed hard with her right fist. A soft pop followed, and water gushed from the bottom of the bag, drenching her feet.

"Krat," she exclaimed, backing away from the quickly spreading puddle. The punching bag swung like a pendulum, shedding water like an out-of-control fire hose.

Carl Lingiari was sitting on the floor in the corner of the room, concentrating on an interface he'd balanced on his knees. "Whoa," he said as he heard Jas's exclamation and saw the spilling water. He scrambled to his feet. "Must have been some punch, Jas," he said, his eyebrows raised.

Her feet had been soaked in the initial burst of water, so she gave up trying to avoid it. She stood in the puddle, her hands on her hips, watching the slowly swinging bag. She drew her arm across her forehead to wipe off the sweat. "No, not really. The plastic bag was too weak. Wish I had some proper training equipment." Pulling off the surgical tape she'd wrapped around her knuckles, she went over to Carl, her feet squishing in her wet sneakers. "What are you doing?" she asked as she trod on the heels of her shoes to remove them. She bent down to pull off her socks.

"Just the usual," Carl replied. "Checking to see if there's been any mention of the Shadows in the media. Isn't it about time you gave the training a rest? You've been going at it a couple of hours now, and you were in here all morning too, weren't you?"

Gazing down at her red, battered knuckles and lifting one lip ruefully, Jas replied, "Yeah, maybe you're right. It's just that I don't have anything else to do. It's so boring here. We've been aboard this ship for three days. Three days. And we can't seem to decide anything. Every discussion we have goes around in circles. We're all cooped up on this starship talking, and meanwhile the Shadows are on Earth killing more and more people, replacing them with replicants, taking over the Government, companies, media, everything." She wrung out her socks over the puddle in the center of the room. "If we don't do something soon, I think I'm going to explode."

"Hard to know what to do until we hear from the Transgalactic Council."

"I know. I know now that the Lees' house is destroyed, any reply from the Council is going to be lost. And I know that we have no idea who Sayen's parents sent the message to." She squeezed her eyes shut in frustration. "I get it. But knowing all that doesn't make things any easier. We have to decide something, and soon. Or else we might as well say we've done our part and wash our hands of the whole problem. Just find ourselves a little corner of the galaxy to wait out the storm, and hope that if we ever return to Earth, it isn't inhabited by Shadows."

"After what's happened over the last few months," Carl said, "that part about finding a quiet corner of the galaxy doesn't sound so crazy. 'Cept I'd just want to pick up Flux first and say goodbye to my old home."

Jas's heart ached at her friend's words. She couldn't imagine what it was like to know your parents had been killed by Shadows. She reached out to softly touch Carl's upper arm. "Whatever we do, we'll pick up Flux. We'll insist on it."

"Yeah. Little fella'll be wondering where I've got to."

They stood quietly for a moment. Jas didn't remove her hand from her friend's arm. They both lifted their eyes and their gaze met. Slowly, they leaned closer. Jas closed her eyes and froze. She was trying to force her way through a sickening dread and not turn away or stop what might be about to happen, to not freeze Carl out as she had done so many times before.

At that second the door opened, and Phelan Lee peered around it.

"Oh, sorry," he said, backing out.

"No, it's fine," said Jas as she hastily drew back from Carl, avoiding his wounded look. Relief eased her churning stomach. "What is it?"

"We're having a meeting." Phelan eyed the puddle in the middle of the dining room. He went to a small hatch in the center of the floor and pushed it down with his foot. The hatch popped open, revealing a floor drain. The water flowed away. "I thought you two would want to come along."

"You bet we would," Jas said, too brightly.

———

They followed Phelan toward the bridge. Jas was still getting used to how much he resembled his sister. Though the two were three years apart in age, it was as if they were male and female versions of the same person. Both looked a lot like their mother.

Phelan was anatomically flawless as his sister, Sayen, no doubt due to the state-of-the-art genetic modding he'd received soon after his conception. The man's physical proportions were exactly balanced, and his face was perfectly symmetrical. His blond hair was even cut to a similar cropped style as his sister's. His personality, however, was quite different.

"Hope I wasn't disturbing anything back there," he said, throwing a grin over his shoulder. "But, you know, there's more comfortable places for that kind of thing than a soggy canteen."

"No worries," Carl replied, "you weren't disturbing anything."

Jas winced at the somber tone of his remark.

Phelan seemed to pick up that he was skirting the edges of a touchy subject. "So," he continued, "can I ask, was there a special reason you wanted to flood my crew's dining area, Jas?"

"Sorry about that," she replied and went on to explain about the makeshift punching bag and the accident.

"You went to all that trouble just to make yourself some training equipment?" Phelan asked.

"Yeah, I did. There's nothing aboard. I like to stay in shape, and I wanted to pass the time. I hope that was okay. I'll unroll the mat. It should dry out in a few hours."

"Yeahhhh," Phelan said, drawing out the word. "The mat's no problem. I was only wondering why, if you wanted something to train with, you didn't just use the ship's printer."

Jas nearly drew to a halt at her own stupidity. Of course Phelan had a printer on board. Every starship she'd worked on had carried a printer to create essential items or spare parts for repairs in an emergency. But because they were expensive to run, printers were locked away. Crew members were only allowed to use them with special permission. It hadn't occurred to her to ask Phelan if he had a printer. "Krat. That was kind of dumb of me, wasn't it?"

"Kinda." Phelan gave a short laugh. "Just kidding. You couldn't have been expected to know that, I guess. But for the record, you can use whatever the crew use aboard my ship. No need to ask. You're friends of my sis, and what's mine's yours, okay? I should've made that clearer sooner."

"Thanks, that's generous of you," Carl said. "How's Sayen doing?"

Phelan had fallen into step beside them. The three walking abreast took up all the room in the narrow corridor. Space was at a premium aboard Phelan's mining ship, the *Bricoleur*.

Sadness dimmed the man's usually bright features. "Not so good. My parents' deaths have hit her pretty hard. She was very close to them both, especially to our mother. Sayen hasn't said so, but I think she's so cut up because, when it came down to it, Mama chose our daddy over us. I think that hurts her almost more than the fact that they're gone."

Reminded of the scene of their escape from the Shadows on the burning rooftop, Jas shuddered. The noise and heat of the flames, the sight of Mr. Lee bravely firing at the host of aliens speeding toward them, and Mrs. Lee pushing Phelan into the shuttle, forcing them to flee and leave the couple to their fate: these were things she'd never forget.

Two

The bridge was the second largest room aboard the mining ship, aside from the equipment bay and the hold. Phelan sat in his captain's seat, throwing a baseball from hand to hand, as he always did when he was thinking. The crew and guests ranged around the space, standing or sitting where a spare seat was available.

Jas wondered if Phelan had excelled at the ancient sport of baseball as he and Sayen had no doubt done at most things while they were growing up. He threw the ball at the ceiling and caught it on the rebound. At the place where the ball had hit was a smudge of dirt, evidence of the captain's long habit. She wondered if the practice irritated his crew as much as it did her.

It was hard to tell. No one, apart from Phelan and the pilot was human. The whole company was there, from the lowliest miner to the second-in-command and engineer, Flahive. Everyone was looking bored after three days of inactivity. Everyone except Flahive. It was hard to tell how the engineer was feeling because he—if his species consisted of hes and shes—was encased head-to-toe in a pressure suit. Flahive came from a high-g planet, and if he didn't remain inside the suit, his entire body would rapidly expand, eventually killing him.

Flahive's suit gave an indication of his species' tripoidal anatomy.

He had three stumpy legs and got around by jumping along on the foremost two while the rear leg kept balance. Carl had said he reminded him of a 'roo'. Flahive's three upper limbs were equally spaced around his torso, about halfway between his legs and dome-like head. At the end of each upper limb was a highly flexible pad, and the alien could manipulate the one at the back just as easily as the two that were closer to his front, as he was demonstrating at that moment by working on the interface on the panel behind him. What his face looked like, Jas had no idea, for it was hidden behind a smoky panel.

The miners were all one species. Hairy and cylindrical, they stood about half Jas's height. They didn't appear to have any method of holding or touching anything, and Jas had never figured out how they worked the mining equipment. She supposed they had some kind of retractable appendages.

The ship's navigator was an android similar to the servants of the Lees' household. She acted and sounded human, but Jas had guessed what she was from her extremely deferential attitude and limited conversational ability. The android was also extremely attractive, and it had crossed Jas's mind that navigation wasn't the only reason Phelan had her on the crew list.

Sayen had propped herself on the edge of an instrument panel as they were waiting to begin the meeting. Her face was pale and her head low. Makey was peering over the pilot's shoulder at levels she was adjusting on her screen. A young woman, the pilot was very reserved and quiet and had rarely contributed anything to the discussions they'd had on what to do next.

Thunk went Phelan's baseball on the ceiling of the bridge. On the rebound, it slapped into his palm. As he went to throw it again, Jas resisted the urge to snatch it in midair, run to the nearest airlock, throw it in, and press Purge.

They were waiting on Erielle, the crippled underworlder. It felt like an age ago since Jas had first met her, though it was only a few weeks.

The bridge was crowded, and Jas wondered why Phelan had

decided to hold the meeting there rather than the larger dining room. Maybe he was about to make a big decision, and he needed his spot on the ceiling.

The bridge doors slid apart, and Erielle walked through. Jas sat up in surprise. The underworlder had been getting around on crutches since her legs had suffered severe laser burns, but she'd replaced them with a frame of slim metal rods that encased her from her waist to her ankles.

"Looking good," Phelan said to the underworlder. "It worked then?"

"Yeah. Thanks for the suggestion, hun. I really appreciate it. Hey, everyone, what do you think of my new leg supports?" For the first time in weeks, Erielle smiled.

Sayen looked up, and her face brightened momentarily. "You look sneck. Did you print them?"

Erielle nodded. "Your brother suggested it. My legs are still kratted, and they always will be unless I get them fixed, but with these supports I can walk normally. I can even run. And I'm a little more comfortable."

Makey went over to the underworlder and squatted down to inspect the metal scaffolding around her legs. "Wow. I bet these make you stronger than you were before." He straightened up and turned to Phelan. "Can I have some too?"

A general laugh echoed around the bridge. Phelan shrugged. "I don't see why—"

"How about you concentrate on getting your body into shape first?" Jas interjected. At Makey's crestfallen look, she added, "Supports are great for helping people with problems, but they don't match the flexibility or responsiveness of natural legs. You wouldn't want to be wearing leg augmentation in a fight. Am I right?" she asked Phelan.

"She's got a point, kid," Phelan replied. "Though if you were running away..." He paused at Jas's frown and gave a chuckle.

Carl stood up to give Erielle his seat, and as the older woman sat down, Phelan cleared his throat. "Okay, we all know why we're here.

We've argued it out, we've thought about it, we've argued some more. We aren't getting anywhere. Some of you think we should skedaddle back to the Outer Rim and carry on like nothing's happened." The miners fidgeted and mumbled. "Some of you want to return to Earth and start rooting out these Shadows wherever we can find them."

"That's right," Erielle said forcefully.

"Though it isn't clear how you'll tell who's a Shadow and who isn't since this scanner you've told me about went up in flames," Phelan said.

"We'll figure out a way," said Erielle. "People are dying down there."

"And if we return to Earth we'll likely die too," Sayen said. "There has to be something more useful we can do. If we can just contact the Council...whoever received my parents' message packet must have informed the rest of them. They must—"

"As I've said all along, the Transgalactic Council must receive a million messages a day from crazies all around the galaxy," said Erielle. "Why would—"

"No." Sayen rubbed her tired-looking eyes. "My parents had connections at the Council, and we sent them the evidence."

"You *think* you sent them the evidence," Erielle said.

"We sent them the evidence," Sayen replied with an edge in her voice. "Not everyone in authority is out to get you, Erielle. If we can't trust the Council to help us, who can we trust?"

Erielle opened her mouth to speak, but Flahive cut in. "Please, if you both don't calm down I'll have to ask for a minute's silence and reflection." The voice his comm unit generated was male, deep, and smooth. As always happened when the alien spoke, soft lights illuminated his face plate. Flahive had given the same warning at every discussion they'd had when things had gotten heated. Jas hadn't yet figured out why, but Phelan never reacted or seemed to think there was anything out of the ordinary about it.

Thunk. The captain caught his ball and tossed it from one hand to the other. "Listen up, folks. I'm gonna lay it on the line for y'all.

Here's my problem. I have a duty to my sis and her friends, I have a duty to my crew, and I have a duty to the good citizens of Earth. Only thing is, all my duties aren't lining up. I can't help one of you without hurting the other. If I help Sayen, I'll be taking my crew into danger. If I try to keep y'all safe by hiding out somewhere until this all blows over, I'm neglecting to help my fellow human beings, and that isn't right.

"So, after listening to all your arguments, I'm gonna act like the captain of this ship that I am and make up all your minds for you. Or, leastways, I'm gonna make a decision and y'all can decide which way you're gonna jump.

"I'm not comfortable sitting here in orbit above our infested home planet. If these Shadows' reach stretches as far as you tell me, and as it sounds like they're especially keen to find you, they might figure out who I have on board soon enough. The *Bricoleur* isn't a combat ship. We won't be winning any space battles. So we need to move, and soon. But where to go? The Council's spread across the galaxy. We don't know where my parents sent their message, so until we figure out who we should be talking to, we can't go to the Council yet. It seems to me the logical thing to do is to sit tight while we try to find out what's happening."

"But if it isn't safe to stay in orbit above Earth..." said Jas.

"I didn't mean to stay right here, like a duck waiting to be shot. We only need to stay in the vicinity. Somewhere close by. Somewhere hopefully not infested with Shadows yet."

"I get it," Makey exclaimed. "We're going to Mars, aren't we?"

THREE

Phelan's plan was to cancel the contracts of anyone in the crew who wanted out and shuttle them to Earth or Mars as they desired. Everyone had been mulling about the problem for days, and it didn't take them long to state their wishes. The pilot said she wanted to return to Earth and check on her family, and she hoped that would be okay now that Carl was there to fly the ship. Carl was happy to take over the position. He only asked that he could first make a quick trip to his family home to pick up his alien friend, Flux.

The miners were disgruntled about Phelan's decision to halt his mining operations. They didn't want to go to Earth or Mars, nor have their contracts canceled early. Phelan listened to their protests, throwing and catching his baseball the entire time.

Finally, he offered to pay early termination bonuses and to provide them with tickets from Mars to their home planet. After putting their hairy heads together and talking in their strange, buzzing language, they reluctantly agreed. They filed out, muttering among themselves like a crowd of angry wasps. The pilot followed.

Flahive said he wanted to stay on, providing that Sayen and Erielle could sort out their differences. It turned out that the point was moot because, avoiding Sayen's teary gaze, Erielle asked to be set down in the Shadow-infested state capital that had long been her home. At Erielle's words Sayen said nothing, but stalked from the room, her head bowed and her lips set.

The underworlder rested her chin on her hand and sighed. The older woman's hair had grown out from the buzz cut she'd worn when Jas had first met her. The effect softened her hard features a little, though the suffering and pain she'd endured ever since she'd been dragged into the battle with the Shadows was still evident in her face.

"I know what you're all thinking," Erielle said. "If I go back to Earth, it'll be a suicide mission. But they're my people down there. All their lives they've been shunned and despised for not being modded, or for not conforming to the system. Ignored. Rejected. When the Shadows make their move, and it comes to a fight, who's going to be looking out for them? No one. They might not be pretty, and they might not be smart, and most of them sure as hell aren't trustworthy or responsible, but I spent all my life trying to help them. I'm not going to abandon them just because that's the easy thing to do."

"I can see why Sis likes you so much," Phelan said. "You're a brave woman."

Erielle smiled grimly. "Not brave. Just resigned."

"It's going to be hard on Sayen," said Jas.

"I know. I must seem like a callous bitch. Believe me, I don't want to put her through any more pain so close to her parents dying. I don't mean to hurt her. I know it might not look like it sometimes, but she means a lot to me. I'll go talk to her."

"I'm coming with you," Makey said.

"You're coming with me to talk to Sayen?"

"No, I'm returning to Earth too."

"What?" exclaimed Jas. "No. No way."

"Yes, I am. You can't tell me what to do with my life. I'm not a kid anymore. I can do what I like."

"You can't go, Makey," Jas said. "It's insane. You'll get killed."

"It's like Erielle says. People on Earth need our help. We can't just forget about them."

"We aren't forgetting about them. We're doing everything we can to help them. Sacrificing yourself isn't going to help anyone."

"I won't be sacrificing myself. I'll be with Erielle, and we'll help keep each other safe. She always wanted me to join the underworlders, and she's right. Everyone on Dawn was an underworlder. I owe it to my mam and sister to help them."

He sighed. "It's funny. All my life I dreamed of escaping my home planet and traveling the galaxy. And maybe I'll do that one day. But I couldn't look at myself in a mirror without shame if I ran away from the Shadows again like I did on Dawn. Don't get me wrong. I'm grateful you helped me, Jas and Carl, but if I'm honest, a day hasn't passed that I didn't regret leaving. Everything I've done has been to try to make amends for what I did. It's not enough. I have to go back to Earth and continue the fight against the Shadows there. I'm sorry, but it's just the right thing for me to do."

With a tiny metallic hiss from her leg supports, Erielle got up and went out. Makey went with her. Only Phelan, Carl, Jas, the android, and Flahive remained.

"I'll program a jump to Mars," the android said and turned her slim, shapely back to them as she bent over her screen.

"I'm hoping the Shadows haven't arrived there yet," Phelan said. "We need to restock on supplies, so we have to go planetside. What do you think, Jas? Is it likely to be safe? Have you been back recently?"

Jas rubbed her eyes, trying to get the image of Makey being dragged into a Shadow trap out of her mind. "I haven't been back since I was twelve years old. I made it as far as orbit once, but that's it."

Phelan whistled. "Not been back since you were twelve years old, huh?" *Thunk.*

A muscle in Jas's jaw twitched.

"I sense you're extremely worried about Makey, Jas, and very conflicted about returning to the place of your birth," said Flahive.

"Perhaps it might help you to go to Mars as a way of examining your feelings and achieving a resolution to them."

"I'm sorry?" Jas said. "You sense I'm...*what?*"

"Flahive." Phelan gave the engineer a little shake of his head.

"Ah, that was inappropriate of me," Flahive said. "I apologize, Jas. I'm very sorry. I was just trying to help."

A look of puzzlement passed between Carl and Jas. The engineer's opaque face plate was enigmatic.

Phelan sighed. "I guess now that we're all going to be shipmates for the duration, I should tell you about Flahive. Or do you want to tell them yourself?" he asked the engineer.

"I find it best if I do the explaining, Captain, if you don't mind. It's certainly not the first time, and I doubt it'll be the last that I have to reassure other species about my ability."

Why would they need reassurance? Jas wondered. She didn't think she was going to like what the alien had to say.

"Firstly," Flahive said, "I want to make it very clear that I cannot read human minds."

Jas had been right. She didn't like the sound of where Flahive seemed to be heading with his explanation.

He went on, "However, I do pick up on strong emotions. Not everyday, minor feelings of contentment, annoyance, dissatisfaction, that kind of thing. But joy, elation, despair, hatred, love, passion, fury, those I can sense. I sense a kind of echo of them. At times, the effect is quite uncomfortable."

The alien's objections when Sayen and Erielle had fought began to make sense. He was an empath.

"I know this can make some humans feel self-conscious or embarrassed, but I've never truly comprehended why. Strong emotions can be an opportunity to initiate much-needed change. They aren't something to be avoided or hidden away. Sometimes emotions bring people together, or advance the individual to enlightenment of some kind. When I sense powerful feelings, I try to encourage an exploration of those feelings if I think it might help that person."

Oh, brother.

"Okay, I think you've explained enough," Phelan said. "Don't worry," he said to Jas and Carl. "You'll get used to him being around. You won't even think about it after a while. I don't." *Thunk.*

"I'll get used to him knowing exactly how I feel?" Jas spluttered. "All the time? He'll be picking up on our emotions all the time we're aboard the ship? Or are you limited by distance?" she asked Flahive.

"My ability *is* limited by distance," Flahive replied.

Jas made a mental note to stay as far away from the alien as she could.

"But it stretches as far as the confines of this ship."

"Great," Jas said.

Phelan gave a short laugh. "Calm down. It isn't a big deal."

"Yes, you should probably calm down," Flahive repeated.

"Don't tell me how I should feel," exclaimed Jas. But Carl was laughing at her now.

"Besides," continued Phelan. "We need Flahive. If something goes wrong with the engine, he's the only one who can talk to it."

Carl's laughter died. "He can *what?*"

Four

They were in Mars orbit. The *Bricoleur* was quieter with Erielle, Makey, the pilot, and the miners gone. Four days had passed since the last of them had left. Flux's addition to the crew had caused a temporary lifting of the spirits, but the atmosphere had quickly returned to a subdued and pensive state.

Carl was the only person aboard who had been planetside, but he hadn't stuck around. He'd remained at Valles Marineris Spaceport just long enough for the miners to disembark the shuttle before flying back.

He was worried about Sayen. After Erielle had left them, her mood had sunk even lower. She was rarely seen outside her cabin, and she ate very little at meals—when she turned up to them at all. She'd grown worryingly thin, and her eyes were shadowed in their sockets. Her depression was bringing her brother down too. Phelan spent most of his time with her, though when the two were seen together he would be the one doing the talking. He would reason with her, or go over stories of their childhood, or just generally try to cheer her up. His naturally buoyant temperament was less and less evident as time wore on.

Carl decided to pay her a visit and take Flux with him in the hopes that the quirky alien's presence might lighten her mood. He rang her door chime twice before she answered, and when she opened her door it was evident she'd been crying. "I'm sorry, Carl. This isn't a good—"

Flux took off from Carl's shoulder and flew into her cabin, alighting on the corner of her bunk.

"Got anything to eat?" the creature asked, his Australian-accented voice high-pitched.

"No, Flux. I don't have anything. Maybe you should try the dining room?"

"Nah, nothing good in there. How about I scout around for some cockroaches?" He flew down from her bunk and crawled underneath it, pulling himself forward with the hooks on his wings.

"There are no roaches in my cabin," Sayen exclaimed. Her cabin was extremely neat and tidy—almost too neat and tidy, as if no one were living there. The surfaces were completely bare and there wasn't a smudge or speck of dust in the place.

"I bet there are," came Flux's voice from under the bunk. "Y' can always find one if you look hard enough."

"Sorry about him," Carl said. "Is it okay if I come in, just for a minute?"

Sighing, Sayen stepped back to let Carl in. She told the door to close.

"Can I get you a drink?" she asked as she went to the dispenser on her wall.

"No, that's okay," Carl replied. As Sayen filled a beaker with water, he noticed that her hands were red and raw, as if she'd been washing them excessively.

Carl took the only chair in the cramped room, and Sayen sat on her bunk, her elbows on her knees and her head bowed. Scratching sounds were coming from beneath her bunk where Flux was searching.

Now that he was there, Carl wasn't sure what to say. *How are you doing* seemed trite.

Sayen broke the awkward silence. "Carl, I know why you're here, and I appreciate it and all, but there isn't anything you can say or do that's going to make me feel better. Phelan's tried his best, but he can't bring Mama or Daddy back, and now that Erielle's gone too..." She paused and swallowed. "It's like the light's gone out of my life, and there's nothing I or anyone else can do about it."

"Nothing under here," Flux said, crawling out from beneath Sayen's bunk. He climbed up the side and onto her mattress, gripping her blanket with his feet and wing hooks. "I'll try up there," he squeaked, launching himself into the air. He flew across the cabin to the top of a cupboard on the opposite wall and disappeared into the gap between it and the ceiling.

"There's no roaches there either," said Sayen.

"I wouldn't be too sure about that if I were you," came Flux's voice.

Carl rolled his eyes at Sayen and was pleased to see the corners of her lips twitch into a half smile, but the moment was soon over.

"Your brother seems to be coping pretty well, at least," he said.

Sayen shook her head. "He's hurting. He just won't show it. We aren't much alike in that way. He doesn't easily show how he feels. Mama and Daddy's choice of modding for him was a little too far on the tough and adventurous side, they always said. I think they overcompensated with me. Made me too emotional and timid."

"Maybe you were a little like that, at one time," Carl replied, remembering her as he'd first known her when she was navigator aboard the *Galathea*. "But that doesn't sound like the Sayen I know now. The Sayen who broke into the secret files the Government was keeping on Shadows wasn't emotional and timid. And neither was the Sayen who saved me and Makey after the truck crashed and we were surrounded." He would never forget that lasting image he had of her appearing on top of the flaming truck, herself in flames.

"Seems like a long time ago," said Sayen. "I was a different person then."

"It just shows, though, doesn't it? We aren't set in stone. People can change. Modding's only one part of who we are. We can still choose how we act and how we react when we hit hard times. We don't have to accept that's how we'll be forever."

Sayen frowned. "I guess so."

Flux flew down and landed on Carl's shoulder. "No luck," he said disappointedly. "You keep your cabin too clean," he said to Sayen.

"Er...sorry about that."

The creature began to pick through Carl's hair.

"You're not going to find anything in there either, mate," Carl said, brushing away a curl that had flopped over one eye.

"You never know," Flux replied, leaning in to peer at Carl's scalp.

This brought a small chuckle from Sayen. Carl thought he would take advantage of the momentary break in her mood with a change of subject. "Hey, did you know about the *Bricoleur's* engine?" he asked.

"The Oootoon drive? Yeah, I know about it. Phelan had to argue long and hard with our parents about buying the ship when they were loaning him the money to start up his business. They didn't think the greater efficiency of an Oootoon engine was worth the necessity of always having an empath aboard."

"So it's true that the engine's alive and can communicate?"

"Oh yes. You could talk to it too, if you wanted to. You have to open the engine casing and touch it. I did it once, when the ship was delivered." She grimaced. "What's inside doesn't look like much. It's just a thick yellow liquid, but I wouldn't recommend touching it. You immediately hear all its thoughts, and it's like being inside the head of someone with multiple personality disorder. Confusing and creepy." She gave a slight shudder. "Took me a little while to get over it."

"Right...why does the engine need an empath?"

"An Oootoon drive will take you wherever you tell it, in hops like a starjump engine, only it's a fraction of the size and it doesn't need any fuel. The last I heard, no one's figured out how it does it. But if the engine's damaged or something upsets it, you have to have a way of talking to it, or it might stop working. Like I said, talking to it isn't easy, but empaths like Flahive can do it. Flahive doesn't need to touch the Oootoon to communicate with it. And he doesn't just feel its emotions like with us; he can hear what it's saying if he 'tunes in', as he puts it."

"Wow," Carl said. "I've never heard of anything like it."

"Humans are still on the fringes of galactic society. We've only had interstellar travel for a couple of hundred years, whereas some alien species have been exploring the galaxy for eons. We've barely touched the surface of what's out there. You should hear some of the stories Phelan has to tell about what he's seen and done."

"Sounds like I should. Ow." Carl frowned and looked up from beneath his brows at Flux, who had just pulled his hair.

"Sorry, mate," the creature said. "Thought I saw something."

Carl gently removed the animal from his shoulder. "Maybe you should give it a rest for a minute," he said, sitting Flux on his knee.

"Yeah. A rest sounds like a good idea." Flux climbed over Carl's lap and pulled open the top of Carl's shirt before climbing in, saying, "You two carry on. Don't mind about me."

Flux made himself comfortable inside Carl's shirt. Carl winced as his friend's claws tugged at his chest hairs. Holding open the top of his shirt, he peered inside. Flux had curled into a ball and wrapped himself in his transparent wings. In a moment, his eyes began to close and his mouth opened, revealing two rows of tiny, sharp teeth. The creature's breathing became deeper and more regular.

"It's good to have him back," he said to Sayen quietly, "but I'd forgotten how much of a pain in the arse he can be."

"I can hear you," Flux said.

Carl smiled at Sayen, and she grinned back.

FIVE

Jas fastened her safety belt, breathed in and exhaled slowly as Carl piloted the shuttle away from the *Bricoleur*. Breathing deeply didn't do much to slow her racing heart. Thinking rationally, it made sense for her to be the one to go planetside. She was the only one with Martian citizenship, which meant that she could enter and move around in Mars Territory freely, providing she passed the health check at immigration. Her coloring also meant that she would blend in easily with the local population and remain relatively inconspicuous. She was the ideal person to assess the place for signs of Shadow infiltration.

On the other hand, if the Shadows had arrived on Mars and were looking for her, she could quickly find herself in hot water. But with Mars' much lower population, little deep space traffic, and far tighter controls on who entered and left, she didn't think it likely that the Shadows had penetrated its defenses.

Yet it wasn't fear of Shadows that was making Jas's stomach clench into knots as Carl flew her to Valles Marineris Spaceport. All her life she'd avoided dwelling on her childhood, which had begun on Mars. Her unknown parents' death had been the first in a series of experiences that had marred her early years.

After being forced to travel to Earth so her bones wouldn't be permanently weakened by Mars' low gravity, things had gone from bad to worse. Global Government policy at the time had mandated that Martian children were separated from their peers to better enable their integration into Earth society. The intention was good, but the effects were poor. Jas had been relentlessly bullied at her Earth institute for cared-for children. Then a traumatic experience while at training college in Antarctica had been the final straw.

Jas's past was a place she'd never wanted to return to, in word or deed, but here she was, traveling back in time as well as space.

"Touchdown in five," came Carl's voice over the passenger cabin speakers. Jas jumped a little as she was jolted out of her musings, surprised that so much time had passed so quickly.

She could have sat next to Carl in the co-pilot's seat, but he hadn't offered and she hadn't asked. He'd been a little cold toward her since that time in the dining room when they'd nearly kissed. She didn't blame him. He'd made his feelings clear and deep down, she reciprocated them. Yet she'd been acting like a nervous sixteen year old, moving ahead only to shy away as soon as anything at all serious began to happen.

What's wrong with me?

Jas shook her head slightly. She knew exactly what was wrong. What she didn't know was how to fix it.

It was night time in Valles Marineris, and the spaceport was a triangle of brilliant lights at one end of the valley. Points of light ran out from the triangle, marking the overground tunnels of the Loop, which led to the colony settlements. Spreading patches of silver and red, they ran across the valley floor and up into the surrounding foothills.

The lights burned brighter as the shuttle vibrated and descended vertically to the landing pad. It came to rest outside a utilitarian, gray building with the words Valles Marineris Immigration Control stenciled across it in red.

The roar of the shuttle engines quietened, and the vibrations ceased. Jas undid her safety belt, but she hesitated, hoping for something before she disembarked. After a moment, her silent wish came true. The door to the cockpit opened and Carl's lanky frame filled it, leaning against the edge.

"All set?" he asked.

"Yep. Ready as I'll ever be." She got up and retrieved her bag from the locker.

"Remember," Carl said, "if you need to leave earlier than we arranged, just send the word. The *Bricoleur's* right above. I can be here in a couple of hours."

"I'll remember. Hopefully, it won't come to that."

"Yeah. Hopefully. Have you figured out where you're gonna go yet?"

"First, I'm going to find a place to stay. Then in the morning I thought I'd try to talk to the governor. See if there's been any comms from the Council. Maybe the Territory officials know about the Shadows already. It's a long shot, but it's worth a try."

"Hmm, yeah. Got any plans to go anywhere else?"

"You mean am I going to go back to the place where I grew up? Maybe. I haven't made up my mind yet. It's been so long, everyone I remember will have moved on."

"What about the colony?"

"The disaster site? No, I don't think I'll bother. They must have rebuilt it decades ago. I don't see any point in going there."

Carl looked doubtful, but he didn't say anything else. The pause began to turn awkward, so Jas shouldered her bag. "I'll be off."

"Okay."

Another pause. Jas wanted nothing more than to step over to Carl and hug him, but her feet wouldn't take her where her heart wanted to go. Instead, they turned her around and carried her to the exit.

"See you soon," she said over her shoulder, unable to meet his gaze.

"Yeah. See you soon. Good luck, Jas."

Six

D r. Sparks was a temperate man and rarely experienced extreme emotions, but after his long secondment investigating the Paths, he was nearing the end of his tether. The death of the administrator who had tried to cut them while they were aboard Polestar's satellite quarantine station had intensified the company's scrutiny of the creatures. Rather than releasing Sparks to his usual duty as medical officer aboard prospecting starships, Polestar had insisted that he accompany the Paths to their more specialized labs on Mars. Anything that could kill had potential to be a weapon, of course.

What Sparks didn't understand was why it had to be *him* doing the experimenting. Other Polestar scientific officers were better qualified and more experienced in research work. Three of them had been assigned to research the Paths alongside him: Graydon, Adrieux, and Rincker. Two women and one man with little to say outside of scientific discussions.

Sparks assumed it was a security issue. They were keeping him on task to limit his ability to divulge secrets. He wished he could air his sense of grievance about his secondment, but there never seemed to be an appropriate opportunity. Maybe they had an NDA to sign. He'd gladly do it for the opportunity to escape the research facility and return to what he did best: practicing medicine. But he never felt comfortable enough under their withering stares to express his dissatisfaction nor broach the subject of moving on.

When it came to the highly lucrative and explosive nature of weapons research, he also wasn't sure what Polestar was capable of doing in order to keep a discovery under wraps. It wasn't like he felt under threat day to day, but he knew the company was ruthless when it came to safeguarding its profits.

Each morning Sparks felt unsure that he could endure one more day of research on the cryptic Paths. Nothing he nor his colleagues had done had yielded quantifiable, statistically significant results beyond those he'd observed and recorded on the quarantine station. The odd, periodic *fading* of the creatures, the weird euphoric trance of the research assistant, Rogers, and the administrator's death remained unexplained.

All the researchers had managed to do was to induce either a temporary coma or death in animals that threatened the Paths. However, because the animals they'd used were dumb creatures incapable of vocalizing their experiences, no one was any wiser as to exactly *what* the Paths were doing or how they were doing it.

Sparks and his fellow scientists had recorded elevated heart rates, blood pressure, and brain activity of comatose animals, and the cessation of heart function in those that died. The simple difference between the Paths' response lay in the degree to which they felt threatened.

After yet another morning of boring, fruitless experimentation, Sparks was eating lunch with his colleagues. All four were intent on their interfaces as usual. The lack of meaningful conversation made alternative sources of entertainment necessary.

Sparks was reading about the recent appointment of a new Martian Governor. The man in question was a natural, and he made no effort to hide it. In fact, he was known for championing naturals' right to work and to freedom from discrimination. The politician had cited what Sparks believed to be flawed research. The studies supposedly demonstrated that natural selection was more likely than gene modding for high intelligence to give rise to geniuses like Einstein, Hawking, and Casson. Researchers proposed that humankind's understanding of the genetic foundation of intelligence was still incomplete, and that as yet poorly understood environmental factors could play a large role in the determination of intellectual ability.

The notion that random gene selection and upbringing could produce anything superior to sophisticated modding was preposterous to Sparks, and he unconsciously snorted in derision as he read the article.

Graydon noticed his reaction. A phlegmatic woman with a horsey face and long, lank hair, she'd always held an antipathy toward Sparks.

"Something funny?" she asked.

"Er, no, not really," Sparks replied.

"Hmpf," Graydon said and returned to her interface.

Ordinarily, Sparks would have left it at that. He knew his views on modded individuals versus naturals weren't politically correct, and over the years he'd become accustomed to being circumspect about to whom he aired them. He was sure that many others shared his opinion that genetic modification produced human beings who were superior in every way to their counterparts, but that few dared speak the truth about the matter. He'd learned to keep silent unless he was fairly sure he was speaking to a like-minded individual.

Today was different. Weeks of boredom and frustration made him careless.

"It's this new governor," he blurted, so loudly that all three of his colleagues took notice. "I mean, what were people thinking? Why has he been voted in? I don't understand it."

"What don't you understand?" asked Graydon. Her dark look should have warned Sparks to moderate his words, but he was intent on getting all his resentment and irritation off his chest.

"What I don't understand is, why would anyone elect a natural? I mean, what does a natural have to offer? Compared to someone whose parents actually *cared* about how their child turned out?"

Graydon put down her interface and folded her arms over her chest. Her eyes were hooded. Rincker was gesturing with his hand for Sparks to cut it out, but he took no notice.

"You think someone who was modded would do a better job as governor?" Graydon asked.

"Isn't it obvious?" Sparks replied. "Do I need to spell it out? Genetic modification creates better human beings. That's what it's *for*," he added, as if explaining to a child. "That's the whole point, isn't it?"

Sparks finally began to notice the woman's severe expression, and the weight of comprehension settled over his stomach. "Of course, not that *all* naturals are inferior. Only...only..." He swallowed. "Only some. I mean, it stands to reason, with the genetic variation involved in natural selection, that modification is required to avoid..." His words dried up and a flush crept from his neck to his face.

Rincker cleared his throat in the uncomfortable silence. Graydon carefully pushed back her chair and stood. Without a word, she left the table.

"Need I tell you?" Rincker asked Sparks.

"She's a natural." Sparks groaned and buried his face in his hands. After a moment he pressed his palms down on the table. "How was I to know? I mean, who could have guessed that someone in her position could have gotten where she is without modding?"

Rincker raised his eyebrows. "Don't you think you've said enough?"

Sparks clenched his jaw and returned to scrutinizing his interface, though he didn't register what was written on the screen. He was too preoccupied with his feeling of somehow being duped.

————

Later, Sparks was sure that Graydon had something to do with the decision that came down from above to use one of 'their own' to test the Paths' threat response. It made no sense, of course. Scientists didn't experiment on themselves. They used volunteers or occasionally prisoners. But the word came, apparently, that as none of the animal tests had yielded useful results, a scientist was required to move the experimentation to the next level.

As the tests were top secret, the person had to be someone who was already involved in the study and understood the required observations. There was no drawing of straws. Sparks was told by the others that he would be the one to approach the Paths with a scalpel, as Rogers had on the quarantine station before falling into a coma.

In vain he'd searched his colleagues' faces for signs of sympathy or concern for his well-being. Sure that any attempt to avoid the task would result in his incarceration, or worse, he had no choice but to agree. He only hoped that the Paths would induce the euphoric coma Rogers had experienced, and not their other response when under threat.

Brusquely, his colleagues attached electrodes to his chest, fingers and scalp. They would transmit data as the experiment took place. Sparks needed no readouts to tell him how his body was reacting. He was shaking and sweating so badly he could hardly hold the scalpel.

They placed a safety helmet over the scalp electrodes and pads to his knees and elbows to help prevent injury if he should collapse. In Sparks's opinion their efforts to help protect him were almost comical.

The Paths were in their sealed chamber. Weeks after their removal from the mysteriously buried starship on the hostile aliens' planet, they had survived miraculously with no food or water. As the scientists had discovered, they were apparently also unfazed by prolonged exposure to extreme temperatures and a vacuum.

Sparks gazed with hatred at the innocuous-looking, inverted, fungus-like bags. The creatures had caused him so much suffering, he would have gladly shoved the scalpel into them and cut them to shreds if it weren't for the fact that such an action would inevitably result in his death.

On Sparks's right, his colleagues were watching him through a thickened glass panel. Their faces were impassive. Sparks's rage rose up against his treatment as a test subject. *He* should be on the other side of the glass, patiently observing what was going on.

Graydon gestured at him. He scowled and took a step closer to the Paths. They remained predictably still, but Sparks began to experience heightened sensations of panic and fear. Though he knew the feelings originated with the aliens, they felt very real to him.

What wouldn't he give to swap places with Graydon? It should be *her* in here, not him. He was modded. He was better. His life was *worth more*.

She was frowning at him and gesturing for him to move closer. She spoke, and Sparks lip-read, *Get on with it*. It was as much as he could do not to lift the scalpel and shake it at her—threaten her with it rather than the Paths.

If he got out of the chamber alive, he'd get his revenge. He'd make her pay. Flames of anger coursed through his veins. He would get the experiment over with. Turning back to the Paths, he strode toward them, almost running in his haste.

He didn't even feel his head hit the floor. He was in nirvana, and he never wanted to leave.

SEVEN

J as put down her bag and went to look out the window of the viewing platform in her hotel room. The rocky Martian landscape spread out to the left beyond the distant spaceport. A shuttle was taking off, the brilliant glow of its rockets slowly fading as it forced its way up through the thin Martian atmosphere. On the right were the snaking lines of the hyperloop tunnels linking domes that marked the entrances to underground towns, factories, and farms. The small, pale sun was setting on the far side of the thinly spaced domes, and the sky was rapidly changing from pink to black as hard, white stars came out.

Mars hadn't changed much, from what Jas could remember. She wasn't surprised. A couple of decades wasn't long in the terraforming process. The modded soil bacteria that scientists had seeded the planet with were doing their job, but enriching Mars' atmosphere with sufficient oxygen to make it breathable would take centuries, if it were actually possible. Many doubted the planet could ever sustain an atmosphere anywhere near equivalent to Earth's.

Colonization had begun prior to the invention of interstellar flight, but it really took off when global warming had reached its peak and millions of refugees were fleeing famine, natural disasters, and ruined local environments. Richer countries closed their borders, and for many, Mars was the only escape.

Jas recalled what her dead Martian friend, Ozment, had told her: the planet had also provided a haven for those escaping increasing division in societies. Genetic modification had become the new privilege, but not all parents could afford the high cost of altering their offsprings' genes just after conception, or they had a philosophical objection to the process. Unmodded children tended to grow up poorer and more disadvantaged. Though the newly formed Global Government hadn't been slow to outlaw the requirement to reveal one's genetic status when applying for jobs or educational courses, modding generally produced smarter, more creative and sociable, physically enhanced individuals. Their advantages were clear, and *natural* became a slur.

Those who rejected the new social order, or who were rejected by it—underworlders—had come to Mars in droves.

In recent years, however, galactic colonization had taken off. Beyond the Solar System were planets far more favorable to life than Mars. The flood of new Martians had dried to a trickle, and then reversed, as they abandoned their cold, dry, barren world for friendlier planets. Jas wondered if Mars would eventually be entirely deserted, and the underground settlements would one day be as empty of life as the surface; if Valles Marineris and the rest of the municipalities dotted over the planet would become no more than ghost towns, inhabited by the memories of long-dead Martians who had eked out pitiful lifespans in harsh conditions.

She hadn't anticipated returning to her original home, yet if she were to ever find out more about her origins, now was her chance. Until she spoke with Ozment, she'd never considered that her deceased, anonymous parents might have been underworlders. The records of her birth had been lost in the colony disaster that claimed their lives, but it would have been easy for her to find out her genetic status. Like many things in her painful past, she chose not to dwell on it. She'd chosen to stay out of the whole modded/natural debate.

She just didn't know if she could bring herself to investigate her past. Facing an attack of hostile aliens on a far-flung planet seemed a more inviting option.

An interface embedded on the wall of the hotel room beeped, distracting Jas from her musings. It was the hotel reception. She accepted the call. The receptionist who had checked her in appeared on the screen. Like Jas and all other Martians, his skin was deep olive, and his eyes and hair were reddish-brown.

"Hi. Is your room to your satisfaction, Ms. Harrington?"

"Yes, everything's fine."

"Great. I hope you don't mind, but I just checked your passport details, and I saw that it's been quite a while since you visited Mars?"

"That's right."

"In case you haven't yet read the room information, I thought I would just let you know that the Rad X protocol still applies. Please try to limit your above-ground time. In the event of a solar storm warning, stay underground until further notice. You'll find your bed access to the right of the screen."

"Okay, I've got it."

"Thank you. Our dining room is currently open and closes at nine. Breakfast starts at seven-thirty. Let us know if there's anything else we can help you with. Enjoy your stay."

The screen turned dark.

Jas had forgotten about the radiation exposure avoidance protocol. All Martians received mandatory gene therapy to help protect them from the sun's radiation. It gave them their unusual coloring, but it only went so far. Exposure to radioactive solar and cosmic particles still increased the risk of cancer over the long term and prolonged exposure could cause radiation sickness.

The hyperloop to the hotel had been above ground, but the journey had taken only around half an hour. She could easily get to Valles Marineris 5 and back within a couple of hours. The question was, did she want to visit the site of her parents' deaths and the largest disaster in the history of human colonization? She didn't have to. She was there to find out what the Transgalactic Council were doing about the Shadows. No one would say anything if she didn't go.

Her mouth went dry at the thought of visiting VM5, though she knew that, realistically, she had nothing to fear. The settlement had no doubt been rebuilt years ago. Not a trace of the devastation would remain. VM5 would consist of the same drab domes and tunnels as the other towns, connecting a few thousand underground homes, shops, workplaces, and factories.

Would it hurt her just to go and see it? Maybe the experience would do her good. All her life she'd been running away from her past. Her long habit had cost her the sense of any place being her home. It had also cost her friends, and now it was looking like it might cost her Carl.

She smiled at the irony of the situation. Her job required her to be the bravest person aboard a starship. She was the one who was expected to walk first into unknown danger. Yet in reality, she was a coward.

Moving swiftly before she lost her resolve, she pressed the interface to call reception for transport information. Though the idea made her legs go weak, she would visit VM5.

————

The hyperloop gate warbled as Jas swiped her card and passed through. In some ways, returning to Mars was like stepping back into the past. Credchip technology hadn't reached the colony. For Jas, this was fortunate as she no longer carried a credchip beneath the skin on the inside of her right wrist. A scar was all that remained from where an underworlder had forcibly removed it, but Phelan had supplied her with ample funds to preload onto a credcard.

The single-carriage hyperloop module arrived within a few minutes. Jas went aboard. She had her choice of the ten seats in the small, empty carriage. She sat down uneasily, wondering why there were no other passengers. Martian society shared many similarities with Earth's. Weekday evenings were commuter time, and Jas had expected at least some workers returning to VM5 from jobs outside the settlement.

As the module stopped at more stations, a trickle of people got on and off. Jas's only respite from her growing disquiet was the way that she was ignored by the other passengers. She was just another Martian. No one took any notice of her. She'd never quite gotten used to the double takes and sidelong glances her appearance attracted among Earthers.

VM5 was the farthest point on the loop. The carriage was once more empty when Jas arrived. The doors hissed open and she alighted. It was like being ejected into a scene from a history vid. She was surrounded by plain metal walls, devoid of even the simple, old-fashioned interfaces and their scrolling ads she'd seen at other stations on her journey. The gates were from an earlier era too. The station was deserted.

Dread grew in Jas. Her trip was intended to reassure her that time had moved on, that the colony had been rebuilt and repopulated, and the terrible disaster had been forgotten. The idea had been, as far as she'd formed one, to convince herself that it was time for her to move on too.

She hesitated at the gate. *Krat it.* She wasn't going to run away any more. Setting her jaw, Jas swiped her card. The gate chimed. Even the sound was different from the rest of the hyperloop. She stepped through and left through the only exit.

A few minutes' walk along a bare tunnel that sloped gently down, taking her underground, brought her to a set of closed, plain metal doors and a booth. What was going on? Why was the settlement shut up? Where was everyone?

An attendant was in the process of closing down the booth. He stopped what he was doing at Jas's approach and glanced at his screen. "Sorry, closing in five minutes. Not a lot of point going in now. Maybe come back tomorrow?"

Jas stood before the man, her hands gripping the edge of his desk. He looked from her hands to her face. His expression took on the appearance of mild alarm. "Er...it's five minutes until—"

"I heard you." Jas's mind was whirring so much she struggled to know what to say. "I just need to...could you help me?"

The man's alarmed look deepened. "Are you feeling all right? Maybe you should sit down?" He moved aside to offer her his chair.

"I'm okay. I just need to know..." Jas's grip tightened. "What's going on? Where are the inhabitants? And why's everything so outdated?"

"Oh." The man's features relaxed. "I think you're a bit confused. This is Valles Marineris Five, the scene of a colony disaster. If you go back to the Loop, it'll take you where—"

"I *know* this is VM5. What I don't know...wait." Everything began to slot into place. The old-fashioned station and tunnel, the attendant in his booth. "Is this some kind of museum?"

"Yes, that's right," the man said, as if he were talking to a five year old. "No need for any alarm. Just head back to the—"

"No. I'm where I want to be. I meant to come here. It's just that I wasn't expecting this. Didn't they rebuild after the disaster?" She tried to remember back to her time in the Martian institute for cared-for children. She couldn't recall anyone telling her what happened to VM5. No one had told her it was being turned into an attraction.

"No, VM5 was never rebuilt. I'm surprised you don't know that. Have you been away from Mars for a long time? No, they made the place safe and it stayed as it was for a few years. But no one was willing to invest in repair and renovation. It was cheaper to excavate another settlement. As time went on, there were calls to demolish it. Raze the site. Then finally they put it to a vote, and the Territory elected to preserve it in memory of those who'd died and as a warning to future generations about what could happen if they don't put safety first.

"But," said the man, swiping his interface closed and putting on his coat, "VM5's closed right now. You can take a tour tomorrow, if you come back."

Jas looked at the closed doors at the entrance to VM5, then back at the man. The shock of finding her birthplace hardly touched since her parents' deaths was dissipating a little. It was being replaced by a compulsion to go through those doors. The feeling was so strong that she was nauseated. She knew that if she left, she might never find the courage to return.

"I want to go inside. Now. I can't come back."

"I'm very sorry," said the attendant. "We're definitely closed. VM5 opens at ten tomorrow and every day except Sunday. You're welcome to return during opening hours and take a tour."

Jas didn't move.

After a moment, the man left and walked a short distance up the tunnel.

Jas still didn't move. "Please?" she said to the departing man's back.

He stopped and turned. He tilted his head. "It really means that much to you? Can I ask why it's so important that you see VM5 right now?"

Jas glanced back at the closed doors once more. She swallowed. "I was born somewhere in there. My parents died in the disaster, but I survived and...I...just...need to go in."

EIGHT

parks's transition from scientist to guinea pig had been abrupt. After what had felt like an eternity of bliss, he woke up in a hospital bed within the research facility. At first, the quiet, regular beeps and flickering glow of lights on the monitoring equipment were confused with the serene vision passing through his mind. He thought the sounds and lights were only another manifestation of the perfect beauty and splendor he'd seen since trying to take a scalpel to the Paths. As more and more of his dream faded, the terrible realization that it was all ending hit him.

A ceiling came into focus high above, and Sparks gradually became aware that his mouth and throat were very dry. He worked his tongue and lips, trying to generate some moisture. He moved, weakly, and discovered that plastic tubes had been inserted into him to supply water and nutrients and to drain his waste.

He closed his eyes and tried to will himself back to the place he'd left. It had felt like an actual place that he'd been in, not a dream, even though he had the evidence of his physical body being on a hospital bed. If only he could slip back into a coma, maybe he wouldn't ever have to leave that wonderful place again.

It was no good. The last threads of paradise broke and scattered, and Sparks was back in the medical center within the research facility on Mars. Despair overwhelmed him. He groaned out his frustration and unhappiness. The sound of his voice, or perhaps the alterations in his brain waves, blood pressure, or heart rate registered by the monitoring equipment brought a nurse to him.

The man pushed open the door to his room and locked eyes. But before entering, the nurse lifted his lapel to his lips and spoke softly into the comm button pinned there. A professional smile then spread over his face and he completed his entrance.

"Mister Sparks, how are you feeling? It's good to see you awake."

Mister Sparks? He tried to voice his objection to the word, but all that would come out of his mouth was an angry croak. He tried to lift his arms to gesture, but they were so weak that even the light blanket that lay over him restrained them.

"Take it easy," said the nurse. "Take it easy. Everything will feel strange for a little while, until you get your strength back." He went to a monitor, bent down to peer at the screen, and adjusted something. His head turned briefly to the door, as if he were expecting someone.

"Water," Sparks managed to whisper, but the nurse either didn't hear him or was ignoring him. With a great effort, Sparks cleared his throat. "Water," he repeated, louder.

The nurse straightened up and turned to him. "You'd like some water? Sure. Just a sip. Don't want to shock your system." He filled a paper cup from the wall dispenser and pressed something at the bottom of Sparks's bed with his foot. "Coming up," he said, as the bed began to vibrate and the section below the upper half of Sparks's body began to slowly rise.

The nurse held the cup to Sparks's lips. He was taking a small mouthful of water when his fellow researchers arrived. *He* thought of *them* as his fellow researchers, anyway. It wasn't at all clear whether they thought of him in the same way. As they came in, without ringing the chime, their small smiles seemed smiles of satisfaction that they could glean more information from their now-conscious subject, not smiles of relief at his recovery.

"Sparks, you came around. Great," said Rincker. "How are you feeling? You must tell us all about it." He nodded to the nurse, who pressed a screen. They were recording him—recording the results of their experiment.

This attitude from the people he had worked with for the previous few weeks compounded his misery. Where was their respect for a fellow scientist? Where was their gratitude to him for becoming a test subject? Sparks cleared his throat once more. "Must I?"

His question threw the scientists into confusion. They straightened up from their hunched, eager stances over him. A look passed between them.

"Yes, of course you must," said Graydon. "That was the whole point of what you did. Don't you remember?" She said to the others, "Maybe he's suffered some memory loss." She took out the interface she was holding under an arm and tapped at it.

Sparks was determined to cling to the last shred of dignity he had. "My memory is perfectly fine, and I didn't sign any kind of agreement about taking part in this experiment. So unless my understanding of the legislation covering human experimentation is inaccurate, I don't believe I'm under an obligation to tell you anything. I signed nothing. I agreed to nothing. I gave up none of my rights. I could get up right now and walk out of here, and there's nothing any of you could do to stop me."

Though he tried not to show it, he quailed a little as he spoke his final statement. He'd been—he was still—conducting weapons research. He wasn't at all sure that he was as free to leave at any moment as he'd stated. He'd been bluffing, or threatening, or perhaps wishing. He wasn't sure which.

"Oh, come now," said Adrieux. "There's no need for that kind of attitude. We're all in this together, aren't we?"

"Are we?" Sparks asked. "It seems like I'm the one in this bed after having risked my life to carry out an experiment on the Paths, and you three are safe, sound, and healthy, standing around me in your lab coats. It doesn't look to me like we're all in this together."

Rincker pursed his lips and glanced at the others. "Okay, I hear you, Sparks. You just woke up. You aren't in the mood to talk right now. We get it. Let's leave it...a couple of hours? Maybe you'll feel better then."

They left. Sparks was under no illusions about what the man's conciliatory remarks were about. He was still, in their eyes, no longer a colleague but a test subject. Any concern they'd felt toward him as another human being was gone. These were hardened weapons research scientists. It took a certain detachment to do their job effectively, and these three had it in spades. While he'd been a fellow researcher, he'd been a real person to them. Now that he'd become the source of information about a potential weapon, they didn't, or perhaps couldn't, see him in the same light.

"I'll put this here," said the nurse, placing the paper cup on the table next to his bed. "We can begin your recovery program now. It's best to begin it as soon as a patient wakes up. Back in a moment."

The door slid closed behind the nurse. Left to his thoughts, Sparks began to calm down a little. He mentally went over his responses to the scientists. Had he been too hasty in denying their wishes? They were ruthless in their pursuit of results. They would stop at nothing to find out what they wanted to know about the Paths.

A heavy weight settled over him. Had he put his life in danger? If he refused to take part in the research process, what might happen? What did the scientists have the authority to do? Did he already know too much to be allowed to return to his normal duties? The Paths could kill. There was no doubt about that. Would the scientists use him to push them to the limit?

Sparks cursed the day the aliens had been brought aboard the *Galathea*. All his life, he'd done as he was told. How had he ended up like this?

He longed to return to that heavenly place of his coma. Hope flickered within him. The prospect of the Path-induced trance was inviting. If he gave the scientists a little information, he could suggest that he repeat the experiment to find out more. It would be risky, yes, but he knew how far to push the aliens before they reacted. He wouldn't overstep the mark.

At the very least, his plan would buy him time until he could figure a way out of the predicament, and he would return to that wonderful paradise again.

He searched around for the call button and summoned the nurse. The man appeared within seconds. His time seemed to be devoted entirely to Sparks's welfare. Of course it was, Sparks realized. He might now only be a test subject to the other scientists, but he was an extremely important test subject.

"I want to speak to my colleagues," he told the nurse.

After weeks of being ignored and sidelined by Graydon, Rincker and Adrieux, he was going to become an object of their rapt attention. His only hope was to milk the situation for all it was worth.

NINE

Jas and the attendant at the VM5 entrance waited for his mother. After hearing Jas's story, he'd called her, explaining that she would be very interested in meeting Jas and he was sure that Jas would be interested in meeting her.

The woman couldn't have lived far away, for no more than fifteen minutes after the attendant had finished his call, a short, round figure came bustling down the tunnel. She was late middle-aged. Her nose and chin approached ahead of the rest of her.

She was in a hurry, and she arrived puffing and panting. Leaning on her son's desk, she gripped her side with her other hand as she caught her breath. She repeatedly looked Jas up and down and nodded to herself as she gasped. When she could finally speak, she moved to Jas and shook her hand, clasping it warmly with the other. "Name?" she asked.

"Harrington. Jas Harrington. But I was given my name by the institute where I grew up. I don't know my real name." It felt weird to say it, though it was true. Jas had never really considered that, for a brief time, she'd had a different name. Her *real* name.

"Hmm...Backra Smart," said the woman. "And this is my son, Tony. Did you introduce yourself, Tony?" Before Tony could answer, she went on, "'Course he didn't. Never does. Got no manners. So is it true, what he said? You were born on VM5? And you've come back to see the place after all these years? Well, well, well. Glad you came. So very glad. Please, come inside. Come in. Come in." She went to the doors, but they remained closed. "Tony, open the place up, son."

"But it's..." Tony half-protested before a look from his mother silenced him. He huffed and went to his desk, opened his interface, and keyed in a code. The tunnel was silent but for Backra's continued panting. The click as the lock opened and the swoosh as the doors slid apart were loud.

Backra scurried through in her rolling gait while Jas hung back. Stopping and looking over her shoulder, Backra gestured for Jas to follow. She called to her son, "You wait out there, Tony, in case the inspector comes. The kid would only get in the way," she said softly to Jas as she stepped inside VM5. In spite of her racing heart, Jas suppressed a smile. The *kid* was at least as old as her.

As they went a little farther in, movement-sensitive lighting flickered on. Jas caught her breath. They really had left the place as it had been after the explosion. Jas and Backra stood in a wide lobby, or what remained of a lobby. The walls were entirely black and charred. In places, the heat from the blast had melted the metal, revealing scorched, bare Martian rock.

Noticing Jas's expression, Backra nodded. "It's quite something isn't it? I used to conduct tours, you know, until Tony took over. Been through the place tens of thousands of times. But you never quite get used to it. What would you like to see?"

"I don't know," Jas replied. "I don't know what there is to see."

"Most visitors are interested in the site of the explosion. What there is left of it, anyway. But I'm guessing you'd like to see the residential areas? They're more interesting in my opinion. Though very sad, of course. Come this way. And tell me all about your connection to VM5. Tony didn't explain it clearly. You were really born here?"

Corridors branched from three sides of the lobby. The remains of signs were just discernible next to the corridor entrance that

Backra led Jas to. All she could make out on the carbonized surface were the figures and letters, 6-AE.

"Yes," Jas replied as they set off. Above, lights strung on bare wires looped along the ceiling. "That's what I was told anyway. I've never bothered to dig into my past or check anything out, but I remember when I was young, a carer told me that I'd been born here and that I was the only survivor of the disaster."

"Hmm...maybe I'm imagining it," Backra said, "or maybe my mind's playing tricks now that you've mentioned that, but I think I remember you."

"What?" Jas exclaimed.

"Sorry, dear. I don't mean I knew you as a baby. No. I think I remember hearing that only one person who'd been inside at the time of the explosion survived, and that it was a baby. But I never heard anything official. It wasn't surprising. So much was kept from us about what had happened."

"What do you mean? What was kept from you?"

"Easier to ask what *wasn't* kept from us. I don't think anyone really believed what they said had caused the explosion, for instance. The official explanation didn't make any sense. Oxygen levels beyond safety limits? Electrical fire? Equipment was basic at that time, it's true, but even then we had alarms to tell us if the atmosphere levels went out of balance. We had automatic fire dampeners." Backra sighed and shook her head. "People asked questions, of course. But the more questions were asked, the tighter the Territory Office closed their lips. Wait for the official investigation, they said. Then we'll have answers.

"But the investigation took years, and everyone was busy just struggling to survive. By the time the findings were announced, most people had moved on with their lives. Things were hard enough as it was without embarking on a wild goose chase trying to track down what had really happened. But I could never let it go. Still can't. So it warms my heart, you see, to meet you. To meet someone who made it out alive."

They'd reached a junction, and Backra paused before saying, "This way."

"Can I ask why it means so much to you?" Jas asked. They were passing doors that starkly contrasted with the blackened corridor. They were modern, and they had clearly been placed there to seal away what lay beyond them. Jas hoped they would stop in a moment. It was a lot to take in at once.

"I worked here," said Backra. "My settlement, VM4, was finished, and the VM5 colonists needed some extra help putting on the finishing touches. I'd come over every day to help fit out living quarters and get them ready for new arrivals. They were flooding in at that point. Mars isn't exactly anyone's first choice any more, but at the time it was popular. You could get a ticket to Mars cheaply. Government subsidies. They were glad to see the back of the likes that came here. I liked to meet the new settlers. I liked to hear stories about Earth. I still missed it badly then, even though things weren't good there. Took me quite a while to get used to being a tunnel rat. Don't know if I ever quite made it. Ah. Here we are."

They stopped outside a room. A plaque had been fitted to the wall, simply stating the room's number.

"Only a few rooms are open, but they all look much the same anyway." She opened the door.

It was a simple, two-bedroom apartment, utterly burnt out. Charred furniture remained and blackened lumps that might once have been toys strewed the floor. Though decades had passed since the fire, the smell of burnt metal and plastic still hung faintly in the air. It reminded Jas of the odor of burning defense units, except that it wasn't mixed with the sickening scent of barbecued meat. Thankfully, that smell no longer lingered.

"Do you want to know exactly what happened during the disaster?" Backra asked. "Or would that be too close to the bone?"

"I want to know," Jas replied quickly. Now that she'd taken the first step she wanted to go the whole way and find out all that she could. She *needed* to know.

"Right. Well, stop me if it gets too much." Backra folded her hands together in front of her and began to speak as if reciting from memory. "When the oxygen ignited, fireballs swept down the corridors. They think they were carried on updrafts leading out and into the Loop. Everyone in the open areas was killed instantly. The fireballs ignited everything they touched, and due to the high oxygen levels, a fierce fire quickly started. It consumed the rest of the place within minutes. The high temperatures and volatile gases killed anyone who was still alive after the fireballs passed. If it's any comfort to you, their deaths would have been very quick. I'm sorry."

Jas had a vision of the apartment as it had once been. Very ordinary, but fresh and new. Through an open door leading to a bedroom, she saw a figure holding a small baby. From outside came the sound of a massive explosion. The ground juddered. A mug of coffee on the living room table tottered and fell. The explosion was followed by a deep, soft whoosh as a fireball passed outside. The spilt coffee began to steam. Screams and shrieks followed from outside. The figure hesitated before running to a safety capsule and thrusting the baby inside.

Why didn't the person get in with their baby? Did they think they had time to find the other parent? Did they want to make sure their partner was safe? In Jas's mind, the figure closed the capsule lid. The lock clicked shut. As the person turned and took just one step, a wave of heat overwhelmed them and they fell.

Backra was quietly waiting, giving Jas time for her thoughts.

"You said you can't let go of what happened," Jas said. "Why? Do you think the Territory Office were hiding something? Was there a cover up?"

Backra's mouth drooped sadly. "I knew those people who died, though I didn't work among them long. They were good people. Kind, honest, and brave to come all the way to Mars to make a new life. I couldn't get used to the idea of all those hundreds of lives gone in an instant. Still can't get used to it, even after all these years.

"Was there a cover up? Yes, I'd say there was. There was a lot of foot-dragging that went on, and apart from the general findings of the inquest, the files were sealed. They won't be available to the public for another eighty years. Anyone who was an adult at the time of the disaster will be dead by then. No one will be around to take the blame. And, like I said, that the fire happened at all is very fishy. If I were to be completely honest with you, I wouldn't be surprised if it was deliberate."

"You think it might have been arson?" Jas asked. "But, why? Why would someone want to kill all those people? That's the act of a monster."

"Because they were underworlders, that's why. Every single blessed one of them. This was before your time. You won't remember, but naturals were hated. I mean really hated. A lot of people thought they were holding back the advancement of the human race. Polluting it with random gene selection. Allowing genetic diseases and weak traits to continue after we finally had the chance to stamp them all out. That was why underworlders ended up in places like this, where they could live their lives in peace. But it wouldn't surprise me if someone had thought they were doing everyone a favor by wiping out a whole load of them at once."

Jas's knees were weak. She wanted to sit down, but there was nowhere for her to sit.

"I'm sorry," Backra said, seeing her expression. "I'm upsetting you with my ramblings. Don't take any notice of me. I'm just an old woman, full of nonsense. Let's go somewhere else. What else would you like to see?"

"I don't think I want to see any more," Jas said. "I think I've seen and heard enough."

TEN

Jas needed people. She actually needed Carl, but he was hundreds of miles above her somewhere among the unwavering stars in the inky Martian night, and he was probably tired of her and her endless dithering. Strangers would have to do. Voices, color, movement, laughter. She needed all these things.

She was back at the hotel after thanking Backra for her kindness and the stories she'd told. The evening was getting old. She should have gone to bed, but she knew she wouldn't sleep. She wouldn't be able to erase that charred room or Backra's theory on what might have killed all those people, her parents among them, from her mind for a while.

Jas was also getting used to the idea that she was a natural. If everything that she'd been told were true, there didn't seem much doubt about it anymore. She wasn't sure how she felt. She hadn't been disadvantaged. She'd been fairly successful in her life without any modding. Yet she also didn't think she had much in common with underworlders as she knew them. Backra's revelations had left her feeling like she didn't fit in anywhere.

Jas smirked wryly to herself. Same as usual, then.

She called reception. The previous receptionist's shift had

finished, and a new face greeted her. "Yes, Ms. Harrington? How can I help you?"

"Can you tell me the closest bar?"

"Certainly. I'll send directions to the closest establishments. Is there anything else I can help you with this evening?"

"No, that's it."

"Great. I'd like to remind you that the hotel's main door is locked at midnight. If you arrive after this time, please contact the night staff via the security panel. Guests are not allowed to invite non-paying guests into their rooms after midnight. Have a good evening."

The receptionist seemed to have an idea about why Jas was going to a bar, but all she wanted was to not be alone.

———

The Loop conveyed Jas to a bar within fifteen minutes. As she went in, she was relieved when no eyes turned toward her. If she'd done the same thing on Earth, she would have immediately become an object of attention. Here, she was just another lanky, red-haired Martian out for the evening.

The map the receptionist had sent her included seven or eight bars within the vicinity of the hotel. Drinking was a popular pastime on Mars. Buggy racing was another, Jas recalled. Out on the red, rocky, dusty plains, youths would ride their wide-wheeled buggies as far as battery life allowed, and sometimes farther, knowing they wouldn't make it back. Like on most colony worlds, suicide rates among Martians were high, especially among adolescents whose parents couldn't afford to send them to Earth for several years to harden and strengthen their bones. Doomed to life on all-but-lifeless Mars or another low-g planet if they were lucky, many young Martians simply gave up.

Scanning the bar, Jas noticed that a good number of young Martians also sought oblivion in alcohol. She wasn't sure if the drinking age was lower here than on Earth, but some of the bar's patrons were surely below it. The law was a nebulous thing in the colonies.

A human bartender was serving. She wasn't sure if he was there for the personal touch or because Mars was really that far behind the times.

The bar seats were all occupied, but it didn't matter. Though Jas needed people around her, she didn't feel like talking. She took her ordered beer and found a dark corner to sit in. Stretching out her long legs under the small table, she rested her head against the wall behind her and watched the crowd.

The hum of conversation began to take its effect and some of the tension of the last few hours began to ease from her. Jas sipped her beer and tried to mentally tease out the implications of what Backra had told her. Had VM5 been sabotaged to explode? Had all those hundreds of colonists been murdered? Had there been a cover up about it?

Jas didn't know what to do if Backra's suspicions were correct. She didn't have time to deal with a decades-old mystery. If the Shadows weren't in the process of taking over Earth, probably as a prelude to taking over the galaxy, she might have dug further, but as it was, she had more urgent problems to fix. Avenging her long-dead parents would have to wait.

Taking another sip of beer, Jas relaxed a little more. The visit to VM5 had been traumatic, but she was glad she'd gone through with it and seen and heard what she had. For so many years, she'd dreaded the prospect of revisiting her past. It'd seemed to contain too much pain and unhappiness, but, on reflection, seeing VM5 had given her a sense of release. It was as if she'd opened her closet door expecting to see ghosts and monsters but found only dust and cobwebs.

An argument was breaking out at the bar. The bartender was cutting someone off. It was easy to see why. The man could barely hold himself upright on his bar stool. There was something about him that looked odd. Unlike the plainer clothes of the men and women sitting around him, he was wearing a suit.

"I shouldn't have given you your last drink," said the bartender. "That's it. Go home."

"I haven't got a home," slurred the customer.

Jas's beer glass was at her mouth, but she stopped mid-sip. She put down the glass and swallowed the half-mouthful of beer. She knew that voice. She was sure of it.

"No home to go to," continued the drunk man, "'less you count that horrible lil' cubicle at the facility. Nowhere to go. If I go back there, they'll put me in with those things again." He raised his hands as if confessing something shameful. "Not saying I don't like it. I do. But...but..." Sobs began to choke him. "I could *die*. I could *die*. And they don't care. Nobody cares." He slumped onto the bar, his head on his arms. His shoulders began to shake with sobs.

The customers on either side of the man patted him on the back. "Let him sleep it off a bit," one of them said to the bartender. "He isn't doing any harm."

The bartender shook his head like he didn't approve of the idea, but he walked away to serve someone else.

Since the moment Jas had realized who it was, she hadn't taken her eyes off Sparks. She didn't particularly want to reacquaint herself with him, but the odds of seeing him on Mars were so large that she couldn't help watching him. His temporary friends returned to their conversations and failed to notice him slowly slipping from his barstool.

When she realized what was about to happen, she wasn't quick enough to save him. Sparks hit the floor, a misshapen heap of sadness and regret. Jas got to him just after he fell. The disturbance resulted in a brief lull in the buzz. The bartender leaned over the bar to see Jas squatting next to the nearly unconscious man.

"Do you know him?" the bartender asked.

Jas wasn't sure she wanted to take on whatever responsibility an honest response might place on her shoulders, but she nodded, reluctantly.

"Then take him home for me, will ya? Or I'll have to call security."

Even if Jas had known where Sparks lived, she didn't want to take him home. Maybe if she could sober him up a little, he could make his own way back to his place.

"I'll just move him over here if that's okay," she replied. "He isn't that drunk. He's just tired."

The bartender raised his eyebrows. "Yeah, right. Look, I don't care what you do as long as you keep him outta my way and as long as he doesn't puke or piss himself. Okay?"

"Yeah, got it." Jas turned her attention to Sparks. His eyes were open, but he was in a world of his own, mumbling to himself. He was focused on something invisible behind her.

"Sparks," Jas said, "get up." She grabbed him underneath his arms and began hauling him to his feet.

Sparks'ss gaze drifted to her face, and when he saw who she was he started so violently that she almost dropped him. "H-H-Harring-ton?" His surprise seemed to jolt him out of his drunken stupor. His body grew less floppy and he tried to get his legs underneath him.

"Yes, it's me," Jas said. "Now get on your feet and come with me over here if you don't want to get thrown out."

Sparks made the few steps to her table without too much help. He sat opposite Jas, rested his elbows on the table, and rubbed his face. Some of his slightly haughty demeanor began to return, as if the shame of Jas seeing him in the state he was in hurt his pride. "Harrington. Who'd have thought it?" He smiled ruefully. "I may have had a little too much to drink."

Jas wrinkled her nose, recalling the former physician of the *Galathea's* condescension towards alcoholics and other addicts. "Yeah, I think you may have. What the krat are you doing on Mars?"

ELEVEN

"Come on, Sis," Phelan pleaded. "It'll be fun. Now that the core shipment's gone planetside, we can use the hold. We can play in two teams. Right, guys?"

He scanned the faces of everyone sitting at the table in the dining room, his eyes asking for their support. With Jas on Mars, the ship's crew was down to the captain, Sayen, the android navigator, whose name was Prosper, Flahive, and Carl. Prosper was in her cabin. Carl wasn't sure what she did in there, probably recharge or something. Flahive joined them at meals to chat, though he didn't eat human food. Sayen had told Carl that he had a machine in his cabin that cleaned waste from and added nutrients to the liquid in his suit.

Carl wasn't sure that Phelan's transparent attempt to cheer his sister up was such a good idea. She'd been looking a little better since he'd paid her a visit with Flux, but expecting her to take part in some weird new game might be too much.

"What is this game?" Carl asked, easing the pressure on Sayen. "Can you explain it again?"

"It's simple," Phelan replied. "Each team has one person as an attacker and one person as a target. The aim is for the attackers to hit the targets with a ball. Whenever the target's hit, their team gains a point. The side with the most points loses. There are a few more rules, but that's about it."

"So the attackers can get hit without gaining points?" asked Carl.

"That's right. And the targets can *catch* the ball and throw it to their team mate or at the other team's target, but if they get hit, their team gets a point."

"Sounds kind of painful to be the target," said Carl.

"No," Phelan said, waving his hand dismissively. "The ball's pretty big and soft. And it's difficult to throw hard in zero-g."

"Zero-g?"

"Yeah. Did I forget to tell y'all that part? We have to turn off artificial gravity to play. Oh yeah, also you can't touch a surface and hold the ball at the same time."

It did actually sound like a lot of fun, and they'd spent days aboard the ship with nothing to do. Flying the *Bricoleur* using its Oootoon Drive to Mars had been the only interesting thing Carl had done. But Sayen didn't look like she was feeling up to it.

She was bent over her breakfast bowl, her elbow on the table and her chin in her hand while she idly stirred her cereal with a spoon.

"Sayen?" Phelan asked. "What do you think? The bots must have about finished cleaning the hold. I told them to do it over an hour ago. It'll only take me a minute to print the ball."

Sayen lifted her spoon and plopped it in the bowl. "What the hell. Why not?"

"Yes," Phelan exclaimed. He got up. "Y'all meet me at the hold in half an hour."

"Print some helmets too," Sayen called as he was leaving.

"Aww, why?" her brother retorted. "It isn't that dangerous."

"From the sound of it, it could be," Sayen said. "And our visas to go planetside aren't through yet, so we'd be relying on your sick bay if someone has an accident."

"My sick bay's pretty good."

"If you want me to play, Phelan, print some safety helmets."

"Okay, Bossypants."

After Phelan had left, Carl said, "You sure you're up to it, Sayen? I can say I don't want to play if it's too much for you."

"No, it's okay. I don't mind. I want him to stop worrying about me."

"That's very wise of you," said Flahive. "The captain is experiencing strong negative emotions at the moment, somewhat at odds with the impression he's giving."

"You probably shouldn't tell us that," Carl said.

"I don't know. He's only stating the obvious, to me anyway," Sayen said.

"You, however," Flahive said, "seem to be feeling a little better."

"Yes, I think so," said Sayen.

"Are you going to play?" Carl asked Flahive.

"I'd like to, but my suit is too restricting. I think the captain has Prosper in mind as the fourth player."

———

Flahive was right, though Phelan said they needed the alien's services to act as a referee. He'd printed helmets for everyone but Prosper, who didn't need one as her metal/silicon skull was tough enough. Carl hadn't spoken much with the android. She could hold a simple conversation, but that seemed to be as far as her abilities went.

"I think it'll be fairest if me and Carl play against Sayen and Prosper," Phelan said. "Prosper's the strongest and fastest of all of us, so that way we'll be evenly matched."

"You think I need Prosper on my side to stand a chance of beating you two?" Sayen asked, a glint in her eye.

"Come on, Sis, you're easily the weakest of all of us. But with Prosper working with you, it evens everything out. Let her be the attacker, and you be the target."

"I've got a better idea," Sayen said. "You and Prosper against me and Carl."

"Well that doesn't make any sense," Phelan replied. "I've played this before and Prosper could beat any of us with both hands tied behind her back. Together, we'll beat you two easily. It'll be boring."

"Humor me, okay?"

"If you're gonna insist, you can have it your way." Phelan handed out the helmets and closed the hold door.

Carl and Sayen went to the opposite end of the large, square, metal-walled room. Ordinarily, it was used to store the precious metal-bearing ore that Phelan mined.

"Does Phelan know about your enhancements?" Carl asked Sayen quietly as they went.

"No," Sayen replied, a small smile brightening her sad face. "When we were growing up, Phelan always beat me at everything. He never let up or gave me a chance, even though I was younger and a girl. Let me play attacker this round, okay?"

Carl chuckled. "Go for it."

They put on their helmets and after giving a warning, Phelan turned off the gravity. Everyone rose gently upward. Carl and Sayen were at the back wall of the chamber, ready to push off. Flahive was in the middle. Prosper had the ball.

"Go," Phelan shouted. Prosper threw the ball hard at Carl, but Sayen was ready. She caught it, and almost too fast to see, with a flick of her wrist she threw it at Phelan, who was still fastening his helmet strap. Even at the distance across the hold, the look of shock on his face as the ball hit him square in his chest was comical.

"Phelan and Prosper, one point," announced Flahive, his deep voice echoing around the chamber.

"Prosper," complained Phelan. "Pay attention." He hadn't seen the first interaction and lay the blame on the android.

"I was," said Prosper. "The ball was traveling too fast for me to intercept it."

Phelan pushed off from the wall to grab the floating ball and pass it to her. "Loser goes first," he called to Carl and Sayen and whispered something to the android. Prosper nodded and took aim.

She wasn't aiming directly at Carl, her target, but at the ceiling.

Almost too late, Carl realized what she was about to do. The ball left the android's hand. He tried to figure out the angle of the ricochet. He nearly made it out of the way, but not quite. The ball was coming straight for him. At the last millisecond, Sayen snatched it before it hit his shoulder.

"Whoa, fast work, Sis," exclaimed Phelan, sounding a little puzzled.

The words had hardly left his lips before the ball bounced off his helmet after flying across the hold in a blur.

"Phelan and Prosper, two points."

"Whaaa…?" said Phelan.

Carl was fighting the urge to laugh. Sayen turned a somersault and pushed off from the ceiling. She hit the floor with her hands and rebounded. "Loser goes first, right?" she called. "What are you waiting for?"

Phelan was floating lazily near the ceiling, his brow creased into a frown. Pushing off with one hand, he grabbed Prosper's arm and pulled her close.

"Hey, no delays," Sayen said. "It's your turn. Hurry up. Look, your target's right here." She pointed at Carl and winked. "Take your best shot."

Phelan gently pushed Prosper down so that she could reach the ball, which had come to rest a few meters away. He was propelled into a spin. Prosper didn't take aim this time. As soon as she took hold of the ball, she threw it all in one smooth motion. It hit the side of the hold, ricocheted across, bounced off the floor, and came flying toward Carl.

Sayen's hands were clasped together in a double fist. She used them like a racket to return the ball. Phelan was still spinning. When he was facing away from them, the ball hit him on the butt, pushing him gently into the wall.

"Phelan and Prosper, three points," intoned Flahive.

Carl couldn't control himself any longer. He roared with laughter and so did Sayen. Their guffaws were multiplied as they echoed around the bare hold walls. Prosper seemed to get the joke, for she smiled, and Flahive's deep chortles provided a bass note to the cacophony.

Phelan took the joke in good humor and laughed a little himself, though he continued to look puzzled.

Suddenly, he held up a hand. "Hey, guys," he called. "Can it for a minute. A comm's come through."

As the laughter died down, the warble of the interface screen next to the door could be heard. Phelan pushed off from the ceiling and hung upside down at the screen as he accepted the message.

"It's Jas," he said. "She says she hasn't found out anything about Shadows or the Council, but she's stumbled across something else. Do you guys know anything about aliens called Paths?"

TWELVE

Their visas came through the next day, and Carl, Sayen, and Flahive went planetside to meet Jas, Sparks, and the weapons researchers, leaving Phelan and Prosper to look after the ship. Flahive's companionship was desired by all concerned. The scientists at the research institute were especially pleased to hear that an empath was at hand to communicate with the Paths and perhaps shed some light on them. Flahive, too, was interested to talk to the aliens. He didn't recall hearing of them before and wanted to find out all about them.

Carl landed the shuttle at the spaceport and waited until Sayen and Flahive had disembarked before moving it into the hangar. He then went to join them at immigration control. The health check was thorough and included passing through a device that he was sure was a Shadow scanner.

His gaze quickly zoomed in on Jas's tall, shapely figure waiting for them at the gate. She was a welcome sight to his eyes, even after just a couple of days apart. The strength of the hug she gave him after they stepped into Mars Territory lent him some hope for the future.

"Great to see you," she said, "but let's get you below ground quickly. Have you got your Rad X counters?"

Carl held up his arm. After passing the health check, an immigration official had stuck a square of plastic to the inside of his forearm. It was a set of bars that would change color to signal radiation exposure. Currently, the lowest bar was green, and the one above it was pale yellow. The official had told him that if the top bar turned red, he needed to get underground and then to a hospital immediately for radiation treatment.

"Good. You should all be fine. There aren't any solar storms forecast, but it doesn't hurt to be careful. Let's go." She led them to the Loop station, where they caught a train to the research facility. On the way, she related her chance encounter with Sparks.

"It'll be good to see Doctor Sparks again," Sayen said.

"Will it?" Jas asked. "I never understood why you liked him so much."

"He's a great doctor," Sayen replied.

"If you were one of the elite, maybe," said Jas. "He was a misborn to the regular crew."

"That's a little harsh, Jas," Sayen protested. "He had a wonderful bedside manner. He was never in a hurry. He always listened."

"Huh, you never saw his bad side," Jas said. "Anyway, he's changed. You'll see."

When Sparks met them at the research institute reception, Carl saw what Jas meant. The doctor was thin, and though it had only been a few months since they'd last seen him, he looked noticeably older. What was more he had a haunted or hunted, air about him. One of the two. His grin as he greeted them was ghastly.

"Sayen, how pleasant to see you again," Sparks said. "And Carl. And you must be Mr. Flahive. I'm very pleased to make your acquaintance. Step this way, please, everyone. My colleagues are very keen to meet you." He'd brought security clearances for them, which he gave out as they passed inside.

"Have you been studying the Paths ever since we got back from the Polestar mission?" Sayen asked him.

"I have. First aboard a quarantine satellite and latterly here, after an unfortunate accident prompted the removal of the Paths to a more secure setting."

"An unfortunate accident?" asked Flahive.

His booming voice took Sparks by surprise, and he hesitated before answering, "Yes. Our alien friends induced a coma in a technician, and soon after that incident they killed an unauthorized person who entered their chamber."

"They killed someone?" exclaimed Jas. "You didn't tell me that. Flahive, maybe you should reconsider your offer to help."

"Oh, there's no need," Sparks said. "They're quite safe. They only kill when they're under severe threat. Communicating with them telepathically shouldn't cause any harm. I have to confess, I was extremely relieved to hear of your acquaintance, Mr. Flahive. I have high hopes that you may offer the breakthrough we've been looking for all this time."

"I can't promise anything," Flahive replied as he thumped alongside them, "but I'll certainly try my best to help. I believe we're getting close to the creatures? I'm picking up some strong mind waves."

"Excellent," Sparks said. "Excellent. Yes, we're nearly there."

At the end of the corridor, three people in lab coats hovered. As they approached the scientists, a lank-haired one came forward, holding an interface. Though Carl possessed zero telepathic ability, he sensed a great dislike between Sparks and the scientist.

Ignoring the humans, the woman went directly to Flahive. Without any ceremony, she said, "You're the empath, Flahive?"

"Yes," he replied a little late, as if he were concentrating on something else.

"I need you to read through this document and sign it. You have to understand, our work here is top secret. You can't repeat a thing of what we're about to tell you, nor anything that you learn or see involving these creatures."

"Please let me see your document," Flahive said. He manipulated the interface in his flexible disc appendages. The English words disappeared and were replaced by his own written language of spots and splashes. "I'm sorry, this may take me some time to read."

Flahive bent his face plate over the screen and very slowly scrolled down. They waited. The woman scientist looked back at her colleagues, who were impatiently fidgeting at the entrance to the room that presumably held the Paths.

Carl was interested to see the unusual aliens again, though he didn't want to get too close, remembering the powerful emotions that they emanated. Everyone who got within their range of influence was affected. They seemed to be far enough away at the moment as he wasn't feeling anything unusual.

Flahive moved the document down another couple of centimeters. Carl marveled at how slowly he read. Everyone was getting bored standing around with nothing to do. Carl pulled out his personal interface and opened the screen.

"I'm afraid your device won't work in here," Sparks said. "The facility broadcasts a dampening field. For security."

Sighing, Carl slid his interface back into his pocket.

"It's all the same as you would expect," the woman scientist said to Flahive in a blatant effort to hurry him. "I can read it out to you if you'd like."

"Just a little while longer," said Flahive. "I've nearly finished."

But he hadn't nearly finished at all. They stood and waited for at least another ten minutes by Carl's estimation, though it was hard to tell now that his interface wasn't working. Sayen yawned and leaned against the wall. Jas folded her arms and tapped her foot. The woman scientist rolled her eyes at her colleagues.

Finally, Flahive was finished. He shifted the document back into English and returned the interface to the scientist.

"You have to sign it here," she said, holding it back out to him.

"I'm very sorry," Flahive said. "After reading through the terms and restrictions you wish me to agree to, I've decided I'm not prepared to go ahead with communicating with these creatures."

"What?" spluttered Sparks. "But...you have to. He has to, doesn't he?" he asked the woman, a childish whine creeping into his voice.

The scientist was glaring at Flahive. "No, not strictly speaking, he doesn't. If you'll wait a moment, I'll talk with my colleagues. Maybe we can ease some of these requirements. I'll see what we can do."

"No need," said Flahive. "I've changed my mind. I'm no longer interested in going ahead with this project. Could someone show me the way out?"

"Wait a minute," said Jas. "Are you sure? The Paths...I found them in a significant place. Maybe you can find out something important for us."

"Maybe I could have, but I'm afraid that isn't to be. I'm leaving now. Is the exit this way?"

No matter what anyone said, Flahive wouldn't deviate from his abrupt change of mind. With an air of anti-climax, Carl, Jas, and Sayen left the research facility with the empath.

"Are you sure you won't change your mind?" Sayen asked when Sparks had sadly said goodbye and they were outside. "What did you object to in the document? They seemed prepared to negotiate. Maybe we could go back tomorrow."

Flahive paused and turned back to the facility. He waited until Sparks had gone inside and the doors were closed. "There won't be any need to return. Not to talk with the Paths at any rate. A remarkable species. We had an interesting conversation as I was pretending to read that ridiculous agreement. I believe I may be able to shed some light on these Shadows, and the Paths, and what's been happening both here and in their universe."

Thirteen

Jas took them to the bar where she'd met Sparks so they could talk. It was, as she'd predicted, nearly empty. It wasn't yet lunchtime. A few regular patrons were dotted around the place, sitting separately, their heads down and their minds on their beer and inner thoughts. Mars was a place of regrets and unfulfilled dreams, it seemed to Jas. How many had nursed hopes of a better life, only to find themselves trapped on a dry, barren world? A world that attracted no investment now that cheaper interstellar travel had opened the gateway to planets that offered richer, more easily exploited resources?

The bartender was cleaning the bar when they went in. He paused and did a double take at Flahive in his high-pressure suit and smoky face panel, but after a moment he continued wiping. Jas ordered everyone but Flahive a drink.

"Your friend not joining you today?" he asked as he made the drinks.

"You mean that guy I helped last night?" Jas asked in return. "No, he's working. And he isn't my friend."

"Right. Well, thanks for lending a hand with him." He put a full glass down on the bar in front of Jas. "I don't mind the regular drunks; it's the noisy, falling down drunks I don't like."

"Sorry about that, but, like I said, he isn't my friend."

"Whatever you say." The bartender put down another full glass. When the order was filled, Jas handed over her card. As he gave it back, the bartender didn't let go as Jas took it, so they were both holding it. "I get off at two. If you fancy going for a late lunch, meet me outside." He released Jas's card.

She couldn't help but smile to herself as she took the drinks to the table where the others were waiting.

"Something funny?" Sayen asked.

"The bartender just asked me out on a date," Jas replied as she gave everyone their drinks.

"Ha," Sayen chuckled. "That's nice and flattering. Did you tell him you can't accept because you're on a mission to save the galaxy?"

"Huh, no," Jas said. "It was more strange than flattering. I'm not used to being asked out. I'm more used to negative attention. I keep forgetting that here I'm normal."

"Maybe we could get on to what Flahive wants to tell us," Carl said edgily.

Jas sat down.

"I'm not sure where to begin," Flahive said. His deep voice boomed around the bar, causing heads to turn. He seemed to do something to his translator, for the next time he spoke it was at half the former volume. "I think it's best if I begin by asking you a question. Where did you first encounter the Paths?"

Jas explained how she'd found them deep within a Shadow trap and, under Haggardy's orders, transported them to the *Galathea* as a new resource for Polestar. She also explained how they'd ended up on Mars, according to Sparks.

"Their initial location makes a lot of sense to me," Flahive said, "based on what the Paths said."

"So you can talk to them?" Jas asked. "We only pick up on their emotions."

"I can converse with them," Flahive replied. "And when you say you pick up on their emotions, you should understand that they also pick up on yours. The best way to describe the phenomenon you humans quaintly refer to as telepathy or mind-reading is that feelings and thoughts are like music and lyrics. The analogy is accurate in that distance is inversely related to the strength of the signal received, and also in that the music of a song—the emotions—are easier to make out than the lyrics—the thoughts. Unfortunately for humans, you're all but deaf when it comes to perceiving emotions and thoughts, though you do transmit rather loudly."

Carl asked, "So how come we feel what the Paths feel?"

"On this plane," Flahive replied, "the Paths are extremely handicapped except for their—for want of a better word—telepathy. Their signal is even louder than a human being's. So loud, in fact, it's equivalent to them shouting at the tops of their voices. Hearing them was almost painful. I had to ask them to whisper."

"Wait," Sayen said. "What do you mean, *on this plane?*"

"I mean in this dimension. The Paths are from another, um, *place.* Another universe, I think, or perhaps something different from a universe. It's all a little confusing to me, even after talking with them for some time. I'll explain it as well as I can, then please feel free to ask me any questions. I may not remember it all perfectly. I couldn't write anything down under the scrutiny of the scientists."

Flahive settled in his seat. He took up a whole bench, and, as always, he looked uncomfortable. His third leg stuck out at the front, which prevented him from sitting close to the table.

"The Paths are from a place that has no physical structure. According to the known laws of physics, it doesn't exist. This place has no atomic particles, no forces, no time, nothing. I'm not sure if the word *place* even applies. I'm afraid the Paths didn't seem to have words to describe their home. They could only tell me about it in terms of what it *isn't,* not what it *is,* because even language doesn't exist or have any meaning there.

"The next thing they told me may be the crucial key to understanding and defeating the aliens you call Shadows. The Paths said that Shadows also come from this place that isn't a place. They create traps in our universe so that they can cross over. They absorb their victims, including their brains, which hold their memories and personality, and recreate that person, only with a Shadow mind. The Paths said that the Shadows are all one thing, but also many things together. They also said that they're aware of what the Shadows are doing, and they're trying to stop them, but here in the physical world, they're nearly helpless.

"They didn't actually tell me this," Flahive went on, "but from what you've said, the Paths appeared in the Shadow trap because they wanted to fight the Shadows or try to warn their victims. Or it may have been because that was where it was easiest for them to pass through. I'm not sure."

"Whoa," said Carl.

"I thought I might find you all here," said a voice. "Do you mind if I join you?" They'd been so intent on what Flahive was saying, no one had noticed that Sparks had come in.

Jas wondered how much he'd heard.

Sparks didn't wait for an answer. He pulled up a chair and sat down.

"Doctor Sparks," Sayen said. "Did you hear what Flahive was saying about the Paths? They're fighting the Shadows too."

Jas shook her head at her.

"Oh, come on, Jas," Sayen said. "We're all on the same side, aren't we?"

"No," Jas said, "I don't think we are."

"You're right, in a way, Harrington," Sparks said. "However, *I'm* not your enemy." He turned to Flahive. "Am I right in understanding that you were pretending to read that agreement while, in fact, you were speaking to the Paths?"

Flahive didn't answer, possibly waiting for an indication from one of the others as to whether or not he should tell Sparks what he knew.

"Carl, what do you think?" Jas asked.

He shrugged. "I don't know. He's working with the research team. I don't know whose side he's on."

"He's on the side of humankind," Sayen said. "We all are. We should go back to the research facility and tell them what Flahive found out."

"I wouldn't advise that," Flahive said. "I don't think those humans who have been working with the Paths are very good people." He didn't say more, but it was evident that that was the reason he'd indulged in subterfuge. The Paths must have told him something that caused him to distrust the scientists.

"They aren't good people," Sparks exclaimed so vehemently it made the others jump. "They are *not* good people. That's why I came here to find you. I wanted to ask you if you could help me get away from here."

Sparks proceeded to spout a torrent of words explaining his experiences over the last months and what the other scientists had been forcing him to do. From what she could gather, Jas concluded that the doctor had been turned from a researcher into a lab rat.

"The coma experience is pleasant enough while it lasts, I confess," Sparks said, "but the Paths are capable of killing. They killed a member of staff on the quarantine station. They've killed animals that we set on them. I just know that those misborn colleagues of mine are going to push me to take more and more risks until the Paths kill me too. And then they'll dissect me like they did all the other animals."

Sayen's eyes had grown round. "Jas, Carl, we have to do something."

"Why don't you just quit?" Jas asked.

"I can't," Sparks replied. "I've tried. Yesterday, when you met me here, I'd been to the spaceport. I had all my things packed. I was ready to give up my job, everything. I was ready to return to Earth with little more than the clothes on my back and start again. But I was stopped from boarding the shuttle. *Travel permission denied*, they said. Since when did we need permission to travel? And where could I flee to on Mars? Where could I hide? They'd find me in a second. Please, could you smuggle me aboard your shuttle, Lingiari? I'll pay you anything."

"You didn't tell me this," Jas said. "You told me you'd been working with the Paths. That was all."

Sparks replied, "I was hoping I had my ticket out when you said you knew someone who could help with understanding the Paths, Harrington. I thought if we had a breakthrough in our experiments, it would take the pressure off and I'd be allowed to leave. When your friend refused to help, I despaired. That's why I came to find you. I wanted to persuade him to reconsider."

"Okay, okay. So you can't leave, but wait a minute," Jas said. "Back up. What did you mean when you said, *the coma's pleasant enough while it lasts?*"

With so much for them to talk about, the group remained at the bar until the evening.

Fourteen

"What? No," Phelan said. "I'm not risking my shuttle...I'm not risking my ship...on anything so hare-brained."

"You have to," said Sayen. "The Paths could be the key to defeating the Shadows. They could be the key to everything that's been happening. We need to get them out of that facility. Then Flahive can talk to them. They could hold vital information. They're our link to the dimension where the Shadows come from. We can't leave them down there in the hands of those weapons scientists."

Jas, Carl, Flahive, and Sayen had joined Phelan on the bridge of the *Bricoleur* after leaving Sparks on Mars with a promise that they would consider his request for help.

"Sis, this isn't like rescuing you from the roof of a burning building," said Phelan. He threw his baseball at the ceiling and caught it. "Mars has defenses. If we swoop into their airspace without clearance, they'll shoot us out of the sky."

"We've got clearance, mate," Carl said. "I've been planetside three times. It won't look unusual if I take the shuttle down again."

"So you're going to land at the spaceport?" Phelan asked. *Thunk.* He sighed. "Okay, tell me your plan."

Sayen grinned. "With Sparks's help, we break the Paths out of the research facility, take them aboard the shuttle, and bring them up here. Then jump somewhere. Quickly."

"Just like that, huh?" said Phelan. "You're gonna break into a top-security facility, steal highly classified experiment subjects, *somehow* get them through export screening at the spaceport, and bring them up here?"

Sayen nodded. "That's the plan."

"Seriously?" *Thunk.*

"We'll have to do it really fast."

"You're certainly a lot faster than I remember you being, Sis, but I don't think being fast is going to cut it this time."

"Phelan," Jas said, "I understand your reluctance, but ever since we found the Shadows, we've had to take risks. We've risked our lives I don't know how many times. Believe me, I'd rather face Martian security and a handful of mad scientists than Shadows."

Phelan remained indecisive. He threw his baseball.

Sayen leapt into the air and caught it before it reached the ceiling. "*I* don't understand your reluctance," she said as she hit the ground. "You don't sound like the Phelan I know, who ran away to space at eighteen, or the man who makes his living mining uncharted planets on the Outer Rim. What's the problem, Brother? I don't get it."

Phelan looked intently at Sayen, and for a moment the confident, carefree mask fell away. In its place was the look of a man who loved his sister very much and couldn't bear the thought of losing her, the last family he had.

Wordlessly, Sayen tossed him his baseball and went over and hugged him.

Jas thought she heard Flahive give a small sigh of contentment. She supposed there was an upside to picking up on the emotions of others.

"Captain," Flahive said, "though this proposal is risky and the consequences of our capture are unknown, I believe we should make the effort. In the short time that I had to speak to the Paths, it became clear to me that these creatures are of great importance not only in defeating the Shadows, but also in helping us understand the nature of their universe. It's little short of a crime that they've been shut away and experimented upon. To try to use their special ability as a weapon is immoral. It's deplorable, in fact. The Paths are suffering, and we have a duty to rescue them."

Phelan said, "I hear what you're saying, Flahive, but I'm also wary of bringing these creatures aboard my ship if they're killers, as everyone's saying."

"I think I may be able to shed some light on that also," Flahive replied. "Doctor Sparks was saying that he enters a kind of trance or coma when he does something to threaten the Paths, and that they kill any living thing that might cause them serious harm. I didn't discuss this reaction with the Paths as I wasn't aware of it at the time that I spoke with them, but if I had to guess, I'd say that they aren't intentionally killing their victims. I believe that the Paths' only defense is their access to the dimension where they usually live. I believe they are stopping their victims' actions by sending them temporarily or permanently into their own dimension."

"Krat," Jas said. "You could be right. It's about the only power they have here. It's the only thing they can do to help themselves."

"So are you saying," Phelan asked, "that as long as they don't feel threatened, they won't hurt us?"

"I'm confident of it," Flahive replied. "If I'm here to translate for them, they'll trust us. No one will come to any harm."

Phelan sighed and rubbed his forehead. "I think I'm probably gonna regret this, but okay. Okay. Y'all can go and get these Paths and bring them aboard my ship, though where we'll go after that, I've no idea."

"Thanks, Phelan," Sayen said, giving him another hug.

"Whoa, hey Sis, those are some powerful arms you've got yourself there. Ease up a little."

"Sorry." Sayen released Phelan and turned to the others. "When are we going to do it?"

"No time like the present," Jas said. "How about tonight?"

Fifteen

Phelan had provided an encrypted comm line to make the arrangements with Sparks. The doctor would meet them at the entrance to the research facility at ten o'clock, when everyone but the security staff would have left. Sparks would say he was working late. Though his status had dropped in the eyes of his colleagues, he retained the necessary clearances to admit guests into the building.

The plan for how they would get the Paths out of the facility was a little fuzzy. They would have to get them past the security guards. How they would do that was unclear. Phelan had the standard complement of weapons you would expect to find on a starship that regularly trawled lawless parts of the galaxy, but there was no way they would get them through customs. Even to try would arouse suspicion. They would be going in empty-handed and would have to rely on speed, bravado, and a lot of luck to see them through.

How they would convince the spaceport officials to allow them to take the Paths aboard the shuttle was another unanswered question. They would have to cross both those bridges when they came to them, Jas concluded as she strapped herself into her shuttle seat, ready to make the descent to the Valles Marineris Spaceport. Things were going to get worse, not better, for the Paths. This would be the best chance they had to rescue them. They had to take it.

Flahive was a concern. Jas had thought that, coming from a high-g planet, he would be fast and strong in Mars' low gravity, but his awkward method of locomotion made him slow. She wondered if his species was aquatic and so walking on land was unnatural to him. His presence was essential, however, if they were to reassure the Paths that they meant them no harm and if they were to avoid the potentially deadly consequences of scaring them.

She was pleased to have Sayen along. Her super speed, strength, and imperviousness to heat and cold made her a valuable team member in any raid. Carl would remain with the shuttle in case they needed to make a quick getaway. They had button comm links to stay in touch.

With Sparks, they had four people to bring the Paths to the spaceport. They should be able to manage it, Jas guessed. If she recalled correctly, the creatures were waist high and half as wide, but they were hollow and light to carry. She hoped the emotions they would emanate as they were being taken away would be positive ones.

"Touchdown in five," came Carl's Australian drawl over the cabin speaker. Jas wished she'd had more time to talk to him since visiting VM5. Delving into her past on Mars had been less painful and more cathartic than she'd imagined. She felt she'd gathered a little courage, maybe enough to acknowledge her feelings about him.

The shuttle landed, and fifteen minutes later they were through all the checks and on their way to the research facility. Sparks met them at the door, his manner very calm and professional. Jas marveled at his acting ability. He had to be nervous and worried, but he didn't show it. Then she recalled how Sayen would rave about his skills as a physician. The man had had long years of practice exuding an aura of confidence.

"Thank you so much for reconsidering your decision," Sparks said as he ushered them in. When a security guard approached, frowning suspiciously, he told the man, "You remember our guests from yesterday? They're paying us a return visit. No cause for alarm."

Ignoring the guard's unconvinced look, he swept them over to the unstaffed reception desk. "We have to go through the formalities, of course. Let me check you in." He tapped at a screen and handed them temporary security passes. They went through the secure inner entrance.

So far, so good, thought Jas.

"As soon as I'm within range, I'll explain to the Paths why we're here," Flahive said. "They should be fully prepared for our appearance and not alarmed."

"Great," Jas said, scanning the surroundings for signs of activity. The place seemed to be as Sparks had predicted it would be: utterly deserted. She couldn't hear anything but the sounds of their footfalls and Flahive's soft *bump, thump, bump, thump.*

In a few minutes they were back where they'd been the previous day, at the junction that led to the Paths' confinement chamber. Sparks's scientist colleagues had gone home, however, and the corridor was dim and silent. The doctor approached a wide door with a security panel at eye height to one side of it. He looked into the panel and pressed a button. An almost inaudible click signaled the opening of the lock.

Inside, looking exactly as they had when Jas had first seen them in the Shadow trap, were the Paths. Their odd, inverted bag shapes were just as incongruous as they had been then. She became aware of a sense of great calm and happiness. The Paths were radiating their emotions. Flahive must have done a good job of explaining what they were going to do.

Lifting the Paths was like picking up elongated, suede balloons, though they weren't rigid. The creatures were soft, velvety, and light. They partially collapsed wherever they were held, which was fortunate. It meant that they could carry all of them without too much difficulty.

Their arms full of Paths, they made their way down the corridor toward the exit. Everything had gone smoothly up until then, but that was the easy part. The hard part was going to be getting the Paths past security and then onto the shuttle.

"Do you know what we can say to the guards?" Jas asked Sparks.

"I've no idea," he replied. "I've wracked my brains, but I can't think of a single reason that would justify myself and three strangers removing experimental organisms from the facility. I was hoping you might think of something."

"Krat," Jas said. "We can't fight them. We don't have any weapons, and I don't want anyone to get hurt. But if they see what we're doing of course they'll try to stop us. We'll have to distract them. Is there something you can do to set off an alarm? If they aren't well-trained, they'll both leave their posts to investigate."

"Hmm, good idea," Sparks said. "I think I might be able to manage something."

"Hurry up," Jas said. "We're nearly at the entrance."

Sparks was glancing around as if looking for something. He said to Flahive, "Could you ask the Paths if one of them would mind if I used them as a water receptacle? Just for a short time."

Flahive was silent for a moment, then replied, "They say that wouldn't be a problem."

"Excellent," Sparks said and disappeared with his Path into a restroom. The sound of running water came from the room, and Sparks reappeared, carrying an inverted Path that was now heavy and round with water. "Could one of you open that, please?" he asked, nodding toward a door on the opposite side of the corridor.

Sayen pushed the door open. Inside the room were ranks of interface screens. It was some kind of classroom or study room. Sparks took a few quick steps and upended the Path over the screens, sending a torrent of water over the electronic equipment. It did the trick. A whooping alarm sounded, and the corridor lights flashed.

"In here," called Sparks, carrying his now-deflated, soggy Path into another empty room.

When they were all inside, Jas held the door open a tiny crack. They waited. After a few moments, a security guard ran past and into the room Sparks had flooded. Just one security guard. *Krat.* The other one must have stayed at his post at the entrance. She had one more ace up her sleeve. She would have to play it. "Run for the entrance, everyone," she said quietly. "Sayen, don't get too far ahead of us. When we're in sight of the guard, let me go first."

They sprinted the final few tens of meters to the lobby and burst through the door. Sayen stepped to one side and let Jas go past. One guard stood at the entrance. As they appeared, he turned and gaped. Jas screamed like a banshee and bore down on him.

The sight and sound of the tall, shrieking Martian carrying a weird alien and flying toward him made the guard's eyes grow round and his mouth gape. His hand went to his weapon, but he fumbled it. In the second of extra time it took for him to get over his surprise, Jas was on him. A quick, well-placed punch knocked him out cold. A moment later, they were past the unconscious guard and out in the street.

"Run," shouted Jas.

Sixteen

Flahive's *bump thump, bump thump* was growing fainter. Jas turned and saw the alien was falling behind. He was too slow. The tunnel they were running down was long and straight, and the guard Jas had knocked out would be coming around within a few seconds. They had to get out of his line of fire.

Telling the others not to wait, and that they would meet them outside the spaceport, she dropped back.

"Please, take my Path and continue without me," Flahive said. His translator didn't convey the strenuous effort he was making, but his leaps were growing shorter and his legs were wobbling.

"No," Jas said. "You can make it. Let me help you." She wrapped an arm awkwardly around his wide frame under his three upper limbs.

"Here," said Flahive, trying to pass her the alien he was carrying.

"I'm not taking it," exclaimed Jas. "You can do it. Come on." She pulled him along another few steps.

"It is too late," said Flahive. He slid from her grip and collapsed.

Jas hadn't heard the laser shot, but as Flahive hit the ground, she saw the damage. A hole had been burned in the back of the empath's pressure suit. A white, wet mass was bulging from the hole, which grew rapidly wider.

"No," yelled Jas.

With the last of his strength, as his body forced its way out of his splitting suit, Flahive lifted the Path he was carrying, holding it up for Jas to take from him. Something fizzed passed her ear. She was being shot at. In the distance, two guards were leaving the open entrance to the research facility. The unconscious guard had woken up and the other had returned from investigating Sparks's distraction. Both were firing at them.

She grabbed the Path from Flahive. A low groan came from the alien's translator. His suit split from top to bottom down the back, and a jelly-like, partially translucent mound erupted like foam from a shaken bottle of soda.

"I have asked...them...to help," were Flahive's dying words.

Holding Paths under each arm, Jas fled, shielded from the guards' sight by Flahive's remains.

———

Sayen and Sparks were waiting for her just outside the spaceport. Their alien baggage was attracting considerable attention from passersby.

"Where's Flahive?" Sayen asked.

Jas couldn't answer. She could only shake her head. She didn't only have her own grief to deal with. The Paths she was carrying were radiating sadness. She swallowed and said, "We have to get to the shuttle immediately. We have only moments until the guards at the research facility raise the alarm and they close the spaceport."

"How the heck are we going to explain the Paths?" Sayen asked.

"I'm all out of ideas," Jas said. "We'll have to try to bluff our way through."

"I don't like this," Sparks muttered. "I don't like this at all. I tried to leave once and they wouldn't let me. My name's known to them. I was hoping you'd thought of another way."

"Krat, Sparks," Jas said angrily. "We're doing our best. A friend just died. We can't perform miracles."

"It *will* be a miracle if we don't get stopped and arrested," Sayen said.

"Let's just try, okay?" said Jas. She couldn't think straight. She couldn't shake the image of Flahive's terrible death from her mind.

They were inside the spaceport and making their way to the security gate. Though they were receiving many curious glances and outright stares, none of the spaceport staff seemed to be aware that they were wanted for stealing highly sensitive potential weapons —yet.

Jas's heart seemed about to thump its way out of her chest as they neared the gate. The clerk's face was a picture as she watched them approach. What could they say to her to convince her to let them through? Should they force their way in and make a run for it? It was a couple of hundred meters at least from the security gate to the hangar where Carl was waiting in the shuttle. *Carl.* She'd forgotten to contact him.

Jas lifted her comm button to her lips. "Carl, we're in the spaceport. Just outside security. We've got the Paths."

"How're you gonna get them to let you through?" he replied.

"Krat knows."

"You can do it, Jas. I'll bring out the shuttle. I'll be waiting for you."

The people in front of them in the line passed through security. As Jas, Sayen, and Sparks stepped up, the clerk put her hands on her hips and raised her eyebrows.

"And what, might I ask, are those?" she asked, staring at the soft, brown aliens they carried.

"Er...they're..." Jas said. Her mind was absolutely blank. She looked at Sayen.

"They're...they're...ornaments," Sayen said. "Souvenirs of our visit."

"Really? Where'd you get them? What are they?" The clerk looked glum as she spoke. The Paths' emotions were affecting her. Jas cursed inwardly. If the clerk was feeling bad, she'd be even less likely to let them into the departure area. When no one seemed able to answer her, she said, "You'll have to take those to the screening office."

"Damnit," Sparks said. "I knew this would happen. I'll never be able to—"

Before he could finish, the clerk's eyes suddenly rolled back in her head, and she fell down in a dead faint. Gasps and exclamations came from the line behind them. For a moment, neither Jas, Sayen, nor Sparks moved. Then Sayen blurted, "It's the Paths. The Paths've put her in a coma."

Hope leaping up within her, Jas shouted, "Let's go," and sped past the unconscious clerk.

Spaceport staff came running up on the other side of security, attracted by the commotion of the crowd. The ones that ventured near the Paths fell like ninepins, creating more confusion.

"Carl," Jas yelled into her comm button, "we're on our way."

Within moments, they were racing down the tunnel that led to the landing pad. *Had Carl gotten permission to take off?*

"Jas," came his voice from her button, "I can't get permission to take off. It's pandemonium in the control room. No one will talk to me. Don't go down the embarkation tunnel. There's another shuttle at the end of it."

"What? No," exclaimed Jas. "We're nearly there. We've nearly made it. There has to be a way."

"There is," Carl said. "But you've got to go outside."

"We can't. We'll freeze, and we won't be able to breathe. There aren't any atmosphere suits in here."

"It'll be safe. It's only a short distance to the landing pad, and as long as I'm on it, the other shuttle can't take off. You can hold your breath while you run. There'll be an emergency airlock in there somewhere. Go through it, and run to me. I'll have the door open."

"The airlock's here," cried Sayen, who had overheard Carl's words. She was doubling back. "We just ran past it."

Jas reversed, and Sparks was hot on her heels. They skidded to a halt next to Sayen. She was reading the instructions to open the airlock.

"Just smash the emergency button," Jas yelled.

Sayen cracked the glass over the emergency panel and pressed the button. With the harsh, metallic clank of long-unused parts, the airlock opened. They stepped inside, and the door closed, sealing them in. In another moment, Sayen located the button to open the outer door, which would lead them out into Mars' frigid, thin atmosphere.

"Ready?" Sayen asked.

"No," Sparks replied. "I think we should—"

"Hold your breath," said Sayen as she punched the button. The outer door slid back. Jas fought not to gasp as the icy cold atmosphere swept inside. A short distance away was the familiar sight of the *Bricoleur*'s shuttle. Less than a one-minute run, Jas estimated. She and Sayen could do it. She wasn't so sure about Sparks.

She pointed, and they ran.

Sayen reached the shuttle way ahead of Jas and Sparks. She disappeared into the dark space of the entrance. A moment later, she reappeared without the Paths she'd been carrying and came back to them.

Jas's lungs were screaming at her to breathe. Darkness was blurring the edge of her vision. A thud came from beside her. Sparks had fallen.

But Sayen was there. She picked up the doctor and hoisted him over her shoulder. Jas groped for the dropped Paths. She had them. There were only meters to go. Sayen was already carrying Sparks into the shuttle, her petite frame comically dwarfed by her impossibly large burden.

With the last of her strength, Jas forced her legs to move. In a daze, she took her final steps into the shuttle and crumpled to the floor.

SEVENTEEN

Warmth and feeling returned to Jas's extremities as she sat in the passenger cabin and caught her breath. Gradually, the ache in her lungs and throat eased. She was dimly aware of the movement of the shuttle as they went up through the Martian atmosphere and pressure forced her down into her seat. She hadn't even fastened her safety belt.

Carl was flying to the *Bricoleur* faster than he had on the other trips. Were the Martian authorities already on their tail? Jas tried to ease her mind. There wasn't much she could do if that were the case. Their escape was now in Carl's and Phelan's hands.

Sparks sat across the aisle. He was white and trembling. The Paths were immobile, as always, lying where they'd been put, on seats and on the floor. The g-force of the flight was compressing their soft forms. Jas wondered what they were thinking.

Sayen caught her eye and gave her a thumbs up. She smiled back. They couldn't have made it without her. Jas was glad her friend had been able to move on a little from her terrible grief and depression.

After what seemed a long time, the g-force eased. They had to be approaching the *Bricoleur*. The shuttle's vibration calmed, and Jas's stomach pushed against her diaphragm as their motion abruptly slowed. They came to a stop. The clank of the access hatch joining the ship echoed through the cabin.

As the hatch scraped open, Sparks scrambled from his seat. Ignoring the Paths, he ran through the opening and into the *Bricoleur*.

"I'll take these, then?" Sayen asked his departing back. She gathered together as many Paths as she could carry. "Can you bring the rest, Jas?" she asked before she left too.

Jas got up and began to collect the remaining Paths. Carl came in from the pilot's cabin.

"What happened to Flahive?" he asked.

"He got shot by a guard. The burn pierced his suit." Her chin trembled.

Carl looked downcast. "When I saw he wasn't with you, I knew something bad had happened. I thought, I'll have to go without him."

"You did the right thing."

Jas continued to pick up Paths. With Flahive's help, they'd done what they'd set out to do. They'd saved the Paths from experimentation, and now they might be able to use them to defeat the Shadows, though Jas wasn't sure how, now that they had no way to talk to them. She was physically and emotionally exhausted after her brief time on Mars. Yet she was glad they'd gone there.

Carl was watching her. He opened his mouth to speak then seemed to change his mind.

"Were you going to say something?" Jas asked.

"We should go through to the ship. We've got to jump. Mars won't let us get away easily after that little stunt."

"Was that all you were going to say?"

Carl shook his head. "Now's not a good time."

Jas winced at the ache in his eyes. Her heart was in her throat. "Maybe it is."

He looked up, hopeful. "What *is* there to say, Jas? You know how I feel."

"I do." Her pulse was thumping in her ears. "And...I feel the same." She carefully put the Paths down.

Carl moved closer. "You said once, until we get rid of the Shadows, it wasn't a good idea to move ahead with a relationship."

"I did say that."

"But," Carl went on, "isn't that a good reason *not* to delay being with someone? Because we don't know how much time we have left."

He was right. Jas couldn't argue with him, and she didn't want to. But that old dread she felt was rising up in her again. She knew where it came from, and it was something that a trip to Mars couldn't fix. She looked down.

"Jas," Carl said softly. He brought his face close to hers, so that his lips were millimeters from her mouth. But he stopped. He didn't kiss her. He was waiting for her to make the move. She had to decide.

She was frozen. Her feelings for Carl were equally matched by her terror of repeating the emotional devastation she'd experienced once before.

The moment was over. With a barely audible sigh, Carl moved away from her.

Jas couldn't bear it. She couldn't bear to let him go. Before Carl could move out of her reach, she grabbed him and kissed him. He held her close, his hands pressed into the small of her back. She was in his arms, his lips were on hers, and she didn't want the feeling to ever end.

"Guys," someone exclaimed.

With a terrible wrench, Jas and Carl moved apart.

"Sorry, guys." Phelan was standing in the cabin. He'd entered unnoticed by either of them. "We need to jump, now. Mars patrol ships are only ten minutes away."

"Krat," Carl exclaimed and ran out. "Get to your jumpseats, both of you," he shouted behind him as he left.

"Where are we going?" Jas asked Phelan as they ran to the bridge.

"Ganymede."

"Ganymede? Why?"

"That's where the Council told me to go."

"You heard from the Council?"

"A message packet came through while you were on Mars. They traced me through my parents' records. They're going to meet us there. Prosper's plotted the jump, but we need to get out of here fast."

They burst onto the bridge. Carl was already in the pilot's seat. Everyone was strapped in and waiting for them.

"Get in your seats," Carl barked, his hand hovering over the controls. The screen at the front of the deck displayed the surface of Mars. Four patrol ships were in view and growing rapidly larger.

Below them was Valles Marineris, Jas's birthplace, a place she had feared returning to for so long, only to find that the ghosts of her past existed mostly in her head.

They jumped.

SHADOW BATTLE

ONE

They'd been waiting for longer than an hour in the cold, bare meeting room at Ganymede Outpost for the Transgalactic Council officers to arrive. Jas rubbed her arms and tried for the hundredth time to find a comfortable position on her hard plastic chair.

"I thought *they'd* be waiting for *us*," she said to no one in particular. "Why did they tell us to meet them here if they weren't here already, or nearby? If they set out from halfway across the galaxy after they sent their message, we could be waiting for days, or weeks."

The rest of the crew of the starship *Bricoleur* were ranged around the room. Carl, the pilot, had given up on attempting to fit his lanky frame into the too-small seats, and was leaning against a wall, his arms folded across his chest. A bulge around his middle was the sleeping form of his alien friend, Flux, inside his shirt.

"They won't be coming by ship," he said. "Council staff travel by Transgalactic Gateway. It's instant."

"Is it?" Jas had heard of Transgalactic Gateways, but she didn't know much about them. Their use was restricted to Council business only and the technology was a well-kept secret. "So how come they're taking so long?"

"Krat knows," Phelan Lee, captain of the *Bricoleur*, muttered.

Next to him, his sister, Sayen, yawned. Jas envied the woman's skin augmentation, which made her impervious to air temperature extremes. There was no way Jas could feel sleepy in that icy room. Though the government station at Ganymede Outpost had been built deep beneath the surface of the frozen moon, she'd detected little increase in warmth during the long descent by elevator.

Jas had also detected a little frostiness in the official who had met them on their arrival. It had caused her to wonder if Shadows had infiltrated the facility, but it seemed safe enough for the time being. Jas speculated that it might be living in freezing conditions that had made the Ganymede staff stand-offish.

"Well I've had just about enough of this," exclaimed Dr. Sparks, rising from his seat. "I'm exhausted. I'm going to ask where our quarters are so I can get some sleep."

"You can't," said Sayen. "You know all the important information about the Paths. You have to be here for the meeting."

"I don't think it'll matter too much if I slip off for a while," replied the doctor. "As Jas said, it could be hours until the Council officers arrive. It's been a long, harrowing day and I can't keep my eyes open a moment longer. Someone can come and get me if they want to talk to me."

"Don't go," said Sayen. "If we have to find you and bring you back here, it'll waste time."

As Dr. Sparks and Sayen bickered back and forth, Jas frowned. She'd never liked the doctor and the more she got to know him the colder her feelings grew. Not only was he a bigot, but despite the efforts she and others had made to rescue him from his informal imprisonment on a Martian scientific research station, he hadn't yet expressed any gratitude to them nor any sorrow about the alien empath who had died to save his life.

Sparks said, "It doesn't matter what you say, I simply have to rest. Just send someone for me when the officers arrive." He went over to the door, but when he opened it, the Ganymede official who had greeted them at their arrival was outside. She drew back, her eyebrows rising at the sight of Sparks.

"Um...the Council managers are here," she said. "They're on their way over. Could you move some chairs and tables back to make room for them?"

The woman indicated the furniture in the half of the room nearest the door. Jas wondered how large the creatures were.

They stacked chairs and tables in the corner while the Ganymede official stood at the open door watching the corridor. Her face broke into a smile as the Council officers presumably approached, though her smile was actually more like a grimace.

Jas sat down once more as scratching sounds from outside signaled the officers' imminent appearance. The odor of vanilla invaded the room.

As the first officer appeared through the door, Jas sat up in her seat. She'd encountered many aliens during her career in deep space security, but nothing compared to what she was seeing then, not even in her worst nightmares. Coated in a bronze exoskeleton and walking on ten pairs of articulated legs, the Transgalactic Council officer was massive and insectoid. On either side of its head were two huge compound eyes, and it had sharp mandibles for a mouth.

The alien was followed into the room by another of the same species, though this one was a little larger at around two and a half meters tall and wide. The third to enter the room was larger still, and its carapace was golden. The vanilla scent they gave off was strong and threaded with spicy undertones.

"We apologize for keeping you waiting," said the golden alien. "We had some urgent matters to address before we left." Subtle flowery aromas wafted across the room. Jas wondered if the creatures used their pheromones to communicate.

"I'll be back in a little while," the Ganymede official said before leaving them alone to talk.

Jas had battled long and hard and many people had died and been injured to get word to the Transgalactic Council that Earth was being invaded by Shadows right under the nose of its government. Her hard, uncomfortable seat was forgotten as she leaned forward to hear what the Council was going to do to help her fellow humans.

"Firstly, we must introduce ourselves," the golden one went on. "My English name is Martha, and my colleagues are Rahul and Peter."

As the humans also introduced themselves, Sayen sent Jas a sidelong smile. The aliens' appearances were certainly at odds with their mundane names.

"For reasons I will explain shortly," Martha went on, "we do not have much time. The message we received from you about the invasion of Earth was short, and we require more information. If one of you could briefly outline your first encounter with the organisms you call Shadows and the related events up until you arrived here, we would be most grateful."

The others turned their eyes to Jas. She was the one who had first discovered the existence of the Shadows on a far distant planet what felt like a very long time ago. She took a breath. She didn't know how she was going to tell the Council officers everything that had happened over the last few months *briefly*, but she began to speak.

As simply and concisely as she could, she narrated the important incidents, like the fight aboard the prospecting ship, the *Galathea*, the battle on the colony world, Dawn, and their encounters with Shadows on Earth as they attempted to inform the Council about the invasion.

The officers were silent throughout her story, though judging by the aromas that drifted around the room, they were speaking with each other as they listened. Sayen, Carl, and even Dr. Sparks added in extra points as Jas spoke.

When she related their re-encounter with the Paths on Mars, Rahul interrupted her. "Pardon me, but may I ask where these Paths are at the moment?"

"They're aboard my ship's shuttle in the docking bay on the surface," Phelan replied.

"I see," Rahul said. "It seems to me that, according to what you told us about finding these creatures within a Shadow trap but unaffected, they are extremely significant. We must speak with them urgently. They may be the breakthrough we've been looking for. Their information may give us an advantage in the battle."

"Battle?" Sayen asked.

"Yes," Martha replied, "we are about to engage militarily with these dreadful invaders. Regarding your story, we had thought that Earth had so far evaded attack, but apparently we were wrong. I would like to thank you for everything you've told us. Your information is most useful. I will record the coordinates of the planets you mention before we leave. Now, we have only a short time remaining, and I must use it to explain the galactic situation with the Shadows."

The creature settled down on its many legs.

"The Transgalactic Council first became aware of these invaders several Earth years ago, though it took some time for us to understand the nature of the menace. At first, it appeared that hostilities between galactic civilizations were increasing. Throughout the galaxy's history, there has never been a time it was entirely at peace, but attacks and invasions were the highest they'd been for a long time. Our military arm, the Unity, stepped in as a peacekeeping force wherever possible, but its resources were stretched thin by the numerous conflicts.

"It was not until we were alerted to thousands of individuals who claimed that their family members, friends, and colleagues had been taken over by unseen forces that we began to suspect that these aggressions were not exactly as they seemed. Our investigations also revealed the presence of Shadow traps on many worlds that were in conflict with other civilizations. The coincidences mounted up.

"Further investigations continued, and as soon as the realization dawned as to what was actually happening, we responded. So far, we've identified hundreds of planets that the Shadows have taken over. The Unity, together with the military forces of so-far unaffected planets, are attempting to destroy the invaders and rescue surviving citizens. We have reclaimed some worlds, but for every planet we free from the Shadows, another two appear in its place. As we speak, the Unity is on the verge of yet another battle. We came here directly from a meeting to finalize the battle plan."

"But what about Earth?" Jas asked. "What are you going to do to help the people of Earth?"

"According to the information you supplied," Martha replied, "we are in no doubt that Earth is indeed in the midst of a Shadow invasion, but I am afraid that your world is one of many civilizations in need of our aid. We cannot do anything immediately, but when the Council can spare the resources, we will do all we can to help."

"What?" Jas exclaimed. She thought of Erielle and Makey, her friends who had returned to Earth intending to fight the Shadows there. Were they even still alive? How long would they have to wait before help arrived? She stood up. "That's not good enough. Earth needs help *now*."

Carl said, "Jas, I don't think—"

"No, Carl," she said. "This is wrong." She swung around to the aliens. "Why do you think we went through so much to contact you? Earth's a Council ally, isn't it? Humans are entitled to its protection. People are dying as we speak. You have to help us."

The Council officers didn't reply immediately. Scents of warm chocolate and acetone filled the air as they talked among themselves.

Martha said, "We understand your position and we sympathize with Earth's plight. Be assured that we will do everything in our power to fulfill our obligations to come to its defense as soon as we are able. But at the moment we simply cannot. A massive fleet of ships controlled by Shadows is currently approaching a highly strategic region of the galaxy. Every vessel at the Unity's disposal has been amassed to stop them. If the Unity prevails in the ensuing battle without heavy losses, we may be able to dispatch a force to address the situation on Earth."

Carl straightened up from his position leaning against the wall. "Is it too late to join the battle?"

"I'm not sure," Martha said. "I doubt that engagement with the enemy has commenced yet. Why? Do you wish to fight?"

Carl said, "I'd like to, especially if it means Earth might receive help quicker. I'm a pilot."

"What?" Jas exclaimed. "Wait a minute."

"Do you have combat experience?" Martha asked.

"Yes," Carl replied.

"There may still be time for you to take part in the battle if you leave now," Martha said. "We can open a Gateway to the Unity recruitment point. I'm sure the officers would be happy to see a trained combat pilot. There is a scarcity of them."

"No," Jas said. "Carl, don't go."

Two

The Transgalactic Gateway opened in the meeting room. Though it was Jas's first time seeing one, she was too distracted by Carl's imminent departure to take much notice. It had all happened so quickly.

He avoided her pleading gaze as the green mist that heralded the Gateway began to form.

"Carl," Jas said. "please don't go. It's too soon. We've only just arrived from Mars. You need to rest up. It's too dangerous."

He only glanced at her and shook his head slightly, as if telling her not to interfere.

"All right, I'll come with you then," Jas blurted. "I'll fight too. I'm sure the Unity can find something for me to do."

"I am afraid that we need you here for the moment," Martha said. "We need further information on the Paths. Sadly, I do not think this battle will be the last. I am sure there will be many more opportunities to fight the Shadows in the future. For now, you can be the most useful to us by telling us more about the Paths."

Jas was numb. It had been only hours before that she and Carl had kissed for the first time after a growing closeness between them that had lasted weeks. She hadn't imagined that he would be snatched away from her—that he would *choose* to leave her—so soon.

"Carl, please," she murmured, her heart tearing in two. Phelan, Sayen, and Dr. Sparks looked away, embarrassed.

The green mist had coalesced and began to lazily swirl into a spiral.

Finally, Carl turned to her. His face grave, he stepped over and touched her upper arm. "I'm sorry, Jas. I have to do this. The Shadows killed my parents. I have to fight them."

"Please prepare to step through the Gateway," said Martha. "It will be open for only a few seconds."

"Don't worry about me," Carl said. "I'll be back as soon as it's over." He kissed her briefly and returned to his position in front of the whirling mist.

The ache in Jas's chest was unbearable. A thousand words rose to her mind and were dismissed. She couldn't speak as she struggled to understand why Carl had to leave her. Maybe if she'd had a family, she tried to tell herself, she would do the same. But she had no family. She only had him.

The scene blurred before her eyes. She didn't see the moment when Carl stepped into the mist. She only heard the others' quiet goodbyes. By the time she wiped her vision clear, he was gone.

After a moment or two, Jas realized that Martha was talking to her.

She swallowed. "What did you say?" she asked the alien.

"I said, I would like to see these Paths. I know of approximately two thousand and seven hundred sentient species who live in our galaxy, yet I have never heard of anything that matches your description. And according to what you have told us, these creatures have extensive knowledge of the Shadows."

Jas was still too upset to say more, which Phelan seemed to notice, for he answered in her place. "If y'all want, Jas and I can go collect them from my shuttle."

"That would be most convenient," Martha said.

"Come on," Phelan said to Jas. "Give me a hand."

Leaving the meeting room and returning to the elevator that would take them up to the surface proved enough of a distraction to calm Jas down a little, which had no doubt been Phelan's intention. In spite of his brash, slightly insensitive demeanor, Sayen's brother was as warm-hearted as his sibling.

The two of them stepped through the bare metal elevator doors and stood side by side as they began to ascend. Phelan's hands were clasped behind his back and his eyes were focused ahead. "Looks like we'll all be joining in a Shadow battle soon enough."

Jas nodded. "I think you're right."

"I would have volunteered too," said Phelan, "but I wouldn't have had any idea what I was doing. I've only ever captained the *Bricoleur* on mining expeditions. I've never been in combat."

"I'm pretty sure neither has Carl."

"What?" Phelan turned to her. "Then why did he say he had?"

She shrugged. "So they'd let him go fight, I guess."

"Krat. Well, I'm sure he'll be fine anyway. He's a damn good pilot."

"He is." Ever since she'd known him, Carl had always flown expertly. Jas recalled how he'd saved the lives of the crew of the *Galathea* by crash-landing the starship onto K. 67092d and later lifting off from the planet's surface. But the best pilot in the galaxy could still be shot down.

They were at the top of the elevator shaft. The doors opened, revealing the walkway that led to the docking bay and the *Bricoleur's* shuttle. Now that Carl had gone, Jas wondered how they would return to Phelan's ship, which was in orbit above Ganymede occupied only by the android navigator, Prosper.

She looked out of the walkway windows on each side. It was always daytime on tidally locked Ganymede. Jupiter was reflecting the Sun's rays onto the moon's frozen wastes. The icy expanse that surrounded them reminded Jas of her college days on Antarctica.

"You okay? You look like you're gonna faint." Phelan was looking at her, worried.

She took a deep breath and exhaled, releasing the memory of the time someone else had left her abruptly and without warning. "I'm okay. Let's get these Paths. The sooner the Council figure out what they can tell us, the sooner we can all move on."

Phelan opened the airlock and they went inside the small shuttle. The Paths were, unsurprisingly, exactly where they'd left them. They so closely resembled large bag-shaped fungi, it was hard to believe that it was only through their enigmatic activities at the Valles Marineris Spaceport that Jas, Sayen, and Sparks had escaped Mars.

Jas's mood lifted as they approached the Paths. Though she knew her feelings were influenced by emotions radiating from the empathic aliens and were a reflection of their reaction to her appearance, she was glad of the effect.

She and Phelan gathered up the brown sacks. Their arms full, they returned to the waiting Transgalactic Council officers.

THREE

Dr. Sparks had explained his experiences with the Paths in detail to the officers by the time Jas and Phelan returned with them. Jas hoped that the officers were telepathic and could speak with the aliens, but after a lengthy pheromone exchange, Rahul announced that this was not the case.

"We appear to only sense their emotions," he said. "It is most frustrating. These creatures do not appear to be very skilled at telepathic communication."

"Flahive didn't seem to have much trouble speaking with them," Sayen said. "In fact, he said they were so loud he had to ask them to whisper."

"You have a companion who is able to communicate with these beings?" Martha asked.

"Had," said Jas. "He was killed on Mars."

"Oh dear," said Rahul. "That is sad and most unfortunate for us. May I ask where this person originated?"

"He was Cruthian," Phelan replied. "He was my engineer. The *Bricoleur* has an Oootoon engine."

"Ah yes," Rahul said. "Everything becomes clear now. High-gravity planets such as Cruth tend to promote the evolution of exceptional telepathic talent." The insectoid alien waggled his head, causing his antennae to wave around. More odors emanated from the Council officers as they continued their discussion in silence.

Jas had been standing since she and Phelan brought the Paths to the meeting room, but suddenly exhaustion threatened to overwhelm her, and she sat down. It seemed that every muscle in her body was aching.

The Council officers began questioning Dr. Sparks about the Paths once more, but Jas barely listened to the conversation. Memories of Carl occupied her thoughts. She remembered the happy-go-lucky co-pilot of the *Galathea*, the tetchy friend on Dawn, his sleeping form at her place on Earth, him driving Ozment's truck. How long would it be before she would see him again? How would she find him among the thousands of pilots fighting in the Shadow battle?

Sayen interjected loudly into the Council officers' conversation with Sparks, telling them they needed to hear what Flahive had told them in the bar after meeting the Paths but before the doctor had caught up with them. The pheromones of the Council officers faded as Sayen related almost word for word what Flahive had told them about the Paths existing in another realm outside the physical universe, and how the Shadows also existed there.

"This is truly remarkable. Incredible, in fact," exclaimed Peter. "What you are telling us is the stuff of mythological tales and beliefs. We simply must find out more. These Paths may not only be our key to defeating the Shadows, they may enlighten our understanding of the very nature of existence itself."

"Look," Jas said to the aliens. "That might be true, but I don't think we can tell you any more than we already have. What happens now? Are you taking the Paths with you? Can I join in the fight against the Shadows? I was a security chief aboard a starship."

"If you do not mind waiting a few more hours," said Peter, "I would like to—"

"I do mind," said Jas. "Whether the Paths have secrets to the universe to reveal or not isn't relevant to us. We've told you about what's happening on Earth and we've brought the Paths to you.

There isn't anything else we can do. It's past time that we went into battle."

"Now wait a minute," Sparks said. "Speak for yourself. I'd be very happy to help the officers for a while longer."

"You would," said Jas.

"Jas," said Sayen, frowning.

"Please, please," said Martha. "Do not argue. We wish to resolve the question of what the Paths can tell us as quickly as you do. Unfortunately, the high-gravity civilizations where empaths who could speak with the Paths live are within the section of the galaxy currently controlled by Shadows. Though we could open a Gateway to one of those planets to try to recruit an individual to help us, the likelihood that we would encounter a Shadow is high. We must find another way to communicate with them. But I have an idea."

Once more, the Council officers exuded odors as they talked among themselves.

"For krat's sake," Jas said in an undertone to Sayen after a short while. "How much longer do you think they're going to keep us here?"

Before Sayen could reply, Martha spoke. "We would like to try something that could be a little dangerous. I am afraid that our physiology prevents us from performing this experiment ourselves, but we believe a human would be highly effective."

"What? What are you talking about?" Jas asked. Her patience had entirely dissipated and any effort at civility had gone with it.

"You are familiar with the equipment the Council uses to test the presence of Shadows?" Rahul asked.

"You mean Shadow scanners?" said Jas. "Yes. I already told you that we stole one from a spaceport. What have they got to do with this?"

"Our fight against the Shadows was greatly aided when we discovered the one difference that distinguished them from their victims," Peter said. "A Council operative who was coated in invisibility spray —a human invention, I believe—saw an aura around Shadows that no other things living nor inanimate exhibited. Through a series of experiments, we discovered that it was the tiny amount of mythranil included in the invisibility spray that enabled the wearer to identify Shadows in this way. Using this knowledge, we incorporated similar trace amounts of mythranil into prototype Shadow scanners and found this made them foolproof at detecting the Shadows' auras."

At Peter's revelation, Jas's mind flew back to what Carl had said when they rescued Sayen from the Shadow holdout in Antarctica. He'd mentioned seeing that same aura. "So, what are you saying?" she asked. "I still don't get how that's going to help you find out more about the Paths."

"We are, of course," continued Peter, "perfectly aware of the illegal uses and effects of this powerful narcotic. It sends the user into a euphoric, trance-like state lasting several hours."

Sparks, who had been sitting in a corner of the room, his chin resting on his hand, apparently thoroughly bored now that the conversation had turned from him, suddenly gasped and stood up. His eyes popping, he pointed a trembling finger at the Paths. "I understand," he exclaimed. "I know what you mean. Of course. Of course. It makes perfect sense. That was where I went. That was where they sent me."

"What are you babbling about, Sparks?" Jas asked.

"When the Paths are threatened, they defend themselves by sending the thing threatening them to another place mentally," the doctor replied. "The body remains, but the mind of the attacker has departed. The place they send their attacker's mind is the place the Paths come from. The effect is to make the threat go away temporarily. If they feel sufficiently threatened, they send their attacker away permanently, and the attacker dies. I see it now."

"Does anyone here have the faintest idea what he's talking about?" asked Jas. "And if so, could they please explain it to me?"

"I think I understand," said Sayen. "The Paths have no physical power here, but their mental power is strong. They can control our minds and transfer them to another plane, where the Paths and the

Shadows come from. But I don't understand the connection with myth."

"Let me explain," Martha said. "The narcotic mythranil is well known for its ability to transfer the mind of the user to another place, figuratively speaking. But from what we now understand about how the trace presence of myth in an observer of a Shadow confers the ability to see their aura, we can speculate that the drug's effect is not figurative, but literal. The user mentally travels outside the physical universe to the realm where the Paths and Shadows exist."

"So..." said Sayen. "You're thinking if someone goes to this place, they could connect with the Paths on their home territory?"

"That is indeed our conjecture," Martha said.

"Sorry," said Sparks, "I'm not threatening them again. It's out of the question. Besides, I don't remember noticing anything resembling the Paths while I was in my trance."

"It would be foolish for the Paths to approach a threat within their own domain," Rahul replied. "But we are not proposing that anyone threatens them. That would be unethical. We have a different method in mind, but unfortunately we are unable to do this ourselves. We require a human volunteer."

"I'll do it," Jas said. Whatever it was, she didn't care. Nothing seemed to matter much anymore.

"Excellent," Martha said. "We will send for the mythranil immediately."

FOUR

The conjoined Shadow minds rippled as their thoughts spread out across the Void. More and more victims in the physical realm had wandered or been driven into traps, and more Shadow replicants were created and crossed over. The small trickle of movement had become a flood.

In the place where spacetime existed, mental contact between Shadows remained difficult. There, they were confined to solid bodies, separated from each other and shaped by—haunted by—the memories and personalities of their victims, which they retained from the copied brain matter and coding of their cell structures.

Their numbers had grown so great that extensive coordination was vital, now more than ever. This need had been identified and was being addressed as they moved toward the final stage of their plan: domination. When spacetime prevented efficient contact, they used the technological communication systems of the beings they had destroyed. It brought great pleasure to the Shadows to operate the marvelous contraptions of the physical plane, especially the vessels that carried solid bodies from place to place. They had gathered a great number of these. The battle was upon them, and they could use the vessels to good effect.

On worlds where the Shadow presence was sufficiently large,

they had seized control of the planet and hastened the destruction of the remaining sentient beings. Among other civilizations, where their numbers were yet inferior, the Shadows bided their time. They had strategized their victim selection so that, though Shadows were not the majority on these worlds, they held key positions within powerful organizations. When the battle was won, these planets would also fall under the weight of the victorious invaders, undermined from within.

The alliance led by the Transgalactic Council had vastly underestimated the extent of the Shadow presence. It would have a surprise waiting when the worlds it was supposedly defending rose up against it; when the friends they did not suspect turned upon them. But until the right moment, the Shadows had to operate carefully.

Meanwhile, though the physical realm was falling quickly under their attack, opposition within the Void was growing stronger. It was inevitable. Their presence was reduced as more and more Shadows split from the fusion and crossed over to the other side, while the might of their Void opponents remained the same, immensely strong and fighting the Shadows' efforts at every turn.

When a few parts of the opposition had managed to slip through and emerge in a trap, the Shadows had feared that they would also have to fight them on the physical plane. But there, the opponents were weak and ineffectual. Though the Shadows could not force them to return to the Void, they did not have anything to fear from them in the physical universe.

Unlike the victims the Shadows took. *They* had much to fear.

FIVE

"Don't do it, Jas," Sayen said. She'd caught up to her friend at a Ganymede Outpost airlock. Jas was already wearing an environment suit and she was getting ready to go outside.

Jas lifted the visor of her helmet. "Huh? I'm only going for a walk. I hate being cooped up in here with nothing to do while we wait for the myth to arrive."

"That isn't what I meant," said Sayen. "You shouldn't take that drug. You've never done it before. Some people die when they take that stuff. You don't know what could happen. What if they get the dosage wrong?"

Jas shrugged. "Someone has to take it. If the Council officers are right, I might be able to find out the Shadows' weaknesses."

"Then let me do it," Sayen said. "My augmented body's more robust than yours. I can probably tolerate the myth better."

Jas shook her head. "Phelan has already lost both his parents. It isn't fair that he should risk losing you too. I don't have anyone who'd be too bothered to lose me."

"That isn't true, Jas, and you know it."

"Isn't it?"

"Of course not. Phelan and I couldn't bear to lose you, but more than that, what about Carl?"

"What *about* Carl?" Jas's gaze turned to the wintry landscape through the airlock window. "I thought he cared about me, but he didn't hesitate to leave me when he had the chance. I guess I was wrong about him."

"Oh, Jas." Sayen sighed.

"I'll be outside for a while," Jas said. "Could you tell them to radio me when the myth arrives?" She snapped her visor closed and pressed the airlock's inner door.

"Wait," Sayen exclaimed, but the door slid into position and Jas turned her back while waiting for the atmosphere exchange to take place.

Sayen hadn't donned an environment suit in years, not since her safety training to become a deep space navigator. By the time she'd zipped up and snapped everything into place and passed through the airlock herself, Jas's long legs had already carried her more than a hundred meters away from the station. Sayen hailed her friend over the radio, and Jas paused and turned. She waited as Sayen made her way carefully over the frozen ground, strewn with ice boulders. In the low gravity, she found she could bound over the ground quite quickly.

Jupiter hung threateningly in the sky above, its bands of color interspersed with angry swirls as massive storms tore through its atmosphere. The gas giant's presence was so close, Ganymede seemed constantly about to fall into it, inexorably drawn into the gravity well. Sayen shivered, though her suit's heating was making her feel toasty compared to the chilly station. She withdrew her gaze from the moon's overbearing master as she reached Jas.

"It's a bit much, isn't it?" came Jas's voice over her radio.

Sayen could barely see her friend's lips move through her darkened visor.

"Jupiter?" she replied. "Yeah, just a little."

"It reminds me of K. 98352g. Do you remember? Only there it was the system's sun that took up most of the sky."

"I remember the planet but not the view. I never used to go down to the surface in those days."

"Oh yeah. That's right," said Jas. "You didn't like to, did you? You told me once that while you were on a prospecting mission, you used to pretend you could step aboard the shuttle and go right down to Earth if you wanted."

Sayen chuckled. "Did I say that? It was true. I did used to pretend I was only a shuttle ride from Earth." Sayen swung around to view the desolate gray-white, cratered scenery that stretched monotonously to the horizon. "Were you headed somewhere in particular?"

Jas's laugh sounded in Sayen's helmet and she saw the ghost of her friend's wry smile. "No. Nowhere in particular. Want to come along?"

"I was hoping for the invitation," Sayen replied. As they set off, she imagined how they must look: Jas inside an environment suit large enough for a tall man, and herself, slim and petite, toddling and bouncing alongside her. They crossed the barren ground, passing eons-old ice rocks for a while in silence.

"You know, Jas, I feel like such an idiot," Sayen said.

"Huh? How come?"

"Those Council officers...I think I met some of their species not long ago. I keep thinking that if I'd said something to them at the time about the Shadows invading Earth, maybe it would have saved us a lot of trouble. Some people might still be alive."

"You met those aliens before? How'd you manage that? It couldn't have been on a prospecting mission."

"No, it wasn't. Do you remember when we went to steal the Shadow scanner from the spaceport? With Ozment?"

"Yeah, of course I do."

"We stopped at a park in the mountains overnight. Erielle was still weak and in a lot of pain from the wounds on her legs. I couldn't sleep, and I went for a walk. I ran into some of those creatures."

"You did? I don't remember you saying anything about it."

"There was so much going on, and I was worried sick about

Erielle...and I didn't think it was important. But maybe if I'd told those tourists what we knew..."

"No, don't beat yourself up, Sayen. Just because they're the same species, that doesn't mean the ones you met had any connection to the Council. They probably wouldn't have had any idea what you were talking about."

"Yeah, maybe. I hope so," said Sayen, then, after a moment, "Jas."

"What?"

"You don't really think that Carl doesn't care about you, do you?"

Her friend sighed. "I didn't think so when we left Mars. Now, I just don't know. The minute the Council officers made him the offer to leave, he took it. Like he realized he'd made a big mistake."

"But he wanted to go fight. He wanted to take part in the battle with the Shadows. He's risking his life."

"That's what I mean. He's risking his life just to get away from me."

"Krat, Jas," Sayen exclaimed. She could hardly believe what she was hearing. "What's wrong with you? Are you sick or something? This isn't like you."

"No, I'm not sick. I don't know what you mean."

"You don't know what I mean? What I mean is, where's all this self-pity coming from? You sound like a kratting teenager. Of course Carl cares about you. You *know* that. You spent the last several months avoiding the fact and pushing him away, but you know it as sure as we're standing here."

Jas didn't reply for a moment, then she asked, "So how come he left me?"

Sayen heard an uncharacteristic tremble in her friend's voice. "Jas, I guess I know how you feel. Erielle left me too, remember? And I was just as hurt and angry as you are right now. But she had to go to fight the Shadows on Earth and protect her people. And it's the same for Carl. The Council mentioned the opportunity, and he took his chance. He had to do it, the same as Erielle and Makey did. He probably thought he couldn't live with himself if he didn't try to avenge the deaths of his parents."

"You didn't go," Jas said.

"I wasn't as quick off the mark as Carl, but I will, Jas, I will, when the time comes. I'll never forget what the Shadows did to Mamma and Daddy."

Without a word, Jas set off walking again.

"Wait a minute," Sayen said, hurrying to catch up.

Jas went determinedly on, continuing to say nothing. Sayen glanced back at the lonely steel tower and squat base that marked the entrance to the underground outpost. The station had grown smaller as they'd increased their distance. Though her suit's navigation would lead them straight back to it, the dwindling image made her uneasy.

"Don't you think we should turn back?" Sayen asked. "The myth should be here soon, and rad levels are high on Ganymede. We probably shouldn't stay outside more than half an hour or so."

Jas's breathy sigh came over her radio, followed by, "I'm being really dumb, aren't I?"

"You mean about Carl? Well..." Sayen considered how to put her response kindly, but she knew that Jas could take the truth without offense. "Yeah, you're being real dumb. Can we go back now?"

Jas about-faced and began to stride back to the outpost. Sayen trotted along behind her.

"You know, Jas," she said. "I don't think Carl went to fight in the Shadow battle just for his parents' sake. I think he wants to beat the Shadows because he wants a peaceful future for both of you."

"Really?" Her friend's voice was high and quavering once more.

"Yeah. When we were aboard the *Bricoleur* before we went to Mars, he came to my cabin—to cheer me up I think. I was pretty low for a while after Erielle left. He brought that daft animal with him. We talked a little, and he did make me feel a bit better. Then we got to talking about everything that had gone on."

She paused. "I probably shouldn't tell you this, but Carl cares about you so much, Jas. He told me so. He was all confused at the time we spoke because he thought you two were close, but you always pulled away if anything started to happen. Yet you'd been so free and easy with that officer on Dawn. He couldn't understand why you were so reluctant to be with him, but now that he knows he's important to you, I'm sure he wants to fight for you too."

"He compared my feelings for Idris with my feelings for him?" Jas exclaimed.

"I guess he did. It's natural, isn't it? But it's okay now, right? Because you finally decided you want to be with him."

Jas stopped in her tracks, almost causing Sayen to collide with her. "This is terrible. He's got it all wrong. I didn't hesitate because I didn't like him as much as I liked Idris. I hesitated because...Krat. Now he's gone, and I can't explain why I acted like I did. Sayen, this is awful. What am I going to do?"

Sayen wasn't exactly sure what Jas was upset about, but she tried to reassure her friend all the way back to the airlock. Her efforts didn't seem to do much good. When they were inside and Jas had removed her helmet, Sayen could see her friend remained worried and distracted. It was too late for them to talk more, however, because the myth had arrived.

SIX

Jas had rarely felt as bad as she did at that moment. She was naked and lying under a blanket in the Ganymede Outpost's medical center, waiting to receive the mythranil that might or might not send her to the place the Paths came from. But she didn't feel bad because she feared what was about to happen. More than becoming addicted to the powerful narcotic, more than getting lost in that place beyond the physical universe, more than dying, in fact, she feared never having the opportunity to set Carl straight about what he meant to her.

Ever since the trauma she'd experienced when she'd been at training college in Antarctica, she'd had a certain approach to relationships. She hadn't shied away from them entirely, but when someone was interested in her, she was always careful to keep everything light and easy. She preferred dating on missions when the man was planetside, knowing that, in a few days or weeks, circumstances would force them to part company, usually amicably, after a brief fling. She'd always steered clear of dating shipmates, who she would be unable to avoid until the mission's end, which could be months or sometimes even years in the future.

With Carl, everything had been different. For the first time since she was eighteen, Jas had felt out of control of what was happening to her. Though she couldn't have put her finger on the moment when Carl had become something more to her than just her pilot friend and shipmate, she knew that her feelings were serious, and her vulnerability had scared her.

On Dawn, with Idris, things had progressed as usual up until the Shadow invasion. The lieutenant had been a good person, but Jas wouldn't have thought twice about him six months after departing the colony. Her feelings for Carl, by contrast, were for life. In the past, she'd lost someone who'd meant that much to her. She didn't think she could survive that loss again, so it had taken a long time for her to let her true feelings show.

"Are you ready?" Martha had come in while Jas was lost in her thoughts. The alien's golden head with its shining compound eyes appeared above her. In the claws at the end of one of her front legs she held a hypodermic needle filled with a deep crimson liquid. Her claws looked almost as sharp as the inner mandibles of her mouth, which protruded as she spoke.

"Um, I think so," Jas said.

"I can assure you that I will hit exactly the right spot," said Martha. "Though my species' vision is not as effective as human's, at this distance I can detect the odor profile of your body. The points of sensitivity are clear to me. I will inject the mythranil in the area that gives the greatest effect. The Council is extremely grateful to you for participating in this experiment."

Dr. Sparks entered the room, rubbing his hands together. "I'll do it," he said cheerfully. He seemed to have caught up on his sleep while they'd been waiting for the myth. But still, Jas thought, the massive insectoid alien with razor-sharp mandibles would be a preferable alternative to the doctor.

He took the hypodermic needle that the alien handed him.

"As you wish," Martha said. "I am sure that you are a competent physician. It really does not matter, providing that Ms. Harrington begins the experience and gathers any useful information as quickly as possible."

The Paths had been placed in a corner of the room in case their proximity might create some kind of beneficial effect. Jas's gaze lingered on their brown, baggy forms as Sparks lifted the blanket.

"You do know what you're doing, don't you?" she asked the doctor.

"Of course I do. Tut tut. Such little faith. As a matter of fact, mystical medical theory is one of my specialties. I took additional credits in it. I know all the meridians and adjacent neural structures. Never fear."

She rolled her eyes. She'd always known the man was a quack. But in this case he did seem to be the right person for the job.

"As a matter of fact, I quite envy you," the doctor went on. "If the effects of myth are similar to the trance the Paths put me in during my little sojourn on Mars, you're in for a delightful experience. Now, please remain still. I've found the exact spot."

Jas gasped as a bright point of pain materialized to the right of her groin. She clenched her teeth, fighting the urge to leap up and rip the hypodermic from Sparks's fingers. Myth was supposed to be a narcotic—a relaxing, pleasurable, doped-up experience. Jas hadn't imagined she would have to endure agony to receive a dose.

But in another moment, the pain was replaced by bliss.

———

Jas wasn't sure if her eyes were closed or open, but she could feel as much as see an infinite expanse surrounding her. She was floating in infinity, and she was part of it, endless and unconfined. Whirls of colors she did and didn't recognize spun around her, though she was also a part of them. She was empty and she was whole; she was split into a billion pieces and she was complete. All her desires and needs, worries and fears, were gone. Existence was all and it was perfect. *She* was perfect and free.

She floated forever, but at the very edge of her mind something nibbled. Like a grain of dust in her eye, a tiny piece of gravel in her shoe, an invisible scrap of food stuck between her teeth. It was the sense of a task incomplete. Something she had to do or see, or someone she'd left behind. The tiny speck of irritation marred the perfection. Jas mentally pushed at the thing, willing it to disappear. But it resolutely popped back. No matter how hard she tried, she couldn't escape it.

A disruption appeared in the ever-evolving patterns that surrounded her, and she understood that she was not alone. The colors churned faster, until, "Welcome," a chorus of voices echoed in her mind. The sounds seemed to bathe her in cool waters and enveloped her in such feelings of security and warmth that she forgot to answer.

The voices repeated their greeting, calling Jas to a modicum of concentration. "Hello? Who's there? Who are you?" she asked without speaking.

"We are the creatures you call Paths in the physical realm."

Jas could vaguely remember something related to that name, but she no longer cared about anything. The name's significance slipped from her mind like raindrops through cobblestones.

"Human, you must listen."

Why wouldn't they be quiet? There was that speck of irritation again, niggling at her. "What? Why?" She tried to move away from the beings who spoke, but they were all around her and all through her too.

"Human, we wish to help you, but you must hear us."

Jas couldn't escape the voices. Wearily, she replied, though her voice was also no more than a resonance in her mind. "What do you want to tell me?"

"You are in the Void, and entities from here are invading your plane of existence. They are leaving here for your universe and destroying living things there. We want to stop them. We want to help you."

The relevance of their words still escaped Jas.

They continued, "We do not want the others to continue to leave and take away the brief, time-bound lives of beings on the physical plane."

Concentrating with all her might, Jas said, "I don't understand. Why do these others want to leave here? Everything is perfect."

"Objects from your plane flit in and out of existence here. They notice these things and desire them. They lust for the complex creations that you physical beings use to move across distances. Here, they have no need of them, for there are no distances. Every point is simultaneously connected. So they must move to the physical plane to enjoy them."

Jas's mind began to drift. She couldn't grasp what the things were telling her. She began to relax once more into elation and bliss.

"Human, please listen. Because we do not wish to destroy and replicate a physical life form, we are all but helpless within your realm and cannot exist there indefinitely. You must take this information back with you. Many of the others have left the Void. We believe they spread throughout your realm, much farther than you imagine. We have read the minds of those remaining here and learned that if your side appear to be winning the battle with them, the others will reveal themselves and betray those closest to them. Your defense will fail. You must take this information back with you and warn your kind of the danger."

But Jas couldn't properly understand what they were telling her. Words were gossamer in the Void.

SEVEN

Jas didn't know how long she'd been floating in the Void. Time didn't seem to exist. She'd always been there, and she'd never been there. She could no longer hear the beings. Only a trace of their warning remained in her mind. What had they been referring to? She couldn't remember. It didn't matter anyway.

A moment or a millennium later, she became aware of more entities. Had the original beings returned? Maybe they would tell her their message again.

But these things were not the same. A wave of unease coursed through her. They didn't embody the bliss of the Void. They were its opposite values—negativity, confinement, emptiness. Jas tried to move away from the things, but the dimensionless place offered no escape. Tendrils of fear wriggled into her, invading her joyful bliss.

"We know you," voices said. "Those of us on the other side encountered you there. You have ended our existences. You cannot return to the physical plane to destroy more of our kind. You must stay here. We will keep you here."

The writhing tendrils of fear hardened within Jas, sparking flames of pain. Her mind was brought rapidly into focus. Where was she? What was happening? What were these things she could perceive but not see?

She struggled, her mind a mess of fear. The things that held her tightened their grip. All Jas's years of training kicked in and she tried to fight, but she had no body. She tried to scream, but she had no mouth. Without eyes, she couldn't see her attackers. She could only feel them. She was trapped.

But like the rays of a gentle dawn over the waves of a stormy sea, Jas felt the first beings return. The initial reaction of those that held her was to tremble as the strength of their resolve weakened. The powerful grip that held her slackened.

Then a discordant tone sounded. The things holding Jas squeezed her tighter. Her mind was being crushed. The sensation was agonizing.

All around, a battle broke out as the opposites fought. Colors flashed and disappeared. Voices erupted and were silenced. Jas was lost in a sea of turmoil, and ever the grip of the things that held her grew tighter. The first beings were trying to free her, but the ones that held her were too strong. Ever tighter they gripped. They were squeezing her from existence. They were...

The sensation lessened and transformed to a rocking motion. She was being pushed from side to side roughly. She began to slip from the entities holding her. She was fading away. One last attempt was made to grasp her, but she was gone.

Someone was pushing her. Why was someone pushing her? She heard voices in the far distance. They were familiar voices, and for the first time in what felt like forever, they were coming from outside her head.

"Jas, can you hear me?" It was Sayen.

"It's okay. She's coming out of it now." Sparks.

"Thank krat for that." Phelan.

She opened her eyes. All three familiar faces were hanging over her.

"M' okay," she mumbled. "I'm okay. Quit crowding me."

As they backed off, Jas shakily sat upright on the narrow cot, pulling her blanket over her shoulders. She shivered. Martha's head was poking in at the doorway.

"You've been under for hours." Sayen said. "We thought you were never going to come around. How are you feeling?"

"I'll check you over," Sparks said. "If everyone could leave?"

"Really, I'm okay," said Jas, and for the most part, she felt she was. Except that she was very, very down. She wanted nothing more than to return to the place she'd left. She could see how easy it was to become addicted to myth.

"Did you find out anything?" Phelan asked.

Jas rubbed her face with her hands. "About what?"

Martha squeezed a little more of her bulk into the room. "Could you tell us if you found out anything about the Shadows or the Paths?"

"The Shadows or the...? I know the names..." Exactly what they were, she wasn't completely sure.

"Have you forgotten the nature of the experiment you undertook?" Martha asked.

"Jas, what can you remember?" asked Sayen.

Trickles of memory ran into her mind. She began to recall snippets of things that had happened recently and people she'd met. Erielle. Makey. The Shadows.

"Just give me a minute, will you?" she said. She shut her eyes, trying to remember. Gradually, the last few months came back to her. She remembered what had happened and the reason for her disorientation. Like opening a barely healing wound, she recalled that Carl had left.

"Are you sure you're all right?" Sayen asked.

"I'm afraid I have to ask everyone to leave so I can conduct a thorough medical checkup," said Sparks.

"I'm fine," Jas snapped.

"I apologize for hurrying you," Martha said, "but time is of the essence. If you have anything to tell me about your experience while under the influence of the mythranil, now would be the appropriate time."

"Ough." Jas put her face in her hands.

"Jas, what's wrong?" asked Sayen.

"I can't remember," Jas replied. "I think I met some beings, and they told me something. There were also some other things that were trying to keep me there, and a fight. And then I was back here. But that's it. Everything else is just a few memories of the run. I've no idea if I met the Paths, and if I did, I have no idea what they told me."

"Ah, I see," said Martha. "That is disappointing. No doubt an effect of the drug. However, several doses remain. Though it is probably now too late for any information we glean to help in the current Shadow battle, we could find out something to be used in the future. Perhaps we can try again."

"I don't think it's going to help," Jas said.

"That may or may not be the case," said Martha. "We will never know unless we try."

"I really don't think there's a lot of point," said Jas. "Look." She pointed to the corner of the medical center were the Paths had been placed. It was empty. The Paths had gone.

EIGHT

Sleeping wasn't easy for Jas at the Ganymede Outpost. A chill penetrated from the surrounding rock ice that the station's inadequate heating system couldn't dispell, and the government-issue bedding was no compensation. Earth's Global Government clearly hadn't spent much funding on the station. To them, it must have been only a handy strategic spot in case of an attack from outside the Solar System. The Government had claimed the place, left its stamp, and then forgotten about it.

But it was more than the cold that was keeping Jas awake that night. Every time she closed her eyes she felt disoriented, as if she were floating in zero-g. Her Martian childhood and long years of visiting other planets had accustomed her to sleeping in gravity lower or higher than Earth's, so she knew it wasn't Ganymede's weak gravity that was causing the dizziness. She guessed the sensation was an after-effect of the myth.

She could hardly remember anything of the *run*, as it was called. Mostly all she could remember was a sense of perfect peace and happiness—joy, even. She could see how hard it would be to resist taking another dose of the illegal narcotic, and another, until the desire for myth became all-consuming. Yet she knew that there was something, or rather *someone*, who stood in the way of that ever happening to her. Happy or sad, she didn't want to leave her reality behind while there was still a possibility of being reunited with him.

Pulling her coverlet over her shoulders, she turned on her side, closed her eyes and tried to go to sleep. But her feet were icy. Her cover was too short for her long body. She pulled up her knees, turned onto her other side and tried once more to sleep. Finally, she drifted into a doze.

Behind her eyelids, colors began to shift and swirl. The sensation of floating returned, but Jas was so tired that she managed to ignore it and slipped farther toward unconsciousness. The shapeless, unmoving sack bodies of the Paths appeared in her mind. Only they were no longer motionless. They were moving, spinning around her. Then, the colors behind them began to darken, and a sense of dread crept up on Jas.

The darkness felt significant, though in her fogged mind, she didn't know why. The Paths' movements became agitated, as if they wanted to leave but lacked sufficient physical control. The colors continued to deepen until they were almost black. Jas shared the Paths' fear, but there wasn't anything she could do about it. Her body refused to obey her mind, and she was forced to remain still. Her mouth moved, but her vocal cords would not create any sound.

As well as deepening their hues, the colors—nearly black by then—seemed to encroach. Something terrible was about to happen, and there was nothing Jas could do about it. Suddenly, the darkness was upon the Paths. Jas struggled against invisible bonds to help them, but in a moment they were gone, devoured by the pitch black cloud.

With horror, she realized the cloud had turned its attention to her.

At last, Jas's body responded to her mind's pleas, her bonds snapped, and she sat up abruptly, hitting her head on the low overhang. She gasped and winced, putting her hand to her brow.

What had *that* been about? she wondered. Then some of the content of her encounter with the beings in her run began to filter through to her. She couldn't remember exactly what they'd said, or even if they'd said anything at all, but she remembered the essence of their meaning. She finally understood that the benevolent beings had been Paths, and that they'd been trying to tell her something important.

Jas leapt up and ran barefoot into the corridor. She hammered on the door to Sayen's room, which was next to her own, forgetting that there was a door chime.

"Sayen, wake up! We have to contact the Council. We have to warn them."

After a moment, the door slid open. Sayen was sitting up in her bunk in the darkened room, her cropped blonde hair sticking up at the back. As she turned on the light and smoothed down her hair, Jas went in and repeated herself, adding, "The Paths told me during my run that there are Shadows on both sides of the battle, and if we seem to be winning the Shadows are going to reveal themselves and turn on their shipmates."

"Krat. Are you sure? How do you know? How come you didn't remember earlier?"

"I don't know. It was probably the myth addling my brain. This all came to me just now as I was falling asleep. We have to contact the Council and warn them. Sayen, what about Carl? What if his copilot is a Shadow?"

"Okay, okay. You're right. We have to tell the Council."

Martha and the other Council officers had returned to wherever they'd come from to continue their work while the humans got some much-needed rest. They'd said it was too early to decide what to do with the humans as they hadn't given up hope that a myth run might still yield information about the Shadows.

Sayen swung her legs down and got up. Together, they ran to the operations room of the station, which was staffed by a corpulent administrator Jas hadn't seen before. As they went inside, the man took his feet off his desk and leaned forward, his belly hanging between his knees. "Hey, you aren't supposed to be here."

"We have to contact the Council immediately," Jas said. "Please, open a line to the one called Martha, who was here today."

"Can't do that," the man said. "You have to get permission, and you won't for a line. It's too expensive. I can send a packet if you go through the proper channels."

"No, this is urgent," said Jas. "We need a direct line."

"No way. It's not happening. Do you know how much energy that takes? Nearly as much as the station produces. It's out of the question. What's this about, anyway? Nothing could be that urgent. The Council was only here a couple of hours ago."

"There's no time to argue," exclaimed Jas. She approached the man, her tall frame towering over him. "Open a line."

The administrator's thick neck bent back as he looked up fearfully at the Martian.

"Jas, it's okay," Sayen said, pulling her friend away from the daunted man. "Sir, it's a matter of life and death, not just for humans, but for the entire galaxy. Please, open a line."

The man rubbed his neck and looked from the red-haired Martian to her diminutive friend. "Well, that's a bit different, isn't it? Why didn't you tell me that in the first place? I'll just contact the—"

"You'll contact the Council officers who were here today," said Jas. "Now."

Shaking his head, the man activated his interface with a swipe of his fingertips and pressed the screen in several places. He hesitated and glanced at Jas's towering figure before giving a final prod. The station's lights dimmed.

"Told you this would take us to capacity," he said. "I hope your message really is as important as you make out or you'll get me into a lot of trouble."

Above the screen, a hologram of the golden head of Martha appeared. Her mouthparts were moving, but no sound was coming out.

"Whoops," the administrator said, and he pressed the screen again.

"We appear to be having a communication problem," said Martha. "Could you please repeat your message?"

"The Paths told me there are Shadows on both sides," blurted Jas. "Both sides of the battle. I couldn't remember after my run, but it came to me just now. I'm sure it's true. Please, tell the Unity commanders immediately."

"You are positive?" Martha asked. "Humans dream, do they not? Are you sure that this is not a product of your imagination, filling in gaps in your memory?"

"I'm certain of it. Please, please tell them."

"The battle has been progressing for some time, and there has been no sign of what you say, but, very well, I will pass on your message with all haste."

"Thank you," said Jas. "And one more thing. I want to be there too. I want to take part. Please let me fight in the battle, because I think it's far from over."

NINE

ayen and Phelan were saying a tearful goodbye, and Jas stood with her back toward them, trying not to intrude. She was facing the bare wall of the meeting room, where Martha had said she would open a Gateway. The Council had agreed to Jas's request to join the reinforcements preparing to join the battle with the Shadows. Her background in security smoothed her way. They'd also accepted Sayen on the basis of her space navigation skills and her modified body. But untrained personnel like Phelan, Martha had said, were better off defending their home planets, where their knowledge of the local environment and population was invaluable.

Phelan had argued that Sayen should return to Earth with him aboard the *Bricoleur*. The pain and indecision in Sayen's eyes was clear to see, but in the end she'd decided to fight the bigger fight, saying that her ability to navigate across space was more useful to the galactic effort. Dr. Sparks had elected to take his chances waiting things out on Ganymede.

At one time, Jas would have been glad that she didn't have those ties that were so painful to sever, but in her case that was no longer true. In fact, she was guiltily aware that her drive to join the Shadow battle had less to do with her desire to help defeat them—though that was important to her too—and more to do with her need to find Carl.

Sayen came over and stood beside her as the green motes sparked into existence in the air in front of them. Jas had already said goodbye to Phelan, but she glanced over her shoulder for a final farewell. Sayen's brother was leaving the room, his head and shoulders bowed.

The Ganymede Outpost had arranged for a pilot to fly the *Bricoleur* to Earth. Now that the Global Government had been forced to officially acknowledge the Shadow presence, military forces had been mobilized to repel the invasion. Though it had annoyed her mightily at the time, Jas hoped that she would see Phelan throwing his baseball at the ceiling over and over again at some point in the future.

Neither Jas nor Sayen were taking anything with them to the Unity reinforcements rendezvous point. They *had* nothing to take but the clothes they'd printed aboard the *Bricoleur*. The green dust of the Gateway began to coalesce. Jas shivered. She would be glad to leave Ganymede Outpost behind, for more than one reason.

"Did you recognize the name of the place that Martha mentioned when she agreed to let us fight in the battle?" she asked Sayen.

"Yeah, I've heard of it."

"Is it hot there?"

"As hot as they want to make it, I guess," Sayen replied. The Gateway spun faster.

"Huh? They have climate control?" Jas asked.

"Aboard the *Camaradon*? Of course."

"Aboard? I thought we were going to a planet. You mean it's a—"

"Step through now," came a voice from the other side of the Gateway.

Jas walked into the green swirls. She could see nothing but emerald light. One of her feet seemed to step onto nothing, and then she was through. Her other foot hit a hard, scuffed metal floor.

"Keep walking," barked a voice. "Out of the way. Move it."

Jas withdrew her gaze from the distant walls and ceiling, myriad of shuttles, and plentiful groups of aliens, closed her gaping mouth and did as she was told. She walked through an archway scanner and past a Unity soldier who was reading the scanner results on an interface. She turned her attention to the massive starship shuttle bay the Gateway had brought her to.

Sayen appeared behind her, and together they went in the direction indicated by the Unity soldier manning the exit. As they went toward a line of waiting aliens, Jas looked over her shoulder at the Gateway. More creatures from around the galaxy were stepping through and following them as ordered by the soldier.

"Move up," instructed the creature who was monitoring the end of the line. At the front was another alien, checking an interface. They stood patiently at the end of the line of new recruits. Jas hadn't seen such a range of galactic life all in one place before. Her attention was also taken by their surroundings.

The bay was bigger than anything she'd ever seen. It was bigger than any starship she'd ever worked aboard, in fact. Thirty or forty huge shuttlecraft of a military type were parked down each side. These vessels had no fancy decorations or frills. They were utilitarian craft, not designed to impress with their looks. Several of the shuttles bore the marks of attacks. Repair crews were at work fixing the damage, roughly patching the holes and replacing scorched and melted areas of metal.

Elsewhere in the bay, teams of new recruits were being allocated weapons and put through hasty drills. The Gateway Jas and Sayen had traveled through closed, and the last of the newcomers walked, slid, or hopped to the end of the line.

"It's quite something, isn't it?" Sayen said, her gaze also roving the massive room. "Biggest ship in the Unity fleet, I heard."

"You knew about this ship?" asked Jas.

"Gee, don't you ever watch the vidnews?"

"Step up," said the soldier processing the recruits. They'd reached the front of the line.

"Name, origin, and background," the alien said. It was a quadruped with two prehensile pincers on either side of double orifices in its head. Around its neck hung what seemed to be a translator, for its voice broadcast from the device. The soldier held an interface in its pincers.

It repeated, "Name, origin, and—"

"Jas Harrington from Earth. I worked as chief of security on prospecting starships. I want to speak to someone in authority."

"Chief of security? Good. We can certainly use you. Ever commanded defense units?"

"Yes, but—"

"Even better. Go to the corner of the bay next to the doors to the take-off zone and ask for Lieutenant Yeroch. He has a squadron of units and no idea what to do with them. Here. Take this." It handed her a device similar to the one hanging from its neck. The alien turned to Sayen. "You. Name, origin and—"

"Wait," Jas said. "I have to speak to someone in authority right away." She looked over the alien's head to other figures in uniform moving around the bay, but she didn't know which rank the symbols on their uniforms indicated.

"Top right corner of the bay," said the alien. "That's an order, soldier."

"Jas," said Sayen, "we told the Council what the Paths said. Let them deal with it."

The alien repeated to Sayen, "You. Name, origin, and background."

Jas set off as instructed. Sayen was probably right. The Council would tell the Unity of the potential danger. No one here was likely to take her seriously anyway. She was just another recruit. But whatever happened, she was surely going to keep a close eye on everyone around her.

It was a long walk to the corner of the bay. When Jas looked back at the line of recruits, she saw that everyone had disappeared. She wondered where Sayen had been sent, and with a lurch of her stomach she realized that, like Carl, her friend was also on her way to a dangerous fight. Only with Sayen, she hadn't even said goodbye.

Whoever was in charge of the defense units was clearly having a hard time controlling them. On her way to her destination, she came across several units wandering around aimlessly and getting in the way of the repair crews. She told them to follow her, and the part-organic androids dutifully marched along behind her.

By the time she arrived at the corner of the bay, Jas had collected seven units of varying models and specs. Another group of the towering androids was standing together as she approached, and she spotted an amorphous creature made of a transparent jelly-like substance among them. All the creature's internal organs were visible, including the inner structures of its four eyes, which on the surface looked disconcertingly human.

"What are you doing with my defense units?" the creature screeched. A regular human voice had broadcast the words in an even tone from its translator, but the life form's own high-toned speech almost overwhelmed the English. Jas wasn't sure if it was as angry as it sounded or if that was just how it talked.

"I found them roaming around while I was on my way here," she replied. "I thought I should bring them with me as they don't seem to know what they're supposed to be doing."

"How did you make them obey you?" screeched Lieutenant Yeroch.

Jas replied, puzzled, "I just...told them what to do."

"Huh, they won't do anything I tell them. I commanded them to wait around for a while until we found them a leader, and half of them walked off."

"They did what you told them to," said Jas. "You instructed them to wait around, so they did that as well as they could. If you want them to wait here, you have to tell them exactly that. They do just exactly what you tell them."

"Is that so?" The creature's voice became so high-pitched, Jas winced. "If you're so good at it, you can take over. They're all yours."

TEN

Over the next couple hours, Jas inspected the defense units and got them working as a team. Some were Earth-manufactured and their organic components were human cells, which seemed to make them easier for her to manage. Others were kinds she didn't recognize, and she had to be even more careful than usual to simplify her language to make her meaning completely clear.

Working with such a mismatched bunch wasn't going to be easy, but the tasks her squadron had been tentatively assigned were at least straightforward: defend the starship from boarders and sweep captured vessels for pockets of resistance.

After checking their integrated weaponry and asking for a status report from each unit, Jas repeated marching orders to accustom them to moving together in a predictable, orderly fashion. This wasn't easy for the units, given their range of sizes and shapes. She was grateful that they all seemed to have organic neural networks that enhanced their adaptability and learning powers.

A few of the units reminded her of the AX models she'd commanded on Polestar prospecting missions. She'd even checked their chest plates, feeling a kind of nostalgia for the times when her life had been much simpler and she only had a myth-addicted, greedy captain to deal with.

She remembered the time she'd snuck aboard a shuttle to try to check out a Shadow trap planet after she'd been confined to quarters. Carl had been the shuttle's pilot, and she recalled him finding her hiding in the hold, along with unit AX10.

She sighed. None of the units under her command were AXs, and she didn't know where in the galaxy Carl was.

Jas came out of her reverie almost too late, as the defense units were about to march directly into a shuttle. "Right turn," she said. As one group, they turned. Jas gave a small smile of satisfaction. Even the smallest of them, LK29, who she'd mentally nicknamed Pint-Size, was finally keeping up.

"Put this on," said a voice behind her, making Jas jump. The words had been accompanied by a screech. She turned to find Lieutenant Yeroch handing her an armored suit and helmet. She took the suit and held it up. It seemed roughly the right size.

"You're shipping out in fifteen minutes. Transport 17," Yeroch continued. "You've been assigned to the destroyer, *Infineon*.

"Are we losing the battle?" she asked.

"No," Yeroch replied. "The word is, we're on the verge of victory, though we've incurred heavy losses. They're calling for reinforcements for the final stage. You've been assigned to a human majority ship." He left, repeating, "Fifteen minutes. Transport 17."

———

What Jas had thought were shuttles were actually military transports with starjump capabilities, she realized. Hence their size. She also realized that the scars they bore were from attacks as they carried troops to and from starships taking part in the battle.

The defense units climbed inside Transport 17, their feet clanking on the metal floor. The interior had definitely seen better days. Inside were two long benches on either side of the long, low cabin. The floor sloped slightly, down to a central channel that led to a drain, no doubt to carry away the stomach contents of new recruits unused to starjumping. The channel didn't look like it had been cleaned any time recently, and the smell of the place confirmed the fact.

Bare pipes encrusted with grime ran across the walls. Dirt also dimmed the light shining from square panels in the ceiling. The corner of Jas's mouth lifted as she imagined Sayen's reaction to traveling aboard the Unity's transportation.

The defense units spaced themselves out evenly along the benches, and Jas took the spot closest to the exit. The hatch closed and sealed itself. They were left in silence and dimness. The defense units looked sinister in the half light, but Jas wasn't too bothered about being alone with them. It had been weeks since she'd worked with androids, and she finally felt she was on familiar ground.

Still, her stomach was in knots. It wasn't that she was afraid of fighting in the battle. It was hardly the first time she'd been in combat, though this would be her first military excursion. Her memory of the Paths' message was making her nervous. If undiscovered Shadows on the Unity side were going to turn against their shipmates, now would be the time.

The Shadows had managed another infiltration unsuspected. Jas guessed that it must have taken place long before the Council discovered the invasion. The Unity had scanned her and the other volunteers immediately when they'd arrived on the *Camaradon*, but if Shadows were already on the inside, it didn't matter. The Unity's precautionary strategies were too late, and now, in the heat of battle, it couldn't possibly check all its personnel.

Had the Council made it clear to the Unity that it faced danger from within its own ranks? She had no way of finding out from her lowly position as a new recruit, and she was cut off from contact with any of the Council officers who had come to Ganymede.

At least the Shadows only replicated organic organisms, Jas reflected. She had nothing to fear from her units, but the minute she set foot aboard the *Infineon*, she had to suspect everyone she met.

The transport lurched as the pilot maneuvered it to the take-off pad, ready to fly the vessel to a safe distance from the *Camaradon* before starjumping. Jas told the defense units to fasten their safety harnesses, and she did the same. She slotted her helmet into place and snapped the visor closed, not knowing what to expect when they arrived at their destination. The cooled, purified air that puffed into her helmet was a welcome change from the stench and stuffiness of the cabin.

"LK29, do we have comm?" she asked.

"Affirmative, Corporal Harrington."

Jas had memorized all the units' designations, and she went through her list, checking that she was in contact with each one individually and as a team.

As she finished her check, the pilot's voice came over her helmet's comm. "Jumping in thirty seconds."

Vibrations juddered through her bones as the transport's engine generated power. The vibrations increased until they were almost unbearable. The Unity clearly didn't waste creds on their troops' comfort. Jas set her teeth and gripped her harness tightly. Just when she thought she couldn't bear the reverberations any longer, they jumped.

ELEVEN

As they emerged from the jump, the floor of the transport seemed to drop away. For the first split second, Jas thought it was an effect of the jump, but it soon became apparent it was more than that. She was forced abruptly downward, which caused her internal organs to crush into her diaphragm. She grimaced and waited for the pilot to correct their rapid drop, except he didn't. The transport continued to accelerate in the same direction. The pilot must have spotted something as soon as they'd come out of the jump, Jas realized, and he was maneuvering to avoid it.

Jas guessed they must have emerged into the middle of a firefight, but she didn't want to distract the pilot by asking stupid questions. A jerk to the right accompanied by the transport's left wall buckling inward confirmed her fears. They'd been hit. A moment later, the lights went out. In response, Jas's and the units' helmet lights turned on, their beams lighting the impassive faces of their fellows on the opposite bench.

A gasp came through from the pilot's voice-activated comm. The transport heaved around, and the floor buckled against Jas's feet. She lifted up her legs and told the defense units to do the same. The pilot cried out, there was a thump, and suddenly they were tumbling over and over. Another hit punched straight through the cabin, blasting two units to pieces. Jas felt the tug of depressurization as the air poured out of the ship.

The final hit corrected their spin somewhat, and now the transport lazily turned, powerless and drifting. The hard light of bright stars shone through the holes on either side of the cabin. The air was filled with tiny pieces of what remained of the two destroyed androids, which followed the spinning motion.

"Pilot?" Jas asked. No reply came. She asked again, several times, but he didn't respond.

"Transport 17," she said, hoping the ship's computer would respond to the simple request. She didn't know if she had the authority to use it.

"Yes, Corporal Harrington?"

A sigh of relief passed through her half-open lips. "What's the pilot's status?"

"The pilot is exhibiting no life signs."

Krat.

"How about the ship's engine?"

"The ship's engine received two hits. The second hit penetrated its plating and disabled it."

As the transport made another turn, Jas caught a glimpse of what looked like a far-distant starship, or at least a small area of starship-shaped space that was black among the shimmering sheet of stars. The *Infineon*? Probably, but they had no way of getting there. A jet of light like a falling star streamed past them toward the patch of darkness. As it hit, the light split and spread out, outlining the shape. It was a starship. No doubt about it. And its force field had just repelled a direct hit.

"Transport 17, please hail the Unity destroyer, *Infineon.*"

"I'm sorry, Corporal Harrington. My ship-to-ship comm is not working."

The enemy seemed to have stopped firing at them and had returned its fire to the starship, probably correctly judging the transport to be disabled. Without a pilot, Jas and the defense units would spin forever unless an attempt was made to rescue them, and she thought that unlikely, even if someone had noticed the transport appear out of its jump before it was attacked. With their engines dead and their vessel sitting in an area of space hot with the trails left by energy weapons, they would soon be just about impossible to find. She would only last a few weeks, but the units might continue functioning for centuries.

The transport made another circuit of its slow spin, but its motion was still reacting to its final hit. Jas found it had turned slightly so that she could no longer see the *Infineon*, if that was what the starship was. Now, only the white points of distant suns showed through the holes in the transport. Floating gently against her safety harness, Jas wondered if any of them were the suns of planets she'd visited.

She hated the idea of giving up hope, but the chances of a change in their circumstances seemed slim. She didn't fear death, though dying of thirst—which seemed the thing most likely to kill her in her powered armored suit with its limited water supply—wouldn't be pleasant. But thoughts that she would never have the opportunity to set Carl straight on what he'd meant to her, and that she'd never see him, or Sayen, Phelan, Erielle, or Makey again—these thoughts made her sad.

"Corporal Harrington, permission to speak," said one of the defense units. Jas lifted her eyebrows in surprise. She'd rarely known a unit speak without being spoken to. Her visor display told her it was Pint-Size.

"Permission granted," she replied.

"What is our status, ma'am?"

"Our status is..." Stranded? Waiting to die? "...awaiting further orders."

"Corporal Harrington, our transport's engine is no longer functioning."

"That's correct, LK29."

"Would it be beneficial to our mission if the engine were repaired?"

"Yeahhhh...it would." Jas's stomach clenched. "Are you telling me you can repair it?"

"Please wait a moment, ma'am, while I run a systems check with the ship's computer."

She held her breath.

"The engine is not repairable," announced LK29.

Jas exhaled. *Oh well.*

"But we may be able to power the thrusters directly and move our vessel closer to the nearest friendly starship, the *Infineon.*"

Jas had forgotten that defense units were also walking, talking, fighting power packs. She should have remembered the fact because it was unit power that had kept Sayen alive when a ship they'd been on had crashed. Jas had never heard of units powering thrusters, but if Pint-Size was correct, that might save them. The transport already had momentum. All they had to do was exert a little propulsion at the right moment in its spin to reverse their motion away from the *Infineon.*

"You might? Then do it, LK29. Do it."

Five defense units unbuckled themselves from their safety harnesses and set to work. They opened the access hatch in the floor of the transport and disappeared through it. Jas marveled at the androids' independence and initiative. If she hadn't known it, she would never have guessed they were the same units who'd been wandering around and bumping into each other in the shuttle bay of the *Camaradon* less than a couple of hours previously. They were acting more like soldiers than machines.

Around a minute later, the transport jumped a little. They were doing it. They were powering the thrusters with their own power packs. She didn't know how long it would take, but eventually they should arrive at the *Infineon.* She just hoped it would still be under Unity control by the time they got there.

At each burst of power from the units to the thrusters, the ship's spin was slowly being corrected. The view from the holes in the cabin stabilized, but the new, steady orientation of the ship showed nothing useful to Jas. She had no visual on the starship they were heading toward. Yet she did see more bolts of light speed past the transport. Despite what Yeroch had told her aboard the *Camaradon*, the battle seemed far from won.

LK29's head appeared in the access hatch in the floor. The android clambered out, followed by another.

"Corporal Harrington, our power is nearly exhausted. Permission to substitute fresh units."

"Permission granted," Jas said. "How much—" A violent lurch from the transport snapped her teeth closed and made her bite her tongue. "Ough." She swallowed the hot, metallic blood that leaked into her mouth. *What the krat was that?* At the same time as the lurch, a powerful shock had run through the ship as if something had collided with it. The units who had been powering the engine were thrown into the others sitting on the benches.

"Units, strap in," Jas said.

The unsecured units struggled upright and clambered onto the bench, fastening their harnesses immediately. There was another heavy bump, and the last unit to emerge from the hatch, who hadn't had time to secure itself, flew across the cabin and out through a hole. The tips of its fingers caught the edge, and it began to pull itself in, but a third thump broke it free, and it spun away into space.

A bolt of light flashed through the holes, illuminating every nook and cranny, every stain and smear in the cabin. They were under attack again. Jas clenched her fists in frustration. A unit was lost, and there wasn't anything she could do about it. They were like passive targets in a vid game, just waiting to be picked off.

The flashes and erratic bumps continued for another few seconds, then suddenly it was all over.

TWELVE

The transport was still. Reverberations in the bench and floor told Jas something was locking onto the exit. It opened, and armed suited-up soldiers poured in, passing Jas as they sped to the far side of the cabin. They began checking the units.

One of them kicked a unit's leg and began gesticulating at another who seemed to be the captain. Jas couldn't hear what the soldiers said, but it was clear from their body language that they were frustrated at finding only units inside the transport.

Jas unfastened her harness and floated free. One of the soldiers swung his weapon around and pointed the muzzle at her. She held up her hands, and the officer waved the soldier down and approached her. He grabbed her shoulders and touched his helmet to hers.

"Are you the only person aboard?" he asked, his voice sounding muffled and distant.

"It's just me and twenty-two units," she replied. Her swollen tongue made her voice thick. " Used to be twenty-five."

"Kr—" said the officer as he pulled away. He pointed at the units and thumbed toward the exit, then grabbed Jas's arm and gestured in the same direction.

She joined the soldiers and units as they left the transport. As soon as she passed through the exit, artificial gravity pulled her to the floor. They were inside a large airlock. With some relief Jas saw the name *Infineon* emblazoned on the walls. Soldiers and units crowded in the airlock, and the last to leave the transport sealed its exit.

They waited for the chamber to fill with air. After some moments, a green light shone above the farther exit, and it slid open. Jas lowered her visor and blinked in the strong light, smelling the familiar, slightly sweaty, tang of a starship's interior.

The soldiers pushed past her and the units to leave the airlock. Jas looked around, wondering what she was supposed to do, but everyone seemed to be ignoring her, including the officer who'd spoken to her inside the transport.

"Units, exit the airlock," she instructed, and brought up the rear as the last of them passed into the destroyer.

They were in an equipment room. The soldiers were removing their helmets and stripping down, still acting as though Jas and her units didn't exist. The troops were of several alien species as well as a few humans. Jas went over to the officer before he took off his suit, which was her only way of identifying him. He was human, his dark hair the same length as his short beard.

"Sir, I'm Corporal Harrington, assigned from the *Camaradon*."

The man nodded without meeting her gaze and pushed his suit below his knees before bending down to pull it off his legs. "Got your orders?"

"No, I was just told to bring these units here. We're reinforcements."

"Great. Just great." He turned to his troops. "Back to your stations."

The space troops left, surly and muttering among themselves.

"Sir," Jas said, "is there some kind of problem?"

"You could say that, Corporal Harrington," he replied. "We lost the fighter ships that pushed you to safety. Two good pilots dead. When we saw your transport had its engine shot to pieces, they wanted to be heroes, thinking they were saving troops." He glanced around at the defense units, who were standing still and silent. "We don't have enough pilots. I just hope you and your units are worth it."

The officer hung up his suit. "You can find a ship's uniform over there. When you're ready, report to Commander Torben." He left her alone with her units.

Jas unclipped her helmet and slowly removed it. *Two good pilots dead.* Now she knew why the soldiers had been disappointed and angry to find only defense units aboard the transport.

The bangs and bumps the transport received had been the fighter ships pushing it the remainder of the distance to the ship. Such a maneuver would have taken great skill. Jas's heart froze at the thought that one of the pilots might have been Carl. The enemy must have spotted what was happening and attacked the vulnerable fighters.

"LK29, are you in contact with the *Infineon's* computer?"

"Yes, Corporal Harrington."

"Can you read its data banks? Like, can you find out the names of the pilots on board?"

"I do not have the necessary permissions."

"Okay. Can you tell me where I can find Commander Torben?"

———

Jas had told the units to wait in the equipment room as she didn't know what she was supposed to do with them. She followed Pint-Size's directions through the ship's corridors, heading toward the bridge. The ship was as utilitarian as the transport had been. The metal floor was worn and scuffed with the passage of thousands of booted feet. No signs explained what was down the corridors or behind each door, possibly as a defense against boarders. Jas imagined that the soldiers had to memorize the layout of the ship.

The whine of air filters and the scent of burnt plastic and chemicals told her the ship's force field hadn't been an adequate defense against all the fire targeted at it. A repair bot almost hit her as it flew past on its way to fix something, and at one point she must have been near the ship's hull, for the metal on one side of the corridor was discolored and warped. At the sound of running feet from up ahead, she moved over to allow the approaching soldiers to pass. In another second the group appeared. They were nearly past her when she heard a snippet of dialogue about the fighter ships still in action.

"Hey," exclaimed Jas. "Hey, are you pilots?"

One of the group turned her head. "Yeah. What's it to you?"

"Is there a pilot called Lingiari aboard this ship?"

"No. Leastways, I never heard of him," called the woman, then the group was gone.

Jas finally found the bridge. After the guards had let her enter, she was a little relieved to see that Commander Torben was a Cruthian, like Flahive had been.

Everyone on the bridge was focused on a hologram that hung in midair in the center. Jas noticed the dark-haired officer who had entered the transport was there. He and the other officers sat at controls around the constantly moving image, which displayed four suns and many dots in a range of colors. This was the area where the Unity and Shadow ships had met head on. One color—red—predominated, and Jas guessed that it signified the enemy ships. The other colors had to be Unity ships of various classes or those belonging to the galactic alliance.

Some of the dots were pulsing and moving slowly, others were still and steady. The red dots of many Shadow ships were motionless. If Jas was reading the hologram correctly, it looked like the Shadow forces had nearly been defeated.

Torben lifted an upper limb to Jas as she approached the commander, its disc-like appendage held flat. Jas paused and awaited the commander's attention.

"Enemy ship on the move in sector six," said an officer, lifting her eyes from her interface to the hologram.

Jas saw it: a pulsing red light was moving slowly in the direction of the nearest sun, as if intending to slip behind the star for protection. Though the ship was crawling, it must have been traveling incredibly fast.

"That's ours," said Torben. "After it before it jumps. Prepare all pulses."

The bridge of the *Infineon* shifted beneath Jas's feet as the artificial gravity took a moment to compensate for the sudden movement of the ship. Jas gazed at the hologram. She'd never seen a space battle before. The blinking green light that crawled toward the Shadow ship had to represent the *Infineon*.

"Pulse distance in forty-three seconds," said another officer.

"If it doesn't jump before we get there," muttered someone else.

"Quiet on the bridge," barked Torben. Though her translator moderated her voice to a near monotone, somehow the feeling behind the words was carried through.

"Corporal Harrington?" Torben asked.

Jas was so intent on the hologram, she almost didn't realize she was being addressed. "Yes, Commander."

"We just received notification of your arrival from the *Camaradon*," Commander Torben said. "A little late. You and your units are to sweep defeated vessels. Remain on standby."

"Yes, Commander," Jas replied, impressed by the commander's coolness in dealing with side business when about to engage in battle. Jas wasn't sure if she should leave. She decided she would stay, at least until Torben noticed she was still there and dismissed her.

"Pulse distance in twenty seconds."

"Prepare to engage," Torben said. The officers at the consoles surrounding the hologram fixed their eyes on the image. Their hands hovered over their interfaces. If the *Infineon* had been in the battle from the start, which had been soon after the Council officers had arrived at Ganymede Outpost, they'd already been fighting for many hours.

"Ten seconds."

The hologram zoomed from a general display of the battle zone to a detailed image containing the *Infineon* and the Shadow ship. Now, the dots moved much faster. The red dot was streaking away from the green one and curving into the outer orbit of the sun. The green dot was gaining on it, however.

The atmosphere in the room became tense.

"Five seconds. Four. Three. Two. One."

Three tiny pale yellow dots sprang from the *Infineon*. They traveled faster than the destroyer, and faster than the enemy ship. The red dot responded with some kind of weapons of its own, laying down a trail of defensive fire, a long line of sparks that ranged behind it.

"Evasive maneuver," Torben said.

The deck dropped from beneath Jas's feet as the *Infineon's* pilot took the ship abruptly downward. She became momentarily airborne and grabbed a rail to steady herself. The ship's artificial gravity didn't seem to be working properly. Maybe it had been damaged in earlier skirmishes. The sparks drew closer.

The enemy ship also attempted a maneuver, abruptly changing its trajectory with a speed that would have tested the ship to the limits of its strength, Jas guessed. But the *Infineon's* pale yellow bolts of energy had just enough time to alter their course to match the change in direction of their target. They sank into the red dot and vanished just before the Shadow ship's sparks converged on the *Infineon*. Many passed them, but the tail hit, and Jas heard and felt their dull thumps on the hull.

The red dot stopped moving. Whoops, hollers, and alien celebratory noises filled the bridge.

"Quiet on the bridge," Torben barked again. "Damage report."

"Force field's down again, Commander," said an officer. "Damage to decks five through seven. Details still arriving. Repair crews dispatched."

"Right. Keep me up to date on the situation."

Another officer said, "Commander, the scanners are showing we took out the Shadow ship's jump engine. It's going nowhere."

"Excellent. Good work, everyone," said Torben.

"Unity Command is hailing, ma'am," someone else said.

"Thank you," Torben said. "Please ask Command for permission to put the comm on general broadcast."

"Yes, ma'am." A pause. "Permission granted. Routing to ship's comm."

A voice sounded from the bridge intercom. "Crew of the *Infineon*, this is Commander General Coney. Congratulations. You just took out the last Shadow ship remaining in the vicinity."

And with that, all hell broke loose.

Thirteen

Torben was the first to die. One of the guards lifted his weapon and calmly blasted the commander in the head. As the Cruthian's suit split apart, her body erupted in a massive froth through the gap. Jas was already running at the guard. He saw her and turned, but before he had a chance to fire his weapon again, she drove her shoulder into his chest, throwing him back against the wall. The impact to his head stunned him, and he slid toward the floor. Jas grabbed his weapon as he fell and turned it upon him. His eyes widened briefly before she burned a hole through his skull.

Fights had broken out all over the bridge as the Shadows attacked the non-Shadow officers. Jas focused on the comm officer who had relayed the Command message. The alien was a large quadruped, and he was sitting frozen, watching the battle around him. Jas killed a Shadow who was aiming at him.

"You," she shouted. "Ship wide alert. Shadows aboard. Shadows aboard. Got it?"

The comm officer withdrew his gaze from the dying Shadow who had been about to kill him. He fumbled at his interface.

"Wait," said the dark-haired officer as he took out another

Shadow who was targeting the quadruped. "Implement Operation Penumbra," he barked at the alien.

The comm officer's mouth quivered.

"Implement Operation Penumbra," the dark-haired officer repeated.

He spun and fired at Jas. She ducked, too late, but the energy bolt passed to her left. As she turned, a Shadow crumpled to the ground behind her. He'd saved her life.

"Implement Operation Penumbra," the comm officer said into his mic and immediately slid under his console. The alien's words were repeated through the bridge intercom and no doubt throughout the ship. Jas threw herself under another desk and found herself sharing a cramped space with the dark-haired officer.

Operation Penumbra. In spite of appearances, the Council's warning had gotten through and the Unity had put some kind of plan in place to respond to a Shadow attack from the inside, though Jas couldn't figure out what it was.

Bolts were still flying around the bridge. When they hit Torben's remains, they hissed through the foam. The white mound was a substantial impediment to straight shooting on the bridge. The surviving combatants had all found shelter and were taking random pot shots at each other. The hologram of the *Infineon* and the Shadow ship in space still hung suspended in midair. From her place of temporary safety, Jas had a good view of the image. The red dot had begun to move swiftly toward the *Infineon*.

"Krat," she muttered.

"What's wrong?" asked the dark-haired officer squashed in with her. He pushed her to one side as he reached out to take a shot.

"That Shadow ship we hit is heading right for us," said Jas.

The man glanced at the hologram before taking another shot. "Krat indeed. We need to get out of here."

"You said it." Jas elbowed him out of the way to lean out. She'd timed it just right. A Shadow's head appeared. She shot and hit it. The Shadow had fired at the same time, but its bolt went slightly wide and hit the wall of the console they were hiding behind.

"Ahhh," the man yelped as the metal that he was squashed against grew hot. He tried to move away, but there was too little room. They were jammed shoulder to shoulder. Jas tried to give him a few centimeters of space.

"The problem is," he said, wincing, "we don't know who's a Shadow and who isn't."

"I'm pretty sure the ones shooting at us are Shadows," said Jas. "We were protecting the comm officer so he could get the message out, and they were trying to kill him."

"Good point. So how do we kill *them*?"

"We call for reinforcements," said Jas. She lifted her comm button to her lips. "Units to the bridge. We could do with a little help here."

It was Pint-Size who replied. "Affirmative, Corporal Harrington. We're on our way."

"Now we just need to survive the next few minutes," Jas said.

Another energy bolt must have hit the metal panel her shelter companion was crushed against because his face became a mask of pain.

"Here," Jas said, "swap places."

His eyes and lips pressed tightly closed, the man shook his head. He opened his eyes and reached out to take another shot. "They're on the move," he muttered as he drew himself inside.

Jas took a peek and saw a Shadow run across open space toward the comm officer's station. The Shadow disappeared behind Torben's remains, but Jas had her muzzle trained on the figure, and she shot at where the Shadow was about to be. A heavy thud confirmed the hit.

"Good shot," said the man. His face shone with sweat.

A cry of fear and pain sounded. The man looked out and drew quickly back. "Another one to the Shadows," he said. "And we've lost the hologram."

"Doesn't matter," said Jas. "We know what's happening. We just need to do something about it."

"When we get out of this kratting hole," the officer said. "I just hope we have a live pilot." The ship's pilot had been the first officer the Shadows shot after Torben.

From outside the bridge came shouting and thuds. *Shouldn't be long.* The doors blocked the soft hiss of laser guns, but Jas had little doubt what was happening outside. Her eyes met the officer's as they awaited the outcome of her units' fight with the Shadows.

She peeked out from their hiding place once more and saw the muzzle of a weapon poking out from behind a console, aiming at the bridge door. The Shadow was planning on blasting whoever came through it. Jas ducked back under cover. It would be a difficult shot, but she thought she could do it.

"Cover me," she said to the man, and she leapt out from behind the desk.

He immediately began laying down defensive fire around the room. Jas used the extra second she needed to take careful aim and fired at the weapon muzzle that was targeting the door. The muzzle melted and flamed just as the doors shuddered and gave a metallic groan. A gap appeared between the two halves. The defense units were physically forcing the doors open. The mechanism whined as they pulled them apart.

More Shadows leapt out from their shelters to fire at the defense units. Jas and the dark-haired officer took some of them out, and the units also came through the doors firing.

In less than a minute, the Shadow rebellion on the bridge was finally quelled. Less than a fifth of the officers had been Shadows, but they'd acted immediately when the Unity had seemed on the verge of victory. It had been the same aboard the *Galathea*, Jas reflected. The Shadows had concentrated on replacing those in charge, and those they hadn't managed to replace were the first to die.

The remaining non-Shadow officers emerged from their hiding places, holding up their hands. The comm officer was one of those who had survived the battle, though the quadruped was trembling with shock.

"Back to your stations," said the dark-haired officer. "We're not out of the woods yet."

"The pilots," Jas said to him. "They'll go after the pilots next." She swung around to the units on the bridge. "Go straight to the pilots' quarters and protect them from attack. And bring one here."

FOURTEEN

It was carnage on the bridge. The bodies of Shadows and officers sprawled everywhere, and Torben's remains were slowly collapsing. Several officers had been wounded.

The dark-haired man was talking to the comm officer. As he finished, he turned to Jas and said, "The pilots suffered some casualties too, but they've got the situation under control. One of them is on her way."

"We need to get that holo working," Jas said. The words had hardly left her mouth before the ship shook with a series of explosions. Her ears rang.

"The Shadow ship's firing on us," exclaimed the dark-haired officer. "What's our force field status?"

"Still down, sir," came the reply. "Decks five through seven caught the worst of it again."

"Krat. Where's that holo? Never mind. There's no time. Pulse response, on the double. Evasive maneuv— Krat. Where's that pilot?"

He leaned over the back of another officer to focus on the interface she was looking at. An impact on the ship threw Jas to the floor, along with everyone else still standing.

"Damage to decks one and two, sir. Hull breach."

The dark-haired officer didn't reply. He glanced at the door, which had buckled where the defense units had forced it open. They needed a pilot. Without the ability to fly, they were sitting ducks.

"Pulses incoming," exclaimed a voice.

"LK29, what's the ETA on that pilot?" Jas said into her comm, but at the same time the female pilot Jas had spoken to earlier ran through the door. Without missing a beat she jumped into the vacant pilot seat. She paused, her hands above the screens on the console. "Hmmm...never flown a destroyer before." She scanned the screens intently. "Let's try..." She swiped a screen and pressed another. "Okay, got it. I see unwelcome visitors. Oh no you don't." She pressed decisively and Jas was crushed to the floor as the ship swept upward incredibly fast.

"More pulses on their way."

"Pilot, emergency jump," said the dark-haired officer from his new position on the floor.

"As quick as I can, sir," the pilot replied.

A deep vibration rose through Jas as the engines began to build power. She started to get up, but another hit buffeted the ship, and she was flung to one side.

"Hull breach deck five." The air was growing hazy with smoke from the damaged areas of the ship. Jas blinked and coughed as the acrid air stung her eyes and throat.

"We scored a hit, sir," said the weapons officer, "but they're still coming."

"Fire with everything we've got," said the dark-haired officer. "Fire at will."

The vibrations grew stronger. Jas had given up trying to stand, deciding that she was safest staying where she was.

"Hold on, everyone," shouted the pilot. The ship rolled and pitched. Jas grabbed the leg of a console. Suddenly the artificial gravity went haywire, and she was hanging suspended in midair, holding on with one arm. The side of the bridge was fifteen meters or so below her. Torben's remains and bodies of dead Shadows and officers had slid and rolled to the bottom. Some of the living were among them, struggling to get away from the corpses.

The pilot and other officers who remained in their seats were hanging precariously to one side. The pilot was trying to fasten her safety harness one-handed. Someone fell and landed heavily on a dead Shadow.

Jas reached up with her left hand to grab the console leg and hold on more securely. Her right hand was already slipping. She missed, grunted, and reached again. But the ship was vibrating so strongly, her fingertips couldn't get a grip. Her shoulder felt like it was being pulled from its socket. For the third time, she swung her left arm up and attempted to grasp the leg. For the third time, she didn't make it.

Her other hand slowly opened as she lost her grip. She was holding on with only her fingers, then they too began to slip. Jas looked down, wondering if she could survive the fall if she landed well. The last of her strength left her fingers, and she dropped like a stone.

When she was halfway down, they jumped.

She never hit the bottom. As they came out of the jump, Jas found herself floating in the center of the bridge. The pilot had shut down the artificial gravity as they'd jumped. The other officers were also suspended in midair or in seats, hastily fastening their safety harnesses.

"Position report, pilot," said the dark-haired officer. He was floating, trying to hook a foot under a chair arm.

"Just a minute, sir." The woman scanned her interface.

"You mean you don't know where we've jumped to?"

"No navigator to figure it out, sir. Had to take a chance."

"Krat, Pilot Kennewell, we could've ended up in the middle of a star."

"Well, the chances of that are—"

"Do not answer me back, madam," the officer barked. "You took an unacceptable risk with the lives of my crew. I shall consider your behavior for a formal reprimand."

The already-quiet bridge grew quieter still as even the wounded officers' groans momentarily quietened.

Jas felt for the pilot. As far as she could tell, the woman had saved all their lives. She wondered if the dark-haired officer was just feeling the stress and responsibility of his new command or if he was always a misborn.

After a pause, the pilot said, "Yes, sir."

FIFTEEN

I t turned out that they were only a few light years from the scene
of the battle. The engines hadn't generated sufficient power in
the short time available to take them very far, but they had
escaped the notice of the Shadows, for the time being.

The dark-haired officer asked for ship-wide status reports, and
the ship's crew listed the dead and injured along with the material
damage to the ship. As that went on, someone must have been fixing
the artificial gravity because, not long after the last of the reports
came in, and when it was established that all the surviving crew had
gotten themselves to a safe place, the gravity reactivated.

Jas had propelled herself into an unoccupied seat on the bridge.
She welcomed the return of the sensation of heaviness. She couldn't
remember the last time she'd slept properly. She felt beyond
exhausted and would have given a lot to close her eyes there and then
and rest just for a little while. But there was still plenty of work to be
done.

The dark-haired officer was in one-to-one comm with Unity
Command, and the uninjured officers began the clean-up. Jas
ordered the units to help with taking the wounded officers to the
medical bay, but another officer intervened and said that a better use
of the androids would be helping the repair crews to seal the hull

breaches. She changed her order and sent them to the relevant decks before lending a hand to carry out the wounded officers herself.

The medical bay was already full of injured crew members, and the medics were busily triaging every man, woman, and alien who went in. Jas left them to it and returned to the bridge to help with the more gruesome task of removing the corpses.

By the time she returned, however, the dead bodies were already gone and some kind of order had been established. The dark-haired officer was still bent intently over the comm panel, speaking quietly into his mic. The quadruped had finally stopped trembling.

Technicians were running diagnostics on controls, though more than half of the stations were empty. Everyone seemed busy except Pilot Kennewell. She was resting her chin on her hand and staring glumly into an interface.

"*I* thought you did a great job," Jas said, taking an adjacent seat.

The pilot sat up and glanced at the dark-haired officer. "Better watch your words around Pacheco," she said quietly. "Or he'll consider you for a formal reprimand too." She rolled her eyes. "Hey, wasn't it you who was looking for someone earlier?"

"Yeah. He's a pilot. Carl Lingiari. Have you heard of him? He joined the battle late."

"No. I'm sorry. He must be on another ship."

"I thought so." Jas was disappointed to find him not aboard, but also relieved to confirm that Carl couldn't have been one of the pilots who'd been killed rescuing her and the units.

"You're new, aren't you?" asked Kennewell.

"Yeah, I only arrived from the *Camaradon* a little while ago. Just before the final attack."

"Oh, you're the..." Kennewell's eyes widened.

"Yep. I was the one aboard the transport two pilots died saving." She looked down.

"Hey," said Kennewell, "don't feel bad about it. We all knew the risks when we signed up, and the pilots who brought you to safety volunteered for the job. No one ordered them to do it, and if they hadn't, I wouldn't be sitting here now."

In response to Jas's puzzled frown, she went on, "Your units killed the Shadow pilots who were in the process of picking off the rest of us. If those pilots who died hadn't saved your units, they wouldn't turned up to save *us*, I wouldn't have been around to fly us out of trouble."

"What about Operation Penumbra?" Jas asked. "Wasn't that a response plan?"

"It was, but we only had a few hours to work on it. Commander Torben had begun screening everyone to find out if we had any Shadows aboard, but it had to be done secretly so as not to let the Shadows know that we suspected they were among us. We were also in the middle of a battle. Everyone who passed the screening was armed and warned of the danger. Operation Penumbra was the code sign to let us know that the Shadow rebellion had begun and we were to watch for attacks, defend ourselves, and stun and confine anyone we suspected of being a Shadow. But it was too little, too late."

Pacheco straightened up and took off his earpiece and mic. "Okay, listen up," he said, his tone sharp. The man looked weary, and he had to be in a lot of pain from the burn he'd sustained while he'd been hiding with Jas.

"Things aren't looking too good right now. We lost three ships to the Shadows during that attack from within, which makes seven altogether when we count the ships destroyed during the battle." He sighed and passed a hand across his face. "Unity Command will send lists of the crews lost as soon as they have them. The Shadow attack turned things around somewhat. The battle's over, but no one's won. As soon as we receive coordinates, we will regroup with the remaining vessels."

He stopped and seemed to have nothing else to say.

After a moment's silence someone said, "And then what, sir?"

Annoyance flickered across Pacheco's face. "What do you think, man? That fight was just a skirmish. Now we begin the war."

How long Jas had known that it would come to this, she couldn't remember, but Pacheco's words were no surprise to her. The Shadows were an infestation that, each time you thought you had vanquished them, they would reappear in another place, more numerous and deadlier. Their great strength was their replication of their victims. They could hide in plain sight as the colleagues, friends, family, and lovers of every sentient being they replaced, biding their time until the moment was ripe to rise up and take over.

Jas didn't know how they could stop them, or if they could ever be stopped. The war had only just started and it could be years before it was finally over. She was separated from Carl and from her friends, and she was caught up in the conflict with no end in sight.

All she could do was continue to fight their deadly enemy and hope that, one day, she might be reunited with the people she loved.

SHADOW WAR

ONE

The destroyer *Thylacine* materialized from a starjump, and Commander Jas Harrington immediately leaned forward in her seat. A hologram blinked into life in front of her—a golden globe slowly spinning in mid-air, filling one-fifth of the *Thylacine's* bridge. A dry, cloudless planet.

The planet's name was unpronounceable in English, but that didn't matter. It was one of several worlds that was home to a rich source of mythrin, the raw ingredient of the stupor-inducing, extraordinarily expensive, highly illegal drug, mythranil. As such, the world was extremely likely to have been infiltrated by the hostile aliens known as Shadows.

Infiltrated, and secured.

The Shadows aimed to cut off the Unity Alliance's supply of mythranil so the UA's Shadow scanners wouldn't work and their ability to tell friend from foe would be lost.

"Force field maximum power," said First Officer Trimborn. "Scanning for enemy ships."

Jas nodded. Everyone aboard knew the drill. If the battle scenario played out as it usually did, they had about five seconds.

Four. Three. Two—

"Pulses incoming," exclaimed Trimborn.

The Shadow ship protecting the planet had spotted them and fired.

"Got the origin coordinates," said another officer. "Returning fire."

Vibrations shook Jas's seat and the arm rests beneath her hands. The enemy's pulses had hit the ship, but the *Thylacine's* force field was strong. They had plenty of power, enough for a long, pitched battle. The trick to winning was to destroy the opposition before the power ran out.

"Picking up the Shadow ship," said Trimborn, looking from his screen to the holo. A starship appeared over the edge of the golden globe. Long, slim, and sprouting four curved extensions, the ship was a make that Jas didn't recognize. Like most Shadow ships, it had probably been built by the native population on the planet below and stolen by the aliens after their invasion.

The *Thylacine's* pulses were already streaming toward it.

"Fire again," Jas said. "Full attack."

"Yes, Commander."

"Halve our distance from that ship, Pilot," said Jas.

Pilot Kennewell replied, "Engaging Raptors, ma'am."

Acceleration from the propulsion engines pushed Jas back in her seat as the *Thylacine* sped toward its attacker, following the barrage of pulses it had launched. A similar assault from the Shadow ship clashed into the *Thylacine's* pulses. The bolts of raw energy collided, exploded, and dispersed in the high thermosphere above the planet. The *Thylacine* continued full speed ahead, cutting through the cloud of energized particles, leaving behind a charged wake. Jas hoped the battle was visible to the population below, giving the invasion survivors the news that the Unity Alliance had come to their rescue.

"A second ship's jumped in," exclaimed Trimborn.

The hologram echoed his words. Before the first officer had finished speaking, another starship winked into existence. It appeared directly behind the *Thylacine*, so close that the energy of its starjump hit them full force, rocking the ship.

"Krat," muttered Jas, gripping her armrests to steady herself. There was no way the Shadows could have messaged for reinforcements. The *Thylacine* was dampening their comms. She was confident of that. This was bad luck—a pure coincidence that her destroyer had happened to arrive moments before a second Shadow ship. It was probably there to relieve the first or was intended to double the planet's defenses.

This battle wasn't going to be as straightforward as Jas had hoped. "Fire away at our second target."

"Already on it, ma'am," came the reply. The pulses flew out toward the new aggressor.

The officer should have awaited her order, but she didn't object. Her team were battle-seasoned. She trusted them to use their initiative, and they knew it. The new ship would take about a second to activate its force field post-jump. If the *Thylacine* could score a hit during that time window, it would do significant damage. Waiting for her command would only have wasted precious time.

"Direct hit," said the officer.

The *Thylacine* continued to zoom closer to the original Shadow ship and away from their surprise attacker. The ship they were leaving behind shuddered as their pulses hit it. Jas craned forward, looking expectantly at the ship. They had to have hit it before its force field was full power, but the holo displayed no debris.

"We didn't breech her hull," exclaimed Trimborn.

"Maintain fire," Jas said evenly, settling backward into her seat. "Equal pulses. Both ships." They were now under attack from two directions.

She bit the edge of her thumb. Failure to inflict serious damage when a ship's force field was down was rare. She peered at the new ship. It was another kind that she'd never seen before. In five years of battles, Jas had seen many starships fighting on both sides of the Shadow War. She'd gotten to know most of the models and their specs and capabilities. Only occasionally now did she encounter an unfamiliar ship. Yet here were two that she didn't know. She wondered if the Shadows had begun to design and manufacture their own ships.

The second ship began its pursuit. The *Thylacine* continued on its course, closing the distance with the first ship. They were fast becoming penned in. Jas clenched her jaw. Taking out one average Shadow ship was achievable. The *Thylacine* had done it often enough. Taking out two—one of which seemed exceptionally well-protected—would be tough.

"Pulses incoming," Trimborn said. They were too numerous for the *Thylacine's* pulses to intercept.

The ship vibrated again under the heavy fire.

"Fighters launched from Shadow Ship Two," said Trimborn. Sparks spewed from the side of the second ship, the tiny flecks of light representing manned Shadow fighter ships.

Jas's stomach twisted at the sight. She raised her comm button to her lips. "Squadron Leader Correia, scramble all fighters."

She imagined the Unity Alliance fighter pilots in their single-seater, highly maneuverable ships as they bravely prepared to launch. Starship force fields protected them against high-energy pulses, but close-range, low-energy fighter fire could penetrate the defensive screen. Protracted fighter fire on vulnerable spots could cripple a ship. The *Thylacine's* fighter pilots would protect against these attacks and attempt to destroy the enemy's fighters.

Despite the danger to her ship from the Shadow fighter attack, Jas hated deploying her pilots. Their chances of survival were terrible. In the average Shadow War battle, fewer than sixty percent of UA pilots would make it back to their ships alive. Jas's pilot survival stats were somewhat better, mostly because she did whatever she could to avoid risking her pilots' lives. It was something Admiral Pacheco criticized her for, though she'd never lost a battle yet.

In the current situation, however, she had no choice.

"Kennewell," she said. "As the last fighter leaves, take us hard to port." The *Thylacine's* fighter ships would launch to starboard. She needed to give the pilots room to maneuver, and she wanted to avoid becoming sandwiched between the two Shadow ships.

"Yes, ma'am," Kennewell replied, her hands hovering over her controls.

The ship continued to vibrate as the odd attacking pulse impacted their force field. Their own pulses were also scoring hits, too, gradually wearing down their enemies' power levels.

Inertia pushed Jas to the right as Kennewell swiftly maneuvered the ship. The *Thylacine's* fighters were now visible on the holo, specks of light swirling around, streaming out to meet the enemy's oncoming ships.

"Drop force field power fifty percent. Divert to pulses. Direct all pulse fire at ship one," Jas commanded, judging that the second ship wouldn't fire through the ranks of their own fighters to attack the *Thylacine*. Temporarily diverting her ship's force field power to pulses was worth the risk. They had to hit the first ship with everything they had.

The *Thylacine's* bolts poured across space toward the first Shadow ship. The pulses the destroyer emitted were so intense they looked like one long chain of light leading from the *Thylacine* to its enemy. They swamped the enemy ship with energy.

Trimborn was intent on his scanner. "Their force field's breaking down, Commander."

"Fighter fire at our launch bay doors," another officer said.

Jas's gaze swept the interplay of fighter ships. They were executing a macabre dance in the space between the *Thylacine* and the second Shadow ship. Some enemy fighters had slipped through her pilots' defenses, and sprays of flickering sparks were springing out and onto the *Thylacine*. Her fighters had spotted the attack, however. Several peeled away from the rest and swept back toward the ship.

"We're through," exclaimed Trimborn.

Jas clicked her tongue. Her first officer's speech always became vague when he was over-excited. "We've broken through ship one's force field, Trimborn?"

"Yes, ma'am. Sorry, ma'am."

Then the bridge of the *Thylacine* shook so violently, Jas was almost thrown from her seat. "Force field one hundred percent," she barked as she recovered her balance. "Damage report."

"They've blasted our bay doors wide open," an officer said. "But—"

Trimborn gave a whoop. "We've got them!"

Jas turned to the holo to see if Trimborn meant what she thought he meant. Sure enough, the first Shadow ship's curved extensions on one side had been blown clean off and were spinning away into space. As she watched, another of the *Thylacine's* pulses hit the ship, cleaving the central section in half.

"The Shadow fighters are returning to ship two," said an officer.

As if in response to the first ship's destruction, the specks of light from the second ship were speeding home. Jas frowned. The fighter ships had succeeded in hitting the *Thylacine*. Why were they giving up their attack? Their actions could mean only one thing, Jas realized. But surely it was too soon for that?

As the enemy fighters left the battle scene, the *Thylacine's* did the same, clearing the path for pulses. Not for the first time, Jas was grateful for her smart squadron leader. Once the fighters were outside the ship, both sides' comm dampeners made giving orders impossible. The pilots were trained in set responses to certain events during an engagement.

"Ship two's building energy," Trimborn said.

"Fire at will," commanded Jas. They would make the best use of the remaining time.

Now that the pathway was clear, the *Thylacine* poured pulses onto the enemy ship. But their attack seemed to have little impact. Like its hull, the ship's force field was formidable.

The *Thylacine's* pulses were bathing the enemy ship in light, so that only its outline was visible above the slowly turning golden globe. Everyone on the bridge fixed their gaze on the starship. No one even seemed to breathe.

Then it was gone.

There was a sigh of exhaled breath. The second ship had jumped. Relieved exclamations sounded across the bridge.

"I want a full damage report," Jas barked. "Begin repairs immediately, and scan the remaining ship's debris for signs of life. Trimborn, assemble a team to sweep the planet."

Her tone quietened the room, and heads turned to consoles as everyone went back to their tasks.

Jas frowned. The battle had been much too easy. Why hadn't the second ship stuck around? Her fighters had penetrated the *Thylacine's* defenses, and expended power made the ship additionally vulnerable.

The two new models of starships added to Jas's suspicions. She would have to speak to Pacheco the next opportunity she had.

Her expression turned grim. Her next task was a sad one. After briefly checking that everyone on the bridge was focused on their work, she opened the interface on her armrest.

The screen displayed a list of pilots' names. As the fighter pilots returned to the ship, their embedded microchips would be recognized by the ship's computer. A dot would appear next to each name as the pilots landed. The search for missing pilots would begin immediately. When it was completed, Jas would write to the families of those who hadn't been found. She would tell them that their loved one was missing in action, presumed dead.

Pacheco had told her several times that she didn't have to do this task, but she did it anyway. The reason was, each time that she did it, she was reminded of a pilot she had once known.

Jas performed this service for missing pilots' families because she knew that *she* would have liked to have received that news rather than being left never really knowing what had happened to him.

Two

Jas's office was bare and functional. She had a desk with an embedded interface and a seat. A couple more chairs stood against the wall in case she ever felt the need to invite anyone to sit, but the seats were rarely used. She wasn't a commander who was in the habit of having long conversations with her crew.

With a sigh, she swept the screen of her interface, and it blinked to life. The damage report from the battle was in. She scanned it, her tired gaze moving down the screen. The *Thylacine* had sustained severe damage to the launch bay doors, but repair crews were already working on them. The area would be without an atmosphere until the doors were fixed.

She had sent First Officer Trimborn planetside to sweep the population for Shadows. He and his defense units and troops would work through the government and other positions of influence in the local population, employing Shadow scanners to root out the aliens. Control of the planet would be returned to its sentient species, and Trimborn's team would train key personnel in the Transgalactic Council's Shadow protocol: rigorous, systematic testing for the Shadows' presence in every area of their society.

How the locals dealt with the Shadows they discovered was up to them, providing they ensured the hostile aliens would no longer pose any threat to the galaxy. In Jas's experience, most of the invaded populations chose to put an end to that threat once and for all.

Some armed resistance during the Shadow sweeping process was almost inevitable, but Trimborn had troops, weapons, and armored vehicles. The fighter ships could also operate in an atmosphere if needed. Trimborn was well-practiced at his task, and Jas had every confidence in her first officer, even if he was prone to getting a little over-excited at times.

As she finished reading the damage report, she frowned. The enhanced capabilities of the Shadow ship and its fighter pilots, and its surprise retreat, still bothered her. With a sinking heart, she pulled up the list of pilots. Where there should have been dots, many blanks remained next to the names. She lifted her comm button to her lips.

"Squadron Leader Correia, report on the missing pilots."

"We've finished our search, ma'am. Everyone who's coming back is aboard ship," came the man's reply.

Krat. The list on the display looked more than half empty. "We seem to have suffered higher than average losses."

"Yes, we have, Commander. Thirty-three missing."

Thirty-three of seventy-eight. "How do you account for those numbers, Squadron Leader?"

The man took a moment to answer. "If I'm honest, Commander, I'd say we were outclassed. If it weren't for the fact that the second ship jumped, I don't think we could have lasted much longer."

"I see."

"I've been a part of this war for nearly three years, ma'am," Correia went on, "and the Shadow fighter pilots just get better and better. At the same time, our recruits are younger every time we receive a new batch, and they're worse-trained. When I joined up, I thought the caliber of our pilots was poor and we were scraping the barrel. Now, if it weren't for the fact that we've got a war to win, I would send half of every new intake back to pilot school." The man's tone rose. "They simply aren't ready, ma'am. And we send them out there like... like... "

"I understand, Squadron Leader," Jas said. "I understand. Please let me know when we'll hold the memorial service for the lost pilots."

Correia had recovered his composure. He answered firmly, "Yes, ma'am."

Jas closed the comm link and returned her attention to the screen. She prepared to write the first mail of thirty-three. Pressing on a pilot's name brought up his or her details, including the next-of-kin's mail address and any last messages or requests from the pilot in the event of their death. She always read each entry carefully and crafted personal mails based on what the pilot had written. She pressed the first name:

If I don't make it, please send this message to my parents:

Dear Mom and Dad, don't cry too long or too hard over me. Please don't be mad over what has happened. I did what I had to do, and fighting the Shadows was it. Put on a brave face for those who need you, and celebrate my life.

Jas read the woman's birth date. She'd been twenty-two when she died. Her eyes sad, Jas began to write.

She always referred to the lost pilot's status as 'presumed dead'. If the searchers couldn't find a signal from their chip, the person was almost certainly going to die if they weren't already dead. Deep space was so vast, the chances of being accidentally found were just about impossible. Though Jas recalled a case where the pilot's arm that held her chip had been blown way off into space, and it was only when she managed to comm her ship that anyone knew she was still alive.

Jas had only written two sentences of the first mail when her interface chirruped. The message wasn't marked urgent, so she ignored it. Whatever it was, it could wait until she'd gotten at least one mail written. Almost immediately, however, there was a second chirrup. This time, she checked to see who was messaging her. It was Admiral Pacheco's office requesting a vidcall.

She rolled her eyes. Vidcalls across space required excessive power. A simple mail should have sufficed if he wanted to discuss something, and whatever it was could probably have been handled by his office too.

She pressed her acceptance, and Pacheco's familiar face appeared on her screen. She'd worked with him in one way or another ever since she had volunteered to join the Shadow War and he was first officer aboard the *Infineon*, where she'd been posted. Jas had been commanding a team of defense units, and Pacheco had earned a quick promotion to commander when the *Infineon's* commander had his head blown off by a Shadow.

Jas and Pacheco had both come a long way since then, and the admiral's dark hair had silvered at his temples. Over the years, Jas had developed a comfortable acquaintance with the short-tempered man.

If only the admiral's feelings about her had been similarly neutral.

"Commander Harrington, good to see you, as always."

"Hello, Admiral. Is there something I can do for you?"

The man's features clouded. "Ever efficient and straight to the point. Would it hurt to just chat for once, Jas? It isn't like we're strangers."

She rubbed her brow. "I'm in the middle of something, Pacheco. So, if this is about the meeting, don't worry, I haven't forgotten. Now, I really need to—"

"You're writing to the pilots' families, aren't you? I keep telling you—"

"And I keep telling *you* that I want to do it. Now, please, krat knows how much power this call is using, so..."

"Okay, okay," the admiral grumbled. "Yes, it was about the meeting. But not only that, you'll collect your new intake of personnel while you're here and jump back to your ship with them. You have some newly trained pilots, a team of defense units, a chief engineer, and relief maintenance crew as your current set are at the end of their duty tour, some medics, and—"

"Fine. I'll make sure to collect them. I'll see you at the meeting."

"Wait," Pacheco said. "There's one more thing I thought you might be interested to know."

"What's that?" Jas asked, wondering what else the man would think up to prolong the call. She lifted her hand, ready to close the connection.

"As your intake were talking among themselves, I overheard something I thought you might find interesting. One of them already knows you, someone said. From way back before the Shadow War began."

Jas's hand halted on its downward trajectory to end the call. "Someone who knows me?" Her voice quivered.

Pacheco's eyes narrowed as he studied her reaction. "Yes, that's right. That was all I heard, though."

Someone who knew her. For a brief moment, Jas forgot where she was and who she was talking to. But she didn't dare to hope.

She returned to the present and saw that Pacheco had been watching her silently during her moment of distraction.

"Okay," she said, with some effort. "Thanks for letting me know. I'll see you soon."

She closed the call without waiting for an answer. Her heart was racing and her blood was rushing through her ears, making her light-headed. Could it really be him? It was hardly possible that he'd survived five years as a pilot in the Shadow War. The attrition rate was too high. She hadn't met a single pilot who had been in the war since the beginning.

Her stomach was so tight, she felt sick. It was strange. She thought she'd given up hope of ever seeing Carl again years ago, when she'd accepted the remoteness of the chances of him still being alive. Yet this small remark passed on by Pacheco had thrown her back into a state of ridiculous, stupid hope. A hope she'd tried hard to give up.

THREE

Jas had a few minutes before the Transgalactic Council gateway would open to take her to the Unity Alliance meeting. She checked her reflection in her cabin's mirror, smoothing down the creases on her uniform pants. She preferred the flexibility of a combat suit to the stiff, black material of a commander's uniform. Hers always looked crumpled and untidy.

She had managed to slow her racing heart a little by telling herself over and over again that it was impossible that this person who knew her from long ago could be Carl. She had met and worked with many people over her career as a security officer. Hundreds of crew members aboard the prospecting starships where she used to work, in fact. This person could be any of them. There was no reason for her to suppose that it was Carl.

She checked the time and turned to face the spot in the corner of her office where the gateway would open. The technology was highly confidential. The Council insisted that it was used well away from lower-ranking military.

Minute green specks appeared in midair and were soon lazily swirling around. Jas had gotten used to traveling by gateway since she'd been promoted to commander six months ago, but she took deep breaths this time as the green spots coalesced.

At just the right moment, she stepped through.

She was in the entrance way of a tall building, standing in the bright light of twin suns. Jas stepped quickly away from the gateway to make room for other commanders and captains who would be appearing behind her. Looking up, she saw that her initial impression of the building hadn't been correct. It would have been more accurate to describe the place as a kind of mound. Way above, the massive insectoid Transgalactic Council officials were flying on translucent wings, emerging from and landing at holes in the sides.

The entrance way she stood at was apparently only for species who went around on legs. Jas took a moment to enjoy the feeling of sunlight on her face for the first time in months before entering the edifice.

Inside, she was greeted by a Council administrator—a smaller, less colorful version of the higher officials—who led her and the other military officers through smooth, ceramic tunnels to the meeting room.

Accommodating the range of galactic species who had allied with the Unity, the military arm of the Transgalactic Council, could not have been easy, but the Council managers had clearly grown adept at the practice during the hundreds of Earth years that they'd been organizing the galaxy's affairs. Jas settled down in a seat designed for humanoids and waited for the rest of the UA officers to arrive.

She'd been eager to attend the meeting after her most recent battle, to discuss what had happened with the new Shadow ships. She'd wanted to find out if anyone had had a similar experience and what they thought of it. But Pacheco's news had distracted her a little. She was looking forward to the meeting being over so she could meet this mysterious person from the past who knew her.

The Unity Alliance officers entered the room in dribs and drabs, walking, hopping, floating, and sliding. Jas knew many of them by sight, some by name. During her brief time as a commander, some of the officers she'd gotten to know had died in the course of performing their duty.

She chewed the edge of her thumb, wondering how much longer she had to wait until the meeting would start.

Finally, when the room was bursting with the assorted UA upper echelons, Admiral Pacheco arrived. As he came in, his eyes caught Jas's. His black uniform was in a far better state than hers. Not a crease or piece of lint was in sight. He was wearing his admiral's hat, which he took off and tucked under his arm.

Only an extra star on the breast of his jacket signified Pacheco's rank, but his dignified composure was enough to tell any onlooker of his status. His gaze, as it swept the room, was quiet and serious. The hum of various languages that had started up as the officers waited was quickly silenced.

"Commanders, captains, rear admirals, thank you for coming," Pacheco said. "Time is pressing, so let's keep this short. I want a brief update from each of you on the recent and ongoing engagements in your sectors."

Jas listened for a moment to the incomprehensible sounds being made by the commander next to Pacheco, who had taken it upon him- or herself to begin, before she realized she'd forgotten to turn her comm button to its translation setting. As soon as she made the change, the button relayed the speech in standard English. The commander was reporting on a successful raid on a Shadow trap planet.

From the description, the world sounded similar to K.67092d, where Jas had first encountered the hostile beings that came from the Void, somewhere outside the known universe. K.67092d had been a barren planet, devoid of complex life forms. Nothing but the strange, hexagonal Shadow traps was of any interest in the place, and that of course made them perfect for attracting the attention of unsuspecting visitors.

The commander related how his crew had successfully destroyed all the traps on the planet. At the same time, they had defended the place from attacking Shadow ships that were seeking to stop them.

The next Unity Alliance officer told a different story. This officer's ship had been tasked with discovering new instances of Shadow invasion that had gone unnoticed by local populations. Galactic civilizations were numerous, and many hadn't yet joined the Transgalactic Council. That fact didn't make them off bounds to the Shadows, however, and to truly remove the Shadow threat from the galaxy, the Council had implemented a program to comb its reaches for their presence.

Not for the first time, Jas was reminded of the Shadows' resemblance to an infestation. Insidious and difficult to permanently eradicate, the aliens had gradually crept into every nook and cranny of the galaxy. They hid away, slowly multiplying, until they finally erupted like a nest of cockroaches.

When Jas's turn came, she told the room about the *Thylacine's* most recent engagement. She emphasized the second Shadow ship's superior fighter pilots, hull, and force field, as well as its puzzling disappearance the minute the first ship was destroyed. When she'd finished her short report, Jas looked to Pacheco for a response, but he gave none. He nodded toward the next officer to begin.

Her brows knitted. Hadn't he understood that there had to be implications to what she'd said? She bit the edge of her thumb again, then stopped because it was already sore.

After what seemed like a long time, the final report was given.

"Thank you, everyone," Pacheco said. "Plenty of useful information there. I also have a report to give. I'm sure you can tell from the many positive stories we've heard here, that the war is going well for us. At the last reckoning, the Unity Alliance effort had eradicated the Shadow threat from approximately ninety-five percent of the galaxy. The scanning protocols the Transgalactic Council put in place two years ago have been working, and the sloppy mistakes we used to make, allowing Shadows to infiltrate the scanning process, are a thing of the past.

"Through the excellent efforts of Commander Harrington and the *Thylacine*—"Jas cringed "—we have secured the Council's access to mythrin, which is of course essential in detecting Shadows. Every day we draw closer to our goal of destroying every known and unknown Shadow invasion." He gave a tight smile. "I think it's safe to say we have the misborns on the run. And now, on to our next maneuver."

Pacheco tapped an interface on the wall. The lights dimmed and a panoply of stars shimmered into view in the center of the room. For a moment, Jas was distracted from her personal concerns. It had been a long time since she'd seen a hologram of the Milky Way. She was used to seeing holos of the local star system wherever the *Thylacine* was engaging in battle. It was only rarely that she saw the galaxy as a whole.

The vast expanse of tiny points of light, representing gigantic, blazing suns, took her breath away.

"Through the efforts of the last five years and the sacrifice of many, many brave individuals," said Pacheco, "we have concentrated the mass of the Shadows in this sector of the galaxy." The holo zoomed into an area of thousands of stars. "According to our intelligence, several star systems in this region remain heavily infested with Shadows. In fact, we're confident that this is where most of the resistance and re-emergences in previously swept sectors are organized and provisioned. It's a Shadow stronghold, but it's the last one. If we can wipe them out here, we have a chance of putting an end to the Shadow menace forever. In short, if we win back this region we will have victory. The war will be over, and the civilizations of the galaxy can return to peace."

Pacheco stopped speaking, but no one said anything for a while. Jas, too, was having trouble processing what the admiral had said. The Shadow War had been going on for so long, fighting it had become a way of life to her. She found it hard to believe that the war *could* end.

A strangled sound, which Jas realized after a moment was a kind of laughter, came from a corner of the room. More sounds and voices joined in, rejoicing at Pacheco's announcement. But before things could get out of hand, the admiral raised his arms and asked for silence.

"Let's not be premature," he said. "We have a lot of work to do before we can celebrate. Now, more than ever, we must continue in our attitude of utmost vigilance to prevent Shadows from infiltrating our safeguards. We must continue to protect our people from their invasions. We must continue to crush and eradicate them wherever we find them.

"I've brought you here today to tell you that we're on the cusp of our best chance for a final, decisive blow. Now, I want you all to return to your ships and redouble your efforts. Expect and accept only the best from those you command. If we can maintain the courage, rigor, and determination that have brought us this far, we can succeed in putting an end to this war. When the time comes for the final push, I will send instructions."

Nothing more needed to be said. The Unity Alliance officers slowly filed out of the room to return to their starships. As Jas had seated herself at the back, she was one of the last to leave. Pacheco was thanking or having brief chats with the officers as they left, but he was alone when Jas reached him.

She tensed.

"Commander Harrington, could I have a word?"

FOUR

As always, Pacheco's demeanor lost some of its stiffness now that he and Jas were alone.

"I just wanted to say, congratulations on another successful battle. How many does that make now? Is it eight or nine?"

Jas smiled, thin-lipped. "I've commanded the *Thylacine* for seven battles so far, Admiral."

"Good work. I knew I was making the right decision when I recommended you for promotion."

Jas didn't reply. Was he expecting her to thank him? She'd guessed long ago that Pacheco was at least partly responsible for her rapid rise through the ranks. That and the terrible losses the Unity Alliance had sustained over the years of the war. But the office of commander didn't mean anything to her. She would have served just as conscientiously if she'd been in the lowest ranks. What was more, serving as a commander brought responsibilities that she didn't relish, though she did her best to fulfill them.

The pause was becoming awkward, so Jas said, "I need to go and find my new intake, sir, and the ship that'll take us to the *Thylacine*."

Pacheco nodded. "Yes, of course. I'll go along with you. It's on my way."

Jas sighed inwardly as they left the room together and entered the labyrinthine tunnels of the Transgalactic Council offices.

"What did you think of the meeting today, Harrington?" Pacheco asked.

"I thought it went well, sir," Jas replied. "I was surprised to hear that we're so close to victory. It feels like we've been fighting this war forever."

"Yes, it feels like that to me too, sometimes," Pacheco said. "Do you mind if I ask, when it's all finally over, what you plan to do?"

"I don't think I have a plan. I've been concentrating on fighting for so long, it's hard to think about the future."

"Will you return to Earth, do you think? Or maybe another planet?"

Earth? Jas hadn't thought about Earth in a long while, and when she did, she usually thought of her old friend, Sayen, ex-navigator of the prospecting starship *Galathea*. She hadn't been able to contact Sayen after they'd both volunteered, due to the security ban on personal comms. She had no idea where she was or even if she was still alive. But she knew that if Sayen survived, *she* would be returning to Earth. Her brother and the woman she loved were there. As to where Jas would go when they finally defeated the Shadows...

"I've no idea," she answered.

They went through a round doorway. Pacheco had brought her to a large waiting area where a group of people and defense units were milling about. It was the usual ragtag bunch. Half already in uniform, half in civvies. Some faces were lined and harried, others looked as though they shouldn't have been let out of school. The defense units were a range of models too. Commandeered from private companies, most likely, or judging from the appearance of some of them, snatched at the last minute from conveyor belts at recycling plants.

Jas's heart began to race as she scanned the faces that turned toward her and Pacheco, but after a few moments, it abruptly slowed and was heavy in her chest. In spite of the five years that had passed, she knew she would notice Carl immediately if he were there. He wasn't.

She realized that the group were saluting her and the admiral. She returned the salute, and from the corner of her eye she noticed Pacheco's gaze upon her while he also saluted. Had he been observing her reaction to seeing the new recruits?

"Thank you. I'll take over from here," she said.

"Yes, Commander. Your transport is waiting on the pad. Safe journey."

"Thank you."

Usually, she was tolerant toward the man's unwanted attention, but her sense of disappointment at not finding Carl among the crowd had irritated her. As the admiral left, she went after him into the empty corridor where she could not be overheard. She said, "Pacheco." He turned, and she went on, "In the meeting, you singled me out for praise. Please don't do that. It's embarrassing."

Pacheco raised his eyebrows and gave a slight shake of his head before walking away.

Jas returned to the room and the waiting women, men, and defense units, already regretting her inappropriate words to the admiral. The man couldn't help his feelings for her any more than she could help the fact that she didn't reciprocate them.

"Who's the highest-ranking person here?" she asked.

A man raised his hand and opened his mouth to speak.

Jas interrupted, "Great. Get everyone onto the transport waiting for us on the launch pad in five minutes."

"Yes, Commander," the man replied.

Jas left to make her own way to the launch pad, guessing that the warren of Council offices had to offer a different route. She wanted to be alone and compose herself before joining the new recruits. She didn't trust herself to maintain a calm attitude in her current state.

She was surprised the disappointment of not finding Carl among the new intake had hit her so hard. It seemed her heart hadn't listened to her head saying time and time again he had to have died.

Her circuitous route brought her to the transport a few minutes after the new crew members of the *Thylacine*. The man who had led them had done a good job. Their packs were safely stowed and everyone was strapped into jumpseats in the bare, functional military transport cabin. All they were waiting for before starjumping was her.

She gave a brief, approving nod before strapping herself in and comm'ing the pilot that they were ready for liftoff. From behind came the soft whoosh and click of the cabin doors shutting automatically, and the rumble of the engines shook her seat.

As the transport rose, wobbling a little, into the air, a realization niggled at Jas. Pacheco's tip had led her to a doomed hope that she might see Carl. When she hadn't, she'd lost interest in the question of who the person from her past might be.

The transport forced its way upward through the atmosphere and against the pull of gravity. Jas was sitting at the front of the cabin near the door to the cockpit. She craned her head around her seat while the transport rose higher, but all she could see were a few recruits sitting in the row behind her. They returned her gaze with puzzled expressions.

She quickly straightened up. A commander had to maintain a level of dignity, which was one of the things she hated about the position.

There were no windows in the transport, but long experience told Jas they had to be leaving the planet's atmosphere by that time. If she could look out, she would have seen the curve of the globe and the dark expanse of space above.

The transport completed the remainder of its flight away from the planet to a distance from which it would be safe to starjump. Jas racked her brains to match her brief glimpse of a faintly familiar face with a memory of a past acquaintance.

It wasn't until they jumped she had the answer.

FIVE

She had never quite gotten used to the rough military transport starjumps. Her stomach lurched as they reappeared in space some distance from the *Thylacine*. The destroyer was still orbiting the mythrin-harboring planet. Whenever she returned to the ship from a trip away, Jas felt like she was coming home.

She thought of the *Thylacine* as her ship. She was the only commander the relatively new vessel had ever had, and she had a sense of ownership of it. At five hundred and fifty meters long and half as wide, the *Thylacine* was only averagely sized compared to the rest of the Unity fleet, but the pulse cannons fore and aft were the latest and best technology. What was more, both the massive jump engine that underlay the working and residential quarters of the ship, and the smaller RaptorXs to either side were the fastest-responding that she'd ever known.

The engineer who had just completed his duty tour had maintained the engines in excellent working order, and Jas was confident that the person she suspected was his replacement would do the same. Like her namesake, the *Thylacine* was small compared to other predators of the Unity fleet, but she was deadly.

From behind Jas came the sounds of recruits whose stomachs

were rebelling even more forcefully than hers at their abrupt arrival. She grimaced, and while the transport flew to the ship and through its bay doors, her mind dwelt on the person from her past and the events surrounding their acquaintance—friendship, even, though it hadn't started out that way.

Finally, the transport's engines powered down and the pilot comm'd to say it was safe to disembark. Jas unfastened her harness and stood up, turning to face the recruits. Some of the new crew members were pale and sweaty, and the cabin reeked from the small pools of vomit in the aisles. The cabin doors clicked and opened with a swoosh, allowing welcome filtered air into the vessel.

"Disembark from the back row forward," Jas said, "and line up in your sections outside."

The recruits stood and began pulling out their bags from the lockers, gingerly avoiding the puddles that dotted the floor. As Jas passed by, they stepped aside.

She went down the ramp and out into the launch bay, experiencing a sense of weird displacement caused by traveling by gateway and starjumping. She felt like she could have been aboard the *Thylacine* a few months ago or, as she had in fact, only a few hours ago. While she waited for the recruits to disembark, she checked over the bay doors. The repair crew had done a good job. The only evidence of the damage the second Shadow ship had inflicted was sprays of scorch marks across the inner bulkheads.

Krat. Jas remembered she'd meant to talk to Pacheco after the meeting about the odd occurrences in the *Thylacine's* most recent engagement. He hadn't seemed to pay much attention to the information while she was giving her report, and afterward she'd been focused on meeting the person from her past. She resolved to mail Pacheco later.

The new crew members were filing down the ramp and lining up as she'd told them. Jas scanned the crowd, her gaze finally alighting on the woman she was seeking. She was as stocky and ginger as ever, though fine lines on her pale face showed the passing of the years since they'd last known each other. Wealthier, or perhaps vainer individuals would have paid to have those wrinkles removed. It looked to Jas as though the woman's situation was similar to what it had been when they worked together.

As the woman met her gaze, Jas gave her a very brief smile.

"Who has the list of names?" she asked the waiting recruits. The defense units had organized themselves into a line too. Suddenly, Jas realized she'd spotted another familiar figure. "Wait a moment," she said as she went over to the AX unit. She read the unit's breastplate and looked up at the android's impassive face in surprise. "AX7. You worked with me aboard the *Galathea*."

"Yes, Commander Harrington."

"Do you remember?"

"Yes, Commander Harrington. All my memories are stored in my database."

Two members of the *Galathea's* crew had arrived on the Thylacine.

"I have the list here, ma'am," said the man who'd identified himself as highest-ranking among them earlier. He came over and handed her an interface.

Jas scanned the list. She would look at the details more closely later. At that moment, she was looking for only one name. She read it and the rank next to it. *Chief Engineer.* She nodded approvingly. It was as she expected. It would be good to have the woman aboard.

She told the new recruits to wait for their section officers, then asked her old acquaintance to go with her. They left the bay.

As soon as they were out of earshot of the others, Jas said, "Toirien, what a surprise to see you."

"You too, Jas...Commander," Toirien MacAdam replied.

Jas clicked her tongue. "No need to call me that. At least not while we're alone. I can't stand all that formality, but I have to go along with it."

"I recognized your name when they told me where I was going and who I'd be serving under," Toirien said, "but I wasn't sure it was really you until I saw you. Who'd have thought all those years ago that when we met again you'd be in command of a Unity destroyer?"

"A lot's happened since we were stuck on that Shadow trap planet," Jas said. "A lot." She hesitated. "Did you have to travel far to get to the Unity recruiting station? Are you tired?"

"No, not far," replied the engineer. "I'm not that tired."

"Do you want to join me for a drink and a chat after you settle in? I need to organize a few things, but then we could catch up on old times."

"Sure. I'd like that."

Jas led Toirien through the ship to the chief engineer's quarters and told her where to find her office when she was ready.

When Jas got back to her office, she drafted a long mail to Pacheco, reporting on the recent battle and highlighting the odd activity. She concluded,

Admiral, I'm concerned that the unfamiliar designs of the two Shadow ships, the unusual strength of the second ship's hull and force field, the high caliber of its fighter pilots, and the ship's abrupt departure when it could have remained and possibly won the battle, are all significant.

Now that I've had time to process the details, it occurs to me that the Shadows may be moving beyond their strategy of using the skills, knowledge, and technology of their victims. They may be developing to be better than them. They could be building their own, better, ships, maybe even inventing new genetic enhancement techniques to improve their pilots' skills.

I suspect the Thylacine got off easy. I think the second ship jumped because they'd discovered what they wanted to know—that their technology is superior.

Jas's door chime sounded. She signed off the mail and sent it, then let Toirien in.

"What can I get you?" she asked, going to the drinks dispenser as the engineer took a seat.

"Water is fine," Toirien replied.

"Nothing stronger?"

"No, thanks. I haven't touched a drop of alcohol since that time you caught me off my face aboard the *Galathea*."

"Ha," Jas said. "I remember. Good for you." Toirien's alcohol and substance addiction had been a big problem, interfering with her work and judgment. Jas also recalled the engineer's wish that she could have her children returned to her. They'd been placed in care due to their mother's addictions.

She poured Toirien's water and ordered a mixed drink for herself. As she handed the beaker to the woman, she sat down on the other side of the desk. The engineer indicated Jas's drink and said, "Is it normal to have alcohol aboard a Unity vessel?"

"I allow it for special occasions," Jas replied. "A small celebratory drink when we win a battle helps boost morale. It keeps my spirits up too."

Toirien's expression was doubtful, and she watched with concern as Jas took a sip of her drink. Jas noticed her look and attributed the engineer's unease to her own past history. It wasn't like that for Jas. Not everyone let their drinking get out of hand.

"So," she said, "who's looking after your kids while you're here?"

"They don't need anyone to look after them anymore. They're all grown up now. Fine young ladies. They've both signed up to fight. Joan is a comm technician and Grace has followed in her mam's footsteps. She's serving as an engineer aboard the *Camaradon*."

The *Camaradon* was Pacheco's command—the largest military space vessel ever built and the pride of the Unity fleet. It had been aboard the *Camaradon* that Jas had last seen Sayen Lee.

"It sounds like you set a great example, Toirien. You must be very proud of them."

Toirien's face twisted into an expression of regret. "I didn't do right by my children for a long time, but I hope I've made up for that at least a little over the last few years."

Jas took another sip of her drink, the alcohol easing some of the tension from her muscles. It was pleasant to talk with Toirien and slip into memories of past times. So much had happened since they last met, and her life was so different. She wondered if she was even the same person anymore.

"So, what's been happening with you?" Toirien asked. "How did you go from security officer on a private prospector to Unity commander? That must be quite a tale to tell."

Jas grimaced. "It is, and I'll tell you the whole story some time. But I'm curious to know about Earth. It's been a long while since I was there. What's been happening? How are things now?"

"Hmm...not too bad. You know that Earth was declared Shadow-free late last year? It was a long, hard struggle to root them all out, but we made it in the end. So many people died during their invasion. It was terrible. And toward the end as the entire population was being scanned, it was odd. People were clinging to their Shadow friends and family. Sheltering Shadows and hiding them from the authorities, in total self-denial. They couldn't face the fact that their loved ones were dead. The Shadows went along with the masquerade, of course, because the alternative was execution."

"How could they accept a Shadow in place of the person who'd been murdered?" Jas asked, shocked.

"I know how weird it sounds, but on the other hand, I know how easy it is to lie to yourself if you want to." Toirien glanced at the drink in Jas's hand.

"How's the recovery going?" Jas asked. "Are things getting back to normal?"

"Slowly, to be sure, but, yes, I'd say a kind of normality is returning to people's lives. Things are different now, though. Battling the Shadows has brought people together. Evened things out a little. You don't see the same separation between modded and naturals, for instance. A lot of the people who benefited from the divisions in societies, like the heads of corporations etcetera, they're nearly all dead. They were the ones the Shadows targeted. So it's like most of the very top layer of society was removed, and now people are trying to rebuild with a more equitable system. Basic modding for your baby is a right now, not a privilege. That'll continue to even things up. And there's more acceptance of people who choose a different way of life."

"That's good to hear." Jas recalled the underworlders and their struggle against a society that despised them. She wondered what Erielle thought of the changes.

Her interface chirruped. Pacheco had replied to her mail. "Excuse me a moment." She opened and read his message.

Thanks for your report. I've noted your concerns. Prepare to ship out to the coordinates given at our meeting. The Thylacine *must be ready for action in eighty-four hours.*

Six

When Jas boarded the shuttle that would take her planetside, she was a little worse for wear after a long evening spent with Toirien. She took a seat in the cabin and comm'd the pilot that she was ready to go.

She'd talked with Toirien about old times and old acquaintances, like long-departed, myth-addicted Captain Loba, self-serving First Mate Haggardy, and bigoted Dr. Sparks. The engineer had been entertained to hear of what had happened to Sparks after leaving the *Galathea*. Jas wondered if anyone had told the doctor yet that Earth was finally free of Shadows, or if he was still hiding out the war at the chilly Ganymede Outpost.

She couldn't quite remember how her evening with Toirien had ended, but she'd woken with an aching head and sore stomach. She'd self-medicated to relieve the symptoms of her hangover, but she still felt light-headed and out of sorts. She hoped a visit to see how Trimborn was getting on with his Shadow sweep would distract her from her malaise.

Her first officer only had three days to train the locals in how to uncover the remaining Shadows hiding among them, and he had to do it effectively or the Shadows would regain control and a pocket of resistance would spring up.

The shuttle was sweeping rapidly down through the planet's atmosphere, buffeted by turbulence. Jas stretched her tender muscles and rubbed her eyes. She was tired, but it wasn't only due to her over-indulgence the night before. She'd been tired day in and day out for months—a deep-down tiredness that the longest sleep never seemed to fix.

"Touchdown in five, ma'am," came the pilot's voice through her comm.

Jas rested her head on the back of her seat and closed her eyes as the shuttle made its final approach. By the time it landed, she'd drifted into a light sleep. The sound of the cabin door opening roused her, and the sunlight that streamed in made her squint and blink. It was a brilliant light, and the air that entered the cabin was hot and dry.

Unfastening her harness, Jas stood and straightened her jacket. After smoothing down her hair at the back, she disembarked. Trimborn and a couple of his subordinates were waiting in a neat row a short distance away, but Jas was so blinded by the glaring light, she perceived them only as dark, indistinct figures.

She lifted a hand in front of her eyes to block out the sun, but the gesture didn't help much. The sun's brightness was reflected and seemingly multiplied by the surrounding landscape. She made her way over to her officers, her eyes narrowed to slits. Already, her uniform was feeling tight and uncomfortably warm.

"Good morning, ma'am," Trimborn said cheerfully as she approached.

"Morning...what are you wearing?" Jas asked.

Her first officer and the two other officers with him had cloths draped over their heads and down their backs. They were wearing their uniform hats, so the edges lifted the cloths into mini tents.

"Only thing that keeps the sun off, ma'am," Trimborn replied.

Jas noticed he also had on thick sunglasses.

The piercing light wasn't making her hangover any better. "Is there somewhere we can go?"

"Yes, Commander. This way." Trimborn led her toward a flat

structure raised only a meter or so above the ground. She hadn't noticed it because it was yellow-tinged white, the same color as the rocky surrounding ground.

"You could have told me what to expect, Trimborn," Jas said as they walked together. "I would have come better prepared."

"I...er...I did, ma'am. I left a message as soon as I received notification you were coming down. But don't worry, once we're underground, it'll be fine."

Jas hadn't checked her messages after she'd gotten up that morning.

They arrived at a circular entrance with an overhanging roof, set halfway into the ground. There was no door, only a dark hole leading to the interior. Uneasiness settled on Jas, and for a moment she wasn't sure why. Then she realized.

"This is like a Shadow trap," she blurted. She grabbed at her side, but in her hungover state, she hadn't remembered to arm herself.

"Yes, it is, isn't it, ma'am," Trimborn said. "Gave us the willies at first too. But there's no cause for concern. It's perfectly safe."

But Jas stopped in her tracks, her legs trembling. The last time she'd been near a Shadow trap, she'd been forced to watch people die while she stood by, helpless. And the time before that she'd had to kill the Shadow of someone she'd been close to.

She swallowed, fighting the urge to vomit.

"Commander," said Trimborn, taking off his sunglasses and peering at her, "are you feeling all right?"

She stared at her first officer. His ebony skin was glistening with sweat in the heat. Was he really who he seemed to be? Glancing at Trimborn's two subordinates, she began to back away. She tried to remember how far away and in which direction the shuttle stood.

Could she fight all three officers by herself? She was out of shape. She couldn't remember the last time she'd done any training.

"Commander," Trimborn said, "I think I understand your concerns, but we've followed all the protocols since landing. We are not Shadows."

She continued to step slowly backward out of the shade at the entrance until she was in the now-welcome, brilliant glare of the planet's sun. "I want proof. I want to scan you."

"But—" Trimborn protested.

"That's an order."

He shrugged, sighed, and turned to one of his subordinates. "Pop inside and bring out a scanner, would you?"

Jas and the remaining two officers waited in uncomfortable silence for the woman to return. Jas screwed up her eyes and hunched her shoulders in response to the pounding heat and sunlight.

Time passed, dragging its heels.

"The Shadow presence on this planet is minimal, ma'am," Trimborn said. "It's due to the Shadows' method of capturing their victims, I believe. The natives only rarely go above ground, you see, so it wasn't easy for the Shadows to entice them into their traps. And though the Shadow traps look similar to the local entrances to the underground cities, they look different enough to cause suspicion. Few victims would have entered willingly."

Jas didn't respond. She would talk to Trimborn when she knew for sure he *was* Trimborn.

The returning footsteps of the officer who had gone to collect a Shadow scanner broke the stillness and tension a little. The hand held scanner she'd brought was far smaller and easier to carry than the long, heavy, tube-shaped models the Council had manufactured in the beginning of the Shadow War. The officer handed the scanner to Jas and quickly returned to the shade.

She examined the device, running her fingers along its seams, checking for irregularities, such as if the instrument had been forced open. There *should* have been no way to open the scanners once they were sealed. They were designed to self-destruct if tampered with, so the chance the scanner had been fixed to give a false reading was remote, but it didn't hurt to check.

"Okay, one at a time, come over here so I can scan you," Jas said. "Trimborn, you first."

She ran the scanner down the back of her first officer. The

mythranil inside it would react if Trimborn bore traces of that mysterious dimension where the Shadows existed. The display read *Clear*. Jas exhaled.

"Stand behind me," she told Trimborn. "You next."

It took just a few minutes to establish that neither of the remaining two officers were Shadows. She relaxed, but the headache she'd forgotten about returned. She handed back the scanner. "Okay, let's go in."

The entrance led into a tunnel not unlike the ones at the Transgalactic Council offices, except the walls were heavily decorated. The brilliant reflectiveness of the native rock, which seemed to be some kind of quartz, had been cut into complex, sophisticated patterns. As well as being entrancing to look at, the many angled surfaces seemed to have been cut to capture every last particle of light that entered from the surface, and transmit it deep underground.

As Jas's eyes adjusted to the gradually dimming light, she became more and more fascinated by the decoration, until she was compelled to stop and look at it more closely.

"Don't touch it, ma'am," Trimborn said. "It's devilishly sharp." He raised a hand to display thin scabs on his fingertips. "Not that the locals think so. One of them told me they like to scratch themselves against the walls. Beautiful, isn't it, though?"

"Scratch themselves?" Jas asked. "What are they like? I was thinking they must be a sort of arthropoid species, like the Council officers."

"Errmm...not exactly," Trimborn replied. He shared a meaningful glance with his fellow officers. "At least, not unless they have another stage to their life cycle. But you'll meet them in a moment, Commander. We're nearly there."

They continued for another few minutes, until they reached a slope in the ground that led to a hole roughly half as wide as the tunnel.

"This leads to some kind of governmental area attached to a mine," Trimborn said. "Careful when you get to the bottom." He sat down at the edge of the slope and pushed off. He slid down and disappeared through the hole. The other officers did the same, and Jas followed last of all.

Though she'd encountered a wide variety of aliens over her career as a security officer and then in deep space military service, she couldn't suppress the revulsion she felt when she saw what awaited them at the bottom of the tunnel.

SEVEN

Jas emerged into a domed chamber. At first glance, the place seemed to be full of human-sized maggots. The sentient species of the mythrin-bearing planet were long and plump, and they seemed to be segmented, according to what was visible of their bodies. They wore patterned and plain one-piece skin-like coverings in a variety of styles and colors.

At one end of the creatures was a star-shaped opening that they flexibly moved, and surrounding the opening was a circle of black dots. The dots seemed to be eyes, because they turned toward Jas, Trimborn, and the others. Folds of skin swept over the dots, covering and uncovering them, apparently randomly.

The creatures moved by edging forward on their lower halves, born along on waves of movement that originated at their heads and progressed down their bodies. It was this style of locomotion, plus the fat, segmented bodies, that turned Jas's stomach. The natives' resemblance to maggots was so strong, she found it hard to push the thought out of her mind during her entire visit.

Though she'd forgotten her weapon, she had, at least, remembered her comm. She switched on its translation function and fought the urge to step back as the aliens edged closer, uttering greetings and thanks for releasing them from the Shadows' control of their planet.

Around the walls of the chamber, hammocks were slung for some reason, and they were filled with yet more of the creatures. At Jas's and the other officers' appearance, they had begun to wriggle out and drop to the floor with soft squelching sounds. These individuals also edged over eagerly, so closely that they were rubbing up against each other.

Trimborn introduced Jas to the creatures, then said, "Ma'am, this is Head of Nest of this nation." He added under his breath, "The translators can't seem to handle their names, but it doesn't appear to matter."

"The Unity Alliance accepts your thanks," Jas said, "but it's unneeded. As members of the Transgalactic Council, you are entitled to military aid in the case of invasion. We only regret that we couldn't free your planet sooner. May I ask how the implementation of the Shadow Sweep protocols is progressing?"

"Well, well, very well," the Head of Nest replied. "Your scanners are working very well. We've found many Shadows. They are very delicious. Thank you. Thank you."

Jas's already sensitive stomach turned over. She caught a glimpse of Trimborn's smirk from the corner of her eye.

"You're...welcome. I'm glad to hear that things are progressing quickly. I'm here to inform you that I must withdraw my team from your world soon. We can supply you with more scanners if you need them, but after the training period is over, you must cooperate with the other nations of your planet to detect any remaining Shadows. Are you confident that your citizens will be able to implement the protocols effectively?"

"Yes, yes. Your trainers teach very well. We understand what to do, and we will do it. Thank you. Thank you."

Jas nodded. She would have to see Trimborn's assessment report before taking the alien's word for it.

"One more thing," she went on. "The Shadow ship that we destroyed, was it from this planet?"

"Yes, yes. It was from here."

"So it was one of your starships?"

"No, no. Not one of ours. The Shadows built it here. Imported materials. We don't build starships from metal. We make them from..." Jas's comm emitted a tone that meant it was unable to translate the word.

"I see," she said. "Thank you for the information."

She concentrated on the Head of Nest—the one non-moving alien in front of her. The creatures' squirming around was increasing her nausea.

"Um," she said, trying to think up a reason to cut the visit short. "I appreciate you taking the time to meet with me, but I have urgent business to take care of, so—"

"Yes, yes. You're very busy. We understand. But we would like to show you a little of our home and what we do here, if you can spare the time. Thank you. Thank you."

Jas hesitated. Right now, she wanted nothing more than to return to the baking overground, the shuttle, and the *Thylacine*.

"I think I know what it means," Trimborn said. "It's very interesting, ma'am. Won't take long, I think."

Jas studied her first officer. A trace of the man's earlier smirk remained. Was he setting her up for something? But she was feeling too under the weather to think up a suitably polite refusal to tell the Head of Nest. Political diplomacy was just about her worst skill as a Unity commander.

She swallowed.

"I would love to see more of your home," she said.

Along with its group, the creature turned and squirmed away. Jas assumed she was supposed to follow, and set off after them, checking that Trimborn and the others were coming along too.

"What's this about?" she asked Trimborn quietly as he drew level with her.

"If it's the same thing they showed us before," he replied, "they're taking us to see their mythrin mine. I thought it was fascinating. Well worth an hour or so, if you can spare it, ma'am."

She took a deep breath and exhaled, which made her feel a little better. "Okay. Let's do it."

The Head of Nest had brought them to a door like an old-style camera lens. It opened automatically as they neared it, and the eyes of the aliens glowed to light up the dark tunnel beyond. This tunnel was smooth white rock, lacking the decoration of the entrance tunnel. The surface lightly reflected the beams from the creatures' eyes, creating a shimmering effect.

In other circumstances, Jas thought to herself, she would have enjoyed exploring this planet—its unsightly sentient species aside.

She and her officers followed the undulating Head of Nest as the tunnel sloped sharply down, until Jas was leaning backward in an effort not to slip. The creatures didn't seem to have a problem with the angle. In fact, some of them began wriggling along the walls in defiance of gravity.

When the floor finally evened out, they stopped. They'd arrived at the end of the tunnel, though in the walls opposite were two smaller holes, linked by a strip of highly polished, flat ground.

The Head of Nest said, "Waiting, waiting. Thank you. Thank you."

A sound of rushing wind was coming from one of the holes in the wall, and within a few moments the source of the sound appeared. It was a torpedo-shaped cart made of a hard, stony material, and it hovered a centimeter or two above the ground.

Following the Head of Nest's lead, Jas got in the cart along with her officers. The seating was made to fit the locals' body shape, so they had to recline on it rather than sit. As soon as everyone was in, the cart whooshed off.

Jas looked around, trying to understand how the vehicle was moving.

"I couldn't figure it out either, ma'am," Trimborn said.

They were borne along at an increasingly fast speed until the ceiling and sides of the tunnel whizzed past them. Jas was careful to keep her head well down and her arms and legs tucked in. The long, low body shape of the natives made their danger of being hurt much lower. Whenever the vehicle tilted upward or downward at a sharp angle, the creatures' bodies or clothing also prevented them from slipping out, while Jas had to grip on to the edge of her seat. She was reminded of rare visits to amusement parks when she was in the institute for cared-for children on Earth. The experience did, at least, take her mind off her nausea.

The ride slowed as quickly as it had begun when they arrived at a landing place. Jas climbed out of the cart, her legs wobbly. They were in a similar place to the one they'd just left, but the rock surface was more roughly hewn.

"This is one of our oldest seams," the Head of Nest told her, "yet it remains productive. Yes. Yes."

The creature led them down yet another tunnel. This one bore markings along the ceiling, which seemed to be notices or signs. Jas wondered how much farther they had to go. Her neck ached from stooping in the low tunnel. Trimborn had said the trip would take an hour or so, and they'd already been traveling for around twenty-five minutes.

As she was about to ask if their destination was much farther, the Head of Nest stopped.

"Here it is. Here it is," the alien announced.

Jas and her officers were at the back of the group. She looked around, wondering what she was supposed to be seeing. Trimborn nudged her. The aliens in front of them were shuffling sideways, creating a gap for them to pass through. She went forward.

The Head of Nest said, "Welcome. Welcome. See."

She followed the direction of its glowing eyes to a spot on the wall. A tube was fixed there below a tiny crack. The tube was the same color and material as the wall, which was why she'd failed to see it at first.

"That's it, ma'am," Trimborn said, arriving at her side.

"That's it?" Jas asked.

"Yes. Look inside the tube."

She leaned forward until her forehead was nearly resting on the wall. Deep down in the tube, a liquid glinted in the glow from the assembled aliens' eyes. The liquid was a delicate, pale pink. She noticed that at the edge of the crack above the tube, a drop of the liquid had swelled. As she watched, the drop fell. Simultaneously, the collected aliens' bodies trembled.

"This is it. This is it," the Head of Nest said. "Mythrin is our world's main source of income. We do not use it. Our bodies do not metabolize it. We only collect it and sell it. Very valuable. Yes. Yes."

The color of the mythrin was much paler than the deep scarlet of mythranil, but that made sense. Mythranil was the refined drug and mythrin was only the raw ingredient. Yet seeing the drug in its natural state made Jas shiver. The narcotic sent the user temporarily to the home of the Shadows, the Void, and it was vital for its use in Shadow scanners.

Also, they'd come a distance of kilometers deep underground to witness the collection of a single drop. No wonder the drug cost so much.

As they traveled back through the mythrin mine, Trimborn told Jas what he'd learned about mythrin from the natives of the planet: that only a particular combination of rare factors, including unusual geological formations and eons-long processes, would result in small amounts of the chemical oozing out of the rock.

"They didn't even know they had mythrin on the planet," he went on. "A couple of geologists who were scouting around found it. They tried to keep the discovery a secret, but the locals soon figured out what they were mining. Booted the geologists off the planet, or possibly ate them. They were vague about that part. Anyway, the local governments weren't slow to exploit the new source of income. Now, according to one Head of Nest anyway, no one living on the planet need ever work again. Except for the miners, of course, and they receive double income."

Trimborn chattered on after Jas had thanked the aliens and said goodbye. He went with her to the shuttle. She barely registered what he was saying, and as she returned to the *Thylacine*, her mind was deeply occupied.

The sight of the mythrin hadn't only caused her to feel wonder. Though it had been five years since the one time she'd experienced the effects of mythranil, her memory of the experience remained strong. Her close proximity to its raw ingredient had created in her a deep desire to use it again.

The feeling of need for the illegal drug, together with her alcoholic binge the previous evening, her constant tiredness, and her inability to consider her future, as if she just didn't care anymore what happened, brought her to another personal truth: she was beginning to fall apart.

EIGHT

When Jas arrived at her office aboard the *Thylacine*, a mail from Pacheco was awaiting her. He was requesting a face-to-face meeting, but this time he would come to her. The time he proposed was soon.

Jas sent her acceptance. The timing wasn't great—she would have preferred longer to prepare her thoughts—but she was glad the admiral had taken her concerns about the Shadow ship seriously. She left a note on the general system to say where she could be found, and waited.

The green motes of the gateway appeared in the air in the corner of her office. When the spiral was swirling strongly, the black-uniformed leg of the admiral appeared, soon followed by the rest of his body. He gave her a nod and took off his hat. Behind him, the gateway disappeared like water running down a plug hole.

"Jas," he said, coming forward.

"Admiral Pacheco," Jas replied. "Thank you for coming. I guess you must be very busy with the battle coming up. Please take a seat." She sat behind her desk. "I take it that this is about my mail? Did any of the other commanders notice anything similar? What do you think about it? Are you going to modify the battle plans?"

Pacheco was putting his hat down and hitching up his trousers before sitting as Jas spoke. He gave her a quizzical look and an embarrassed half smile. He rested his hands on his knees.

"I read your report, Jas, and I agree what you saw is odd, but the battle plan is complex, involving thousands of Unity Alliance ships and hundreds of thousands of personnel. We're too far along to change anything now, even if your observations are correct. What do they mean anyway? That the Shadows have their own ships and very well trained pilots? I'm not sure how that's going to change anything that we should or could do."

"Of course it should affect what we do. If they're building their own ships, we could try to find out their specs. We could gather more intelligence in Shadow-controlled planets. If this is our best chance to defeat them, like you said, shouldn't we make the best preparations we can?"

"Does something make you think we aren't already gathering intelligence on Shadow-controlled planets?" Pacheco asked. "I can tell you we've received no information about them building their own ships. Why would they need to when they can just take their victims'? It takes years to build new ships. Don't forget they only have the knowledge and skills of the people they murder. If they were designing new ships, we would have seen more evidence of it than a couple of vessels in a minor battle. Battleships aren't exactly easy to hide."

"But what if they have?" Jas asked. "The technology I observed on one of the ships was much better than ours. If we go ahead without knowing more, the next battle could be suicide for us."

"If they do have a few starships that are better than ours, the sooner we annihilate them, the better." Pacheco tutted and shook his head. "Jas, you're not getting it. It's too late to do anything now. The countdown's begun and the wheels are turning. A little under three days from now, every available ship in the Unity Alliance fleet will jump into strategically decided coordinates, and the battle will commence. The last battle, I hope."

Her tension deflated with disappointment. She was sure there was something to be learned from what she'd seen, something important and worth acting upon, but it was clear she wouldn't persuade the admiral of it.

"Then," she said with a frown, "why are you here?"

Pacheco picked up his hat and began turning it in his hands. He looked down at it as he seemed to think about how to answer her.

"Let's forget about me being an admiral and you being a commander for a moment, okay?" he said at last. "We go back a long way, Jas, don't we? Do you remember when we first met?"

Her heart sank. So *this* was why he'd come. Couldn't the man take a hint?

"Yes," she replied, "of course I do. You were serving on the *Infineon*, and I'd been sent there in command of a team of defense units. Some of the ship's pilots died rescuing us when our transport was attacked."

Pacheco nodded. "I was quite upset about that. We were short of pilots as it was, and to lose some over a handful of defense units and a single greenhorn, well, it didn't seem worth it. Not that it was your fault."

Jas replied. "I don't think it was my fault either, but I felt bad about those pilots too. And all those who have died since."

"I know you do. I know," Pacheco said softly. His gaze returned to his hat.

She was squirming with embarrassment on the man's behalf, though she didn't know what she could do to avert him from the course he'd set upon.

"When the Shadows in the *Infineon's* crew revealed themselves, and the fight erupted on the bridge," he continued, "and Commander Torbin was killed, you and I were pinned down in one spot together...do you remember?"

"Yes, you got that horrible burn on your side from metal heated by laser fire."

"That wasn't so bad." He paused. "I changed my mind about you during that fight. I saw how hard and how bravely you fought. I knew the effort to save you had been worth it."

She sighed. She wasn't so sure about that.

"And since then," Pacheco said, "we've served together most of the time. How many of us are left who have been in the war since the start, do you think? Not many, I guess."

He gave a huff of frustration and put his hat down on the seat next to him.

Here it comes. Jas looked with sympathy into the man's dark, troubled eyes.

"What I'm trying to say is," Pacheco said, "over the years, I've grown to care about you. Probably more than you think. And I wanted to come here and tell you so because in a few days' time we'll both be involved in something that's going to decide the fate of the galaxy. Who knows if either of us will survive?

"It seemed important that I tell you how I feel," he continued as Jas was wishing she could disappear into the floor. "I guess I'm here to find out if there's anything I can hope for when it's all over. I'm not sure exactly what I mean to you, Jas, but I don't think you feel the same way about me as I do about you. That's what's always stopped me from saying something. But I believe it's wrong to sit on these things forever. So here I am."

He looked up, all the dignity and demeanor of his office and rank stripped away.

Her heart ached for him, but not in the way he clearly hoped. She opened her mouth to speak, but he interrupted her, her expression apparently telling him everything he needed to know.

"It's someone from your past, isn't it," he said heavily. "Someone from before we met. I noticed you've never gotten together with anyone in all this time. I saw how eagerly you scanned your new recruits after I told you an old acquaintance was among them, and how your face fell when you didn't see whoever it was you were hoping to find."

"My private life is my own concern," Jas said quietly.

The admiral's disappointed features became hard and set. He stood and picked up his hat. "So you *are* clinging to the past, like I thought. In that case, you're a fool. You're wasting away your life on a memory when you could be happy. If you would just give someone else a chance, you could be loved. Did you ever consider that?"

Her hands clenching into fists at his attack, Jas also moved to stand but in her haste she banged her knees on her desk. She gave a gasp of pain and sat down again, her hands on her lower thighs. "Krat, Pacheco. Things aren't that simple. I don't get to choose how I feel."

The admiral stepped toward her and stood over her, his black-suited figure shading out the overhead light. "You're living in the past, Jas. Living on dreams." He squatted down, looked up into her eyes, and continued in a more conciliatory tone, "When we win this battle, things will go back to normal. People will return home and pick up the pieces. Build new lives. Start anew. We always worked well together, Jas. You can't deny it. We think alike. We have a good rapport. When all this is over, you and I would make a good team. And I know you don't hate me. If you would just stop shutting me out, we could have something good going for us, don't you think?"

She looked down and didn't answer. She couldn't answer. In some ways, he was right, but so was she when she'd said she didn't have a choice about how she felt.

He gave a sigh of exasperation and stood up. "So that's it, is it? We go into battle with no hope for a future? You're content with that? What's the point then? Who is it you're fighting for?"

Still, she had no words of reply, but the response that popped into her mind was, *not me.*

NINE

The pilots had assembled in the launch bay as Jas had requested prior to what she hoped would be the final battle. The old hands would know what was coming, but she made them attend anyway. Her words were just as important however often they heard them.

She always spoke to the pilots on the eve of every battle. Though it tortured her to look into the eyes of the men and women standing before her, knowing that many of them would be dead within a few short hours, she felt they were owed this personal address. It was the very least someone like her, who would be within relative safety behind the force field and heavy hull plating of a starship, could do.

They deserved acknowledgment of the risk they were taking, and for many, of the sacrifice they would make, so that others could live in peace and safety.

For Jas, it meant more than that. She forced herself to look into the eyes of the people she was effectively sending out to die because she didn't want to become hardened to their fate. She wanted to be sure those women and men were real to her, so she would never deploy them unless it was absolutely necessary.

The pilots were dressed in their flight suits and standing to attention. The fresh recruits' uniforms were new and colored a deep, rich gray. Older pilots were identifiable by their lighter gray suits, faded a little with time.

"At ease, pilots," Jas said. "This won't take long." She put her hands in her pockets. "As you know, tomorrow we begin a new battle. I can't emphasize to you enough how important it is that you have one hundred percent confidence in your ships. Before you go to bed tonight, I want each and every one of you to be absolutely certain that your ship and all your equipment is in perfect working order."

Her comm button bleeped, but she ignored it.

"If you're uncertain about anything, or if you want to run another diagnostic, ask a technician. If any of them complain they're too busy or not on duty, report them to me. Have you got that?" She stopped her pacing and glared at the pilots, who gave a few hesitant replies of *Yes, Commander.*

Her comm button bleeped again.

"*Krat it*," she muttered under her breath. Lifting the button to her lips, she barked, "What?"

It was Trimborn. "Commander, Navigator Curlio's violently ill. I've sent her to the sick bay."

"What?" Jas repeated. "What's wrong with her?"

"I don't know, ma'am. She keeled over at her station. She's running a fever and delirious. The doctor's assessing her at the moment."

Jas hoped the woman's illness wasn't serious and that, whatever it was, it wasn't contagious. The ship's crew coming down with a virus just before going into battle was the last thing she needed. As it was, the best-case scenario was her navigator would be out of commission for the next few, crucial, hours.

She ran through her mental list of the ship's company, trying to think of a replacement. She didn't know of anyone aboard with recent experience of navigating a destroyer, and when she asked Trimborn, neither did he. They could use someone who had out-of-practice navigation skills, but there might still be time to find a better solution.

"Direct comm Admiral Pacheco, Trimborn," Jas said, "and explain the situation. Maybe someone's available who can replace Curlio at short notice."

"Yes, ma'am."

She closed her eyes for a moment to refocus on her speech to the pilots.

"You've got the hardest, most dangerous job of all to do tomorrow," she continued. "I'm sure you realize that, but you're still here, and that says a lot. You chose to join this war, and you chose the riskiest way to serve. Every one of you standing in this bay is already a hero. I want you to understand that I and everyone else aboard this ship knows it and we appreciate what you're doing.

"I also want to thank you, now, for your service, and to tell you that I will do everything in my power to bring every single one of you home again to your families and loved ones. Good luck, everyone. Dismissed."

At her command, the pilots broke formation. Some began to walk away, but a few came over to her. The first held out his hand. He was a short, slightly tubby man with silvered stubble. He was wearing the fresh uniform of a recruit, yet he looked too old to enlist. Jas guessed the recruiting officers made exceptions for those with flying experience.

She shook the man's hand. The woman who was with him also held out her hand, and the next pilot, and the next. The ones who were leaving noticed what was happening, and they came back to also shake her hand.

She was so moved, she couldn't speak. Her lips drawn to a thin line, she shook each pilot's hand. When they were all done, she waited where she was and watched the courageous women and men leave the launch bay. She hoped they would spend the next few hours as well as they could before they began the fight of their lives.

TEN

Sayen Lee was deep in concentration when her comm sounded. She was sitting at her cabin's interface screen manually calculating starjumps. It was an old habit from the days when she worked aboard prospecting starships. The mental exercise calmed her and distracted her from excessive worrying about her brother, Phelan, who was heavily involved in rooting out the remaining Shadows on Earth.

She'd been figuratively kicking her heels aboard the *Camaradon* for the last two weeks, and she'd gotten increasingly bored. Admiral Pacheco had assigned her the role of second navigator after the frigate she'd served aboard last had been incapacitated in a skirmish. But the *Camaradon's* first navigator was entirely competent at his job as well as irritated by her hanging around. Effectively, she had krat all to do.

"Navigator Lee," came the admiral's voice over her comm. "You're being reassigned. Get ready to ship out. You'll be leaving by gateway in thirty minutes."

"Yes, sir," Sayen replied. "Permission to ask where I'm going, Admiral?"

"The *Thylacine*. Their navigator's taken ill and they don't have a suitable replacement."

"Thank you, sir," exclaimed Sayen, but the admiral had already broken the connection.

The *Thylacine* was Jas's command. Sayen was sure that was what she'd heard. Throughout the Shadow War personal comms had been strictly forbidden for security reasons. The risk of vital information leaking out was too high. As a result, Sayen hadn't sent or received a word from her friend for five years. It had only been when Jas's rapid rise to the rank of commander became a topic of gossip that Sayen had known she was still alive.

And now, after all this time, she would see her again.

It took Sayen only ten minutes to prepare to leave. It didn't take long to pack when all your belongings were neatly arranged in drawers and your cabin was already spotless and tidy. She shouldered her regulation duffle bag and trotted through the ship to the gateway door.

She knew the destination well. It had been at the same gateway door that Sayen had arrived aboard the *Camaradon* when she'd signed up to fight all those years ago. She recalled the massive bay holding the huge military transports and the crowds of volunteers of all species who were flooding in to join what everyone had seemed to think would be a short fight.

She and Jas had been assigned to different vessels, and her last glimpse of her tall, Martian friend had been as she left to command a team of defense units. Jas had been upset that her sweetheart, Carl, had volunteered before them. Sayen also hadn't seen Carl for five years. She hoped that he and Jas had met again in the intervening time.

She navigated the *Camaradon's* passageways with ease. To give herself something to do during her enforced break from work, she'd explored the battleship from top to bottom. It was an impressive vessel, nearly a kilometer long. Its size meant that it required two sets of starjump engines, and they were positioned to each side of the central working and living areas. The largest pulse cannons were fixed onto the engines to better utilize their energy generation capabilities if the ship's stored power ran low. During a space battle, the

Camaradon could continue firing long after lesser vessels had exhausted their power.

Sayen arrived at the gateway entrance. The alien guard in charge scanned her embedded chip and said, "You're early, but you can go now if you want."

Sayen nodded, excited at the thought of being reunited with her old friend. They'd been through so much together.

The guard started up the gateway. It was only the second time Sayen had traveled via the Transgalactic Council's classified technology, usually reserved only for high-ranking individuals on urgent business. At the guard's signal, she stepped into the mist and out into the reception area of the *Thylacine*.

She'd half-expected Jas to meet her, but there was only a young first officer who introduced himself as Trimborn. She guessed Jas didn't know who Pacheco had sent as a replacement navigator.

"Boy am I glad to see you," Trimborn said. "We were waiting all night for the admiral to send us a replacement navigator. I guess he's busy preparing for the battle. I'll show you to your cabin. After you drop off your stuff, I'll take you directly to the bridge. We don't have long before we go into battle, and I'm sure you'll want to familiarize yourself with the *Thylacine's* controls."

"I would, thanks," Sayen replied.

She matched the officer's quick pace as they did as he'd said. As they went along, she took in the attitude of the crew and the general state of the ship. Everyone seemed to know what they were doing, and there was no slouching about or time wasting. All seemed in good order. The *Thylacine* was shipshape and ready for battle. But then Sayen expected no less with Jas in command.

She thought she'd have a little fun with the first officer.

"Hey, Trimborn," she said, "would I be out of line to ask what Commander Harrington's like? I heard she has quite a reputation."

The first officer twisted his lips in a slight grimace as he considered his answer. "Let me put it like this: the commander's a bit of a dragon, truth be told, but the crew have a helluva lot of respect for her. Some commanders I've served under seemed to think of losing crew as unfortunate but necessary collateral damage, but not Harrington. You know that when it comes down to it, she's got your back, if you know what I mean."

"Yeah, I know what you mean," Sayen replied. "I think so too."

"Wait a minute," Trimborn said, "I thought you hadn't served under her."

"I haven't, but I know her from way back before the War started."

Trimborn sucked air between his teeth and looked at her from the corners of his eyes. "I guess I'm lucky I didn't say anything worse. Is what I said going to get back to her?"

"Don't worry. Commander Harrington wouldn't give a damn whether anyone thought she was a dragon. She might even take it as a compliment."

She put her duffle bag on the bunk in her new cabin and followed the first officer to the bridge. The bridge doors parted, and Sayen stepped through into the familiar setting. Over the years, she'd served aboard several Unity ships. The sight that interested her was the figure sitting in the commander's seat with her back toward her.

Sayen would have recognized Jas's tall figure and short, reddish-brown brown hair anywhere.

"Commander," Trimborn said, "our replacement navigator has arrived."

"Good," Jas replied without looking around. "Take your seat, Navigator. We're running through pre-engagement checks."

"Yes, Commander," Sayen replied with a smile. She went to the empty navigator's station and sat down. With a sweep of her hand, she activated her interface and bent over it, wondering how long it would take for the penny to drop.

When she glanced in Jas's direction, she saw her friend staring at her, the light of realization dawning on her face. Her mouth opened then shut abruptly as she appeared to remember where she was.

For the next hour, Sayen and the rest of the officers on the bridge ran through the battle prep, testing and retesting their controls. Jas led them through it, her demeanor calm. Occasionally, her and

Sayen's gazes would meet briefly, but they stayed in their professional roles while the process was completed.

"Thanks, everyone," Jas said finally. "Please remain at your stations while we await the order to jump. Shouldn't be long now. Navigator Lee, I'd like to speak with you for a moment."

Sayen got up to follow Jas out of the bridge, but her pleasure at meeting her friend again was tinged with concern.

While the officers had been carrying out the checks, she'd had time to see how much Jas had changed. When Sayen had known her, she'd exuded vitality and strength. But her impression of her old friend this time around had shocked her. Jas was thin, and she'd lost her previously firm, well-muscled physique. What was more, stress and exhaustion were written into her features. She looked like she hadn't slept properly in days.

Worse than all this was something else, something that underlay all of the other signs of a long-serving, overworked Unity commander. What jumped out at Sayen about Jas was that she seemed to be living with a deep sadness.

ELEVEN

As soon as they reached a passageway that was empty, Jas grabbed Sayen into a hug. She was half-tempted to lift the petite woman off of her feet and swing her around, but she guessed that Sayen might find that undignified.

As she let go of her, she exclaimed, "When Pacheco said he was sending me another navigator, I didn't guess for a second it would be you. Where have you been all this time? What have you been doing? Ough." She let out a gasp of frustration. "Why does it have to be now, right before a battle, that we get to see each other again? I wish we had more time to talk."

"Me too," Sayen replied. "But forget what I've been doing, what have *you* been doing? You're a commander now. That's amazing."

Jas made a self-deprecating *meh*. "I had inside help, I think. Look at you, though. You haven't changed a bit. You look exactly the same as you did five years ago."

"That's no surprise," Sayen replied. "The doctors who created my enhanced skin told me it doesn't age, so I'm gonna look like this until I die."

A crew member appeared around a bend in the corridor, and both women became silent. Jas had hunched over to talk quietly to her short friend, but at the sight of the man she drew herself up. As soon as he had passed them and disappeared around the next bend, she returned to her former position.

"Guess what," she said, "Toirien MacAdam's aboard too. Do you remember her? She was the only engineer aboard the *Galathea* who survived the Shadow attack and the crash."

Sayen said, "Yeah, I remember hearing about her. How's she doing?"

Jas briefly filled her in on Toirien's life story since she'd returned to Earth. "It seems weird that the three of us should come together again just before this final battle. There's even an old defense unit from the *Galathea* aboard." She looked pensive.

"The final battle?" Sayen asked, her eyes wide.

"Krat," Jas said. "I was forgetting you didn't know. I'm not supposed to tell the crew, but yeah, this next engagement is the final push. We've got them on the run, Sayen. We're almost there. The remaining Shadow force is confined to one small sector of the galaxy. We've wiped them out everywhere else, and if we can defeat their last ships now, the war's over for them. We'll have to do some mopping up, but that'll basically be it. Every Unity Alliance ship in service is being deployed. The *Camaradon's* leading the fight."

Jas's comm bleeped. It was Pacheco. "Commander Harrington, prepare to starjump at thirteen hundred and fifty."

"Affirmative, Admiral," Jas replied. They had a little under half an hour. As always before an engagement with the enemy, Jas's heart began to race, but it had already been beating fast while she'd been talking to Sayen, and not only because she was excited to see her old friend again.

"How's Phelan?" she asked, skirting around the question she was burning but also fearing to ask.

"He's okay," Sayen replied. "Busy finding the remaining few Shadows on Earth. That was the last I heard from a recruit who'd heard of him. It's hard to keep track of what's happening when no comms are allowed. I hate having no contact with him."

"And Erielle?"

Sayen heaved a deep, sad sigh. "Erielle died not long after she returned to Earth with Makey."

"Oh krat, Sayen. I'm so sorry."

"Thanks. I found out a couple of years ago when I was allowed a short trip home. She died not long after she got back. It was Shadows among her underworlders. An inside job, not an open fight." Sayen's shoulders were sagging, but she straightened up as she added, "But Makey's doing well. He survived the fight for the control of Earth, and now he heads some kind of underworlders' council, negotiating for the rights of naturals."

"That's good to hear," Jas said. "Good for him. He was always a special kid."

"Yeah, he was."

After a slight pause, Jas finally found the courage to ask about their other mutual friend, but as she spoke, so did Sayen.

"Have you seen—" Jas asked at the same time that Sayen also asked,

"Do you know what—"

They both stopped speaking. Jas realized what Sayen's question meant.

"You mean you don't know what's happened to Carl?" she asked.

Sayen shook her head. "I haven't seen him since Ganymede Outpost. Have you?"

"No," Jas replied. "Not once."

"Jas, I'm really sorry."

She swallowed. "I guess that's it, then. He couldn't have survived all this time."

Sayen touched her arm. "You don't know that. Have you searched the personnel records?"

"I don't have security access, and the records are all over the place anyway. He's gone, Sayen. He has to be dead."

"Don't give up hope. Not while there's still a chance."

"He's a pilot, Sayen. Do you know of a pilot who's been around since the beginning of the war? What are the chances that he's still alive?"

Sayen looked down and gave a slight shake of her head. "I don't know what to say. I can't believe it. I thought you'd tell me that you'd seen him."

"And I guess you were my last hope." Jas continued to herself, "Pacheco was right."

"What do you mean?" Sayen asked.

"Just something the admiral said." She heaved a large sigh. "We don't have long before we jump. Let's go back to the bridge."

TWELVE

Admiral Pacheco adjusted the collar of his uniform and placed his arms gently on his arm rests. As he surveyed the officers at their consoles on the bridge of the *Camaradon*, his body thrummed with tension. He was careful not to let it show, however. During his long career serving with the Unity, he'd learned that a crew took their cue from whoever was in charge—commander, captain, or admiral. If he wanted his women and men to feel confident, confidence was what he had to exude.

Not that he wasn't confident. Though it had taken five years to get to this point, the Unity Alliance had been successful in slowly gaining ground and destroying their enemy, forcing them into this corner of the galaxy. In the forthcoming battle, the UA had every chance of delivering the final, crushing blow.

He wasn't tense because he thought they were in danger of losing. It was because he was responsible for the maneuvers of more than sixty starships as they battled the Shadows.

It was the largest number of ships that had been under his command all at once, and it would take every ounce of concentration and skill to do his job. The battleground was vast. He was only one of many peers performing the same role across the sector. In all, the

Unity Alliance had amassed more than one thousand starships to fight this final battle.

Save for a few frigates busy stamping out flares of Shadow resurgence on distant worlds, the entire Unity fleet was present. But the Unity ships numbered only in the hundreds. The rest of the force was made up of Alliance vessels and crews from across all of galactic civilization. The many and varied alien species from high- and low-g planets, water worlds, ice giants, desert orbs, and the other multitude of homes to sentient life scattered across the galaxy, had come together to defeat their common enemy.

It was a coordinated effort that would be remembered for thousands of years to come, providing they won the day. And they would. Pacheco was sure of it.

After the battle, he planned to leave the service. Too long a career space officer, he was tired of fighting. If only Jas Harrington's affections didn't lie with some probably long-dead lover from her past, he pondered. He wasn't a man to form frivolous connections. His feelings toward the Martian had grown over the years that they'd worked together aboard his first command ship.

Their first encounter had been rocky but, as time went on, he'd learned to appreciate her steady, effective approach to her work as well as her personal integrity. Before long, he'd realized he was giving her responsibilities much above her rank because he knew with certainty he could always rely on her.

When career progressions meant they'd parted ways, he'd soon missed her presence on a professional level and, in the quiet of his bunk at night, he'd realized he also missed *her*. He wished she could reciprocate his feelings. He wanted to relieve that constant melancholic look she always wore. He wanted to make her happy.

Pacheco shifted in his seat and checked the time. Fifteen minutes before his fleet was scheduled to jump to their designated positions and attack the Shadow ships known to be hiding out at certain coordinates. The *Camaradon* was going to engage with the leading ship. Everything was in place. The battle plan was laid out. All they had to do was follow it. What would happen afterward, Pacheco wasn't sure. Perhaps he shouldn't give up hope of winning Jas over just yet.

The doors opened, and Fleet Admiral Tarsa entered the bridge. A Haidiren, she was encased in her water-holding suit, her grass-green head poking from the top into a transparent, globe helmet. Pacheco and his officers stood to attention and saluted.

The alien's v-shaped lips quivered, which her translator related as, "Admiral Pacheco, I came in person to wish you and your officers good fortune in the forthcoming engagement."

"Thank you, Fleet Admiral," Pacheco replied.

"Your planning has been meticulous. We have every chance of success. I am now withdrawing to my private rooms to oversee the battle as a whole. If I have instructions for you, or if you wish to consult me, we will use the ship's comm."

"Very good, Fleet Admiral," said Pacheco.

"Good luck, everyone," Tarsa said to the bridge generally. "You couldn't wish for a better leader than Admiral Pacheco here. I leave you in his capable hands."

As the Fleet Admiral left, his officers returned their attention to their consoles and Pacheco took his seat again. They had ten minutes. He checked with his first officer that he was ready to bring up a holo of the battleground the second that they jumped.

"Yes, Admiral," came the reply, with a slight hurt tone underlying it.

Pacheco tutted softly over his officer's response. Some people were over-sensitive. Of course, the man knew his job, and Pacheco hadn't meant to imply that he didn't. He tapped his armrests, his fingernails hitting the interface screens. Time seemed to slow down.

Five minutes.

"Prepare to engage jump engines, Pilot," Pacheco said.

"Yes, Admiral," came the woman's reply.

"Power up pulse cannons," said Pacheco to the weapons officer.

His neck ached with tension. He rubbed it. He breathed in deeply before exhaling long and slow. "Ready, everyone."

The seconds ticked away on his interface display. The air seemed syrupy and hard to breathe. The stress in the room pressed down.

The battle that could unlock a future of peace for galactic civilization was about to begin.

Pacheco's display read zero.

"Jump."

Thirteen

The *Thylacine* was ready to starjump across the galaxy to the remaining Shadow-controlled region. As she sat on the ship's bridge for the countdown to the jump, Jas was reminded of the fact that the ship would pass momentarily through the Void on its journey. She had learned that fact during her myth run at Ganymede Station. The Paths had told her that glimpses of the starships of the physical universe dipping into the Void while they starjumped had enticed the Shadows to devise a method to cross the barrier and find out more about this plane that was new to them.

Up until then, no one had known or even guessed the Shadows' motivation for their invasion, but the knowledge didn't seem to matter. It wasn't as if the sentient species of the galaxy could give up using starjump technology. Traveling the vast distances across space would be impossible without it. The energy required to power trans-galactic gateways was so great that transporting large numbers of people or large amounts of goods wasn't economically viable. Jas wondered if traveling via gateway also meant stepping briefly into the Void.

It was unfortunate that the jump drive had resulted in enticing the Shadows to enter the galaxy, but she had no compassion or sympathy for the creatures. They were responsible for the deaths of millions, and one man in particular whose loss she would never recover from. She could never forgive what the Shadows had done, and she relished this opportunity to grind them to dust beneath her heel.

They jumped.

Starjumping such a large distance always left everyone disoriented for a moment. Jas blinked as the bridge came into focus around her.

A holo popped up. As Pacheco had told her, a large Shadow ship was in the vicinity. It was bigger than the *Thylacine,* but they had the element of surprise. With a grim smile, Jas imagined the reactions of the Shadow captain and his crew when they registered the *Thylacine's* presence, heavily armed and force field up.

"Pulse cannons at the ready," Jas said. "Fire."

A battery of pulses flew from the *Thylacine's* cannons, arcing across space, toward the Shadow ship. The first arrived before the ship's force field was fully employed, and the holo displayed a satisfying splash of light directly across its hull. The following pulses hit soon after, spreading out across the force field and dissipating into space.

"Second degree hull damage on the enemy ship, Commander," Trimborn said, his gaze intent on his console.

Score one to the *Thylacine.* The following battle might be long and hard until they finally subdued the enemy vessel, but they already had an advantage.

The return pulses weren't slow in coming, but the *Thylacine's* force field shrugged them off.

Jas leaned forward in her seat to look at the holo of the Shadow ship more closely. "Trimborn, is that a—"

"Class three destroyer, ma'am," the first officer replied. "Unity ship."

He looked up from his screen to give her a wry smile. Class three destroyers had been phased out of production because they had a notorious weakness: their new model, RaptorY engines were prone to exploding if the surrounding hull were breached, and the explosion would take out the entire ship.

Jas's face registered grim satisfaction. "Kennewell, take us aft of that ship."

"Yes, Commander."

The pilot fired the *Thylacine's* more trustworthy RaptorXs, and maneuvered the vessel on a course to bring them behind the Shadow ship.

The Shadow in command seemed to guess their intent, for the enemy ship began to swing around in response to the *Thylacine's* maneuver.

"Ha," Jas said, slapping her knee. "Looks like we're in for a game of cat and mouse. Kennewell, get us behind that ship, whatever it takes. Trimborn, maintain full pulse barrage." While it was under sustained attack, the ship wouldn't be able to build the power to jump.

Abrupt acceleration crushed Jas into her seat as Kennewell powered the *Thylacine* on a vertical trajectory. The officers who were standing bent at the knees and gripped their consoles. A violent lurch of the ship threw everyone to the right as the holo displayed their rapidly moving vessel speeding closer to the Shadow ship.

"There it goes," Trimborn said, remarking on the Shadow ship's rapid descent, almost off the display.

"I'm after it," Kennewell said, and Jas was airborne for a moment as the *Thylacine* plunged toward the enemy vessel. Bolts of light were passing between the two ships as pulse after pulse shot out of them.

"Force field eighty percent," Trimborn said. The *Thylacine's* power reserves were beginning to drain. Jas bit her lip. If they could last longer than the enemy vessel, they'd win in the end, providing—

"Ah, krat," Jas said, forgetting her dignity as a commander for a moment as sparks of light flowed from the Shadow ship. The enemy hadn't been slow in deploying its fighter ships. And it appeared to have over a hundred of them.

"Direct pulses at those ships, Trimborn," Jas said, hoping to take out enough to force them to retreat.

The *Thylacine's* pulses changed direction and began cutting through the cloud of fighters. But the pulses could only take out a handful at a time before disappearing into space. Meanwhile, the enemy ship's pulses rained down on the *Thylacine*. The force field was holding for the time being, but the ship shuddered and shook as the pulses impacted.

"Force field forty-six percent," Trimborn said.

Kennewell was doing her utmost to bring the *Thylacine* to the rear of the Shadow ship, but the enemy also clearly had a pilot who was excellent at playing the mouse.

"Force field thirty-five percent," said Trimborn.

With a heavy heart, Jas spoke into her comm, "Squadron Leader, scramble all fighters." Lifting her head, she said, "Trimborn, return pulse fire to the enemy ship."

Pulses wouldn't stop the enemy's fighter ships, and no matter how fast Kennewell piloted the *Thylacine*, the large ship was no match for their speed or maneuverability. They would soon be close enough to fire at her.

The *Thylacine's* fighters erupted from her launch bay. A collective gasp sounded on the bridge as a pulse from the Shadow ship cut a swathe through its own fighter ships, destroying the sparks like a jet of water on a fire. The Shadows were killing their own pilots to target the *Thylacine's*.

Sayen turned a white, stricken face to Jas.

"Looks like they're prepared to do anything to win this battle," Jas said grimly.

The Shadow fighter ships were drawing nearer, and the *Thylacine's* moved to engage with them. Another pulse flew from the Shadow ship, wiping out not only Shadow fighter ships, but the *Thylacine's* too.

"What the krat are they doing?" Trimborn burst out. "What's the point of sending out fighters just to destroy them?"

"As long as a few get through," Jas said, "and none of ours

survive, they could cause us some serious damage. And if we go after the fighters directly, that prevents us from targeting their ship."

She bit the side of her thumb and stared at the holo.

She barked, "Kennewell, for krat's sake, get us below that ship." The *Thylacine* would draw some of the Shadow ship's fire. But as they moved, the Shadow's faster fighter planes were right on their tail.

"Commander," Sayen said. "What if we jump?"

Jump? They couldn't do that. It would mean leaving their fighters behind in the hands of the enemy. Unless she meant...

"Can we do that, S—Navigator?" Jas asked.

"It'll be close," Sayen replied, "but as long as our fighters stay at the fore, they should be protected."

"Do it," Jas said. "Trimborn, cut pulses. We're going to jump."

"Jump, ma'am?" the first officer asked.

"Jump engines powering, Commander," Kennewell said.

Sayen bent over her interface, rapidly calculating the jump.

"Prepare for full pulse barrage the second we jump," Jas said. "No force field."

Kennewell was watching Sayen, waiting for the coordinates. Without lifting her head, Sayen raised a hand and pointed at the pilot.

But she shook her head. "Still waiting on the engines."

Without their pulses targeting those incoming from the Shadows, the *Thylacine* was taking a brutal beating once more. On the holo, their ship was a ball of light as the pulses spread out across her force field. The Shadow fighters had also broken through the defense laid down by the *Thylacine's* pilots.

"Force field eighteen percent," Trimborn said. "Damage to hull, port, and starboard."

Jas prayed her squadron leader would notice the *Thylacine* was building to a jump and guess her intention. Her gaze was fixed on those tiny flecks of light that represented the lives of more than eighty women and men. If their fighters were too close when they jumped, they would be killed. One or two lingered in the unsafe zone. *Come on. Move.*

"Force field seven percent."

"Get out of the way," Jas exclaimed, hitting her arm rest.

As if in response, the *Thylacine's* fighter ships that were in danger began to peel away, fleeing the vicinity like fish escaping a shark's mouth.

"Jumping in fifteen seconds," Kennewell said.

The officers dropped into their seats and fastened their harnesses.

"Five seconds," said Kennewell.

"Remember that barrage, Trimborn," Jas said. "Don't waste time on the force field."

"Yes, ma'am," the first officer said, and then they jumped.

The *Thylacine* reappeared less than a heartbeat later right behind the Shadow ship. Trimborn unleashed the full might of her pulse cannons on one spot—the site of the RaptorY engines. The Shadow ship's force field was still strong, but not strong enough to protect the ship from the concentrated power of the *Thylacine*. The captain also took too long to realize what was happening.

A single pulse sped from the enemy ship in their direction before its force field collapsed. The *Thylacine's* next attack penetrated the hull, hitting both RaptorY engines. As soon as the breach appeared, without waiting for the order, Kennewell pulled the *Thylacine* violently away, throwing everyone on the bridge forward.

Another pulse from the Shadow ship and the blast of its explosion hit the *Thylacine*, throwing it backward even faster. Kennewell didn't slow the ship down until they were safely beyond the explosion zone.

"Hull breach," Trimborn said. "Losing atmosphere decks two and three. And we're on fire."

They'd sustained some damage, but they'd done it. The Shadow ship was nothing but scattered debris.

"Direct comm to Admiral Pacheco," Jas said.

The comm officer pressed his console and spoke into his mic. He nodded and took off his earpiece before holding it out to Jas. She strode over, held the earpiece to one ear and spoke into the mic.

"Mission successful, Admiral. The Shadow ship's destroyed."

"Then get over here," came Pacheco's reply. "The *Camaradon* needs you."

FOURTEEN

The *Thylacine's* engines began building to starjump again. Jas spoke to the repair crews who were sealing the hull breech, telling them they had three minutes to get everyone behind sealed bulkheads. As she spoke, her eyes were on the holo. The surviving fighter pilots were streaming back to the safety of the *Thylacine's* launch bay, though the remaining Shadow fighters were engaging them in dog fights.

With their mother ship gone, they were as good as dead. They had nothing to lose. And if Jas left without them, her fighters were in nearly the same predicament, though if the *Thylacine* made it through, they would return to search for them.

Sayen was busy calculating their next jump from the coordinates given by the *Camaradon*. Jas wondered what the problem was. The Unity's fleet ship had never been beaten in battle. She had never even had her hull breached, as far as Jas was aware. And Pacheco knew what he was doing when it came to space battles. Maybe their intelligence had underestimated the enemy's firepower.

"Trimborn," Jas said, "what power capacity are we at?"

"After this jump," he replied, "I estimate seventy-three percent."

Not too bad, but not great either. Not for entering another

intense engagement. Pacheco knew that, yet he'd still asked them to come. Things had to be bad.

"Sending coordinates," Sayen said.

"Got them," said Kennewell. "Engine three minutes from jump, Commander."

Jas gripped her arm rests and stared down at the list of pilots' names ever present on her screen. The dots were missing from a large percentage, and as she watched, one of the lights wavered and went out. Looking up at the holo, she saw the fighter vessels approaching, dogged by fire from the Shadow fighters.

"Trimborn," she said, "can you aim a pulse at those Shadow vessels without risking hitting our own ships?"

He frowned over his console for a moment before replying, "Yes, ma'am."

"It will delay our jump a few seconds, Commander," the comm officer said.

Kennewell scowled at him.

"I'm aware of that," said Jas. "Do it." She watched as the short pulse from the *Thylacine* obliterated the tail end of the Shadow fighters. The *Thylacine's* fighters were already arriving at the ship and entering the launch bay. The remaining pilots fought off the Shadows still chasing them.

"Jumping in one minute," Kennewell said.

Their fighters were going to make it. Jas checked with the repair crew that everyone was in a place of safety, and she told the rest of the ship to get to their jumpseats. She comm'd the Squadron Leader to tell his pilots to remain aboard their vessels for the jump.

Jas leaned back in her seat and passed a hand over her eyes. The adrenaline from the battle was fading, leaving behind a deep fatigue. She felt like she could sleep for a month. *Just one last effort,* she told herself. Just one last fight, then it would all be over. Sayen could return to Earth and her brother, Toirien could be reunited with her daughters, and Pacheco could find someone else to moon over.

What she would do, she didn't know, but neither did she care.

"Here we go," Kennewell said, and Jas felt the familiar falling sensation.

"Krat, would you look at that," exclaimed Trimborn as the holo of the battle scene flickered to life.

The *Thylacine* had appeared to one side of a flurry of pulse fire. Pacheco had brought them right into battle, and it soon became obvious why. The *Camaradon* was under severe attack.

Jas's heart froze at the sight. A mere few hundred thousand kilometers from the *Camaradon* was a ship bigger than any she'd ever seen. It dwarfed the massive Unity ship like a planet did a moon. The ship's make was also entirely unfamiliar.

Her mind flew back to the *Thylacine's* battle with the unfamiliar Shadow ships. The Shadows *had* been building their own ships. They'd moved on from using their victims' knowledge and skills and begun to innovate and create. Had the ships Jas encountered been mere test vessels for the technology of this new, gargantuan ship?

"Attack that ship," she shouted, leaping out of her seat. "Full pulses."

Her hand rose to her mouth. Had they been tricked? Had the entire battle been the Shadows' idea? Had the *Camaradon* and the other Unity Alliance vessels been lured into a trap?

Her eyes rose to the holo of the Shadow ship that overhung the bridge. She scanned the vessel for any familiarities—sensor arrays, drive assemblies, cannons—anything that could give her a handle on what they were dealing with. But the ship was a mystery to her. Even its firepower was different. A long stream of energy burst from it, not the familiar bolts of pulses.

The *Camaradon* was being raked by this raw firepower, and its own barrage of pulses were being trapped and eradicated by the wavering energy beam before they could even hit the Shadow ship.

As they watched, more Unity Alliance ships blinked into existence, called to the *Camaradon's* aid, yet they looked like fleas hopping around a dog.

The *Thylacine's* pulses attracted the attention of the energy beam. It flicked toward them, and the pulses were gone. The familiar burst and dissipation of charged particles was missing, however. Had the beam absorbed the energy? Were the *Camaradon's* pulses being converted and returned to it as firepower?

"Stop firing all pulses," Jas said. "Comm the Admiral."

"I can't, ma'am," the comm officer said. "Our comms are being scrambled. Everything that leaves or enters our system."

Krat. Jas got up and went over to the holo. The behemoth Shadow ship dominated the display but Unity Alliance ships surrounded it on all sides. The number of ships indicated that the UA had been successful in most of their individual battles, but that wouldn't mean anything if they lost the *Camaradon.*

The Shadow ship was bigger and the Shadow's technology was better, but the UA had to win this fight. If they didn't the enemy would begin to push back, retaking the planets that had been cleaned of their presence, infiltrating new worlds. All the battles of the previous five years, all the lives that had been lost would have been for nothing.

But how could they defeat the Shadow's devastating ray?

As Jas watched the holo, tiny sparks began to stream from the belly of the *Camaradon.* Pacheco had launched his fighter ships, sending individual women and men in their tiny craft against that terrifying beam of light that was possibly being fed by pulses from the UA side.

But Pacheco had the right idea. If pulses couldn't break through the Shadow ship's defenses, the only chance the UA had of destroying the ship was the force field-penetrating, low-energy fire of the fighters. If they could wreck whatever it was that was creating that ray, the *Camaradon* and the UA still stood a chance.

Jas and everyone else on the bridge held their breath as the tiny sparks representing the brave *Camaradon* pilots neared the Shadow ship. The enemy's beam was still flickering over the battleship like electricity in a Van de Graff generator. Jas desperately hoped that the fighters would escape the beam, but as the sparks swooped nearer, forks of light split from the ray and took out the leading ships.

The remaining fighters took evasive action, diverting from a direct course toward the Shadow ship and splitting into different flight paths. But no matter what course the pilots took, the beam seemed to sense their presence, sending out long trails of light that split from the central ray.

All around the bridge something between a gasp and a groan sounded. It was a massacre. The pilots were going like lambs to the slaughter. They couldn't evade the dreadful ray, and they couldn't get close enough to the Shadow ship to employ their firepower.

There was nothing, nothing anyone could do to protect them or fight back.

Suddenly, the Shadow's beam broke through the *Camaradon*'s force field and hit the hull around one of its starjump engines. Jas's chest constricted. If the ray broke through the hull, the ship would be incapacitated, unable to jump. If it couldn't escape, it would be destroyed, along with the two thousand or more lives aboard.

Jump, for krat's sake. Jump. Yet she knew jumping was impossible for the *Camaradon* now. Her hands were fists.

"What should we do, ma'am?" Trimborn asked. His tone caused Jas to turn to look at him. The man's usually sanguine expression had turned to fear. He was reading the next steps of the battle the same as she was.

The *Camaradon* was halfway to being lost. Pacheco had been expending all the ship's power on pulses and her force field. He couldn't afford to drop what remained of the force field either, or it would mean immediate annihilation. It would take ages for the ship to build the power to jump, and meanwhile the Shadow's beam was targeting the very engines that might save it.

Jas wouldn't fire at the Shadow ship—that only seemed to help it. There was nothing they could do. Her first responsibility was to her crew.

"Kennewell, prepare to jump."

"Yes, Commander."

"Jas," Sayen exclaimed, her face stricken, but there was no time to explain.

It would take several minutes for the *Thylacine* to generate jump power. When the engines were at maximum capacity, they could remain in that state for several more minutes. At the current state of the battle, that should be long enough to do something to help if the opportunity arose. Though the longer they waited before expending the massive amounts of energy, the more danger they were in of simply exploding.

"Navigator," Jas said, "plot a course for as far away from here as we can go."

Sayen nodded, understanding that Jas was going to wait until the last possible second before they jumped, requiring the *Thylacine's* engines to top out their power.

How long would it take before Pacheco realized the battle was already over?

"Open launch bay doors," Jas said, then spoke into her comm. "Squadron Leader, maneuver all fighter ships to the back of the launch bay. Prepare to receive survivors."

"Yes, ma'am." The man's tone was relieved.

Trimborn's sharp intake of breath caused her to look up. Light flared blindingly from the holo of the *Camaradon*. The Shadows' beam had broken through the hull of one of its jump engines and released the energy Pacheco had been building to jump.

That was it. He had to abandon ship now. Around the holo of the Shadow ship, UA vessels began to wink out of existence, their captains and commanders retreating before the dreadful ray was turned on them.

Come on, Pacheco. Save your crew.

If only the Shadow ship wasn't scrambling their comms, Jas could have ordered the remaining *Camaradon* fighters to retreat to the *Thylacine*. Some were returning to their stricken ship, some were continuing to brave the terrifying ray. Jas wished they'd see sense and give up their hopeless attack.

Pacheco, come on.

"Ready to jump, Commander," Kennewell said.

Jas's gaze frantically searched the belly of the *Camaradon*. Any evacuees needed to leave immediately if they were to reach the

Thylacine before she would have to jump. She exhaled. A few specks had appeared. Fighters that Pacheco must have told to turn around when they arrived. They headed in the direction of UA ships, but some were jumping before they could reach them.

Thankfully, some were heading for the *Thylacine*.

Larger specks appeared. The evac ships. These held one hundred. Some of the crew were getting away, but Jas thought it would take longer than the *Camaradon* had to launch them all.

As an evac flew from the *Camaradon's* belly, it attracted the notice of the Shadow's beam. A lick of lightning, and one hundred lives were lost. Somewhere on the bridge, a voice cried out.

"Ma'am," Kennewell said, "the jump engines are becoming unstable."

Jas didn't reply. She was biting the edge of her thumb. Blood was running down her hand to her wrist.

"Commander," Kennewell said.

Jas opened her mouth to answer, but at that moment another evac ship appeared and began to streak toward the *Thylacine*, one of the few UA ships remaining in the vicinity.

"Squadron Leader," Jas said into her comm. "An evac's on its way to us. Tell me the second it arrives."

Everyone on the bridge was frozen, transfixed as the evac drew swiftly closer.

"Ma'am," Kennewell said, a note of desperation in her voice.

Jas ignored her.

"Commander," Trimborn exclaimed, "the *Camaradon's* going to blow."

Jas ignored him too.

The Squadron Leader's voice sounded from her comm. "Evac ship's aboard, ma'am. Launch bay doors closed."

"Jump."

FIFTEEN

Sayen was helping with the survivors from the *Camaradon*. Most were in shock, but very few were injured. The first evac ship had been filled with the injured. The evac ship that the Shadows' beam had destroyed.

Twelve fighter pilots had made it to the safety of the *Thylacine's* launch bay. Along with the hundred of the *Camaradon's* crew who had made it to the evac ship that made one hundred and twelve. One hundred and twelve out of two thousand. Sayen hoped that other evac ships had reached UA vessels before they jumped. Jas had said they would return to the battle scene in an hour to look for survivors. Fighter ships had twenty-four hours of life support. There was a slim chance that some pilots were still out there, or even an evac ship or two that had escaped the Shadows' notice.

It was a slim hope, but Sayen clung to it as she walked among the survivors, who were sitting and standing in groups in the launch bay: technicians, engineers, troops, and general maintenance staff. Sayen handed out blankets and energy drinks, which were accepted with shaking hands. Most of the survivors were silent, others were crying.

She didn't see Pacheco until she was nearly upon him. He was sitting by himself, looking the most shocked of all.

"Admiral," Sayen said, holding out a drink she'd opened. "Are you okay, sir?"

He looked from the drink to her face for a moment as if not hearing or understanding what she'd said, then recognition dawned in his eyes.

"Navigator Lee," he replied, his voice choked. "Thank you." He took the drink. "Is Commander Harrington on the bridge?"

"Yes, sir."

"Thanks." He stood up unsteadily and walked away, his hand drooping, spilling his drink in a trail along the floor. Sayen went after him, concerned about his state. He stopped and turned to her. "She made me leave, you know."

"Sir?" Sayen asked.

"The Fleet Admiral. I wanted to stay. A captain should go down with his ship. I was going to stay. But she made me leave. She told me there was nothing I could have done. It was false intelligence. A trap to take out our best ship. The Shadows will make their move now. They've begun to push back. I have to help coordinate our response."

"Yes, sir."

"You do understand? I had to leave. I didn't want to abandon my ship."

"Yes, sir. I understand completely."

The admiral nodded to himself. "Don't worry. I know the way." He left the launch bay.

Others of the *Thylacine's* crew had also come to the bay to help with the survivors, and to search for family members and loved ones. These latter went from group to group asking for news. Sometimes the news wasn't what they wanted to hear, such as that the person they were looking for had been injured and on the first evac ship. Crew members were hugging and crying.

Sayen recognized a ginger-haired woman, and she went over to see her.

"Toirien," she said. "Jas told me you were aboard."

"Umm...," Toirien replied, her freckled face turning pink.

"I'm Sayen Lee. From the *Galathea*."

"Oh, right. Hi," Toirien replied, in a tone that said she still didn't know who this strange woman was.

"Navigator Lee. Do you remember?"

"Oh," exclaimed Toirien. "I remember. You were the one in stasis in the sick bay while we were trapped on the Shadow planet."

"Yes, that was me. But I was also the ship's navigator for the mission."

Toirien shook her head. "I'm sorry. I didn't really take any notice of who was who aboard the ship. I mostly kept my head down and got on with my job then. I was fighting my demons."

"Demons?"

"Never mind." Toirien held out a hand and they shook. "It's good to meet you finally. I just wish it was in better circumstances. I came here to look for my daughter. She was an engineer aboard the *Camaradon*, but someone just told me she was transferred to another ship before the battle. Now I don't know where she is."

"I'm sorry," Sayen said, "I hope she's okay. I hate to ask you this, but could you help me with something if you have time? I want to find berths for these people."

"It'd be my pleasure. The engines are ready to roll, and I was starting to feel a little useless. I don't know how to help these people."

Sayen found Trimborn, who was inputting the survivors' details into the ship's system, and explained what she wanted to do.

"Be my guest," Trimborn said, handing her an interface. "That was next on my list. While you're doing that, I can organize people to help the doctor with triage and dispensing sedatives."

Sayen and Toirien searched the *Thylacine*'s system for spare berths or other potential sleeping accommodation and assigned the survivors to bunks. They would need somewhere to sleep after the doctor's sedatives began to take effect. A period of recovery was needed, though what would happen after, Sayen didn't know.

"Toirien," she said, "you got to know the commander quite well while you were on the Shadow planet, didn't you?"

"Yeah, pretty well. I like her, though she's got a tough side to her."

"Would you say she's changed a lot?"

"Krat, yes," Toirien exclaimed. "I don't know how she's still standing, to be honest. Never seen someone look so bad who wasn't sick in bed. If I didn't know better, I'd say she was on something."

"Really?" Sayen asked. "You think the commander might be on drugs?"

"No, that's not what I said. From the way she acted toward me on the *Galathea*...Sayen, I have to confess, I used to have a bad drug and alcohol habit, so I know what I'm talking about. What I said was, *if I didn't know better.* Jas Harrington hates drugs, and, anyway, she isn't the type to take them. She's no thrill seeker. But she looks just as exhausted and ill as if she were on something strong and had been for a long time. I should know. I used to mix with those people. I was one of those people."

"I think she looks bad too," Sayen said. "I'm worried about her, Toirien."

"It must be the stress of command that's wearing her out."

"No, I don't think it's that. Or at least, that isn't all of it. Jas used to be a strong person. All that's gone now. It's like she's only just holding on."

"Well, I don't want to add to our commander's troubles..." Toirien looked around and took Sayen's upper arm, pulling her into a quiet spot in the corridor outside the launch bay. "Talking of drugs, I think we may have a problem aboard this ship."

"Seriously?"

"As I said, I used to be in that scene, and I see all the signs. There's myth or something similar doing the rounds."

"Myth? But it's so expensive. How could ordinary Unity crew afford it?"

"I've no idea, but I swear there's some intense dealing going on. I think one of my engineers might be an addict, but I'm not sure. I don't want to formally accuse her. If I'm wrong, that kind of mud sticks."

Sayen ran a hand through her hair. Myth was the scourge of the galaxy. "Have you said anything to the commander?"

"I didn't want to burden her when I don't have any proof."

"Yeah, she has enough on her plate. Thanks for telling me. I'll mention it to her if I find the right moment."

"Okay." Toirien scanned the interface. "Hey, there's an empty bunk in this cabin."

Sayen filed away Toirien's tip about drugs aboard the ship. It was definitely not a good time to give Jas more to deal with. In an ironic kind of way, Sayen realized, it was good for Jas that the war wasn't over. She had a suspicion it was the only thing keeping her friend going right now.

Sixteen

Pacheco was familiar with the layout of the *Thylacine*, but he'd gotten lost on his way to the bridge. He suddenly noticed he was wandering the corridors on the lower decks, which were empty and quiet.

Ever since abandoning the *Camaradon*, he'd felt light-headed. Everything around him seemed surreal. Images of the battle flashed constantly through his mind, making it hard for him to concentrate on his surroundings and what people said to him. They sounded like they were speaking to him through cotton wool or from a far distance.

He'd never lost a ship before.

He recalled the *Camaradon's* jump into the remaining Shadow-controlled sector of the galaxy and the discovery of the gigantic Shadow ship. Its sheer size had been impossible to grasp. His first officer had checked and rechecked the scanner readings.

A ship that large had never been built before in the history of the galaxy. Pacheco hadn't even thought it was possible to build a ship so big.

He had barely had time to register that it was real and the scanners weren't lying before it unleashed its onslaught. The Shadow's terrible ray had tested the strength of the *Camaradon's* force field from the very moment it struck.

He stumbled over his own feet and fell against the passageway wall. He gripped it for support, shaking his head. But he couldn't shake the memory of the behemoth dominating the holo on the *Camaradon's* bridge, or of the fearful faces of his officers when they'd realized what they were up against.

The Unity Alliance had been too confident; too sure of its intelligence. Reports had said that the Shadow flagship was in the vicinity, and the reports had been correct. But they had completely underestimated the size of the craft. It had all been a ruse to trap the Unity Alliance into committing its best ship to an unwinnable battle.

Their final, decisive blow against the Shadows had turned into a crushing defeat.

Pacheco told himself he'd fought the best he could, but the words sounded empty in his head. His view of the *Thylacine's* passageway disappeared and was replaced by the sight of the *Camaradon* firing pulse after pulse at the Shadow ship, and the awful ray wiping them up as if they were mere annoyances, all the while pouring its dreadful energy at the *Camaradon's* force field.

In his mind, the rest of the fleet appeared after their battles once more, called to the *Camaradon's* aid. But their pulses were also useless against the enemy. The Shadow ship had never seemed to even weaken. Where the ship derived its power from, Pacheco couldn't understand. He wasn't a scientist, but he was sure that such amounts of energy were impossible to generate and expend so rapidly.

His legs shook and he dropped to his knees. He slumped against the bulkhead, his eyes closed, reliving the memory of the last, desperate measures before their inevitable defeat. He'd sent out the fighter ships in an all-but-doomed attempt to break through the Shadow ship's defenses. He relived the realization that the *Camaradon* would never generate the energy to jump unless its force field were turned off, and that it would mean a quick, fiery death for everyone aboard.

Yet if they couldn't jump, the *Camaradon* was lost.

The Camaradon was lost. Pacheco drew his hand down his face. It came away wet.

The Fleet Admiral had been the one who had given the command to abandon ship. Should it have been him? Had he insisted on fighting too long, when it was clearly hopeless? Had lives been lost needlessly because of him? He would never know. He also didn't know if it had been his false optimism that had made him keep the *Camaradon* fighting, thinking that, somehow, the battle would turn in their favor, or if it had been pure arrogance and stubbornness—an unwillingness to believe he could ever lose.

The flashing emergency lights and klaxon of the final minutes echoed in his mind. He saw the fighter pilots seeking refuge in other UA ships before they jumped. He recalled giving the order to evacuate the sick and injured first, and the horror as the Shadow ship annihilated their vessels. He relived the last desperate, hopeless rush to the evac ships, choosing probable over certain death.

His final memory was of the fleet admiral's insistence that he leave, telling him that the UA needed him if they were to fight back. Then came the sole moment of peaceful, dreamlike wonder as the fleet admiral had knelt down, and bowed her head. It had dissolved into hundreds of pieces, which floated gently in her helmet.

Somehow, Pacheco's recollection of that moment of gentle death steadied his racing heart and whirling mind. Even in her last moments, the fleet admiral had held onto hope. As Pacheco understood it, she had entered the reproductive cycle of her species, and pieces of her could grow into a new Haidiren.

Would they survive the explosion and the cold and vacuum of deep space? Perhaps thousands or millions of years in the future landing on a watery planet and beginning to grow? Pacheco didn't know, and it didn't matter. The fact was, the fleet admiral had demonstrated that in the direst circumstances, hope can survive.

He blinked. He was back aboard the *Thylacine*. The empty passageway had come into focus around him. His hat lay upside down on the floor, having fallen off unnoticed. He picked it up and replaced it on his head before pushing himself to his feet.

With some effort, he concentrated on walking toward an elevator that led to the upper decks and the bridge. He needed to find Jas—Commander Harrington. He had to contact the ships that had survived as well as the Transgalactic Council. The *Camaradon* was lost, but that didn't mean the war was over.

The elevator doors opened as he approached. He told it where he wanted to go, and it sped upward. He took the opportunity to check his appearance in the shiny steel of the walls. He straightened his hat and smoothed his uniform.

The elevator doors opened. The passageways were busy there, near the bridge. He ducked across the crowded thoroughfare and went quickly to the nerve center of the ship, where Commander Harrington was sure to be.

His arrival on the bridge caused a minor stir.

"Admiral," Trimborn exclaimed as Pacheco entered and the bridge doors slid closed behind him.

Pacheco waited a moment while the man recovered from his apparent surprise and offered his salute. He returned it as the other officers on the deck offered theirs too.

Jas was standing. Despite everything that had happened in the last few hours, despite everything he'd been through, his heart still leapt at the sight of her.

She said, "Admiral, I'd like to speak with you in private if I may."

They went out into the busy passageway, and Jas took him to a quiet area.

"Where have you been, Pacheco?" she asked. "We had a ship-wide alert going. Navigator Lee said you left the launch bay over an hour ago. Where's your comm button?"

He looked down at the breast of his jacket. His button had been torn off in the crush aboard the evac vessel.

"I...I... needed to take some time to reflect. I didn't know I didn't have my comm."

Jas tilted her head and peered at him. "Are you okay?"

"I'm fine, Commander," he replied. She was acting like he was some kind of weakling. "Thank you for your concern."

"I'm glad to hear it, *Admiral*."

"Have you been in contact yet with the Transgalactic Council over the results of the battle?" he asked, ignoring her tone.

"Of course I have. They gave us coordinates to report at in twelve hours. We don't have any serious casualties that need better medical care than we have aboard ship."

Pacheco's mind replayed the destruction of the evac ship carrying the *Camaradon's* wounded.

"Pacheco?" Jas asked. "Pacheco?"

"What?" he snapped.

"I said, do you have any instructions for the *Thylacine*? Are you sure you're all right? You zoned out for a moment there."

"Commander, I was present for the destruction of the flagship of the Unity Alliance fleet. I am not *all right*, but I expect I shall recover soon. Is that good enough for you?"

"Krat, take it easy, Pacheco," Jas said. "I was only trying to help. Maybe you should see the doctor."

Her words only irritated him further. He wasn't in need of any medication. He was stronger than that.

"And what's more," he said, "I want to make it clear that the fleet admiral *ordered* me to leave the ship."

Jas raised her hands in a gesture of conciliation. "Pacheco, no one thinks you're a coward. You did absolutely the right thing."

He ground his teeth. Though her words said the opposite, it sounded like she was accusing him of running away. A part of him knew he wasn't being reasonable, but that didn't change how he felt. He glared at her, and her expression grew angry in return.

Why did they always end up at loggerheads like this? He wondered. He remembered the years they'd worked together aboard the *Infineon*, after he'd been promoted to commander to replace Torbin.

"Pacheco," Jas barked. "You're zoning out again."

"I'm—"

"You're *not* fine. Go and see the doctor, or I'll have you confined because you're unfit to serve."

"You wouldn't—"

"Yes, I would. Go."

He clenched his jaw and glared, but the look in Jas's eye told him she wasn't going to back down. He spun around and stalked away. *Krat the woman.*

SEVENTEEN

Jas went back to the bridge and, ignoring the inquiring gazes that met her, flopped down into her seat. They'd lost. Just when she thought it would all be finally over, they'd lost. The prospect of the Shadow War continuing stretched out endlessly in front of her. She'd thought she could make it through to the end. Now, she wasn't so sure.

Everybody on the bridge was intent on their tasks, checking the *Thylacine's* systems for damage after the battle, programming diagnostics and repairs, making sure everything was shipshape. But was there any point? How would the Unity Alliance be able to defeat that monster Shadow ship?

The Shadows must have been building it for years, she realized. Safe from prying eyes within their stronghold, developing new materials and weapons and biding their time while the UA slowly drew closer.

As long as the ships it was battling were its own, the UA victory had seemed achievable. No one knew those ships better than those who had built them. They'd been perfectly prepared, exploiting their advantage of knowing exactly what the commandeered Shadow ships were capable of and what their weaknesses were.

But the beings from another dimension were far from dumb. They must have realized long ago what the outcome would be if they continued on the same path. They'd understood they needed to use a different tactic, and they'd chosen the correct one.

The devastation of losing the *Camaradon* was only the beginning. The Shadows had seen the success of their superior technology, and they wouldn't be slow to press on, reversing all the gains the UA had made, retaking the planets they'd lost, restarting stalled invasions.

Jas slumped forward and put her head in her hands. She wanted to fight the Shadows. She wanted her revenge for them taking away the only living man she would ever love, but she was at the end of her tether. She wished she were just an ensign again, or a security officer, so that someone else would bear the responsibilities that rested on her.

She felt so alone. Pacheco, annoying though he was at times, had been someone to rely upon, but even he seemed to have lost it.

"Commander," said a voice.

Jas looked up. It was Kennewell.

"I was wondering when we were going to return to look for survivors," she said in a small voice.

Krat. Jas had been planning to return to the scene of the battle to check for fighter pilots who hadn't made it to a ship.

"What's the time?" she asked the bridge. When someone told her, she exploded.

"Why didn't any of you say anything before? Are you all kratting idiots? What's wrong with you? Do I have to spell every last thing out to you people? Sayen, plot the coordinates to put us a safe distance from the scene of the battle. Can you figure that out? Kennewell, prepare to jump."

Sayen was staring at her, open-mouthed. Jas glared, and the navigator swung around in her seat to her console. Kennewell began hastily pressing her controls. The rest of the officers on the bridge ducked their heads and focused more intently on their screens.

Jas slumped back in her seat and stared ahead, unseeing, hoping the war would end soon, one way or another. For her, it was already over.

Eighteen

Sayen's coordinates put the *Thylacine* at the limit of scanner range from the scene of the battle. The limit of Unity Alliance scanner range, anyway. Sayen hoped that the Shadow ship, if it remained in the vicinity, didn't possess superior scanners as well.

As a precaution, the first thing they did upon arrival was to throw up a maximum power force field.

"I'm not picking up anything besides residual heat from the battle, Commander," Trimborn said, "and a lot of debris. The *Camaradon* blew to tiny pieces."

Jas sighed and rubbed her eyes. "No life signs?"

Trimborn expanded something on his screen, pulling it wider with his fingertips. "Nothing at all, ma'am."

"Take us in, Pilot," Jas said. "Slowly."

She looked awful. Sayen could now see what Toirien had meant when she'd said that her friend looked like she was on something. It wasn't only that Jas had lost weight, she looked unhealthy and weak. In all the time Sayen had known her, no matter how hard things had been, or even when people close to them had died, Jas had never looked as bad as she did right then. She looked like she'd given up on life.

She didn't seem to be despairing; it was more that there was an entire absence of emotion in her eyes. And what was worse, Sayen didn't know what she could do to help her old friend.

"Picking up a ship," Trimborn blurted. "It's just jumped in, ma'am."

Sayen's heart seized up. Had the Shadow ship returned to trap them?

"Ma'am, it's the *Vespira*. She's hailing us," the comm officer said.

"Thank krat for that," said Trimborn, just loud enough for Sayen to hear.

Jas had a short conversation with the captain of the *Vespira*. They agreed to divide the battle area into quadrants and search independently for any signs of life among the debris. It would reduce the time spent searching and also the time any survivors had to wait to be picked up. The battle had been fought far from any star systems, so at least there were no planets to search.

The mood on the bridge was somber as the *Thylacine* undertook its slow, sweeping scans of the scene of the battle. The embedded chips everyone wore didn't emit a signal a significant distance in deep space terms because their energy came from the wearer's metabolism. That meant that the chips stopped emitting a day or so after the wearer died. This had seemed cruel to Sayen when she first learned of it, but she later understood that recovering the bodies of dead crew only to then give them a space burial was seen as frivolous by the Unity.

"I can see one," Trimborn exclaimed.

"You mean you've picked up a signal?" Jas asked tiredly.

"Yes, we've got a live one. It's a fighter pilot. Sending coordinates, Kennewell."

The pilot eased the *Thylacine* closer to the stranded fighter ship, which was floating without power.

Sayen knew the procedure from rescue operations she'd taken part in previously. Another fighter would be sent out to either connect to the disabled vessel, or, if that wasn't possible, to grapple it into the launch bay. Then it was just a matter of retrieving the wounded pilot, hopefully without having to cut him or her from the wreckage.

Sayen turned to read Jas's expression. *She* hadn't entirely given up on finding Carl one day, but it looked as though Jas had. Her face was blank as she looked down at the interface screen on her armrest.

As soon as the *Thylacine* was near the shipwrecked pilot, Jas dispatched Squadron Leader Correia to bring the person in. Everyone on the bridge waited tensely while the rescue operation took place. The only information they had was the holo on Correia's and the stranded fighter ship, which didn't show them much. Trimborn gave regular updates on the signal from the pilot's chip. It gave only minimal information: heart rate, blood pressure, and oxygen saturation of the pilot's blood were all they knew of her or his physical state until the squadron leader made contact.

Jas had a direct comm with Correia, and the rest of the bridge couldn't hear what he said. They knew, however, when a message came through because Jas screwed up her face. The news wasn't good.

"Still in the land of the living, though?" she asked. When she heard the reply, she nodded, then spoke to the doctor, telling him to go to the launch bay to be on hand when the injured pilot was brought in.

Telling Trimborn to continue to scan for more survivors, Jas stood up to leave the bridge. Knowing she wouldn't be needed for a while—Kennewell could map the sweep by herself—Sayen jumped up and went after her.

She trotted along the ship's passageway to catch up to her long-legged friend.

"Do you know who the pilot is?" she asked when she drew level.

Jas shook her head. "The name isn't on my manifest. Must be from another ship."

"Is he in a bad way?" Sayen asked.

"Pretty bad. Burned up and unconscious, Correia said."

"Krat," Sayen muttered. "Are you going to see him brought in?"

Jas nodded.

"I guess if the doctor can't treat him here, we'll have to jump to Unity medical facilities right away."

"Yeah," Jas replied. "That's not why I'm going down to the bay, though."

"Isn't it? Why are you then?"

Jas gave her an inscrutable look and didn't reply.

They arrived at the launch bay just as the doctor was bringing the patient out. Sayen couldn't make out the pilot's face, he was so badly burned. It was a miracle he was still alive. The doctor had put the patient on a life-support gurney and, along with Correia, he was pushing it toward them. A terrible smell of burned flesh hung in the air.

"Excuse me, Commander," the doctor said. "I must get this person to the sick bay immediately."

"Wait a moment, Doctor," said Jas. "Did you scan him?"

"No, of course not. No time. I can go through the formalities later."

He tried to push the gurney around Jas, who was in the center of the passageway. She put a hand on the plexiglass lid, stopping the gurney dead.

"Scan your patient now, Doctor," Jas said.

The man tutted, but he comm'd a medic to bring over a Shadow scanner. "It's a waste of time, in my opinion, Commander. What are the chances of the Shadows burning up one of their own in an attempt to infiltrate our ranks?"

Jas folded her arms and looked at him implacably.

When the medic with the scanner arrived, the doctor opened the plexiglass lid. The sickening smell intensified. Sayen put a hand over her nose and mouth, though it made little difference. The doctor passed the scanner up and down the prone patient. Without looking at it, he lifted the scanner and held it toward Jas, display side facing her.

"Do you see?" he asked.

The display read: *Shadow Detected*.

Jas turned the scanner toward the doctor so that he could read it. As he saw the result, he turned pale. "I, er... " he stammered. Correia took a step backward and stared at the burned pilot in disbelief.

The terrible burnt smell had already made Sayen nauseated. At this latest revelation, she clenched her teeth and swallowed saliva to prevent herself from vomiting.

It had been another trap. The Shadow ship had vacated the vicinity, but they had left behind injured 'survivors' as plants to infiltrate the UA ships. What wouldn't they stoop to? Sayen wondered. Jas must have guessed the doctor would be too caught up in saving his patient to remember, or bother, to follow protocol and scan him.

"Airlock it," Jas said. She stood against the bulkhead and spoke into her comm. "Patch me through to the captain of the *Vespira*."

The doctor was staring down at his blackened patient as Jas talked to the *Vespira's* captain.

"I can't believe it," he said. "How could they do such a thing?"

"I don't know," Sayen replied. "They used to be so similar to their victims, we couldn't tell them apart. But this, this is something beyond regular cruelty."

When the doctor still seemed to be frozen in disbelief, she added, "You'd better do as the commander said."

The doctor's head hung low. He flicked off the switches to the machines on the life support gurney. The equipment and screens turned silent and dark. Together, he and Correia pushed the gurney along the passageway until they came to an airlock. Sayen keyed in the code to open the inner door, and the doctor lifted the Shadow in his arms, still wrapped in a sheet. He went into the airlock and lay the creature almost gently on the deck before returning.

Sayen sealed the door. She started the sequence to open the outer lock. Figures counted down in the display. She didn't want to look, but somehow she wasn't able to take her eyes off the burned Shadow that lay unconscious through the airlock window. Had it suffered when they'd burned it? Had it volunteered or agreed to the deceit, or had it been coerced?

The display reached zero, and the outer doors opened. At the sound or sudden loss of temperature and atmosphere, the Shadow stirred. Horror rising up in her throat, Sayen saw its eyes flick open. Then it was gone, swept into space, the sheet trailing behind it.

Nineteen

Jas went to the meeting at the Transgalactic Council like she was on autopilot. Nothing mattered anymore. She felt like a machine, going through the motions for as long as the war lasted.

Pacheco was also there. He seemed to have recovered a little from the loss of the *Camaradon*. His eyes no longer had a distracted look, and he was as smartly dressed as ever. He was seated with the other seven admirals and two fleet admirals. The large room was packed full of Unity Alliance commanders and captains. Everyone had been scanned twice by separate, randomly picked personnel before entering, and as always, the meeting room was proofed against any kind of surveillance.

Still, Jas couldn't help but wonder if somehow the Shadows had slipped in an informant. Not a Shadow, but someone who had gone over to their side, perhaps on the promise that they and theirs would not be harmed.

The golden insectoid alien who was the current head of the Council—Jas had heard that it was an unelected position, conferred by a lottery system among the qualified candidates—addressed the room.

"Fleet admirals, admirals, captains, and commanders of the

Unity Alliance, I had hoped to have been greeting you in more joyful circumstances. I had mistakenly predicted that our most recent battle with the Shadows was to have been our last. Sadly, we now know that was a false hope.

"Our intelligence reports were not entirely incorrect, but they left out important information. The Shadows drew us into a trap, resulting in the destruction of our most powerful starship. They removed our key instrument in the fight, and now it would seem that they have the advantage.

"For this reason, I would like to suggest a different tactic, which is to be the subject of this meeting. I would urge you not to spend time regrouping, building new vessels, and so on. This is probably what the Shadows expect us to do. But we have discovered that our former strategy was not effective. We must not pursue old tactics. We must try something new. And for that reason, I and the rest of the Council's leaders suggest we must fight back now. We must commit everything we have remaining at this moment. The longer we wait, the stronger the Shadows will become."

"But if we attack now," interrupted a fleet admiral, "what do we attack them with? We have nothing to withstand that monster ship. I've seen the vids of the destruction of the *Camaradon*. That ray they have is like nothing I've ever seen before. Going against it with our current weaponry would be little short of suicide."

"We have a saying among my kind," the golden councilor replied. "When you cannot be the strongest, be the smartest."

"It seems like the Shadows are the ones who have been the smartest so far," grumbled the fleet admiral.

Jas rested her chin on her hand and watched the councilor through half-lidded eyes. It had something up its sleeve.

"We have carefully studied the reports of Admiral Pacheco and the captains and commanders who were present at the defeat of the *Camaradon*," the golden alien went on. "We have detected a theme running between the lines of the reports. In fact, some of the reports overtly stated the observation. The ray the Shadows used so effectively seemed to draw some of its power from the pulses it encountered. We cannot be sure of this, but if it is true, this fact offers us hope."

"How? That makes things worse," said the fleet admiral. "If we're right about that, it only means we can't even fire at it without that energy being fired back at us."

"It would indeed be a hopeless situation if all we were able to do was fire at it," the golden councilor said. "But let us think laterally, just for a moment."

Jas had the impression the Transgalactic Council leader was vastly more intelligent than those assembled around it, and it was simplifying everything while trying not to sound like it was talking down to them.

It went on, "If this Shadow beam can in fact absorb the energy of the pulses it encounters, and then redirect that energy outward, that means the pulse power must be drawn into the Shadow weapon first. And if it takes in pulse energy, what else might it draw in?"

There was a moment of silence while they pondered the councilor's question. What could the Shadow ship take into its beam that could harm it? Then, Jas realized what the councilor meant.

"A bomb," she said.

"Precisely," said the councilor. "If we can disguise a bomb as a pulse, and fire it at the Shadow ship, we could destroy it."

"What kind of bomb?" the fleet admiral asked. "If it absorbs energy, we can't increase the power of our pulses."

"Indeed not," the councilor said. "But we may be able to disguise an anti-matter bomb in a pulse. A poison pill, so to speak. If the beam absorbs anti-matter, the result would be quite spectacular, I believe."

"Do you have such a bomb?" the fleet admiral asked.

"No, but our scientists are working on it as we speak. They believe such a thing can be constructed, though it would be very unstable. No matter. For now, we must act as though the bomb will be ready in time for us to use it. We must find the Shadow ship and prepare for an assault."

The discussion went on for longer than an hour, but Jas sat back and let them argue it out. Some of the UA leaders saw the councilor's idea as outlandish and unrealistic, and were more in favor of a guerrilla warfare style of resistance, similar to what the Shadows had been doing for the majority of the war. Others agreed with the councilor that a single, final, decisive blow was required as soon as possible. They said that their people would rather die than live in servitude and fear.

But the anti-matter bomb was the better idea, Jas thought, and the majority eventually agreed to it.

As she left the meeting to return to the *Thylacine*, Pacheco caught up to her.

"I think we made the right decision, don't you?" he asked.

"Yeah, I guess so."

"You don't sound enthusiastic about the idea."

"I'm not enthusiastic about much these days. This war's been going on too long."

"I got the impression you weren't doing so well," Pacheco said. "I, er, wanted to thank you for making me see sense the other day. I went to the doctor. That post-battle shock isn't to be messed with. I didn't really believe how bad it was until I experienced it."

When Jas didn't reply, he went on, "You know, you might benefit from a visit to the doc yourself. It doesn't hurt to have a checkup. Talk things over, maybe."

She smiled wryly. "Giving me a taste of my own medicine, Pacheco?"

"Think of it as gentle advice from a concerned friend. I've accepted you're never going to feel about me the same way I feel about you, Jas. But that doesn't mean I've stopped caring about you."

For the first time in a long while, Jas was moved. Pacheco's concern touched her. She stopped and looked into his eyes. "Thanks, but there isn't anything the doctor or anyone else can do that's going to make me feel better. It is what it is."

Pacheco nodded. "Well, I'm going to be around to keep an eye on you anyway. Now the *Camaradon's* gone, I'm to berth aboard the *Thylacine*."

Jas's warmth toward the admiral cooled a little. In spite of what he'd said, she had the impression he still hadn't given up hope of something closer between them.

TWENTY

It took the Transgalactic Council only ten days to locate the Shadow's flagship vessel, but their scientists took over six weeks to develop the anti-matter bomb. The idea for the technology wasn't new, and they'd already been working on a prototype when the battle had occurred, so they hadn't had to start from scratch. The greatest challenge, Jas heard, was to envelop the anti-matter in pulse energy for long enough after its manufacture for it to be fired and taken in by the Shadow weapon. Anti-matter was incredibly unstable.

Also, the UA couldn't simply create the bomb, jump to the Shadow ship's position, and fire it into the Shadow's beam. It would have to send a ship that was carrying the bomb-making equipment to attack the Shadow vessel. If the bomb wasn't fired in time from the ship where it was created, it would explode and destroy the ship. So, to disguise what it was doing and to protect the vessel that carried the bomb-making equipment the UA decided to launch a regular attack.

The *Thylacine*, as an average-sized destroyer of the Unity fleet—and therefore unlikely to attract undue attention from the Shadow ship—drew the short straw. Jas's ship was to carry the bomb-making equipment and unleash what everyone hoped would be the final blow, destroying the gigantic Shadow ship.

Six weeks of preparation for the battle hadn't improved Jas's feelings of hopelessness and exhaustion. She'd been busy attending all the meetings and briefings as well as overseeing a full update of all the *Thylacine's* systems and equipment so that the ship was in tiptop shape. She'd also had to deal with a myth problem that Sayen had told her about. Somewhere along the line as they'd been releasing mythrin-bearing planets from Shadow control, the refined drug had gotten aboard. She'd ordered a thorough search of the ship, and screened every crew member, finding and dismissing several addicts. But even so, the time had seemed to pass slowly.

She was responsible for the *Thylacine's* crew and the ship's operation, Pacheco was responsible for the installation of the bomb-making equipment and the deployment of the bomb. That part of the plan was top secret.

Finally, the day before the battle arrived. Jas watched the officers as they went through their checks. A few supplementary crew members were arriving that evening, and Trimborn was responsible for settling them in.

When everything was completed, she left the bridge and returned to her cabin for an early night. As she went through the passageways, the atmosphere aboard the ship was quiet and tense. The anti-matter bomb was a secret, but the crew couldn't fail to have noticed the new equipment being brought aboard. Jas wondered if they had guessed that the *Thylacine* was playing a larger-than-usual role in the battle.

She changed into her unflattering, Unity-issue pajamas, catching sight of herself in her cabin's mirror. She turned away from her wan face and tired eyes and climbed into her bunk. She lay down on her back with one arm over her eyes and mentally went through the battle plan for the next day. She'd had so much trouble sleeping lately, she'd gotten into the habit of drinking to relax herself. But it was the night before a battle and she had to remain sober, even though it meant that sleep would be a long time coming.

A while later, as she was finally on the edge of drifting off, her door chimed. She removed her arm from her eyes and squinted at the clock. Who the krat could it be at that hour? Trimborn wouldn't dare wake her unless it was something serious. Or was it Pacheco? She hoped that pre-battle tension hadn't rekindled his feelings for her.

She thumbed the door comm. "Who is it?"

"Jas, it's me," said a voice. A voice that stopped her heart.

Or was it only that she was tired and on the edge of sleep? She couldn't believe it was who she thought she'd heard. "Who?" she asked again, a tremble in her voice.

"Jas, open up. I have to talk to you."

Was her mind playing tricks on her? If so, she didn't want to be seen in her bunk by a crew member. She didn't give a voice command from where she was, but turned on the cabin's half-light, got out of bed and padded over to the interface screen that would show her who was outside. She swallowed, and turned on the screen.

At first, she almost didn't recognize him. He was standing with one hand on the bulkhead next to the door, his head bowed. She couldn't see his face. His brown curls were gone, replaced by a cropped military cut peppered with strands of gray. He was thinner too. But it was him. It was Carl Lingiari. Her Carl.

As she watched, momentarily too shocked to move, he lifted a hand to press the door's comm button again, but before he made contact, she opened the door. He looked up. Their gazes met. The sound of her thumping heart rushed through her ears. She couldn't speak.

Carl had aged more than the five years that had passed since she'd last seen him. Lines were traced on his previously boyish features, but his warm, kind, deep brown eyes were the same.

"Is it okay if I come in?" he asked, looking a little anxious.

Responding automatically, she stepped back. Carl came into her cabin and she closed the door. She leaned back on it, catching her breath as if she'd been running.

For a moment, they looked at each other in silence. She reached out and touched his arm. She wanted to reassure herself that he was real. She was still unsure if she was dreaming. He was wearing an old, faded flight suit. The material was worn and soft, and she could feel the lean, hard muscles of his arm beneath it.

"Where have you been?" she whispered. "Where have you been all this time?"

"I've been fighting, of course," he replied. "Flying fighter ships, for years." He looked down. "Jas, I wanted to tell you I'm sorry for leaving you like that. When I volunteered, I never thought the war would take so long. I wanted to contact you, but with the ban on personal comms, it was impossible. I didn't even know you'd joined up until I heard about the commander of the new destroyer, the *Thylacine.* After that, I kept asking to be assigned to her, but it never happened until—"

She stepped forward and grabbed him into her arms. She held him close, her senses overwhelmed by the solid, physical presence of the person she'd yearned for for years, until that yearning had turned into only a wishful hope, and then only a sad memory, for what had seemed like forever.

He put his arms around her and drew her closer still. "I didn't know if you still would be glad to see me after I left you," he said, his breath warm on her neck. "I missed you."

"I'm not mad at you," she replied, drinking in his scent and the warmth and strength of his body against hers. "I missed you too." She closed her eyes and tilted her head backward. He kissed her. Tingles ran through her, down to her fingertips and toes. Once more, her heart raced like she'd been running. Her skin prickled with sweat.

They kissed deeply. She felt the muscles of his back slide under her hands as his lips left hers and descended to her neck. She drew in a breath at their passionate touch and the soft scrape of his stubble. Desire for him overwhelmed her. She reached to the top of his flight suit to unzip it. His hands went under her pajama top and moved up her bare back.

For the next couple of hours, they tried to make up for years of unmet needs and unfulfilled longing before they fell asleep in Jas's bunk, their limbs entangled.

Twenty-One

At some point during the night, Jas woke. Elation filled her for a moment, then it was supplanted by fear that the previous evening had been a dream. She moved her hand and encountered a muscled chest. Carl was still beside her, warm and very, very real.

She turned on the cabin's half-light. Her lover was deeply asleep. One of his hands was tucked between their two bodies, and the other rested on her breast, rising and falling with her breathing. Running down his visible arm and the side of his body were long, silvered scars—burn scars. She traced them with a finger.

What had Carl been through in the years they'd been apart? He had always been lean, but now he looked positively gaunt. Barely a trace of fat softened the outline of the muscles in his arms, legs, chest, and stomach. His eyes were underscored with dark circles, and exhaustion lined his features.

What trials had he endured? How had he survived?

With a slight start, she saw his eyes were half open and he was watching her. Not so deeply asleep after all, then.

"Hey," she murmured.

"Hey." He shifted position and briefly kissed her lips.

"How'd you get these?" She stroked his scarred arm.

"It looks worse than it was. I got a bit too close to a Shadow ship. Took a hit. But it was okay. My ship's extinguishers kicked in in time. You've got a war wound yourself." He kissed her ravaged thumb.

"It must have been terrible," Jas said. "I've been so worried about you. I didn't think you could have survived this long—Oh, krat," she exclaimed, half sitting up.

"It's okay," Carl said. "I'm fine. I just haven't had a chance to get the scars fixed yet."

"No, it's not that. I forgot about the battle tomorrow. Carl, you can't go out there." She couldn't send him out with the rest of the *Thylacine's* pilots to face the Shadows again.

"I have to go, Jas," Carl said softly. "It's my job."

"No, I won't allow it. Not now that I've only just got you back. You've done enough. Years and years of flying those fighters and risking your life. I won't let you do it again."

He pulled her down onto the bunk and wrapped his arms around her. He spoke into her ear. "Jas, you can't protect me. It wouldn't be right. What about the other pilots? You can't put me before them."

"No," Jas said, tortured. "No, it isn't fair. Why now? Why us? How much more do we have to give?" She gripped him tightly.

He gently eased her hands open, then stroked her hair. "You know, every time I went out to fight, I thought it might be for the last time, and that I'd never see you again. I'd never get a chance to say sorry and make things right between us. But we've had this night at least, and maybe we'll have many more. There's plenty of people who haven't been as lucky as us."

Jas's earlier happiness had melted away, but fatigue, or maybe hopelessness, sapped her will to fight him. It seemed to be an inevitability that he would fight in the morning. If that was so, she also had something to get off her chest.

"Carl, I wanted to tell you something too. Something that's important to me for you to know." She told him what had happened to her when she was at training college in Antarctica, and how her experience had made her hold him at arm's length years even though she cared about him. She explained that it was because she cared so much, not because she didn't care enough.

"I'm sorry you went through that," Carl said, "but it explains a lot. I wondered why you acted so weird when we were in Antarctica rescuing Sayen."

"Yeah, I can't stand going back there. Hey, did you know Sayen's aboard?" Jas asked. "She's our navigator. And you remember Toirien MacAdam from the *Galathea*? She's here too."

"Really? No, I didn't know. The minute that I arrived aboard ship I came straight to your cabin. Got some weird looks when I asked where you were. I hope I get time to say hi to both of them before the fight starts tomorrow."

Jas heaved a sigh when he reminded her of the trial ahead. Everything that was about to happen had regained meaning for her. Before, she'd only wanted it all to be over. Now, she was desperate for the Unity Alliance to win and for Carl to survive. But he'd been flying fighters for five years. It was hardly credible that he'd lived this long. Could he survive one more battle?

"I didn't know what had happened to any of you for so long," Carl said. "Then I heard about a new destroyer called the *Thylacine*, and its commander, Jas Harrington, who'd climbed the ranks on merit. They said she was one of the best to serve under." He gave a small smirk.

Jas rolled her eyes and batted him. "The ship's named after you, you know."

"Huh?" Carl lifted himself onto one elbow.

"It's a long story, but one of the admirals has a soft spot for me. When the new ship was commissioned and I was chosen to command it, he asked me for suggestions for a name. They went with the one I picked."

"You think I'm like a rare, predatory marsupial?" Carl asked, one eyebrow raised.

"The Tasmanian tiger came back from extinction, right? When everyone had given up hope."

He sighed, wrapped his arms around her, and buried his face in her neck.

After a little while, Jas said, "Speaking of animals, where's Flux? Is he hiding in your cabin?"

Carl sighed again. "He's gone. He left about four years ago. A planet we freed from the Shadows was his homeland, and he said that now a couple of hundred Earth years had passed, the heat would have died down enough for it to be safe for him to go back."

"He'd been in trouble for something?"

"Yeah. He'd been hiding out. On the run, he said, though he wouldn't tell me what for. Looked sheepish when he talked about it."

Jas wondered how Carl had been able to read the expression on the creature's face. "I'm sorry. You must miss him."

"It was for the best. I didn't want to get the little fella killed. He said to come and visit when it was all over."

When it's all over. Jas hoped with all her heart that it would all be over after tomorrow.

"This admiral who liked you," Carl said. "Was it Pacheco?"

"Yeah, it was. How did you know?"

"Most of the others have three heads, or six legs, or slither rather than walk."

Jas chuckled. He was exaggerating, but he had a point. "We got to know each other when we served together on the *Infineon*. He was in command. It was my first posting."

"So...did you guys get together? It's okay if you did. I don't mind. Five years is a long time." Though he was trying his best to hide it, Jas detected a tone that indicated he *did* mind.

"Nothing happened between me and Pacheco," she replied. She didn't mention the admiral's annoying pursuit of her. "How about you? Did you find someone to keep you company between missions?" Now it was her turn to pretend to not mind.

"I couldn't, Jas. Couldn't stop thinking of you." His eyes showed his raw honesty.

Should she tell him she'd been convinced he was dead? It didn't seem a good idea. That was a conversation for another time.

"I love you," she whispered.

"I love you too."

They both slept.

TWENTY-TWO

Jas's alarm woke her two hours before the *Thylacine* was due to jump to the battle zone. Her stomach sank at the thought that, this time, Carl would be among her fighter pilots. The sound of her alarm hadn't disturbed him, and she studied his tired features with concern. He needed a week of sleep before he would be in a state fit to fly, but she knew he wouldn't allow her to exempt him from duty.

The fact that *she* was the person who might be sending him out to risk his life again seemed unbearably cruel. Just when she thought the Shadow War couldn't ask any more of her, it made another request.

She eased herself out of Carl's arms and went quietly to take a shower. She would delay waking him until it was absolutely necessary. She would leave just enough time for him to eat and dress before the battle hour.

Running her fingers through her hair as she came out of the shower, she was happy to see he was still asleep. But as she was dressing, he woke.

"Good morning, Commander," he said from the bunk as she was buttoning her uniform jacket.

She clicked her tongue. "Don't be an idiot, Carl."

"You look sneck, Jas. And sexy." He got out of the bunk and came over to her. He held her upper arms and leaned forward to kiss her, but stopped.

"Krat," he said, concern overtaking his amorous look. "You're trembling. What's wrong?"

She wrapped her arms around him and pressed her face into his shoulder. "I guess I'm scared."

"Scared?" He rubbed her back. "Jas, you're the bravest person I know."

"No, I don't think I was ever that brave. I just never had much to lose. Not until now."

They stood silently in each other's arms for a while. Jas lifted her head and kissed Carl on the lips. When he kissed her back, though her heart was sad, her body responded. Her breathing quickened and she lifted a hand to unbutton her jacket at her neck. She pulled Carl closer with the other. He helped her with her buttons, and soon they were back in her bunk.

Their lovemaking was more tender and gentle this time. She forgot about anything else. She even forgot where they were and that time was passing—until the loud ringing of her door chime drew her quickly and painfully back to reality.

"Krat," she exclaimed, extricating herself from Carl's embrace and checking the time. "I'm supposed to be speaking to the pilots right now."

"Who's at the door?" Carl asked, picking up his flight suit from where he'd dropped it the night before.

She gave him a worried look. She hoped it wasn't who she thought it was. She hoped it was Trimborn, or Sayen, or anyone else but that person. As she picked up her jacket, she noticed the comm button flashing. How many times had she been called without answering?

She hastily fastened her uniform, then opened the interface screen next to the door. Her stomach fell. It was the last person she wanted to see in the circumstances. Pacheco was right outside, his uniform perfect, and not a hair out of place. He looked annoyed. She winced.

"Carl," she said, "I have to go."

He was pulling his flight suit over his shoulders. He nodded. "Me too."

Jas took a breath and opened her door. She rushed out, knocking Pacheco's shoulder and spinning him around.

"I'm sorry. I'm on my way to the launch bay."

As she ran, she glanced over her shoulder. Pacheco had managed to catch the door before it closed and was looking into her room. Carl appeared, zipping up his flight suit.

Jas cringed and ran on, wishing she'd had time for a better parting from Carl.

Twenty-Three

Carl tried to step around the admiral who was waiting outside Jas's room, but the man blocked his path. He peered at the breast of Carl's flight suit and said, "Pilot Lingiari, I don't think we've met."

Carl finished pulling up his zipper. He guessed this was the admiral who had the hots for Jas. He didn't like the look in the man's eye. It was the look of someone about to throw the first punch, and Carl didn't have time for scrapping with love rivals. He had a ship to fly.

"No," he replied, "I don't think we have." Saluting and asking permission for this or that didn't seem appropriate in the circumstances. "Excuse me." Carl tried to sidestep the admiral again, but the man put a hand on his chest. Carl looked down at the hand and up into the admiral's eyes.

"Being in the commander's cabin first thing in the morning is unprofessional behavior," the admiral said, not blinking. "You're aware that fraternizing while on duty is a court martial offense for both of you?"

Carl tilted his head and looked at the admiral from under his brows. "What I'm doing in the commander's cabin is none of your business, mate."

The two men locked gazes for a long moment. Anger and pain flitted across the admiral's features, but they were followed by something like resignation. His hand dropped to his side, and Carl took the opportunity to leave. He walked briskly away. He should have been in the launch bay with the rest of the pilots ten minutes ago.

After he had gone twenty or so paces, the admiral called out, "Lingiari."

He stopped and turned.

"You're a lucky man," the admiral said.

Carl paused before replying, "I know."

He jogged through the ship to the launch bay, where the rest of the pilots had already assembled. He snuck behind the fighter ships and slipped in at the back of the group of men and women. Jas had begun speaking to them already. She was talking about how hard and dangerous their job was and that everyone aboard the ship appreciated their service.

She hadn't changed much in the five years since he'd last seen her. She didn't keep herself as fit as she used to, and the strain of command showed on her face. But he found out the previous night and that morning that she was still the same Jas he'd fallen in love with.

She'd said she was scared. He was scared too. Not of the forthcoming battle. He'd lost count of the number he'd flown in the Shadow War. He would try to fly his best as he'd always done. He couldn't do more than that, and that attitude had stood him in good stead until then.

But he knew what Jas had meant when she'd said she was scared of what she had to lose. Now they were together again, he felt the same way. He would have given a lot to jump the *Thylacine* to Earth, fly Jas down to his parents' old farm, and live out the rest of their years quietly. Maybe have a kid or two if Jas was willing. He could teach them to fly.

There had been a time when he'd only dreamed of piloting starships across the galaxy, looking sneck in his pilot's uniform, and flirting with his female shipmates, who he'd imagined would all fall at his feet, of course. That time seemed long ago, and he felt like a different person now. Whether it was living through the Shadow War that had caused his change of heart, or because he'd fallen in love, he didn't know. It didn't matter. He only had to get through today, and maybe his new dreams would come true.

Jas was finishing up her speech. Her gaze had passed over him all the time that she'd been talking, but as she wished them good luck, her eyes met his. For a brief moment, she had the same expression she'd had in her cabin when he'd felt her trembling. The neutral look of command fell away, and her vulnerability and fear showed through.

He wished they'd had time for a proper goodbye. Or maybe it was best that they hadn't.

She turned and left the launch bay. The squadron leader ordered them into their cockpits, ready to respond instantly to the order to join the battle. Carl climbed aboard his fighter and strapped himself in.

It wasn't much of a consolation, but he'd always loved the Unity fighter ship's design. A high cockpit protruding to the front, giving excellent visibility if his scanning equipment failed, and streamlined body with two aerodynamic engines for flying in an atmosphere as well as space. Six low-energy laser emitters faced forward, two on each wing and one on either side of the cockpit. Carl knew these planes' capabilities like the back of his hand.

Just one more flight. Or maybe it wouldn't even come to that.

He yawned and put on his helmet, but opened the visor, which turned off the air and power. Reserving those for when he absolutely needed them had saved his life a couple of times. There weren't many more lonely and isolated experiences than floating in a disabled fighter ship in deep space, waiting for and hoping that someone would be back to pick you up before your oxygen or heat ran out.

The squadron leader's head appeared at Carl's window. "Lingiari?" came the man's voice through his comm. Carl nodded. The man made the universal *open up* gesture. Carl gave the voice command to unlock the hatch, and with the clunk of heavy metal, the ship complied.

"What's up, sir?"

"Step out, pilot. Gotta scan you."

Carl unfastened his safety harness and swung out of the cockpit. The squadron leader ran a Shadow scanner up and down his body. He read the display and nodded. "Just a precaution after your late arrival last night. Can't be too careful. It seems a bit odd to me that we're getting special attention. The *Thylacine's* the only ship with the full complement of pilots. It's like we've been singled out for something."

Carl shrugged, but the man was right. It was a little strange that the authorities had gone to the trouble of reassigning himself and two other pilots to the *Thylacine* at the last minute. The ship was an ordinary destroyer. There was no reason it should be shown any special favor. Jas hadn't said anything about the battle plan.

"Anyway," the squadron leader continued, "glad to have you aboard, Lingiari. I read the service record that arrived with you. I was impressed. It looks like the Unity have sent us their best. You've been in this war longer than I have. Not many have survived so long."

"I've been lucky, sir."

"Takes more than luck to survive the number of firefights that you've seen. You could probably teach *me* some maneuvers, but there's no time for that now. You were never promoted to squadron leader?"

"I was offered, but I prefer just to fly."

"Probably wise. Let's get through today, then I'd be glad to share a beer with you later when we celebrate winning this kratting war."

Though the man's words were light, his eyes told of the pilots he'd spoken to in the same manner for the last time.

"I'd be happy to," Carl replied.

The squadron leader ordered him to return to his ship. As Carl refastened his harness, he mulled over the man's suspicions about the role the *Thylacine* was to play in the battle. But after a while he gave up trying to figure out what it might be.

Whatever Jas's task was, it didn't make any difference to him. He would have to do the same job as always: get close enough to the Shadow ship to penetrate its force field with low energy fire, and destroy whatever he was told to destroy. Then get out of there fast before he was caught in the blast if the ship exploded.

For the time being, however, all he had to do was wait. He settled down to mentally replay his recent moments with Jas.

TWENTY-FOUR

J as encountered Sayen as she went from the launch bay to the bridge. In a quarter of an hour, the order would come to jump to the star system where the massive Shadow ship had been spotted. Jas was in a rush, but at the sight of her friend, she had to stop to tell her the news.

As passing crew members moved out of earshot, she said, "Sayen, Carl's here."

"Carl's aboard the ship?" Sayen exclaimed. "He's alive? That's great. When did you see him?"

"Last night. He came to my cabin."

"Oh," Sayen said, smiling. "That must have been quite a reunion. I'm happy for you."

"I'd be happy too, if it weren't for what we have to do today."

"Oh, yeah." Sayen's smile fell. "He's flying, then?"

"I couldn't persuade him not to. I probably could have thought up a reason to excuse him from duty, but he wasn't having it."

Her eyes softening, Sayen said, "If he's made it this far, he can make it through one more battle. I'm sure of it."

"I hope so. I don't know what I'll do if he doesn't. I'd given up on him. I'd given up on everything. Then he came back. If he doesn't survive this, I don't think I'll have a reason to go on."

"Carl will be okay, Jas," Sayen said. "He's a brilliant pilot."

But nothing her friend said could dispel the fear that hung over Jas's heart, and there was no time to talk more with her.

"We'd better go to the bridge," Jas said.

Pacheco was already there. He was standing—there was nowhere for him to sit. As well as overseeing the battle maneuvers of the *Thylacine*, he would help to orchestrate other ships involved in the engagement.

His expression was pained and tight as Jas and Sayen entered the bridge. He didn't look at Jas as she took her seat. Sayen went to her console. The rest of the officers were already at their stations.

"Navigator," Pacheco said, "Please plot our jump."

"Yes, sir." Sayen swiped her screen to activate it and read the display. "Oh," she said. "K.67092d?"

"Yes," Pacheco said between his teeth. "Is there something remarkable about that, Navigator?"

"No, sir," Sayen replied. "I mean, it's only that I've been there before. It's the planet where the commander and I first encountered the Shadows."

The Shadow trap planet. Of course. Jas thought. The planet's designation had been familiar, but she hadn't realized why until Sayen pointed it out. After all these years, they were returning to where it had all begun.

"Hmpf. Yes, it is a Shadow planet," Pacheco said. "One of the earliest ones from what we can gather. Possibly the Shadows have their reasons for parking their mother ship there, but that doesn't concern us today. We'll be fighting this battle in space."

Jas recalled the harsh, windswept, barren surface of K.67092d and the hexagonal structures that the poor fool, Master Loba, had insisted were not constructed by sentient beings. No one had ever discovered how the Shadows made their traps, but there was no doubt about what happened inside them. Myth-addicted, resource-hungry Loba had paid for his thoughtless greed with his life.

Jas gave a shudder. Of all the planets she'd visited while working aboard prospectors, K.67092d was the last place she wanted to return to. She'd rather go back to Antarctica.

"Coordinates ready," Sayen said. "Sending them over."

Pilot Kennewell gave a nod as they arrived. "Jumping in ten."

Jas relayed the information to the crew around the ship, telling them to take their seats. "Perhaps you should find a jumpseat, Admiral?" she asked. It wouldn't be safe for him to be standing when they jumped. Though the process usually wasn't violent, it wasn't unknown for ships to jump into weapons fire.

Pacheco seemed to wrestle with something in his mind, but he conceded to Jas's common sense and left the bridge.

The tension relaxed a little as he departed. Officers who had been intent on their screens looked up and around at each other. There were some nervous smiles and quiet good luck wishes.

Jas tried to clear her mind, and get ready for the battle, but in truth her thoughts were in turmoil. Depending on how the battle went, she faced a terrible decision. If it made tactical sense to scramble the fighters, she would have to do it. And that would mean putting the life of the man she loved at risk.

Twenty-Five

As soon as the *Thylacine* had made the jump, Pacheco began to make his way back to the bridge. The comm officer had set him up with channels to the ships under his command, though his ability to speak with them depended on how effective the Shadow ship's dampening field was.

In the battle where they'd lost the *Camaradon*, it had been all but impossible to comm the other UA ships through space rather than jump channels, but he had to try. The right maneuver at the right time might mean the difference between victory and defeat. In case he couldn't comm the other ships, all their captains and commanders had been fully briefed on the aims and rationale of the battle tactics in case they were forced to act without instruction.

The battle plan was simple: deluge the Shadow ship with fire to prevent it from jumping, surround it with UA ships to dilute the effect of its ray, and give the *Thylacine* time to create the anti-matter bomb. The *Thylacine* would also need their protection while it prepared the bomb.

Jas had to make sure her ship didn't stand out from the rest. If the Shadows suspected she posed a special threat, all they had to do was target it for destruction with their beam, and the last hope of galactic civilization would be crushed.

That was why the Unity Alliance had chosen the *Thylacine*. There were bigger, faster ships with more firepower, but they would attract the Shadows' attention. The *Thylacine* was a run-of-the-mill destroyer. It wouldn't stand out. It was like a drab brown scorpion with a lethal sting in its tail.

The *Thylacine* was also Jas's ship, and though Pacheco was finally beginning to accept that there would never be anything personal between them, he was still moved to protect her. He'd argued strongly that the *Thylacine* was the right ship for the job.

In a way, he felt a fool. It didn't take a genius to guess that the pilot he'd seen coming out of Jas's cabin that morning was the lost love she'd been pining for all these years. He'd been crushed, if he was honest with himself, to see the man in the flesh. It was one thing to understand on an intellectual level that your love would never be reciprocated; it was quite another to meet your rival face to face.

There wasn't anything special about that man, Lingiari, Pacheco told himself. It was just that he'd made his move first, and Jas wasn't capricious. He knew that. It was one of the things he liked about her.

He was at the bridge. The doors opened and he went in. The battle was already in full swing. The holo of the gigantic Shadow ship hung in the air to the front and center of the bridge. The UA ships ranged around it to the sides and above and below. Farther below, the gray-brown surface of K.67092d with its wide, pale blue oceans slowly turned.

Every ship was firing. Pulses were raining down, but the Shadow ship wasn't using its beam. It must require a period of time to start it up, Pacheco realized. They really had caught the Shadows by surprise this time, unlike at the previous battle where the beam was activated almost immediately.

The Unity Alliance ships were pouring all their energy into attacking the Shadow ship's force field. Pacheco hoped the effort was making a dent in the ship's massive power supply and preventing it from jumping.

He glanced around him as he went over to the comm officer's desk. Everyone on the bridge was performing their tasks like clockwork. Jas sat at the center of the activity, pale and tense. He wondered what was going through her mind. To be reunited with her lover the night before she might lose him in battle had to be tough.

A collective gasp and a flare that lit up the bridge told him before he turned to the holo that the Shadow ship had activated its beam. There it was. The impossibly powerful ray of energy had sprung out and was targeting a UA ship. The Shadows had picked a large battleship out of the numerous UA ships that surrounded it.

The beam bore down, slowly gnawing away at its force field, grinding down its defenses. The battleship ceased firing pulses, as had been the order if targeted by the beam. With luck, the ship would have time to build the energy to jump before the beam broke through.

Meanwhile, the rest of the Unity Alliance fleet targeted their pulses to avoid the ray on their way to the Shadows' force field. If their guess that the beam absorbed the energy from pulses that crossed it was correct, it made no sense to feed it.

The officers were glancing up from their consoles at the battleship that the Shadows had targeted. Jas was also staring at it, her knuckles white as she gripped her armrests.

Suddenly, where the destroyer had been was nothing but empty space. A cheer arose, and Trimborn exclaimed, "They made it. They jumped."

The ray shone out into deep space, fading away at its farthest end. It quickly switched to another ship. This also immediately stopped firing, conserving its energy for its force field and to build up to jump. This ship was smaller, however, and Pacheco doubted it had the ability to withstand the Shadows' beam to the same extent the battleship had.

As if to attract the Shadows' attention, another battleship moved toward the targeted UA ship, but the Shadows didn't take the bait. They poured energy onto the second ship. The battleship inched forward across the holo display, though in reality it was traveling at thousands of kilometers per hour on its RaptorX engines.

Jas murmured into her comm, no doubt checking her engineer's progress with the equipment that was building the anti-matter bomb. Pacheco hoped the bomb was on schedule.

The officers drew in their breath. The Shadows' beam had broken through the second ship's force field, but in another moment it was gone. It was impossible to tell what damage had been done before it jumped. The second ship's crew would soon find out at the other end.

Meanwhile, the battleship that had been trying to distract the Shadows from the weaker ship got her wish. The Shadow's ray flicked to her.

Pacheco had an idea. He asked the comm officer if he had a channel to the other admirals. If they all acted as the battleship had, ordering their ships to fly to the vessel targeted by the ray, they might persuade the Shadows to split their attention. Ten UA ships would withstand a split ray better than one would its concentrated force.

"Sorry, sir," the officer said, "nothing yet, but I'll keep trying."

If they couldn't spread the devastating beam around, the Unity Alliance was playing a losing game. By firing all pulses, the UA ships were expending energy quickly. Few would now be able to do what the first battleship had done and simply jump out of trouble.

They had to last long enough for the *Thylacine* to launch the anti-matter bomb.

Even without Pacheco's suggestion, many of the UA ships seemed to have had the same idea. They flew toward the battleship that was under fire. But the Shadows were not to be tempted. From experience, Pacheco knew the battleship's force field could not last much longer. He caught Jas's worried gaze as they both counted down the seconds.

The beam broke through the battleship's force field. A minute later, her hull began to break down. Soon, she was gone.

"Did they have time to evacuate?" someone asked.

"Concentrate on your job," Jas snapped.

Another ship blinked into existence to the far side of the Shadow ship. It was the first battleship, returning to the fight. The Shadow ship saw her immediately, and left its target to fire again upon the returned ship.

The pulses the UA vessels were pouring at the Shadow ship's force field seemed to make no difference to its resources. The beam didn't lessen, dim, or waver. The ship's power levels were incredible.

Another ship appeared and began firing on the returned battleship. Pacheco's momentary confusion cleared. It was another Shadow ship. The mother ship was calling her children to her. Another Shadow ship appeared, and another. The battle became difficult to follow as the new Shadow ships engaged with UA vessels, forcing them to re-target their pulses.

The returned battleship lost her fight. She burst apart.

How much longer for the anti-matter bomb? Time was dragging. They'd been fighting less than half an hour, yet it seemed much longer. Had something gone wrong with the bomb? Pacheco couldn't ask Jas directly. None of the officers present knew of the UA's plan. The danger that something would be leaked to the Shadows had been too great.

"They're sending out fighters," exclaimed Trimborn.

From the underside of the giant Shadow ship, a cloud of sparks streamed like hornets from a nest. The Shadow mother ship was going all out to attack the UA vessels. Pacheco swung to Jas with a sudden realization. If any approached the *Thylacine*, she would be forced to respond. Not to do so would be odd, and she couldn't afford to do anything to attract the Shadows' attention. The *Thylacine* wouldn't last long under that dreadful beam.

Another UA ship exploded, and the ray sought a new victim. More Shadow ships appeared. The tide of the battle was turning against the Unity Alliance. They had to deploy the anti-matter bomb, and soon. The chances that the *Thylacine* would be next to experience the Shadows' beam grew stronger every moment.

"Fighters approaching, ma'am," Trimborn said, though his words were unnecessary. The contingent of Shadow fighters approaching the *Thylacine* was plain to see.

"Target pulses on them," Jas said.

The *Thylacine's* pulses diverted from the Shadow mother ship and onto the approaching fighter ships. The small specks were undeterred by the bolts that passed through them, hitting only one or two. The *Thylacine* had to use a different method to defend herself from their attack.

Jas's face was wracked with pain as she spoke into her comm, and Pacheco lip-read the words, "Squadron Leader, scramble fighters."

Twenty-Six

Jas could barely concentrate on the battle. Her thoughts and heart were with Carl, who was at that moment flying out of the safety of the *Thylacine* to do battle with Shadow fighters once more. In her mind's eye, she could see him intent over the controls of his ship, guiding it skillfully into space, seeking out the approaching Shadow ships, ready to fire.

Like all the other pilots, he was also tasked with breaking through the Shadow fighters' ranks and attacking the origin point of the Shadows' devastating weapon in the hope of disabling or destroying it, slim though the chances were of their success.

And Carl wouldn't shirk his duty, Jas knew, even though he'd done far more than his fair share of fighting.

Her gaze was fixed on the swirling sparks that were the *Thylacine's* fighters, already drawing near the enemy. The rest of the battle faded in significance compared to those tiny flecks of life. The two sets of fighters engaged, and the sparks began to disappear.

"MacAdam," she said urgently into her comm. "How long?"

"Thirty-seven seconds, ma'am," came the reply.

The anti-matter bomb had been configured to be attracted to the greatest source of energy in the immediate area. It needed no aiming to fly directly to the Shadow's beam. Once released, it would do its job. The question was only whether it would succeed. The idea that the beam absorbed as well as dispensed energy was just a hypothesis. The Transgalactic Council scientists were also unsure that they had effectively disguised the bomb as a pulse, or that it wouldn't explode before it reached its destination.

It was all based on guesswork. If they were wrong, it was all over.

Jas realized she was biting the edge of her thumb and the iron taste of blood was in her mouth. She couldn't take her eyes off the part of the holo where the *Thylacine* and Shadow fighters were at battle.

"Toirien," she exclaimed into her comm.

"It's ready," Toirien said.

"Fire now," Jas blurted.

A pulse flew out from the *Thylacine* toward the Shadow ship. It looked the same as the others, and Jas could only tell it was the bomb because it didn't follow the same trajectory. Rather than targeting the side of the ship opposite the beam, it flew straight toward it.

"Hey," Trimborn said, "what's that? Is it one of ours?"

"Pilot, reverse Raptors," Jas barked. If the bomb worked, there was going to be one hell of an explosion.

Looking confused but obeying immediately, Kennewell pulled the ship sharply away. Pacheco stumbled due to the sudden movement.

With some relief, Jas saw that the fighter pilots had noticed the *Thylacine's* motion and broken off their engagement to return to her. She didn't worry about leaving them behind, despite her speed. Until the *Thylacine* built momentum, the fighters could fly much faster and catch up to her easily.

The other UA ships were also quickly withdrawing from the vicinity of the Shadow ship. Their captains and commanders had clearly been watching for the release of the anti-matter bomb, as their ships began to crawl steadily away.

The bomb reached the Shadows' beam and was gone in a flash. Jas and Pacheco were the only ones on the bridge who understood the significance of the event. Jas stared at the beam, though the brilliant light hurt her eyes. One second passed, and another. The bomb should have reached the ship. It should have exploded.

Nausea rose in her stomach. The bomb hadn't worked. They'd failed. She locked gazes with Pacheco. His dark eyes were full of despair.

Then the Shadow mother ship exploded. The *Thylacine* was thrown backward at ten times her earlier speed. The holo disappeared as the ship's sensors were flooded. Jas gripped her armrests to avoid being thrown out of her seat. Pacheco was already down.

"Hull breached," Trimborn said in a strangled tone, holding tight to his console.

But there wasn't anything anyone could do until the force of the Shadow ship's explosion had dissipated. They waited for the turbulent movement to ease. Gradually, the forces operating on the *Thylacine* diminished. Jas's hold on her armrests loosened, and Pacheco stood up.

"Damage report," she said.

"Where do I start?" Trimborn asked.

She snapped a hard look at him, and he said hastily, "Hull breached decks five through eight. Two RaptorX's out. I don't know about the jump engines. Not getting anything from them."

"How about the sensors?" Jas asked. "Can we get the holo back up?"

She desperately wanted to see what had happened to the fighter ships in that devastating blast.

"External sensors are knocked out," Trimborn said. "They're auto-repairing, but give no estimate on completion time. Internal sensors are operational."

Krat. There was only one way she could tell if Carl had survived. When he returned to the ship, the internal sensors would pick up the signal from his chip.

She stood up. "I'll be in my office," she announced.

"Commander," Pacheco said, "aren't you forgetting something?"

"What?" Jas answered, before realizing her officers were watching and waiting for an explanation of what had just happened. "Oh, yes. We just destroyed the Shadow mother ship."

The women and men around her gaped. They looked to Pacheco for confirmation that their commander hadn't gone mad. When he nodded his agreement, they began to whoop and holler and hug each other.

Jas left the bridge unnoticed as her officers celebrated. She went quickly to her office. Someone on the bridge broadcast the news of the victory around the ship, and the celebrations spread.

Until Jas knew Carl was aboard the ship, she couldn't join in.

At her office, she sat and turned on her interface. The list of pilots was already on the screen. The names refreshed as the computer added the data on the pilots who had arrived the previous night. There was Carl's name. No light was beside it.

It's okay, she told herself. *It's still early.* She couldn't expect to see any of the returning pilots yet. The Shadow ship's explosion must have propelled them all over the place. It might take them hours to make their way back to the *Thylacine*. And some of the ships would be disabled. They would have to sweep for them. Other ships might pick them up.

Jas reassured herself in this way over the next few hours as buttons lit up next to the returning pilots' names. Sayen came to see her and watch with her, but Jas sent her away. She didn't want any distraction from the screen. Pacheco also came in, to see what she was doing. As soon as he realized, he told her he would take over the running of the ship while she was busy. She barely heard him.

Carl didn't arrive with the pilots who managed to return to the *Thylacine* under their own power.

They didn't find him in any of their sweeps. None of the other UA ships had picked him up.

Twenty-four hours later, after a night of no sleep, Jas finally accepted he was gone.

The Shadow War was over, and it didn't mean a thing.

TWENTY-SEVEN

In the days that followed the Unity Alliance's victory in the Shadow War, Sayen had little to do. She spent most of her time worrying about Jas. The *Thylacine* remained at the scene of the battle, in orbit around K.67092d. The ship's defense units and troops were planetside destroying the Shadow traps. There were many, so the task was a long and difficult one.

The rebuilding of galactic civilization had yet to begin, but the mopping up process after the war was underway. The Unity Alliance ships set out to find and destroy the remaining Shadow ships and free the planets in the sector that remained under their control. The UA had to be sure the galaxy was free of the Shadow menace. After that, all sentient species would have to remain in constant vigilance to prevent them from returning from the Void and establishing strongholds again.

Jas remained in her quarters most of the time, delegating whatever tasks she could, refusing to talk to anyone. The first couple of times Sayen had visited, Jas had been polite, saying she was too busy or tired to talk. The third time she'd been more abrupt.

Sayen had been standing outside Jas's cabin, speaking into her comm—her friend wouldn't even open the door. "Jas, please let me in. I just want to talk. It helps, you know. It might not seem like it, but it does."

"I can't see you now," came Jas's reply, "as I've already said. Stop bothering me, Navigator. That's an order."

There was something in her friend's tone that didn't sound quite right. It wasn't that she sounded unhappy—that was to be expected. It was something else.

"Don't be like that," Sayen said. "I thought we were friends. Why are you talking to me about orders?"

"Because I'm your kratting commander. Now do as you're told."

Sayen could hardly believe what she was hearing.

"Jas, open the door. I'm really worried about you. If you don't open up, I'll tell the doctor you're sick and he'll override your door security."

There was no reply, but thirty seconds later, the door opened. Jas stood on the other side, fury written on her features. "What will it take to get you to leave me alone?" she spat.

Sayen reeled back, and not only from her friend's venom. She reeked of alcohol.

"You're drunk," Sayen exclaimed.

"What I do in my private time is none of your business," Jas said. "Now, *will* you go away?"

"No," Sayen replied. "No, I'm not going anywhere. You need help. You can't deal with this by yourself."

"Oh right. What kind of *help* do you think you're going to get me? What do *you* think is going to make me feel better?"

"Jas, don't forget that I've been through this. I know how you feel."

"You...you know how I feel? Is that some kind of joke? You think this is like you and Erielle?" She swallowed. "He's dead, Sayen. Carl's gone, and it's *my* fault. I sent him out there to die. So unless you killed the person you loved, you have *no* idea how I feel, and you have no idea what's going to put things right. Nothing can bring him back and *nothing* can change what I did."

"What? You didn't send him to—"

The door slid closed. Sayen called Jas through the comm a few more times, but her friend wouldn't answer.

She wasn't sure what to do. If Jas wouldn't talk to her, she didn't know who she would talk to. She didn't want to tell the admiral what was going on—he would probably relieve Jas of her duties and her duties might be the only thing keeping her going.

In search of advice and someone to share her worries with, she went to see the only other person aboard who really knew Jas. Maybe together they could figure out how to help her.

Toirien MacAdam was working in the jump engines, running point by point diagnostics, the second engineer said. Sayen went to an engine access hatch and climbed down the narrow ladder. As she went, she was strongly reminded of the time that she, Jas, and Carl had hidden from Shadows in the engine of the *Galathea*. It seemed like another lifetime.

Her vision blurred, and she blinked to clear it as she remembered Carl. She hadn't even had a chance to see him when he came aboard the *Thylacine*. Though it had been five years since they'd parted at Ganymede Station, her affection toward him hadn't lessened. He'd been like a brother to her. Jas wasn't the only one grieving over his loss.

Within the access tunnels to the huge jump engines, the ship's noises were cut off. Sayen heard Toirien's footsteps in the quietness as she walked the steel mesh floor. By following their sound and calling her name, Sayen soon found the engineer.

Toirien listened carefully to Sayen as she explained the situation. She turned to the control panel she was working at and pressed some keys before answering.

"Well, it's certainly strange how things turn around," she said.

"Huh?"

"The last time Jas Harrington and I were working aboard the same ship, it was me who was getting drunk, and worse."

"Seriously?" Sayen said. Toirien had told her of her former addictions, but she hadn't said she'd continued them aboard ship. "Did Jas or Carl know?"

"Oh yeah. Jas knew. She found me off my legs in my bunk one time. Outraged, she was, and rightly so. Everyone was relying on me to get the *Galathea's* engines working again. The only problem was, I knew it. I couldn't take the pressure. And I missed my girls. I...well, it's a long story. It just strikes me as an odd coincidence that mine and Jas's circumstances are the other way around now."

"So...what changed?" Sayen asked. "What helped you give it up?"

"Ha." Toirien smiled wryly. "I don't think what helped me is going to be of any use to poor Jas." She returned her attention to the control panel.

After Sayen had waited expectantly for a moment or so, Toirien relented and said, her face reddening, "It was a myth run."

Sayen's eyes widened. "You were a myth addict?"

"Not exactly. That takes serious creds. But old Loba was, and after he died, his stash was found and distributed around the ship. I got a hold of a dose. I was as low as I could go. And..." Her face went redder still. "You know, now that I come to think of it, I've never told anyone this.

"I went on my myth run, and I had a strange dream. I was floating in bliss, when some beautiful creatures came to me. They took me to my daughters, who were much younger in my dream than they were at the time. They were the same ages they had been when I'd last seen them. I was so happy to be with them again. Then, the strangest part of the dream was that my eldest told me I was being stupid. She said there was nothing wrong with the engines, and that it was only my doubting myself that was holding me back."

Sayen's eyes grew wider and her jaw dropped. "And was it true?"

"It was true. I hadn't trusted myself to interpret the readings I was getting from the engines. They were fine. I hadn't believed the evidence of my eyes. When we tried them, they worked. Carl got us off the planet, and we were saved."

"I remember," Sayen exclaimed. "Carl told me you thought the engines wouldn't start because we were on emergency power after the crash. But as far as I can remember, Jas only said that you finally figured out the engines were okay."

"I don't think she knew any more than that. It wasn't like I went around advertising what I'd done."

Sayen sighed. "It's an interesting story, but I think you're right. A myth run isn't gonna help Jas. That isn't going to help her forgive herself."

"No. I'm sorry, I don't know what to suggest. Maybe with time she'll start to get over it. It's early days. The wound's still raw."

"Yeah, maybe," Sayen said, but from what she knew of Jas, she wasn't sure that was likely to happen.

She thanked Toirien for her time and climbed out of the access tunnels. She decided she would try one more time to talk to Jas and persuade her to see the doctor. If she refused, Sayen would tell the doctor herself. Jas needed help, whether she realized it or not. She headed toward her friend's quarters once again.

But she found Jas before she reached her destination. Her friend was standing in a passageway with her back to a bulkhead. Now that Sayen could see her under the bright overhead lights, she saw that Jas looked worse than she'd ever seen her. She looked like she hadn't eaten in days. Her facial bones jutted out of her skin and her clothes were loose on her body. Her hair was a mess. Her lips were pale, and her eyes were sunken in their orbits. They had a strange, faraway look.

"Jas?" Sayen said. "Did you change your mind? Are you going to see the doc? Do you want to talk?"

Her friend didn't reply. She was looking at her as though she didn't know who Sayen was. Then her gaze shifted straight ahead of her to the opposite bulkhead.

Except it wasn't a wall. It was an airlock.

Sayen's heart froze. "Jas, hun. What're you fixing to do?" She took a step toward her friend. Jas slid an equal distance away. She was looking longingly at the airlock hatch. Sayen's throat was constricting. Could she stop her friend from going into the airlock if it came to it? She probably could, but she didn't want to take that risk.

Her heart sinking, Sayen lifted her comm button to her lips and, not taking her eyes from Jas, she called Admiral Pacheco.

Twenty-Eight

"You can remain in your quarters for the time being," Pacheco said. "Unless you'd rather stay in the sick bay? There would be people around you, and you wouldn't be alone. The doctor could monitor you better."

Jas was on her bunk. Her feet were on the floor and her head was down. She barely heard what the man was saying. She was in civilian clothes, having been relieved of duties for an undefined length of time.

"I really think it would be a good idea for you to stay in the sick bay," Pacheco said.

Why wouldn't he leave her alone? She wished they would all leave her alone. She couldn't be around people. It hurt too much. Everything hurt too much.

"Jas?"

She shook her head. "M'okay." The sedation was making it hard to speak, and she could hardly think. But then again, maybe that was a good thing.

"Right," said Pacheco. "As long as you're sure. You *are* sure you're feeling better?" 'Better' meant that she wasn't going to space herself. Everyone wanted her to be 'better'. Jas didn't want to be better. All she wanted was Carl back, or to never have sent him to his death.

She mustered her concentration. "I'm okay. Really." Anything to make the man go away.

Pacheco moved toward the door. "I'll leave you for a while, then. Navigator Lee will be along to see you soon, in case you need anything." He paused. "Jas, I'm sorry. You waited for your pilot for so long, he must have meant a lot to you. When I saw him coming out of your cabin, I could have put him in the brig. That would have kept him out of the battle. It would have been easy enough. I could have protected him for you, but I didn't. I didn't even think of it. I guess I was just too wrapped up in myself."

At the edge of her vision, Jas saw Pacheco's legs and feet at the door. She wished he would leave. Didn't he understand she had enough of her own *what ifs* to occupy her forever? She didn't need his too.

Finally, he left.

She lay down on her bunk and curled up on her side. After a long time, during which Sayen arrived to check on her, she slept.

When she woke up, she felt terrible. Slivers of pain stabbed behind her eyes, her tongue was thick in her mouth, and her throat ached. She wondered if it was a side-effect of the sedation. She sat up, wincing as the movement caused more pain to dance behind her eyes. Her eyelids squeezed to slits, she checked the time. She'd been asleep around four hours. It was the quiet shift aboard the ship. Most everyone would be asleep.

She pulled up her sleeve to where the sedation dispenser was taped to the underside of her arm, and picked at the edges of the tape until she could peel it off. The dispenser was a lozenge of plastic with a fine mesh opening, through which the sedative was forced into her bloodstream at regular intervals.

Now that the tape was gone, the dispenser was only lightly stuck to her skin. She removed it and put it in the trash. She went to her wash basin and doused her face with water.

Not really knowing what she was going to do, she left her cabin.

Though the doctor had infused calories into her system to make up for her days of self-starvation, taking away her dizziness, her legs remained unsteady from the doses of sedation. She rested a hand on the bulkhead as she went along to keep her balance.

She drew closer to an airlock. She thought she knew the code to open it. It was to access a sensor array for external repair.

If she went through the lock, it would mean a quick end to her pain. To die like that, frozen and floating among the stars, seemed kind of fitting. On the other hand, maybe she didn't deserve a quick end. It seemed too easy after what she'd done.

She passed the airlock by, saving the option for another time.

Wandering aimlessly through the quiet passageways, she realized she was making her way to the crew living sections. These were the dirtier, noisier parts of the ship, where the lowest-ranking crew bunked four to a cabin, and quiet and privacy were scarce. It had been a long time since Jas had lived in those conditions, when she'd been a plain security officer. Young and lonely. Had anything much changed? Now she was older and lonely, that was all.

The area wasn't very familiar. She rarely came this way. She'd hated the way all the lowest ranks would leap to attention when she appeared. She'd felt like she was invading the one place they had where they could relax. But now she was no longer a commander. She wasn't anything. She had no doubts she would be retired on health grounds as soon as the sweep of the Shadow trap planet was complete and the *Thylacine* returned to Unity docking.

She came across a door she vaguely remembered was the entrance to a lounge. She was tired, and she wanted to sit down. Thinking the place would probably be empty at that hour, she opened the door. Four pairs of eyes turned to her. Four crew members were huddled together over something on a low table.

For a second, she and the men and women stared at each other, then one of them shouted, "It's the commander." They all bolted, pushing her down in their rush to leave the room. Dazed, she looked behind her, but they were gone.

She rose unsteadily to her feet and went over to the spot where the crew members had been huddled. A small opaque bottle was on the table, along with some drug-taking paraphernalia. She sat down and picked up the bottle, an idea of what might be in it already forming. The bottle was tiny. After unscrewing the lid, she peered inside. She had to put her head close to look through the small hole, and as she did so, a whiff of vapor from the contents confirmed her suspicion. Just a breath of the substance made her head spin.

It was myth.

Someone had smuggled myth aboard. Her attempts to weed out the addicts hadn't been entirely successful. Automatically, she reached for her comm button to inform Pacheco, but it wasn't there. She'd forgotten to transfer it from her uniform. She looked up at the door. Next to it was a comm console that would also allow her to do the right thing and tell someone what she'd found.

But that small barrier to action had given her time to think. She'd only experienced the effects of myth once—on Ganymede Station when the Council managers had wanted a volunteer to try to communicate with the Paths. But since that time she had never lost the hankering to try it again. The visit to the mythrin mine had concentrated the feeling.

Up until that moment, she'd always managed to resist the temptation.

She put the lid back on the bottle and held it in her palm, cool and smooth. It was so small, it probably only held one or at most two doses, yet aboard the ship it would sell for a month's wages. Jas recalled the experience of her myth run. She remembered how all concerns and fears had fallen away, and she had basked in perfect, seemingly endless bliss.

The prospect of escaping from the hell she was in—real escape, not the dulling of every emotion that the sedative gave—was tantalizing. The idea that she could forget that Carl was gone, if only for a few hours, grew stronger in her mind.

She picked up the paraphernalia, slipped it with the bottle of myth into her pocket and left the lounge.

TWENTY-NINE

As soon as she'd closed her door, Jas took out the bottle of myth and box of needles and swabs from her pocket and quickly stripped off her clothes. She wanted to start the myth run soon or she might be discovered before it was over. She had the feeling she was standing on the precipice of a vast, black abyss, yet she didn't care.

Before lying down in her bunk, she unscrewed the bottle, plunged the needle into the crimson liquid and drew it all up into the syringe. The myth was a deep, dark carmine in the dimmed cabin light, like blood. Her heart raced at the thought of the escape that it held. She'd been right when she told Carl that she wasn't brave. There were some things she couldn't face, and this precious drug was her way out, for a few hours at least.

She lay down, holding up the hypodermic syringe in one hand. Closing her eyes, she brought back the memory of when Sparks had injected the drug into her. The site of the injection was important, she'd heard. She bit her lip. The memory of the bolt of pain that had shot through her when the myth entered her system was still vivid, but it was worth it for what happened after.

She traced the fingers of her other hand down one side of her belly, trying to recall the exact spot. Her action reminded her of her night with Carl, and she whimpered from a hurt more painful than any she'd ever felt in all her years of fighting. She clenched her teeth. Just a few more moments, and the terrible ache would be gone. Her fingers probed farther south until she located the spot where she was certain she'd received her last shot of myth. She opened her eyes and lifted her head from her pillow, gazing down at the area.

She positioned the hypodermic syringe above the spot and hesitated. The tiniest flicker of sense at the back of her mind told her that what she was doing was wrong. But she pushed the thought away as she simultaneously plunged the needle into her skin.

The agony as she pressed the plunger home caused her to cry out, but the sound died on her lips as the drug took effect.

———

She was floating free, unchained from her pain, and it was bliss. Now that she'd returned here, she remembered the Void as clearly as if she'd never left. Its otherness was impossible to put into the language of the physical plane, but she was aware of infinite distance, light, and color.

She was also infinite and without form. She reached out to the vast ends of the Void, then contracted smaller than an electron. She reveled in the endless space, where nothing and everything had happened and time did not exist. Carl had not died. They were together and apart, and it didn't matter. Nothing mattered anymore. She would stay in the Void forever.

After she had drifted for always and for no time at all, something told her she wasn't alone. Presences were approaching her consciousness. Unease rippled through her as a vague memory of something unpleasant about the Void surfaced. There were some beings here who trapped people—who had trapped her. She recalled fighting and an escape back to the other place.

But her senses told her these were not those beings. Her tension eased. These were the ones who had fought for her. These beings had come through to the physical plane to help her and others. She found it hard to remember where she'd come from. Consciousness of the other side was slippery in her mind. That place felt unreal. Here was reality and truth.

The beings of the Void spoke. "We know you," they said. "You came to us in the other place. You saved us when we were weak and helpless."

"Did I?" Jas's unspoken words echoed inside her. "I don't remember."

"You have been here with us before."

"Yes, and now I've come back, and I'm staying."

"You cannot remain. Your kind can never remain. You always go back."

"I'm not going back." Dark gray ripples of disquiet left her and spread out.

"You will."

She twisted and turned, trying to escape the beings, but they were everywhere that she was, around her and within her. She rejected their message. Why wouldn't they let her mind return to floating free and careless?

"Many of the Others are gone," the beings said, "destroyed on the physical plane. We are sad that they harmed so many of you, but we are grateful that their existence has been reduced and they no longer trouble us."

The beings' words were sparking painful recollections in her mind. She wished they would stop. "Please, leave me."

"We will depart if our presence disturbs you, but we came to tell you the one you mourn is here."

The words reverberated through her perception. *The one I mourn?*

"...What?"

"The one whose loss you grieve is here, but he cannot exist in the Void. He is fading."

"What?" Jas's unspoken voice was tiny.

"You ache. You have suffered a loss. We can sense this. The one you have lost is here."

Struggling hard against the mind-numbing effects of being in the Void, Jas said without words, "Carl's here?"

"If that is how you identify him using language, that one is here. We can sense him in you, but he is here too."

"Where? Take me to him."

"He is here as you are, but you cannot sense him."

"Can he sense me?"

"No."

Despair nibbled the numbed edges of Jas's consciousness. Even in the Void there was no escape from it. Her escape was no escape after all.

"Should we return him to your universe?" the beings asked. "He may not survive the transition, but he also cannot survive here."

"You can send him back? I don't understand. Haven't the Shadows got him? Won't he come back as a Shadow?"

"We have the remaining Others under control. We can use their mechanism to push him through at the place where you found us. But the Others use their process to insert their persona into the newly created copy of the one they stole. We will eschew this part. We will not insert a persona."

"No persona?" Jas couldn't grasp their meaning. Carl wouldn't be Carl? Just his body? She struggled to comprehend, but her thoughts were slippery and ephemeral. "Can you explain?"

"The Others recreated only the form of the creatures from the physical plane. They animated the copies they made with their own selves. If we return the one you lost, he will have no self."

She still couldn't really understand. It sounded like whatever they pushed through would have Carl's brain with all its knowledge and memories, but somehow he wouldn't have his personality. She couldn't imagine what Carl would be like if the beings did as they proposed. But just to have him back would be something.

"What should we do?" the beings asked.

"Send him back. Please, send him back."

"We will return him to the place where you found us."

———

She opened her eyes. She was lying naked in her bunk, a hypodermic needle hanging painfully from her upper thigh. She sat up and carefully pulled out the needle. The syringe was empty. As she remembered what she'd done and why, the weight of her entire existence settled heavily over her.

So it had all come to this? All her years of fighting. Everything she'd endured. All the friends that she'd dragged into the fight, only to have them die. And she'd ended up like the man she'd despised— Loba, a myth addict, living only for the next run.

The syringe in her hand fell from her fingers to the floor. Let it lie there. Let them see it. What did she care? Her mind returned to the airlock and its alluring escape.

She rose out of her bunk and went into the shower. Maybe she could wash away some of the disgust she felt for herself. As the hot water started up, she was reminded of the shower she took the morning that she saw Carl for the last time.

She groaned. She rested her forearm on the shower wall and her forehead on her arm while the water cascaded over her. She would never be able to clean herself of what she'd done. She'd never be free of her all-pervading grief. Everywhere she went and everything she did reminded her of him.

Sometime later—she didn't know how long—she turned off the water and got out of the shower. Her efforts to divert her mind from thoughts of Carl were useless, and something about him was nagging away at her like a toothache. A background annoyance that she couldn't bring to the front of her mind.

She put on some clothes and sat on her bunk, slumped forward. Checking the time, she was surprised to see only around two or three hours had passed since she'd injected the myth. As she understood it, she should have been out for at least five or six hours. She rubbed the inner corners of her eyes with her fingertips.

Carl. There was something important she had to remember about Carl. Something about... She squeezed her eyes shut and forced her foggy mind to clear. Snippets of her myth run flashed into her inner vision. The benevolent beings—the Paths—had been there, and there was something else, something to do with Carl. The Paths had told her...what was it?

Jas gasped. Her hands gripped her bunk.

The Paths had told her Carl was in the Void and they were going to send him back.

THIRTY

J as hammered on Kennewell's door. Then she remembered about door chimes and pressed that too. Before the pilot had time to answer, she pressed again.

"Kennewell," she called through the door, "wake up. I want you to take me planetside. Now. Kennewell!"

Jas didn't let up until the pilot's door opened and the tousled-haired young woman appeared, staring at her with sleepy eyes.

"Commander?" she said, covering a yawn with the back of her hand.

"I need you to take me planetside in the shuttle immediately. I have the coordinates."

"But, I, er...Are you sure that's a good idea?" Kennewell's returning memory that Jas had been relieved of her duties was evident in her expression.

"Yes, I'm sure. But if I told you why, you wouldn't believe me. You'll have to trust me. It's about Carl Lingiari, one of the lost pilots. I think I might have a chance of finding him."

"Oh." Kennewell's face turned sad and sympathetic. It was clear she thought Jas was so grief-stricken, she was delusional. Her face brightened as something occurred to her. "Okay, ma'am. Sure. I just need to ask the admiral for permission first."

"No, you can't." Jas took a deep breath and tried to calm herself. She had to convince Kennewell to take her down to K.67092d. She'd known the pilot for years. She was almost a friend. "Look, I know how it looks. You think I'm crazy. I was. I was out of my mind with grief. But I'm not now. And I really, really need you to do this for me. Please. As a favor. I was a good commander, wasn't I? I was fair? Not like Pacheco?"

"Actually, you and he are pretty alike."

"What?"

"Never mind." Kennewell sighed. "I'm probably going to regret this, but the war's over and I'm going home soon, so what the hell. Okay. I'll take you down. Just let me get dressed." The door closed.

Jas waited impatiently for Kennewell to emerge, and when she did, she hurried the pilot toward the launch bay.

"You've cleared this, right?" Kennewell asked as they went along. "It's not like I can just take a shuttle and fly it wherever I want."

Krat. "No, I haven't. What do you suggest?"

"Hmm...well, if Trimborn's on duty, we should be okay. He might turn a blind eye and let me go."

"Really? How come?" Jas was surprised to hear that her first officer would act so unprofessionally.

"We, er, we have a thing going on."

"You do? Well, that's great. I hope it's him." Jas also hoped that Pacheco was still asleep. If he found out what she was doing, he'd probably have her restrained. She was well aware that telling him about her myth run and what the Paths had told her would be useless. He would only think she was still insane with grief and guilt. Sayen might believe her, but she didn't have time to convince anyone. The Paths had said that Carl was fading and that they would push him into the physical plane, but she didn't know when.

Troops and defense units were in the process of destroying all the Shadow traps on the planet. If she didn't get there soon, she might be too late.

The guards at the launch bay were nonplussed by Jas turning up in civilian clothes with Kennewell at her side. Jas put on her best serious commander face and nodded at them as she walked swiftly past. The guards fell for her bluff and didn't challenge her.

It had taken Jas some serious digging to find the coordinates of the crash site of the *Galathea*, but she'd located them in the data files on K.67092d. The shuttle had a copilot's seat, which Jas took. As she sat down next to her, Jas gave Kennewell the coordinates.

She let the pilot do the talking when it came to persuading Trimborn to okay the shuttle launch. Kennewell framed the request in terms of the commander's receiving information about a lost pilot that she wanted to informally investigate. Trimborn didn't sound like he believed her, but he allowed them to go.

Jas closed her eyes and tried to relax as Kennewell piloted the shuttle planetside. She doubted that the Paths truly understood time, coming from a place where it didn't exist. Carl could have already come through into the Shadow trap and be wandering around somewhere that was just about to be destroyed.

But there wasn't anything she could do to arrive faster. At her urging, Kennewell was already flying the shuttle at its maximum speed.

"Commander," Kennewell said, "do you really think you can find this pilot? We did a thorough sweep."

Jas opened her eyes. "We couldn't sweep the place where he's been. I think what happened was that after a dogfight or the explosion of the Shadow mother ship, he crash landed on K.67092d. Maybe he crashed right into a trap or got carried into one unconscious. I don't know. There weren't any Shadows on the planet when I was there, but that was a long time ago. However it happened, he was taken into the Void. Except there are so few Shadows there now, the benevolent beings who also live there have stopped them from returning. They're sending Carl back minus a Shadow's personality."

"But how do you know? Who told you?"

"That's a long story. I hope I have the chance to tell it to you one day."

THIRTY-ONE

Landing at the site of the *Galathea's* crash gave Jas a weird, uncomfortable feeling. In spite of the passage of years, the crash site was plain to see as they came down. A wide, deep trench was carved into the rocky soil, with a yawning hole at the end of it where the starship had slid to a halt and, later, the Shadows had begun to draw it down into their trap.

One thing was very different. A team of troops and defense units were walking away from the trap toward a military vehicle parked about a kilometer away. Jas knew this sight well. The troops were sweeping the planet for traps, and they were about to blow this one up.

Except that she wasn't going to let them.

Before the shuttle had come to a stop, Jas was undoing her harness. She jumped out of her seat.

"Let me turn off the engines, for krat's sake," Kennewell said.

The air was hot with heat exhaust when the pilot finally opened the hatch and allowed Jas to leave the shuttle. Their arrival had had the effect she'd hoped it would. The troops and units had paused and were watching curiously as she ran toward them.

"You can't blow this one up," she shouted as soon as she was within hearing distance. "Someone's inside."

The corporal in charge put his hand on his hips at her words. He was a grizzled old soldier who would have been too far on in years to fight if they hadn't been at war. Jas didn't recognize him. He must have been drafted in for the work from another ship.

The man looked at Jas with narrowed eyes as she reached the group, panting. She was definitely out of shape.

"You mustn't destroy this trap," Jas gasped.

"Says who?" the corporal asked, looking her up and down.

Jas had been hoping to use her former authority to persuade the troops to obey her, but they were all strangers. To them, she was just a Martian in civvies.

"I'm Commander Harrington."

Comprehension dawned in the older man's eyes. "Oh, right." He gave a smirk. He'd obviously heard of her fall from grace. "Sorry, ma'am. We're just obeying orders. Now if you have something from the admiral...?"

Jas clenched her fists. "There's no time for that. If you blow up that trap you'll be killing a man. A pilot. He crashed here." As she spoke the lie, Jas realized how crazy she had to sound. There was clearly no sign of a crashed fighter ship. Carl must have come down somewhere else. It was here that the Paths were returning him.

"Yeah, sure," the corporal said, nodding and winking at his troops, who were barely controlling their smiles. "You should get back to your shuttle, ma'am, or you'll be in the blast zone."

"No," Jas exclaimed. "Listen to me."

But the corporal had signaled his troops and units to follow him. They turned their backs and began to walk away. Jas sized up the group. Five soldiers and three units. She could never take them all. She swung around to look for Kennewell, hoping that maybe the pilot had a weapon on her.

As she turned in the direction of the Shadow trap, she saw him.

Carl was emerging from the hexagonal entrance. His head was down, and he was staggering, but it was him. He was alive.

"Carl," Jas yelled as she sprinted over to him.

Her cry attracted the attention of the troops.

"It's a Shadow," one of them cried.

Jas glanced back, and with horror saw one of them lift his weapon to fire.

"No," she shouted, and put herself between the soldier and Carl. "Don't shoot. He isn't a Shadow."

"Out of the way, ma'am," the corporal yelled. "Get out of the way."

But Jas continued to run. The closer she got to Carl, the harder it would be for them to avoid hitting her if they fired.

Carl showed no recognition of her or what was happening. He walked on, taking small steps, almost shuffling.

"Carl," Jas cried. A bolt flew past her, hitting the edge of the Shadow trap entrance.

She reached him and threw herself at him, pushing him to the ground. He lay beneath her, neither moving nor speaking. She looked back toward the soldiers. They were running over, the defense units bringing up the rear.

"Get away from it, ma'am," the corporal said. "We're under orders to kill all Shadows on sight."

"He isn't a Shadow," Jas exclaimed. "I told you, he's a pilot. He crashed into a trap."

"If he crashed here, where's his ship?"

"He didn't crash here. He's just come out here."

"That doesn't make any sense," said the corporal. "Look, I'm sorry. I can see the man must have been important to you. But if he came out of a trap, he's a Shadow. No question about it. Now please move away from him, ma'am. I don't want to have to make you."

Jas clung to Carl's motionless body as if her life depended on it. Her life did depend on it.

The corporal sighed. "AX7, take a hold of that woman."

"Which woman, Corporal Stormer?" the defense unit asked.

AX7? Jas remembered the designation. The unit was the one she'd worked with aboard the *Galathea*.

"The woman on the ground there," the corporal replied, irritated. "Commander Harrington."

AX7 bent down and grabbed Jas's arms. She found herself lifted gently but inexorably upright and away from Carl. As her grip on his flight suit was broken, he didn't react. He only lay there, face down in the dirt.

The corporal lifted his weapon to fire. Jas screamed, "Nooooo..." She fought with all her might, but she was no match for the metal and silicon of the unit.

The corporal hesitated. He lowered his weapon and glanced at Jas with pity in his eyes. He turned to a soldier. "Run to the vehicle and bring out the Shadow scanner, then we can show her what it is."

They all waited in silence as the sound of the soldier's running feet grew quieter and quieter. The chill wind cut through Jas's clothes, but she barely felt it. Physical discomfort was nothing compared to the agony she now faced of seeing Carl shot and killed in cold blood. He had come from the Void. He carried the trace of that place that the myth in the scanners reacted to. She was certain that the scanner would identify him as a Shadow. Kennewell stood by, pale and grave.

They all thought Jas was sick in the head, and they were humoring her. She struggled in AX7's grip, but the unit's hands were firm and unyielding around her biceps.

The soldier returned, breathless, bearing the scanner. The corporal took the device and ran it over Carl's prone form. He looked at the display. His face grim, he turned it toward Jas. She'd been correct. The display said that Carl was a Shadow.

"It's wrong," she said. "I know how this must look, but, please, you have to believe me. If you kill him, you'll be murdering an innocent man."

"AX7," the corporal said, "take Commander Harrington back to her shuttle."

He was sparing her the sight of seeing the man she loved killed.

"No," Jas shouted. "AX7, let me go." To her complete amazement, the unit's hands fell away. She dropped to the ground. She was free! The unit had obeyed her counter-command. "AX7, protect the man lying on the ground."

The unit marched over to Carl, its weapons sliding out of its arms. It turned and aimed at the corporal and his soldiers.

"AX7," the corporal yelled, "Commander Harrington has been relieved of duty. Her commands do not supersede mine."

"I obey Commander Harrington," AX7 replied.

With a gasp of frustration, Stormer lifted his weapon to shoot at Carl, but before he could fire, AX7's weapon discharged and stunned him. In response, the soldiers fired at the unit, but they were also felled by it.

In less than a second, Kennewell, Jas, and Carl were the only humans remaining conscious. The other two units hadn't moved.

"Thank krat the corporal didn't think to order them to shoot," Jas said to Kennewell, indicating the other units.

The pilot's mouth was open in an O. "Err...What just happened?"

"I'm not sure myself," Jas said. "AX7, why didn't you obey the corporal? Am I still the superior officer according to your data?"

"You are not a superior officer. You are on sick leave according to my data. But I am loyal to you, Commander Harrington. I chose to obey you."

Thirty-Two

Carl hadn't said a thing since Jas had rescued him from the Shadow trap. He lay on the examining bed in the *Thylacine's* sick bay as the doctor subjected him to a battery of tests. His eyes were open, but they didn't focus on anything. If food was placed in front of him, he would eat, and he would drink water that was offered. He would also stand up and walk around randomly, so the doctor kept him restrained to the bed with straps.

Jas refused to leave his side, convinced that he would be executed as a Shadow once he was out of her sight. She also kept AX7 next to her. The unit obeyed her and no one else. How it had overridden its compliance protocols, she didn't know. It was true that the defense units she'd encountered had always seemed a little more independent and individual than they were supposed to be, but this one's behavior was exceptional. She guessed that the time she'd worked with AX7 aboard the *Galathea* had made a long-lasting impression on it, and that its organic components had allowed it to develop to the extent that it could influence its programming. Whatever the reason for AX7's fidelity to her, she was grateful for it.

Pacheco requested her presence in her office, which he'd taken over, but when she wouldn't go, he was forced to come to her. His somber face appeared at the small window in the door to Carl's room. The door opened and he came in, his expression pained. He drew up a seat and sat down, hitching up his pants.

Jas was holding Carl's hand as it lay above the sheet. She looked defiantly at Pacheco.

"Jas." Pacheco rubbed his hands together as he considered his words. "I read Corporal Stormer's report, and I've spoken to Kennewell, and I'm still no wiser as to what's going on here. How about we go somewhere that we can talk about this properly? I give you my solemn assurance that nothing will happen to Pilot Lingiari."

"I'm not leaving him, Pacheco. We can talk here. I'll tell you everything, right from the beginning. And you can confirm it with Sayen Lee and the Transgalactic Council."

"All right then," he replied. "Have it your way." He told the doctor they were not to be disturbed until they were finished. He sat down again and folded his arms. "I'm listening."

It took Jas longer than an hour to tell Pacheco about what had happened at Ganymede Station, about finding myth aboard the ship —he raised his eyebrows as he heard about that—her myth run, and what the Paths had told her.

When she finally reached the end of her story, Pacheco remained doubtful. He turned his attention to Carl. The pilot's gaze was directed upward and was unfocused, as if he hadn't heard a word of Jas's story.

Pacheco shook his head. "I don't know what to make of it. What do you think the Paths meant when they said he wouldn't have a persona? Is this just his body? Is he going to stay like this forever?"

"I don't know. It's like he's in a coma, except he's awake. The doctor can't find out what's wrong with him. But he's back. That's the main thing."

Pacheco looked doubtful. "The problem is, he's officially a Shadow. That's what the scanners say. And that means that he must be rendered safe, unable to endanger anyone else. I don't know where to go from here. I'll have to take it up with the Council."

"Does Carl look like he's a danger to anyone?" Jas asked. "Talk to the Council. They'll confirm what I told you. Help me persuade them to let him go, Pacheco. Please. I just want him to be left alone. I want us to be left alone."

———

For weeks afterward, Jas nursed a secret hope that Carl would suddenly wake up and return to normal, but it never happened. She brought him with her to the Transgalactic Council, where she had to tell her story many more times. Supported by the testimony of the officers who had come to Ganymede Station, she managed to convince the Council that what she was saying was credible, and that Carl was some kind of anomaly—not a Shadow, but also not the person he had once been. He was a replica of the original Carl minus whatever it was that had made him himself.

But in truth Jas couldn't bring herself to believe that the real Carl didn't lurk somewhere inside the shell of his body. He'd returned from the Void looking exactly as he had when he entered it, except that his burn scars were gone. As far as she understood, the Shadows who crossed over from the Void retained the genetic makeup and the memories of their victims. She thought it was those two things that made up human personalities. If Carl had the same genes and memories as he'd had before he was taken into the Void, where was he? She couldn't understand what was missing.

Sayen stayed with her while Jas was arguing for permission to take Carl back to Earth. She was grateful for her friend's presence during the stressful negotiations, especially as she knew that Sayen was longing to see her brother again. The two women had many conversations long into the night about the Shadow War, and about Erielle, Makey, Ozment, and all the other people they'd met and some of whom they'd lost during the course of it. They also talked about what they would do when they returned home.

When Sayen left her for the night, Jas would lie down next to Carl. She would recall the days when she'd first gotten to know him. At first, she'd thought of him as just another crew member, a little awkward and flirty. She hadn't seen his kindness or loyalty or courage. Was it that she hadn't really known him then, or that he'd changed? The War had brought out a lot in people.

She felt like *she'd* changed. She hadn't realized back then at the start how alone and lonely she'd been. As time had gone on, she'd learned that she needed people. And she wasn't lonely any more. It might have looked to outsiders like she didn't have much with Carl, but that wasn't true. She had hope.

The day finally came when the Council relented and told her that Carl could return to Earth with her, providing he remained under her supervision and care for the rest of his life or until he regained a normal state of mind. She didn't need to be told twice. Within half an hour, she and Sayen were packed and waiting to leave on the next ship that would take them in the direction of Earth.

She was excited at the thought of returning to humanity's origin planet. A long time ago, all she'd wanted to do was to leave Earth. She'd looked out to the stars and dreamed of her escape. Now, with Carl, she would make it her home.

EPILOGUE

The man blinked in the bright sun. A hot breeze was blowing, drying the sweat that was forming on his skin. He was standing in the shade of tall trees, which whispered and sighed above and around him in the wind. A faint scent of eucalyptus hung in the air. He was looking out over a wide landscape of tan and brown, dry in the summer heat. The place had once been a farm, but it was overgrown after what looked like many years of neglect.

At the man's feet sat a tall woman. She had her back to him. Her knees were drawn up and her arms wrapped around them as she, too, silently regarded the desiccated view. The woman's hair was short, reddish-brown, and messy. There was something familiar about her.

Flies buzzed near the man's face and he batted them away. Though he wasn't sure where he was or what he was doing here—or even *who* he was—he wasn't alarmed. The scene around him made him feel calm and peaceful. He had a sensation that he'd been far away for a long time, but if he was patient, everything he should know would come back to him.

The man sat down at the woman's side. She turned to him with a sad smile and took his hand in hers. He remembered her name.

"Jas?"

The woman had returned her attention to the landscape, but as she heard him speak, she turned to him again, her mouth falling open. Her grip on his hand tightened. "Carl? You can talk? You know who I am?"

"Yeah," he replied. "I do." Speaking felt weirdly unfamiliar to him. Memories of the woman began to pour into his mind, and he added, "Of course I do."

Happiness welling up in him, he put his arm around her shoulders and pulled her close.

"What's been going on, Jas? How come we're back at my folks' farm?"

Her grip on his hand remained almost painfully tight. "You recognize it? You know where you are?"

"Yeah, but I don't remember coming here."

"I brought you here. Carl, you've been sick for a long time. I can't believe you're finally getting better, but you should take things slowly. Let's sit here quietly for a while and see what comes back to you, okay?"

She rested her head on his shoulder, and he sat with her, watching the still landscape under the hot sun and pale blue sky. Scenes and dialogue began to play in his mind like snatches of once-forgotten movies. The memories were jumbled and confusing at first, but the more he thought, the more shape they took, and he began to be able to slot them into order.

The recollection that his parents were dead snagged at his heart, and he bowed his head.

"How are you feeling?" Jas asked after a while. "Do you remember more now?"

"I do. It's all coming back. A few things I wish I didn't remember too."

"It's all over now, Carl. We won the war. The galaxy's at peace."

"And so after I got sick, you wanted to come back here with me?"

"I thought this was where you'd want to be."

"You were right."

Dealing with the flood of returning memories was tiring him. He lay down in the long dry grass and pulled Jas down with him. She rested her head on his chest. Above them, the afternoon sun slanted through shifting gum tree leaves.

He was silent for a long time.

"Carl?" Jas asked softly.

"Yeah?"

"What are you thinking about?"

"I'm thinking..." He took the grass stalk that he was chewing out of his mouth. "I'm thinking we should get this farm back on its feet."

He felt her nod in agreement.

Later still, he felt a patch of wetness growing wider on his shirt. "Why are you crying, Jas?"

"I'm just glad you're back."

THE END

I hope you loved Jas's story. For another action-packed complete series, try my science fantasy STAR LEGEND.

Sign up to my reader group for a free copy of *Starbound*, the Shadows of the Void prequel that tells the story of what happened to Jas Harrington in Antarctica, and for exclusive notice of new releases, advanced reader opportunities and other interesting stuff.

Copyright